THREADS OF HOPE

Books by Leslie Gould

The Courtships of Lancaster County

Courting Cate

Adoring Addie

Minding Molly

Becoming Bea

Neighbors of Lancaster County

Amish Promises

Amish Sweethearts

Amish Weddings

The Sisters of Lancaster County

A Plain Leaving

A Simple Singing

A Faithful Gathering

An Amish Family Christmas:
An Amish Christmas Kitchen *Novella*

Plain Patterns

Piecing It All Together

A Patchwork Past

Threads of Hope

THREADS OF HOPE

PLAIN PATTERNS • 3

LESLIE GOULD

BETHANYHOUSE
a division of Baker Publishing Group
Minneapolis, Minnesota

Published by Bethany House Publishers
11400 Hampshire Avenue South
Minneapolis, Minnesota 55438
www.bethanyhouse.com

Bethany House Publishers is a division of
Baker Publishing Group, Grand Rapids, Michigan

Library of Congress Cataloging-in-Publication Data
Names: Gould, Leslie, 1962– author.
Title: Threads of hope / Leslie Gould.
Description: Minneapolis, Minnesota : Bethany House Publishers, a division of Baker Publishing Group, [2021] | Series: Plain patterns ; 3
Identifiers: LCCN 2021037685 | ISBN 9780764235245 (paperback) | ISBN 9780764239878 (casebound) | ISBN 9781493436088 (ebook)
Subjects: GSAFD: Christian fiction.
Classification: LCC PS3607.O89 T48 2021 | DDC 813/.6—dc23
LC record available at https://lccn.loc.gov/2021037685

Scripture quotations are from the King James Version of the Bible.

This is a work of fiction. Names, characters, incidents, and dialogues are products of the author's imagination and are not to be construed as real. Any resemblance to actual events or persons, living or dead, is entirely coincidental.

Cover design by Dan Thornberg, Design Source Creative Services

Author represented by Natasha Kern Literary Agency.

Baker Publishing Group publications use paper produced from sustainable forestry practices and post-consumer waste whenever possible.

22 23 24 25 26 27 28 7 6 5 4 3 2 1

In memory of my four grandparents,
Emil and Alice Egger—Fred and Blanche Houston.
Their love of the Lord and their children, grandchildren,
and great-grandchildren inspires me more and more,
the older I grow.

Trust in the LORD *with all thine heart; and lean not unto thine own understanding. In all thy ways acknowledge him, and he shall direct thy paths.*

Proverbs 3:5–6

PROLOGUE

Jane Berger

October 10, 2018
Nappanee, Indiana

Jane Berger stared at the sunshine-and-shadows quilt stretched across the frame in the back room of Plain Patterns, the quilt shop she owned and operated. Jane wasn't sure who to give the quilt to, but she wouldn't worry about that now. She'd know when the time came.

She stepped to her desk in the corner of the room and sat down, her hands falling into position on the old manual typewriter. She'd been struggling for a topic for her next column in the *Nappanee News*.

Along with quilting, storytelling brought her comfort—except when she was trying to come up with a new story to tell. That was the hard part.

And over the last year, it had become more difficult.

She stared at the white paper for a few moments and then stood. Perhaps an idea would come once she was home.

She gathered her purse and coat and then stepped out the front door, drawing in a breath of woodsmoke. Her brother and sister-in-law, who lived in the big house, had a fire going in their stove.

After she locked the door of the shop, she turned her attention to her little home across the road and the maple tree covered with fiery red leaves that shaded it. Autumn was her favorite season. The harvest. The changing leaves. The acrid smell of smoke in the air. The digging of the last of the root vegetables from the garden.

She walked through the small parking lot of her quilt shop and then started across the road. She reached the other side and then, instead of going into her house, she headed to the backyard and settled into a lawn chair to watch the sun set over the field.

At sixty-six, was she in the autumn of her life? She smiled at herself. She could easily have a decade or two more to live. Maybe even three.

Unlike most Amish women, she'd never married. At one time she thought she might, but then the young man who'd been courting her left for Ohio to work for a summer and never returned. She'd had a letter from him saying he'd decided to leave the church and take a job in Kentucky.

Jane never regretted not getting married and having a family. She'd relished being an aunt and great-aunt, being part of the extended Berger family. She'd never felt unfulfilled or isolated.

Owning Plain Patterns had been a creative outlet for her and also a place for women to gather and develop friendships. Writing her column for the newspaper brought her joy too.

But she couldn't help but wonder if there was something more for her. More writing. More research. Perhaps even trips in her future. She'd love to visit Pennsylvania to see where her ancestors settled when they arrived in America in the 1700s. She'd love to go even farther, back to Europe to the places they lived in the Palatinate region in Germany, and before that in Switzerland.

But she didn't know that she was ready to close down Plain Patterns yet. The thought of letting it go pained her. That was something she'd need to decide in time.

Jane took in another deep breath of the cool air, with the hint of smoke, and then exhaled. Her brother, Andy, had finished harvesting his soybeans the week before. He would start on the corn and be done with everything by November. Then there would be weddings to go to and finally Thanksgiving, where the extended Berger family would gather in the big house that Andy and his family lived in and celebrate their gratitude to God for all He provided.

But before Thanksgiving would be November eleventh, and the one-hundred-year anniversary of the end of World War I, the war to end all wars. If only it *had* been the war to end all wars. She shivered at all that had transpired in the last century. It was on anniversaries like this that she missed her parents, her grandparents, and her great-grandfather, Vyt Landis, who had been born the year the Civil War ended. She'd heard hundreds of stories about the past from those particular five people, yet she regretted not asking for more stories, more details. Had she ever asked any of them what they remembered or had heard about life around Nappanee during the Great War?

She'd heard some about the farm depression in the years after the war. Many had struggled to make a living then and keep their farms, all the way through the Depression and then up until World War II.

In fact, she vaguely remembered a story involving her *Dawdi* Berger from that time that had to do with the farm, about him working hard to save it and his father's too. But she'd never thought to ask what he did in the years before, during the war. She knew some young men who had grown up Amish joined the Army during that time, and some even fought overseas. Others had registered as conscientious objectors and had been sent to camps and hospitals to work.

Her grandfather would have been the right age to have been drafted, but she didn't remember him talking about that time or what he did during the war.

Jane stood as the sun lowered, spreading streaks of pink and orange across the horizon. Then the sun disappeared, but the colors lingered.

There weren't many people left to ask about the family stories. Andy had no interest in the past. She had one older cousin, Beth, who might have some information for her. Regardless of what she found out about her grandfather, she'd like to tell a story that had to do with the anniversary of the end of the Great War.

Instead of heading for her house, Jane turned toward the phone shanty on the edge of her plot of land to leave Beth a message. She stepped inside, turned on the flashlight she left on the shelf, and dialed Beth's number from memory.

To Jane's surprise, someone answered. "Hallo. This is Joanna."

It took Jane a moment to gather her wits, but then she explained to Joanna—who was Beth's step-granddaughter and sometimes came to the quilting circle—that she hoped to talk to Beth sometime soon. "Is she up for a visit?"

"You won't be able to come here," Joanna said. "*Gross Mammi* broke her hip, and she's in the hospital in South Bend. That's why I'm in the phone shanty. I'm letting everyone know."

"Oh my." It seemed Jane's questions would have to wait.

"But she was talking about you just this morning. She has a quilt she wants to ask you about. It belonged to your *Mammi* Katie and needs to be repaired. Can you go visit her at the hospital?"

"*Jah*," Jane said. "I'll get up to the hospital as soon as I can."

"She also has a stack of letters she thought you might be interested in, ones that maybe you can use for your column."

"Oh? Who are the letters from?"

"Mammi Katie, to your grandfather. And vice versa. *Gross* Mammi wants to downsize. She's hoping you'll want them."

"Of course," Jane answered. "I absolutely do." Maybe she'd be able to write about her grandmother and grandfather after all.

CHAPTER 1

Tally Smucker

"Tally," *Mamm* called out. "Are you still there?"

"Jah." I stood in the doorway of Mamm's room, fighting back tears as I watched her under the patchwork quilt that I'd helped make when I was ten. "I thought you were asleep."

"I nearly was," she answered, "but then I thought you'd left, and I woke back up."

"I'll stay right here." I leaned against the doorframe. "Until you fall asleep."

Dat had made the furniture in the room before they married over thirty years ago—an oak bedstead and a bureau, along with a table that sat under the window. The blue curtains let in a little light, but the day was overcast and the entire room was washed in gray.

A couple of minutes later, Mamm's soft snore signaled it was time for me to go. I had at least an hour to myself, and the best way to spend it was a walk along the country road that ran adjacent to our farm. Then I'd need to get supper started, get Mamm up from her nap, and put the food on the table by the time my brother, Rich, came in from harvesting the last of the soybeans.

I blinked back the tears I'd been fighting to contain since that morning, slipped on my running shoes, grabbed my coat, and headed through the back porch and out the door into the brisk fall air and down the ramp that Rich had built to accommodate Mamm's wheelchair.

I turned to glance back at our house. Dat had built it too. It was two stories with five bedrooms. Dat hadn't had any children with his first wife, who'd died a few years before he married Mamm. He was forty-four when they married, while Mamm was thirty-six. Even though they were older, they'd hoped to fill the house with children. But God had sent only two, my brother and me. It was one of Mamm's great heartaches to not have more children. It was one of mine now too. What I wouldn't give to have a sister to share my burden.

Mamm had been extra needy all day, wanting me to sit with her at the table instead of washing the morning dishes, then crying a little midmorning when I went out to dig potatoes in the garden, even though I wheeled her chair to the window where she could watch.

She was hungry before I had the noon meal ready and then grew teary again when Rich interrupted her while we ate. After we finished, she wanted to go down for her nap before I had a chance to clean up. I'd made her wait until her usual two-o'clock naptime and then felt bad for being firm with her.

She'd had a stroke three years ago, a few months after Dat died. Some said it was out of grief, which could be true. Dat died from a heart attack at age seventy-two. He'd come in from the field to wash up for supper and then stumbled into the kitchen. I reached for his arm, but he fell to the floor, pulling me down with him. By the time I got to the phone shanty to call 9-1-1, plus the time it took for the ambulance to arrive, plus the time it took to get him to the hospital, he'd passed.

Four months later, Mamm fell too. However, she came home from the hospital—although in a wheelchair. She'd lost strength in one leg, and regardless of the physical therapy, she never recovered.

I was eighteen when Dat died, so my childhood was already over. But I wasn't prepared to be the sole caregiver to my mother. And I wasn't prepared not to like being a caregiver either. I thought it would come naturally, but it was a struggle every single day.

My main respite away from the house, besides my walks, was going to Plain Patterns every few days for the quilting circle. Mamm enjoyed the quilting, while I especially enjoyed the stories Jane told while we quilted. But the weaker Mamm grew, the harder it was on both of us to get out the door and on our way, even though we had a custom buggy for her wheelchair. I guessed those outings would soon come to an end, which would be a loss for both of us.

I wasn't alone with Mamm though. I had Rich, who turned out to be quite able to farm our land and make a living. What would I do without him? But he did little to help with Mamm and seemed oblivious to the work I did to keep up with the house, the cooking, the laundry, and the gardening. He also didn't seem to be able to read my emotions when I was sad or overwhelmed.

I increased my pace as I reached the road, as a blue pickup sped by, its wheels crossing the yellow dotted line for a moment. The driver quickly corrected and kept on going.

Rich drove the metal-wheeled tractor in the far end of the field. He was twenty-seven and hadn't courted anyone, although I'd noticed Joanna Yoder striking up a conversation after church a few times in the last couple of months.

I kept my head down as Rich turned the tractor toward me. He thought my daily walks were frivolous, but a swift pace cleared my mind and gave me strength for the rest of the day, until I had Mamm back in bed for the night.

When Mamm first had her stroke, our old district pitched in and helped us out, just as they had after Dat passed. Rich had help with the chores for a couple of weeks. When harvest came around, the older farmers stopped by to see if he had questions. I believe he offended more than one well-intentioned neighbor with his abruptness and lack of conversation. On the other hand, Rich worked fourteen-hour days, starting long before sunrise and going back out most evenings after supper ended, and didn't need help.

I, however, did.

And at first, help was plentiful. Women in our district reached out. They delivered meals. Helped with spring cleaning the first year and the second year too. They dropped off baked goods from time to time. My *Aenti* Frannie, Mamm's sister, spent Wednesday mornings at our house for a few months.

After a while, I think they all believed I had everything under control and stopped coming by. As shy as I was, I often felt I didn't belong, which made it even harder to ask for help. And physically I did have things under control—barely. But emotionally, I was on edge.

I reached the end of our property and approached our neighbor's house. The blue pickup that had sped by earlier was now parked in the driveway, next to a white SUV. I'd only met the neighbors, Danielle Roman and her little girl, once, about a year ago. They kept to themselves.

As I stared, the little girl ran out the front door of their one-story ranch house. She wore her dark hair in two long braids, and I guessed she was around six or so. Was she home from school already?

The mother, who wore a stocking cap over her blond hair, came out the door, locking it behind her. She wore bright red lipstick, just as she had the time I met her.

The little girl waved and smiled, and then Danielle did too.

Surprised at how friendly they appeared, I paused a moment but then waved and smiled back.

"We're going on a picnic," the little girl called out. I hadn't been told her name before—I'd remember if I had.

Before I could answer, a man climbed out of the blue pickup. He held a basket in one hand, with an orange blanket on top of it, and his cell phone in the other. Danielle, who was nearly as tall as the man, approached him and pointed to the trail on the edge of the driveway, and the two adults started walking along it, toward the woods behind the house. The man appeared to be a decade or so older than Danielle, probably in his late thirties. The little girl skipped along behind them.

Feeling as if I were being nosy, which I was, I picked up my pace even more and hurried on. It seemed a little chilly for a picnic, but they all had on warm coats.

Twenty minutes later, I was on the far side of the loop. I began to run, something I did every day. I breathed in deeply again, doing my best to let go of my anxious thoughts. Running made me feel stronger than I did any other time of the day. It made me feel alert. In control. While caring for Mamm and cleaning and cooking, a numbness would come over me. That all lifted when I was outside in the fresh air, running. Jogging, technically, I was sure. But it felt like running to me. Sometimes it felt like flying.

I took a deep breath, trying to relax into my stride. I'd always struggled with anxiety, but Mamm's stroke had made it worse. My world had shrunk to not much more than the loop that I walked and trips into Nappanee to take Mamm to the doctor and to buy the few groceries we needed, things we didn't grow or raise ourselves. And our beloved trips to Plain Patterns.

I slowed as I reached the road that led back to our farm and then transitioned into a fast walk as I reached our property. I took several deep breaths, rolled my shoulders, and then turned down our driveway. The tractor was parked by the field fence, and Rich wasn't in sight.

For a moment, I feared something was wrong with Mamm, but how would Rich know? It wasn't as if he ever checked on her.

As I neared the house, I heard voices, and then Rich said, "I need to get back to work." He stood from where he'd been sitting on the couch that was on our screened front porch. He wore his work clothes—black pants, a forest-green shirt, and straw hat over his dark hair. Joanna Yoder sat in one of the rocking chairs closest to the steps. She grinned up at him, her dimples flashing. He didn't smile back, but his eyes engaged with hers in a lively way that wasn't typical for my brother.

She saw me and stood. "Tally," she said, "I'm glad I didn't miss you." She started down the steps toward me. Joanna was a year younger than I was, and we were as different as could be. She was an extrovert who exuded joyfulness. I'd never seen her grumpy or even glum. Joanna was in our old church district, had gone to my school, and just recently joined the quilting circle at Plain Patterns, although she wasn't known for her handwork.

Rich was seven years older than she was and seemed pretty boring in comparison. But Mamm often said opposites attract.

Joanna motioned toward the cardboard box on the porch table. "I brought you a loaf of banana bread and a jar of peanut butter spread."

"*Denki.*" I'd give Mamm a slice of the bread for her afternoon snack.

"Well," Joanna said, "I need to get going. *Gross* Mammi's in the hospital with a broken hip, and Jane Berger is stopping by to pick up a quilt my *Gross* Mammi wants her to repair, along with a box of letters."

I smiled a little. Maybe Jane would spin a story from the quilt or letters. Or perhaps from both.

"Will you be at Plain Patterns tomorrow?" Joanna asked.

"I hope so," I answered. "If Mamm feels up to it."

"All right," Joanna said. "I'll be there unless *Gross* Mammi comes home by then. I'm going to take care of her."

I nodded in affirmation.

Joanna started toward the barn, where her horse and buggy were hitched. Rich walked a few steps ahead of her.

Bringing the banana bread by for me had most likely been an excuse to see Rich. I turned toward the porch, climbed the steps, and picked up the loaf. I hoped Joanna was understanding of how Rich could be.

The sound of a vehicle on our gravel driveway drew my attention away from the bread. A white pickup, driven by a young man, stopped. He rolled down his window and waved at me. "Excuse me."

Before I could answer, Rich jogged toward the pickup, calling out, "What do you need?"

With the bread in my hand, I stepped around to the side of the house toward the back door, going up the ramp. I hung my coat and then put the bread on the table. Our kitchen was long and narrow, with counters and a sink on one side, a large china hutch on the other, a table on the side that led to the living room, and a stove that ran on propane just past the counter.

Mamm's room was down the hall. I expected her to still be asleep, but she was sitting on the side of the bed, one hand on the arm of her wheelchair. "I heard voices," she said.

"Joanna Yoder dropped off a loaf of banana bread."

"I heard Rich's voice."

"Jah," I answered. "He was talking with Joanna."

Mamm smiled. "She's sweet on him."

I stepped in front of the bed, put my hands under her arms, and transferred her to the chair. "Wouldn't that be nice if they started courting?"

I jumped as Rich's voice shot through the house. It sounded if he were yelling from the front door. "Tally, would you come out here?"

I stepped to Mamm's doorway.

Rich appeared in the hallway. "Our neighbor's name is Danielle, right?"

I nodded.

"She's missing, and her brother's worried about her. I saw you walking that way a little while ago. Did you see her?"

"Jah, I did."

Rich bobbed his head toward the front of the house. "Go talk with him."

I WHEELED MAMM out to the living room window, where she could see what was going on, and then, leaving the door open, descended the steps.

Rich stood a few feet from the young man, who stood beside his pickup, and said, "This is Kenan Peters."

"Pleased to meet you," I said. "I'm Tally."

"Good to meet you." He wore a Cincinnati Reds baseball cap, jeans, a gray jacket, and heavy work boots, but not farm boots. Perhaps he worked in construction.

"I'm looking for my sister." He motioned in the direction of her little farm. "I stopped by, but no one answered the door, even though her vehicle is there. I'm worried about her."

"Is there another car parked there?" I asked. "A blue pickup?"

His face clouded a little, and he shook his head. "Did you see the pickup earlier?"

"Jah." I crossed my arms against the chill in the air. "About an hour ago. I was out for my walk, and a man arrived in the pickup. Then your sister and her little girl followed the man past the house."

"Thanks." Kenan quickly turned toward his pickup and opened the door, but then stopped and faced Rich. "I might need some help. Would you mind going with me?"

"What are you talking about?" Rich asked.

"It's just a hunch," Kenan said. "My sister has some . . . problems. I might need another adult."

Rich gave him a puzzled look as Joanna drove her buggy by, giving Rich a big wave. He barely lifted his hand in return. I could tell he was befuddled.

"I'll go," I said to Kenan. "I'll meet you over there."

He motioned to the open truck door, but I shook my head. It wouldn't be appropriate for me to ride with him.

His face reddened. "See you there. Thank you."

I turned to Rich. "Would you sit with Mamm until I get back?"

"For a bit," he said. "If she needs me to."

I walked quickly as Kenan pulled his truck around. When I reached the road, I began to run.

When I reached Danielle's, Kenan was climbing out of his truck.

My words were breathy. "They were walking down the trail on the other side of the house." I pointed through the front yard.

When we reached the trail, I led the way. It appeared to go through the field and then perhaps all the way to the grove of trees in the distance.

When we arrived at a chain-link gate, I reached over and unlatched it. As I opened it and stepped through, I gasped. The little girl was curled up by the brush on the other side of the fence, her coat pulled over her head.

I stepped aside so Kenan could get to her.

"Maggie." He kneeled down and scooped her up. She threw her arms around his neck. "Where's your mama?"

She buried her head in his shoulder.

"Maggie," Kenan said, "can you tell me what's going on?"

"She's asleep." With her head still buried in Kenan's shoulder, she pointed to the woods. "Under a tree."

"I'll go," I said. "You stay here."

I started up the trail and then started to jog. When I reached the woods, I scanned the shadowy floor. The afternoon sun was waning, and the woods were growing dark. I squinted. Hopefully Danielle wasn't too far off the trail.

A strip of gray up ahead caught my attention. Danielle's coat. Under her was the orange blanket the man had been carrying, and the basket was beside her. I froze for a moment, feeling as paralyzed as Danielle appeared.

The moment passed, and I began to jog again and then sprint.

When I reached her, I fell to the ground beside the blanket. "Danielle?" I touched her shoulder. "Are you all right?"

She was on her side with her head turned toward me, and her legs, bent at the knee, pointed toward me too. Her hands were both tucked under her head with her blond hair spread around them. Her lipstick was smudged, and she appeared as if she were sleeping.

Fear filled me. Was she dead?

My heart pounded as I took her wrist and felt for a pulse. I found it. Relieved, I put my hand on her shoulder again and shook her a little. There was no response. I shook her a little harder. She turned away from me.

"Danielle," I said again. "Are you all right?"

"Leave me alone," she muttered. "I don't know you."

"I'm your neighbor. Tally."

"Let me sleep."

CHAPTER 2

When I reached Kenan, I stretched out my arms for Maggie. The little girl shook her head and then buried it in her uncle's shoulder again.

He gave me a questioning look.

I spoke softly. "Maggie is right. Danielle is sleeping. She woke up a little and talked to me, but you should check on her and decide if we need to call for help."

"All right." Then he whispered into Maggie's ear, "Stay here with Tally, okay? I need to go speak with your mama."

He turned so Maggie was facing me. I extended my hands, and the little girl fell into them. She was tall but felt light in my arms.

"Thank you," Kenan said as he headed down the trail.

"Maggie, how old are you?" I asked.

"Five." She held up her hand with her fingers spread wide. "Mama says I'm a handful."

I smiled. She seemed like a fun handful.

A flock of crows flew out of a tree in the woods, cawing, most likely scared by Kenan. "How many birds do you see?" I asked Maggie.

"A lot."

I began to count, reaching eighteen before they flew upward and then back to the woods.

"I want to go to my house," Maggie said.

"We will," I replied. "In a few minutes."

"I want Uncle Kenan to cook me supper."

"He will," I said. "Soon." I pointed toward the house. "What is your favorite thing about where you live?"

"The room under the staircase."

"Oh?"

"It's where I hide," she said.

"Why do you hide?"

She shrugged. "Sometimes I just want to be by myself."

I could understand that.

"Tally!" Kenan called out. "Can you help me?"

I turned back to face the woods. He stood on the edge of the trees, waving at us.

I started toward him, still holding Maggie. When he reached me, he said, "Danielle's awake but unsteady. If I hold on to one side and you hold on to the other, we can get her back to the house."

"What about Maggie?"

"She'll have to lead the way." He took her from my arms. "Can you do that?"

Maggie swung her hands behind her back, away from Kenan. "Yes."

"I'll show you where to wait," he said, "so you can be ready to lead. We'll follow."

"All right." Maggie wrapped her arms around Kenan's neck.

He carried Maggie about twenty yards into the woods and put her down. "Wait right here."

She rubbed her arm, under the sleeve of her coat. "I will. I promise."

He bent down and kissed the top of her head. "We'll be right back."

He led the way to Danielle while I followed behind him. He didn't speak, which I appreciated.

When we reached Danielle, she was still on the blanket. Her eyes were closed, and she was breathing slowly.

"Maybe you should call 9-1-1," I suggested.

"Not yet. This isn't the first time I've found her this way."

Kenan bent down and spoke to Danielle, saying, "It's time to go. Maggie is waiting for us."

"Let me sleep," Danielle muttered.

"Nope." Kenan put his arm under hers. "We need to get you back to the house." He lifted her a little and wedged both of his arms under her. Then he stood, lifting her up.

"Don't do this," Danielle said.

"Either we do this, or I call 9-1-1."

"Definitely don't do *that*." Her feet moved a little.

She was now completely off the blanket, so I moved the basket off too. It had a few paper plates and plastic bags of grapes, crackers, and slices of cheese. A small white paper bag caught my eye. I lifted the blanket, shook it, and then folded it, placing it on top of the basket before picking it up.

I stepped to Danielle's side and looped my free arm through hers. Together, Kenan and I started walking her forward. I was five foot seven, and she was a couple of inches taller than me, and also incredibly strong. By the weight of her, I guessed she was all muscle.

Danielle said, "I fell asleep. I'm fine."

"You're not fine," Kenan said. "Maggie was all the way to the gate. What if she'd gotten to the road?"

"Hardly *anyone* drives out this way."

"That's not the point," Kenan said. "She could have been hurt. Or taken. Something horrible could have happened."

"But it didn't," Danielle said. "She's fine."

As we neared Maggie, she turned toward her mother. "Are you awake now?"

"Yes, love," Danielle said. "I'm sorry I fell asleep."

Maggie turned back toward the gate and started marching, the three of us behind her. Danielle shuffled her feet. I wasn't sure I needed to keep holding on to her, but I followed Kenan's lead. When we reached the gate, Maggie stopped. Kenan let go of Danielle, and she slumped toward me. Kenan unlatched the gate, opened it, and told Maggie to head toward the house. "But don't get too far ahead of us."

Maggie walked ahead, her hands swinging back and forth.

Danielle moaned. "I just want to go to *bed*."

"What did you take?" Kenan asked.

"Nothing." She moaned again.

I thought of the small white paper bag in the basket.

Maybe Kenan's question wore heavy on her, because she lifted her head more and moved her feet with determination instead of shuffling along. As we neared the house, she muttered, "Kenan, I'm fine. Please don't make a big deal out of this."

"You said you weren't going to see Dirk anymore."

She didn't respond.

When we reached the house, Maggie opened the back door, which was unlocked, and led the way into the kitchen. Danielle leaned against the counter by the sink, and I put the basket on the counter by the stove.

Maggie took my hand. "Come see my hiding place."

I followed her through a hallway. She opened a door, just taller than she was, under a staircase. She stepped inside and pulled a string, which turned on a lightbulb. I'd read about rooms under staircases but had never seen one. A bookcase filled with picture books was placed against the far wall, and a sleeping bag and pillow were spread across the hardwood floor.

"What a nice place you have," I said to Maggie. "I really like it."

"Uncle Kenan made it for me in the summer, when Mama was sad. He said it would be good for me to have a fort where I could read and play." Maggie stepped toward me. "Mama's sad a lot."

"I'm sorry."

Maggie reached backward and grabbed the chain hanging from the lightbulb. She pulled hard, turned off the light, and stepped out into the hall.

"Are you in kindergarten, Maggie?"

"Sort of. Mama's homeschooling me." She lowered her voice. "She says we need to be together. I have a bunch of schoolbooks. Want to see them?"

I needed to get back to take care of Mamm. Darkness was falling, I hadn't started supper, and Rich would be annoyed if I didn't return soon.

"Sure," I answered.

Maggie walked into the study, which had a large table at one end next to the window. On top was a stack of children's books and a stack of workbooks.

"This is my school."

"How lovely." I wished I could spend all day teaching instead of caregiving.

Maggie lowered her voice. "We only do about an hour of school a day. Mama says it's enough."

"I imagine it is with only one student," I replied. Maggie led the way back into the kitchen. Kenan had started a pot of coffee, and Danielle was sitting on the floor now, but her eyes were open and her head was up. She patted the floor beside herself and said to Maggie, "Come sit by me, baby."

Maggie shook her head.

Danielle wrinkled her nose.

Kenan cleared his throat.

I wasn't sure what was being communicated, but clearly something was, and all three of them seemed to understand the message.

Kenan turned toward me. "Thank you for your help."

I smiled a little. "Let me know if there's anything more I can do. . . ." I wasn't sure what that would be though.

After telling everyone good-bye, I let myself out the back door and headed to the trail along the side of Danielle's driveway. As I started for home, the blue pickup drove slowly by.

I stepped behind a tree and waited. After the pickup had passed, I returned to Danielle's back door. I knocked and then opened it a little. "Kenan," I said. "Would you come here for a moment?"

He appeared immediately, a dish towel in his hands.

"I wanted to let you know the pickup that was parked in the driveway, the blue one, just drove by."

He shook his head a little and frowned. Then he said, "Thank you for letting me know."

I lowered my voice even more. "Also, there's a paper bag in the basket. A small white one, like the kind prescriptions come in."

He sighed. "I'll take a look." He slung the dish towel over his shoulder. "Will you be okay walking home by yourself?"

"I'll be fine."

"Okay," he said. "Thank you again. For everything."

I dipped my head and then gave him a little wave as he stepped back into the kitchen. He looked as if he had the weight of the world on his shoulders, instead of just a dish towel. I retraced my route from a few minutes ago and then walked along the highway. As I reached our driveway, the blue pickup drove by again. I stepped back toward the road and watched it continue on. Finally, it picked up speed and kept going. Hopefully, it wouldn't come back.

When I entered the house, Mamm was in the living room by herself.

"Where's Rich?"

"He's putting the tractor away." Mamm raised her head and met my eyes. "What took you so long?"

"I was helping the neighbor."

"What happened?"

I wasn't sure how much to say to Mamm, partly because Danielle's behavior brought up sad memories for me. Would it bring up troubling thoughts for Mamm too?

"Tally . . ." Mamm's voice had a hint of curiosity. She hated not knowing what was going on.

"It seems Danielle might have some health problems."

"What kind?"

"I'm not sure. . . ." My voice trailed off.

"Tally," Mamm said. "Why won't you tell me what happened?"

"I . . ." I didn't want to worry her, plus I feared I'd sound gossipy.

"Just tell me," Mamm said. "You don't need to explain anything to me. Just give me the facts."

I sighed. "Don't read anything into what I tell you, all right? I have no idea what's going on. There's no reason to judge our neighbor."

Mamm nodded.

I left out the part about the man in the blue pickup, but I did tell Mamm about Danielle being asleep on a blanket in the woods and Kenan and I waking her up.

"That sounds innocent enough," Mamm said. "They went on a picnic. Danielle fell asleep. Mothers of small children get tired. I remember I did."

I remembered too.

"Why would I judge her for that?" Mamm asked.

I shrugged, stepped to her chair, and wrapped my hands around the handles on the back. "Ready to get supper started?"

"Jah. What are we having?"

I was tired of coming up with ideas for meals. It was such endless work. I didn't know how women did three meals a day for, well, forever. I'd done the math. Three meals per day was 1,095 meals a year. For some women, that was fifty or sixty thousand meals during their lifetime, or even more.

Jah, a woman's work was definitely never done and always underappreciated.

"Tally," Mamm said as I pushed her into the kitchen, "what are we having?"

"I don't know. . . ." I pushed her to the table. "I could make a potato, ham, and cheese casserole. With broccoli on the side. And the bread I baked this morning."

Mamm gave me a quick smile. "Good idea. I'll peel the potatoes." It was a task she could still do, although slowly.

"Denki. I'll go get them." I grabbed the flashlight from the cupboard and headed to the basement stairs. I'd been digging potatoes nearly every day and had burlap bags full in the back of the basement. I made a sling out of my apron and placed ten potatoes in it. I'd make enough casserole to have leftovers for the next day. Or maybe I'd make two batches and give one to Danielle.

Except that would mean I'd need to go back over to her house. I decided against making the second casserole. I had enough to do.

As I started back up the stairs, Rich's voice called out my name. I didn't like it when he yelled.

"Tally!" he called out again.

As I stepped into the kitchen, he said, "What's going on?"

"What do you mean?"

"Another man just stopped and asked if I'd seen Danielle in the last half hour."

"Was he in a blue pickup?"

Rich nodded. "Why are we involved in this?"

Mamm looked hurt. "Tally, why didn't you tell me that?"

I turned toward her. "I told you all the important details."

Rich threw up his hands. "What's going on?"

"I have no idea," I answered. Which was true. My heart lurched for Maggie. I knew what it was like not to be able to rely on a mother, on the person you expected to care for you.

And I wasn't thinking about the way Mamm was now. I was thinking about how she was when I was a little girl.

CHAPTER 3

The next morning, after I'd fixed hotcakes and sausage for our first meal of the day and then cleaned up the kitchen and started a stew to simmer all morning for our noon meal, I rolled Mamm to the living room window and then went out to the garden to work for a half hour before hitching the horse to the buggy to go to Plain Patterns. I wore my work coat, a black scarf on my head, and gloves on my hands.

I began digging the last row of potatoes. The ground was muddy from the rain the night before. It wouldn't be long until the first hard frost, so I needed to finish soon.

Working in the garden gave me a few minutes to myself, but I didn't enjoy it. Dat, unlike most Amish fathers, had been our main gardener, and I'd never developed much of a knack for it. The last three years I'd struggled to get the vegetables to grow, but this year had been better.

I missed Dat the most when I worked in the garden and not just because I wished he were still around to do the work. He was at his best when he was planting, weeding, and watering. It was what he did to relax. He enjoyed farming too, but the garden was his happy place. It was what he did after he'd worked all day in the fields, before he came into the house, and often for a while before he went to bed.

I'd sit on the edge of the garden and talk with him, or I'd join him and weed. I didn't mind working in the garden as long I was able to work with him. It was my escape.

Reading was my other escape growing up. I lived for trips into town to the library and would check out stacks of books at a time.

I no longer had Dat, but I still had books. I used to read any chance I could. While I was cooking. Walking to the chicken coop. Before I fell asleep. Lately, I couldn't concentrate as well as I used to, although I still checked out stacks of books from the library. I also bought used magazines at the yearly library sale—all sorts, from housekeeping to medical journals to education journals. I mostly just read at night now, which gave me a break before I started the same endless routine over in the morning. It also helped me better understand the world around me.

It was through my reading that I guessed Rich was probably on the autism spectrum and understood that he wasn't oblivious to my emotions on purpose. In our community, being on the high end of the spectrum wouldn't be noticed, and even if it was, it would not be addressed in most cases. What mattered was if Rich could run a farm and be a husband and father—the God-ordained head of his household. That was definitely something Rich would be able to do. People might find him quirky, but no one would question his abilities.

I also learned more about teaching through reading. I had stacks of old copies of *Weekly Reader* and *Education Week*, along with back copies of *Blackboard Bulletin*, an Amish magazine for teachers, from a woman in our old district who used to teach.

Ever since I was a young scholar, I dreamed of teaching at a one-room Amish school in the area. I was shy, but I loved to share what I learned. While I hesitated to speak up in social situations, teaching was different. I'd had the opportunity when I was seventeen to be a teacher's assistant and found it rewarding. After Dat passed away, I was hired by our district's school board to teach, but a few days later Mamm had her stroke and it became obvious she would need full-time care. I'd accepted the job—but then had to decline it.

I had no regrets. Mamm had to be my priority. It was my duty to honor her by caring for her. But I'd thought she'd get well. I thought I'd care for her for a few months, maybe a year, and then I'd be offered another teaching position. But Mamm didn't get better. And over time I feared I'd lost my skills to be a good teacher at all. I no longer felt as if I belonged in a classroom.

However, I would always feel as if belonged inside a book, inside a story. When I first began to read, I felt as if I belonged with the characters—Heidi, Laura Ingalls, Pippi Longstocking, and even Ramona the Pest. Later, it was with Jane Eyre and Elizabeth Bennet. Jah, I managed to read the English classics too. Dat and Mamm never monitored what I checked out from the library.

When I'd read the same book a second time, which I often did, not only did I feel as if I belonged with the characters but also with the author too, as if we had a connection.

That was how I felt when Jane told a story. As if I completely belonged.

I tossed more potatoes onto the grass as wheels rolled over the gravel driveway. I turned my head. It was Kenan again.

He waved and then climbed out of the truck. "Hi, Tally. How are you?"

"Fine." I stood up and stepped out of the garden and onto the lawn.

"Thank you for your help yesterday."

I smiled slightly.

"I spent the night at Danielle and Maggie's, and Danielle seemed fine when I left just now, but I was wondering if you could look in on her sometime this morning."

"I'm sorry," I said. "I'm taking my Mamm to a quilting circle. But I can check on them this afternoon."

"Thank you," he said, "I'd appreciate it."

It was the neighborly thing to do, but I had no idea what to look for when I checked on Danielle and Maggie. For the man in the blue pickup? For another pharmacy bag? For a sleeping Danielle?

Kenan handed me a piece of paper. "Here's my phone number if you need it. If you see any . . . problems, would you please call me? I don't expect you to do anything except let me know."

I took the paper and shoved it in the pocket of my coat.

"Thank you," he said again.

I wished he'd stop saying that. I simply nodded, ready for him to go.

"Danielle has been going through a rough patch, but she's a good mother to Maggie." He lowered his eyes. "Most of the time."

I glanced toward the house.

Realizing the direction of my gaze, he took a step back and gave me a wave. "Sorry to keep you."

I waved back but didn't say anything. As Kenan drove away, I gathered up the potatoes on the lawn, put them in a bucket, and lugged it onto the back porch. I felt overwhelmed caring for Mamm and paralyzed as far as my own hopes and dreams. How could I help Danielle too?

After I hitched the horse to the buggy, I drove it to the post by the back door. The sun was growing bright, and the day had warmed some. I went into the house, changed my apron, put on my *Kapp*, and helped Mamm get her coat on.

We'd had a special buggy made for Mamm's wheelchair about six months before. The back of the new buggy was a tailgate that unfolded and worked as a ramp. There were also attachments to secure her wheelchair to the floor of the buggy so she wouldn't roll around. By the time I got Mamm down the back-door ramp from the house, up the buggy ramp, and safely in her spot, I was breathing heavily.

When I climbed into the buggy, Mamm asked, "What did that Englisch man want?"

"For me to check on his sister."

"Are you going to?"

"Jah, after we get home from the quilting circle."

"Why don't we stop by now? Maybe they'd like to go with us."

"I doubt it," I said.

"Well, let's ask."

I was a little surprised at Mamm's concern. She'd been mostly focused on herself since her stroke. Actually, she'd been mostly focused on herself for as long as I could remember. I'd long been aware of Mamm's self-absorption, and I'd often despaired at her lack of concern for others. In my exhaustion in caring for her, had I now developed those same tendencies?

But she'd seemed empathetic toward Danielle the day before. I couldn't discourage her interest in someone else, not now. And I couldn't ignore the biblical mandate that I needed to look after my neighbor, even if I had no idea how.

When we pulled into Danielle's driveway, I could see Maggie's face in the front window. She immediately ran out on the porch. "Tally!" She wore a green plaid flannel dress and red cowboy boots.

I climbed down from the buggy. "Hallo, Maggie!" I walked toward the porch. "Is your mother around?"

"She's doing the dishes." Maggie turned toward the door. "I'll go get her."

I waited on the porch, feeling even more awkward than usual. Why had I given in to Mamm? Danielle wouldn't want to go to a quilting circle.

She came to the door, drying her hands on a towel.

"How are you doing?" I asked.

"Besides being embarrassed?" She shook her head sadly. "I'm *really* sorry about yesterday. And you didn't need to check on me today. I know Kenan asked you to."

I didn't verify that he had. "Actually, I came to ask if you and Maggie wanted to go to a quilting circle with me and my Mamm. At Plain Patterns—a quilt shop not too far from here."

"I know where it is," Danielle answered.

Maggie grabbed her mother's hand and pulled on it. "Can we?"

"What about school?"

"We can do it when we get back. I want to ride in Tally's buggy."

I didn't imagine Danielle would want to go, let alone ride in the buggy.

But she surprised me. "May we ride in your buggy?"

"Jah," I said. "My Mamm rides in the back—she's in a wheelchair. But there's room on the seat in the front by me."

"We'll go, then." Danielle smiled broadly, and for the first time I noticed her dimples. She motioned for me to step inside.

I hesitated a moment, thinking of Mamm in the buggy, but then stepped through the door. Mamm would be all right for a few minutes.

"Grab your coat," Danielle said to Maggie.

The little girl ran through the living room, the heels of her boots clicking on the hardwood floor, then turned down the hallway and disappeared. Danielle followed her.

I glanced around the living room, which I hadn't seen the day before. It was sparsely furnished for an Englisch house, with just a sofa and a rocking chair. There were two photos on the fireplace mantel. One was of Danielle with a young man. Both wore some sort of military uniform—Army, I believed. The other photo was of the couple with a baby—Maggie, I guessed. The man appeared to be Hispanic, which explained Maggie's dark hair.

"Come on, Mags," Danielle said. "Hurry! You're going to get a buggy ride."

A minute later, they both appeared with their coats on, and Danielle had a purse slung over her shoulder. She wore red lipstick, which I was beginning to think was some sort of a trademark for her. I really liked the look of it. If I ever had a proper *Rumschpringe*, which I wouldn't, I'd buy a tube. The thought made me smile.

I stepped to the front door, opened it, and then led the way to the buggy. "Danielle and Maggie are going with us," I called out to Mamm as we approached.

"*Wunderbar*," Mamm said.

I lifted Maggie into the buggy. "Sit in the middle." As I showed Danielle where to grab to get in the buggy, she laughed a little and hoisted herself up without any problem.

After I climbed up to the seat, I gestured toward Mamm. "Danielle and Maggie, this is my mother, Regina. Mamm, Danielle and Maggie."

"Pleased to meet you." Danielle turned and reached out her hand to Mamm, who took it.

"Nice to meet you too." Mamm's voice had an unusual hint of levity to it.

As Danielle let go of Mamm's hand, she whispered, "Say hello," to Maggie.

Maggie smiled. "Hello."

"Hallo, Maggie," Mamm replied.

Maggie gave Mamm a wave and then sat up straight with her shoulders squared.

"Would you like to hold the reins?" I asked Maggie. "Once we're on the highway?"

Her eyes sparkled.

I turned on the highway and handed the reins to Maggie. She took them and smiled up at me. "Hold them loosely," I said. "He knows where we're going."

A moment later, Mamm said, "You're doing a good job, Maggie."

Maggie responded with a quick turn of her head and another smile for Mamm.

When we arrived at Plain Patterns, I parked the buggy by the barn and then opened up the back to roll Mamm down the ramp.

"I'll take care of the horse," Danielle said. "Should I put him in the barn?"

"Jah," I answered. "And Denki."

Danielle had already unhitched the horse and was leading him away from the buggy by the time I rolled Mamm down to the ground. I set the brake on the wheelchair and headed into Jane's barn to see if Danielle needed anything, but she was just closing the door to the stall.

"You're a pro," I said.

"I grew up with horses," she answered.

I pushed Mamm around the side of Plain Patterns to the ramp Jane's brother had built, that led to the deck, and then through the back door of the quilt shop, with Danielle and

Maggie following behind us. We entered the back room that housed a little kitchen, a play area for the kids who came with their mothers, and the main quilting frame, which was surrounded by chairs. We'd recently started quilting a sunshine-and-shadows quilt. The design was small squares of fabric—blue, green, pink, red, lavender, and black—arranged by color to form concentric rings of diamonds and then framed by a wide border, anchored with large corner blocks. It had always been one of my favorite patterns.

Jane stood at the little kitchen, starting a pot of coffee. "Hallo!"

I introduced Danielle and Maggie to her. Jane stepped forward and shook Danielle's hand and then said to Maggie, "Let me show you around." As Jane led the way to the play area, she said, "We should have two little ones joining us, but they are much younger than you are. Ruby and Owen are their names."

After I positioned Mamm at her place in the circle, I noticed there was a smaller quilting frame with an old quilt on it off to the side. I stepped toward it. Solid colors of shades of blue and green were pieced into hexagons on muslin. The border was a blue calico print, and the back was a solid blue.

I turned toward Jane, thinking of the quilt Joanna had mentioned yesterday. "Where did you get this?"

"From my cousin Beth. It was our Mammi Katie's."

"It's beautiful."

Jane smiled. "I don't remember ever seeing it before. It's so much more intricate than I would have thought an Amish woman would have made back then. As far as I can tell, she made it before 1920."

"So, you're restoring it?"

"Jah," Jane answered. "Then I'll give it back to Beth."

Other women began to arrive. Arleta and her little girl, Ruby.

Miriam and her son, Owen. Phyllis. Catherine, our bishop's wife. Because of the ever-increasing population of Amish in our area, several districts had been reconfigured a few months ago, and our new bishop was David Deiner, Catherine's husband. We were now in the same district as Jane.

Dorothy, who was in her eighties, arrived with her friend Wanda. And then Joanna. One by one, I introduced them to Danielle. Most of the talk was in English, but Catherine asked Wanda about her son, Tommy, and his girlfriend, Savannah, Dorothy's granddaughter, in Pennsylvania Dutch. "Have they set a date yet?"

"Aww," Danielle said, "a *wedding*. How wonderful."

"You understood that?" I asked.

Undeterred, Catherine said, "So, will there be a wedding soon?"

Wanda just shook her head, and then Dorothy said, "There's no ring as far as I know, but you should ask Savannah. She hopes to come to the quilting circle sometime soon." The Amish didn't do engagement or wedding rings, but Savannah and Tommy were both Englisch, although they went to a Mennonite church.

Jane turned toward Danielle. "Tell us about yourself. As much as you'd like to, of course."

She blushed. "I gave myself away by eavesdropping on your Pennsylvania Dutch. I grew up Old Order Mennonite in Ohio. However, I didn't join the church. Instead, I did the opposite. I joined the Army."

"Oh my," Catherine said. "Your poor folks." Catherine wasn't as judgmental as she used to be, but she still spoke her mind at times. Although her daughter Sophie—who was living Englisch and now engaged—had helped her with that.

"Jah." Danielle sighed. "It was hard on them."

There was a long pause, then Jane asked, "You don't have

to answer this if you don't want to, but how long did you serve in the Army?"

"I don't mind your asking. Six years. I spent one of those years in Iraq. After I was discharged, I used my GI Bill to become a medical assistant, although I'm a stay-at-home mom right now, along with being a part-time farmer."

Jane's face brightened. "Tell us about your farm."

"It's across the road from Regina and Tally's place. It's small, only twenty acres. I have a field of soybeans and a field of corn, plus a small wooded area. I hire out most of the work, so I guess I'm more like a manager than an actual farmer."

Her talk about the farm made me grow even more curious about the man I'd seen in the picture on the mantel. Were they married? Divorced?

A serious expression fell across Danielle's face, making me forget my questions for a moment. "I was hoping to make enough off the crops to help pay the mortgage."

Jane made a sympathetic sound, but the other women concentrated on their stitching.

"God probably wants me to lose my farm," Danielle said. "It's my comeuppance."

Shocked, I didn't know how to respond. What had she done, besides dishonoring her parents by joining the Army?

Jane simply smiled at her, and then after another long pause, as if she were debating on how to proceed, said, "I've been doing research on a difficult time in my family's history. Besides loaning me the quilt to restore, my cousin Beth gave me some old newspaper clippings and a box of letters. The letters were written between 1917 and 1919."

My ears perked up. I'd read enough to know that time period was trying. There was both a war and a pandemic going on.

It was as if I were reading Jane's mind. "During the Great

War, what was later called World War I, the flu of 1918 and 1919 swept through the entire world, including Indiana. Then soldiers came home shell-shocked." She met my eyes. "And then there was an economic downturn, including a farm depression. Many people lost their lives. Some lost their sanity. And then others lost their land."

This story sounded perfect for Danielle. So why was Jane looking at me?

"Would you like to hear it?"

"Of course." I'd never pass on one of her stories.

Now Jane looked at Danielle. "How about it? Do you feel up for a story?"

Danielle nodded and then said, "Death. War. Insanity. Farming woes. What could go wrong? Or, perhaps, what could possibly go right?"

Jane smiled a little, and then took a small notebook from her pocket. "Two of the central characters in the story are Ben and Amos Berger."

Mamm's eyes lit up. "Berger is my maiden name."

Jane smiled. "We're fourth cousins, remember?"

"That's right," Mamm said.

Jane continued, "One of the other central characters is my Mammi, Katie Landis. It's no surprise the story includes my grandmother, since it's her quilt I'm trying to restore"—Jane pointed in the direction of the antique quilt—"and it's her letters I've been reading." She held up her notebook, which looked to be full of scrawled notes. "Katie was nineteen when this story starts, back in 1917. . . ."

CHAPTER 4

Katie Landis

June 6, 1917

The old desk in the corner of the front room was covered with pieces of paper—bills and invoices—along with a stack of newspapers. Katie, following her Mamm's instruction, was tidying up Dat's desk.

He'd gone over to the Berger place. Katie wasn't sure why, but she could imagine him chatting away with John Berger and his sons, Amos and Ben. Together, the four seemed to think they could fix the problems of the world, or at least the problems of Elkhart County, Indiana.

Dat kept up with all sorts of news and often discussed how it affected or might affect their community. He was convinced, and the bishop agreed, that it was important to know what was going on locally and also in the world.

Katie separated the invoices from the bills and arranged the two piles. Then she started to go through the newspapers, all copies of the *Nappanee News*, a daily paper Dat subscribed to. Katie knew Dat had saved these particular newspapers for a reason. Otherwise, he would have used them to start the morning fire.

The oldest one was dated April 3. The front-page headline read, *Wilson Declares War Against Germany*. Katie kept reading. On April 2, President Woodrow Wilson had addressed Congress, saying, *"It is a fearful thing to lead this great peaceful people into war, into the most terrible and disastrous of all wars, civilization itself seeming to be in the balance. But the right is more precious than peace . . ."*

This had happened over two months ago. Why hadn't Dat said anything? She read more of Wilson's speech. *". . . The day has come when America is privileged to spend her blood and her might for the principles that gave her birth and happiness and the peace which she has treasured. God helping her, she can do no other."*

Bile rose in her throat. Privileged to spend America's blood and her might? Katie felt as if she might be ill.

She flipped to the next paper, dated April 7. Congress had approved Wilson's request and declared war on Germany.

The next newspaper, April 30, had an article about a possible Selective Service Act. Not enough men were signing up to fight, which meant the government was thinking about requiring men to fight. Men such as her brother, Seth? He was five years older than she was, so he'd be of age. Men such as their neighbors, Amos and Ben Berger? Even though they were peace-loving and nonresistant and would not fight?

The next newspaper was dated May 19. The Selective Service Act of 1917 had been enacted the day before.

Why hadn't Dat spoken about all of this? Why hadn't Seth?

Convinced it was because they were protecting Mamm, Katie tucked the newspapers under her arm and headed to the front door.

But why hadn't Amos said anything? She thought of him as a—as what? At least as a friend, and hopefully—someday—more.

The day was overcast and warm. Her brother dug a fence post hole in the far field. He didn't notice her. When she reached the Berger farm, Ben waved from where he dragged their pasture. She waved back and then continued marching along.

Katie started to second-guess confronting her father about what she'd read. Would she embarrass Dat by showing up with the newspapers?

"Katie!"

She turned toward the barn.

Amos stepped out of the shadows of the main entrance, his straw hat pushed back on his head over his blond hair. His gray eyes shone bright. "What are you doing here?"

"Looking for my father."

"He's on the porch with Dat. What's with the newspapers?"

She had them all in one hand now and waved them back and forth as she spoke. "War is what's in the newspapers. Why didn't you tell me?"

His face reddened.

"Did Dat ask you not to say anything?"

Amos nodded.

"Because of Mamm?"

"Jah," he answered. "Your Dat didn't want to worry her."

Mamm had a weak heart, caused by the scarlet fever she'd contracted after Katie had been born. She often said she didn't want to be protected from bad news, but all of them did it anyway. The thought of Seth having to go off to war would be a horrible shock to Mamm. But that didn't excuse Dat, nor Amos, from telling Katie.

"Didn't Dat—didn't *you*—think I could keep it private?"

Amos blushed again. "Your Dat asked me not to tell you—yet."

"When were you going to tell me?"

"Today. Your Dat just came over with the latest news. He and my Dat are talking things through. All men between twenty-one and thirty must register for the draft."

Katie exhaled slowly. That meant Seth. And Amos and Ben. Unless . . . "Are there farm deferments?"

"Possibly. That might work for Seth. And for either Ben or me—but not both of us."

Katie didn't need to ask which brother would go. Amos was the risk taker, the one always looking for adventure. Ben was older by a year, but Amos had always been the leader of the two. He was the fastest and strongest. He'd always been the best hunter. The most daring—or perhaps the most impulsive.

Amos could barely contain his smile, and the excitement in his voice was clear. "I'll most likely be sent to an Army fort or camp. Then I'll declare myself a conscientious objector."

Amos hadn't joined the church yet, and there wouldn't be time to if he was called up soon. But he intended to join, and he already adhered to the teachings of the church. He believed in nonresistance, in not fighting or even defending himself.

Amos grinned. "I doubt this will last long. Chances are it will all be over before I ever leave Elkhart County."

"Perhaps . . ." She doubted that. But it couldn't possibly last longer than another six months or so. Once the US became involved, the war would end. She wouldn't begrudge Amos an adventure as a conscientious objector.

"But if it's not over immediately, I'll write to you about everything I see and experience," Amos said. "And then when I come home—"

Katie put up her hand. "Write to me. And then we'll talk when you come home."

AFTER SUPPER, Katie cleaned the kitchen, slopped the hogs, secured the chickens in the coop, and then sat on the porch with her sewing. She was stitching a quilt top, a mosaic pattern made from hexagons. Mamm sat in her rocking chair, darning a pair of Seth's socks, and Dat read the newspaper. Not surprisingly, the front page was missing.

Seth had said he was going on a walk, no doubt to visit Paulina Fisher, who lived two miles away. Katie took another hexagon from her sewing basket and pinned it in place.

Katie heard Amos whistling before she saw him. She started to stand, but Dat was already on his feet, calling out, "*Gut'n Owed*, Amos. How are you?"

"Just fine," he answered. "It's a nice evening."

"It is," Dat said. "Did you come to sit with us for a while?"

Amos paused just a moment and then said, "I was hoping Katie would go on a walk with me."

Katie quickly put the quilt block down. "Is that all right, Dat?"

"Jah," Dat said. "Go on."

"Don't be too late," Mamm said.

She stood and headed down the steps at a quick pace, the ties of her Kapp bouncing on her shoulders. She heard Mamm make a clucking noise. In Mamm's opinion, Katie was always moving too fast.

Amos caught up with her and was silent for a moment before clearing his throat. "I'm a little worried that you didn't seem to want to talk about *us* this afternoon."

"Can't we concentrate on how wonderful it is you may get to see more of this country than northwest Indiana?"

"I appreciate that you feel that way," Amos said. "But I thought you might be upset about me leaving."

"You don't know you'll be going anywhere for sure."

Amos cleared his throat again. "Well, if I do . . ."

"Why would I be upset?"

"Well," he said softly, "I thought you might miss me."

"Oh, I'll miss you." She swatted her arm toward him. "Whose hand will I be removing fishhooks from? Whose eyes will I flush after they've been filled with sawdust? Whose arm will I sling after a fall off the rope swing?"

It had typically been Katie's job to see to the boys' wounds. Well, Amos's. Seth and Ben were much more cautious than he was.

"Katie." Amos stopped walking. "I'm serious. Will you miss me?"

She turned toward him. "Of course I will."

He shook his head. "Will you miss me more than you'd miss Ben if he ended up going?"

Amos had always been her favorite. The Berger brother she aimed to keep up with, as best she could. He was the one she longed to come and ask her for a walk, as he had tonight. But now he was most likely leaving. Jah, she had feelings for him, but he'd be home soon. They would continue their relationship when he returned.

"As I said." She crossed her arms. "We should have this conversation when you return."

"But if we have it now, I'll have more to look forward to while I'm gone."

"Amos . . ." It was hardly fair of him to put her on the spot.

"I don't want to go at all," he said, "if it means you might start courting someone else."

"I'm not going to court anyone else," she said. "I'm going to wait for you. Once you're home, we'll figure out our future. In the meantime, write to me—as you promised—and I'll write back, as I promised."

"Is that as much as you'll reassure me?"

She pursed her lips and then shrugged.

He smiled a little. "You've always been stubborn. I've always liked that about you, from when you were just a little thing."

She relaxed a little. "I had to be stubborn to keep up with three boys."

Amos sighed. "Maybe Ben will go instead of me, after all."

"Don't you dare not go," Katie replied. "You're the one who loves adventures. You're the one who's always wanted to travel. You'll never have another opportunity like this. I'll never have another opportunity to hear about what you see."

"You're right." He gazed back toward the Landis house. "We'll talk when I get back."

THE HEAT OF MID-AUGUST had sent Mamm to her room while Katie finished weeding the herb garden. Seth, waving an envelope, shouted from the lane, "You have a letter. From Amos."

Katie tried to brush the soil from her hands, but without much success. Instead, she wiped them on her black apron as her heart raced.

Seth reached her and handed her the envelope. "The return address is Camp Meade, Maryland."

She slid the letter into her apron pocket.

"Aren't you going to open it?" he asked.

"Not right now." She turned back to the rosemary plant and bent down again, the envelope pressing against her thigh. It was all she could do not to tear it open, but she didn't want to share the letter with Seth. Not yet. She wanted to read it in private first.

Amos had been gone for five weeks, and it was the first letter she'd received from him. She missed him far more than she'd expected and was annoyed he hadn't written sooner.

Once word was out that Amos was leaving, Dat told Mamm about the draft, but by then both Seth and Ben had received agriculture deferments. That seemed to placate Mamm. She wasn't as worried about Amos. "*Ach*," she'd said. "Amos has always been able to take care of himself. Out of the three boys, he'll fare the best."

A half hour later, as Katie loaded the weeds in the wheelbarrow, Ben yelled her name and then asked, "Did you get a letter?"

Katie stood, straightening her back. "Jah, I did."

"May I read it?"

She wrinkled her nose, not sure how to respond.

Ben held up an envelope. "You can read the one to Dat and me."

"I haven't read mine yet," she answered. "I'll come over after supper."

He took a step backward. "All right. I'll see you then."

After she washed up at the outside pump, Katie walked around to the front porch and sat down on the top step. She took the letter out of her pocket and carefully opened the envelope. The letter was folded in thirds.

She opened it. Amos had written in ink at the top of the page:

August 7, 1917

Dear Katie,

I hope this finds you doing well. I think of you often and miss you.

Well, it's finally happened. I'm off on an adventure, but it's not what I expected.

I immediately declared myself a conscientious objector when I arrived at Camp Meade. I expected to be ridiculed;

however, it's been worse than I anticipated. We're segregated, we're not given enough food, and we don't have any blankets.

There are a few other Amish, several Quakers, a few Mennonites, and three Church of Brethren men in my group. All are easy to be around, mostly. The Secretary of War, Newton Baker, visited the camp a few weeks ago. He's the one who insisted we be segregated, hoping the isolation would make us give up our CO status. He addressed us, saying, "Time to give it up, boys." He believes we're "traitors to the cause" and we "need to join the real men."

On a brighter note, I enjoyed the train ride east. You would have loved it. Ohio is hillier than Indiana but just as green. Pennsylvania has more trees. The city of Pittsburgh seemed to go on forever—I couldn't imagine so many people could live so closely together in so much smoke and grime. I would never want to live there but found it fascinating.

Please write when you can. I long to hear from you—news of our families and community, what you're thinking, and everything and anything else you want to write to me.

Sincerely,
Amos

She read the letter a second time, sorry to know that he was being treated poorly. Perhaps she shouldn't have encouraged him to go. On the other hand, he'd enjoyed the train trip and was amongst people who believed similarly to him. He was strong. She had no doubt he could weather the challenges.

He wrote that he thought of her often and missed her.

As much as she missed him?

She feared not.

Mamm and Dat settled on the front porch after supper while Katie finished cleaning the dishes. Once she was done, she slipped out the back door, with the letter in the pocket of her apron. When she reached the Bergers' house, Ben sat on the porch by himself.

"Hallo, Katie." He stood and waved the envelope in his hand. "Are you going to let me read Amos's letter?"

"Jah."

"There's nothing private in it?"

"*Nee*," Katie answered. "Nothing at all." She'd told Amos they needed to wait until he returned home to talk about their future. She was beginning to regret that too.

Ben cocked his head but didn't say anything more. He motioned for her to come up on the porch and then gestured to the chair next to his. She sat and handed him her letter. He took it and handed her his.

Katie feared Amos had written the same thing to Ben as to her, but he hadn't. His letter to Ben was full of questions about the farm, their father, the church, and about the Landis family. *Be a good friend to Katie while I'm gone*, he'd written.

Katie's heart skipped a beat. She treasured each word and then finally handed the letter back to Ben, who said, "Amos is doing what he thinks is best."

"Jah," Katie said. "And I support him."

"He'll be home soon."

Katie swallowed the lump in her throat.

"Can you stay for a while?" Ben handed Amos's letter to Katie back to her without commenting on it. "I can walk you home."

Katie slipped the letter back into her apron pocket. It wouldn't hurt to spend some time with Ben. He knew how much she and Amos cared about each other.

How much they all cared for one another.

CHAPTER 5

A month later, Mamm sat at the kitchen table, snapping beans for dinner, as Katie pulled four loaves of bread from the oven. The weather had cooled enough to bake in the house without causing too much discomfort.

"Take two of those over to John and Ben after we eat," Mamm said. John hadn't remarried after Amos and Ben's mother had died a few years before. They sometimes had help with the cleaning and cooking from a neighbor woman but did most of the work on their own.

"I'll make a couple of peach pies," Katie said to Mamm. "And take one of those over too."

"If you have time to bake today," Mamm said. "I wish I could help you pick the peaches. . . ."

"It won't take me long. The peaches are practically falling off the tree."

Peach was Amos's favorite pie.

She guessed Ben probably liked peach pie too.

By four, Katie pulled the pies out of the oven. While they cooled, she decided to go check the mailbox. She'd written Amos back right after she received his letter but hadn't heard from him since. She'd been longing for a letter each day.

Dat had received a newspaper, and there was one letter—from Amos. Relieved, she tucked the envelope into her apron pocket as Ben headed toward town in a freight wagon loaded with haybales. She guessed he was heading to the train station to send the hay to Elkhart or even on to Chicago. He waved and smiled. For a moment, she feared he'd stop and ask to read the letter, but of course he couldn't know she'd received one. He kept on going.

When Katie reached the house, she settled again on the front steps and quickly extracted the letter from the envelope. Holding it close to her face, she read it quickly.

September 3, 1917

Katie,

You are the first to know that I've taken the Secretary of War's advice and "joined" the men. I was doing groundskeeping work near the shooting range and soon realized I was a better shot than any of the soldiers. I could remain a CO and clean toilets, scrub pots, and pull weeds—or I could join the Army and spend my time shooting, marching, and doing calisthenics.

That is what I've chosen to do.

Tomorrow I leave for Chickamauga, Georgia. I expect that will be as far as my adventure goes. No doubt the war will end before I see the Atlantic Ocean.

I don't expect you or anyone else back home to understand. Nor God. Nor myself, really.

If I thought I might actually be called to shoot anyone—to kill another human being—I wouldn't be doing this. But when all I'll be doing is target practice, I can't see any reason not to join the Army when my only other choice is a life as a groveling CO.

I know I am impulsive, but I put much thought into this decision.

I'll soon be home, and I am still looking forward to our talk about our future.

Amos

Katie held the letter at arm's length and read it again, this time slowly. When she finished, she dropped the letter and watched the paper fall to the bottom step and then to the ground.

She buried her hands in her face and began to cry. Not tears of sadness, but hot tears of anger. How could Amos be so selfish?

Finally, she dried her face with her apron and then picked up the letter and shoved it in her pocket. Had he thought about consulting her before making a decision that would affect both of their lives? Obviously not. Clearly, he'd only been thinking about what was best for him for a short time, not what was best for their future.

She'd misjudged Amos. He wasn't the man she thought he was.

A sob shook her as she opened the front door and stepped into the house.

"Katie?"

She squinted in the dim light.

Mamm sat in her rocking chair. "What's wrong?"

"Nothing."

Mamm shook her head. "What's happened?"

Tears stung Katie's eyes again. "I've had another letter from Amos."

"And?"

"He's joined the Army, as a soldier. He's sure the war will be over before he's shipped overseas and that he won't be forced to fight."

"Oh dear. Do John and Ben know?"

"I'm not sure." Katie guessed from Ben's smile from the wagon that he didn't.

"Don't tell them," Mamm said. "Don't tell anyone. It's not up to you."

"What should I do, then?"

"Take the pie over to Ben."

Ben. Not *John and Ben.*

Katie exhaled slowly.

Mamm tilted her head to the side. "Obviously Amos isn't committed to you. Nor is he committed to the Lord."

"But he hasn't joined the church yet. He won't be shunned."

"It doesn't matter," Mamm said. "He's a soldier now. He's turned his back on all he was taught. He can't be trusted."

As the tears started to roll down Katie's face again, Mamm's expression turned sympathetic. "You must trust the Lord."

Katie nodded. She knew that. She hadn't joined the church either, but she would. No doubt about it. No matter what Amos had done.

"He's gone against the *Ordnung*," Mamm said. "I doubt he'll ever come back home, not after this, whether he ends up fighting or not."

Katie again lifted her apron to dry her tears. Mamm was most likely right. Amos wouldn't fit in, not at all. And she couldn't imagine him joining the church after living as a soldier. Religious persecution, which included forced conscription into the military, had forced their ancestors to leave Europe for the freedom of the New World. How could he, in return, embrace the military now?

"Staying busy is best." Mamm leaned forward in her rocking chair. "Why don't you take that pie over to Ben now?"

"He headed into town," Katie said. "I saw him drive by."

"Then take it after supper. You and Ben will have more time to talk then." Mamm began rocking again. "When do you plan to join the church?"

"I'll talk with Deacon Samuel about taking the class."

Mamm bobbed her head in approval and continued rocking as Katie stepped into the kitchen.

Amos was living with Englischers now, with soldiers—no, *as* a soldier. It went against everything they'd been taught their entire lives. She couldn't join her life with his, not now. Not ever. Mamm was right. She couldn't trust him.

IN OCTOBER, Katie rode into Nappanee with Dat and a wagonload of onions to ship to Chicago on the train. The sun shone brightly, but there was a chill in the air.

"I think we'll get frost tonight," Dat said.

He slowed for a wagonload of logs turning into the lumbermill on the edge of town. "Have I ever told you about the oak log I sold to the mill?"

Katie remembered the story well but said, "Tell me about it."

"It was thirty feet long and thirty-five inches wide. They milled nearly two thousand feet of lumber from it." He whistled. "When the Amish settlers first came to Indiana eighty years ago, they burned the trees to clear the land for crops. Imagine how much all that lumber would be worth now."

When Katie was a little girl, Dat had hauled wagonloads of logs to the mill, enough to build their new house. It was one of Katie's first memories. She'd stood with Seth, Amos, and Ben and watched the men work. The four children had picked up scraps of wood, filling buckets full and then dumping them in a pile to be burned. When the men were done for the day, the children picked up nails too, which were reused. It had been great fun.

Most of her early memories included Amos and Ben. They'd all gone to the same school, which taught both Englisch and Amish children. Katie had been shy around the Englisch children, but Amos wasn't. He was two years ahead of her and became a leader during the recess time when it came to playing kickball and then baseball when they were older. He'd always been strong and athletic.

The Berger boys had been like brothers to her, along with being good friends, until a year ago when Amos asked to drive her home from church one Sunday. That's when she knew her relationship with him had changed.

Would he have been as eager to join the Army if they'd already made plans to marry? If she'd agreed to have that talk about their future?

Dat and Katie rode in silence for a short time and then, as they reached the bricks that paved Main Street, he said, "John had a letter this morning from Amos. He's joined the Army and is in Georgia now."

Katie straightened her back. Ben hadn't said anything to her, so she'd assumed Amos hadn't written to tell them his news, but apparently he finally had.

"Do you know anything about that?"

Katie answered quietly, "Not much."

"But you knew?"

Katie nodded.

"For how long?"

"A few weeks."

"I'm guessing you have your reasons for not saying anything to me, but John asked if you knew, and I answered no. I thought you would have told me. . . ."

"I'm sorry, Dat."

"You have nothing to be sorry about." He gripped the reins a little tighter. "You have no obligation to tell me your personal business. I won't correct the mistake I made with John unless he asks."

Katie sighed in gratitude. She didn't want to talk about Amos with anyone, but especially not his father. Nor Ben.

Dat cleared his throat. "However . . ." His voice trailed off.

Katie waited for him to say more.

Finally, he said, "I'm not saying this to influence you one way or another. I have no idea of your feelings for Amos or why Amos would have done such a thing. Maybe he regrets what he's done. Maybe he will in time. Maybe he never will."

Katie couldn't imagine what Dat was getting at.

He pulled back on the reins as they neared the train station and then turned the team of horses toward where the produce freight was unloaded. "Just remember that Amos is a good man," Dat said. "Someday he'll come back, and he'll need friends, whether he joins the church or not. Pray for him now. Don't turn your back on him later."

She didn't answer her father. She couldn't agree with Dat that Amos was a good man. He'd betrayed his upbringing. He'd betrayed her.

After a long pause he said, "Katie, did you hear me?"

"I did, Dat." She sighed, fighting back tears. "I'll remember what you said."

An hour later, Katie stepped into Hartman Brothers General Store and headed to the notions section. She needed another spool of blue thread for her mosaic quilt.

The store was the largest in the county, and people rode the train all the way from Goshen to shop at it. As she headed across the store, she heard someone call her name. Ben stood at the dry goods counter, a bag of sugar in his hands.

He waved. Katie smiled. She continued on to choose a spool of thread.

As she paid at the notions counter, Ben approached, carrying his parcel.

"Are you in town by yourself?" he asked.

She shook her head. "Dat's waiting in the wagon."

"Will you be home this evening?"

Where else would she be? Katie nodded.

"Want to go for a walk?"

"All right."

The clerk gave Katie her change and a small bag with the thread.

"Did I tell you how much I enjoyed that peach pie you brought over this past summer?" Ben asked.

"You did."

He grinned as he bounced up on the balls of his feet. "I was just thinking of it again this afternoon."

"I'm going to make apple pies tomorrow," Katie said. "And bread."

Ben's eyes grew larger. "And . . ."

"Are you asking if I'll bring over a pie?" Katie teased. "And loaves of bread?"

He grinned.

"Of course I will." Katie smiled. "Don't be silly."

"Dat said yesterday that either he or I need to marry." As soon as he said the word *marry*, Ben began to blush. But he managed to add, "Or else we're bound to starve."

Katie felt her face grow warm too, but then she forced herself to smile again. "Well, is it a race, then? To see who can find a wife first?"

Ben laughed. "If that's the case, I'd guess Dat will be the winner."

Katie chuckled, feeling awkward. She tried to turn her response into a joke too. "I'd bet on your Dat too."

Ben blushed even more as they stepped out into the cold air. Ben waved at Dat, who smiled.

"Nice to see you, Vyt." Ben exhaled and then asked, "I was wondering if Katie could ride back with me."

"That's fine." Dat turned toward Katie. "If you'd like to."

"I don't mind." She couldn't turn Ben down—not when he was so earnest. She'd never have a future with Amos, but perhaps she could have one with Ben.

"I'm parked around the corner," he said.

"I'll see you at the house." Dat waved.

She tucked the small bag in her apron pocket and pulled her coat tight against the chill. When they reached Ben's wagon, he helped her up to the bench, and then unfolded a wool blanket and spread it over their laps.

As the wagon wheels rolled over the brick street, Katie's eyes stung from the cold. She expected Ben to bring up the letter from Amos, but he didn't say anything about it. In fact, he didn't say anything at all.

They caught up with Dat on the outskirts of town, just before the lumber mill. Ben still hadn't said a word. It wasn't until he stopped in front of the Landis home that he finally spoke. He said, his voice soft, "I'd like to see more of you."

Katie's heart skipped a beat. "You'll see me tomorrow. I'll bring the pie and bread over."

"All right," he said. "See you then."

As he helped her from the wagon, he gave her a quick smile. Optimism rushed through her for the first time in months. Ben wasn't Amos—but he was a good man.

She walked around the side of the house and up the steps to the back porch. When she stepped into the kitchen, an envelope with Amos's handwriting sat in the middle of the table. Seth must have gotten the mail.

She hated that she was drawn to the letter.

Katie headed through the house with the letter in hand, then up the stairs to her cold bedroom. After she'd closed the door, she sat on her bed and opened the envelope, pulling out the letter.

October 1, 1917

Katie,

I'm sorry to be writing to you again, but I don't know what else to do. I've undoubtedly made the biggest mistake of my life—turning my back on how I was raised. Perhaps, without meaning to, even turning my back on you.

I sent a letter to Dat, which I now regret. It would be better if he didn't hear from me. It would be better for you if I didn't write to you either. But here I am—writing to you.

It was hot when I first arrived in Georgia, but now the evenings are cooling. I'm in the far northwest corner of the state, near the border with Tennessee.

Several of the other soldiers have accused me of being German because of my accent. I've told them I'm just a farm boy from Indiana, but they don't believe me. All of us Amish children were taught all of our lives to "not be of this world." How did I possibly think I could fit in? I was never intended to.

There's no one I can talk to here, and no one else I can

write to back home who might understand—not that I expect you to either. But I thought perhaps you would listen.

If you can find it in your heart to pray for me, I would appreciate it. If you can find it in your heart to write me back, I'll doubly appreciate it. And I would appreciate your friendship too, if I haven't completely destroyed your trust.

Your friend,
Amos

Could Katie let go of her anger enough to pray for Amos? God commanded that she forgive others. Perhaps praying for Amos, as Dat had asked her to do, would ease her anger and lead her to forgiveness.

Perhaps praying for Amos would do her more good than him. But there was no reason she couldn't, as Mamm suggested, spend time with Ben. She would try her best to do both.

CHAPTER 6

Tally

Look at the time." Jane pointed toward the cuckoo clock on the wall. "It's eleven already. Time to let you ladies go home."

The two younger children played with the toys, but Maggie had been standing between Danielle and me for the last hour, listening intently to Jane.

I wished Jane would keep telling her story, but it was time to head home. I needed to get dinner on the table for Rich.

The other women started to disperse, including Joanna, but Danielle put her hand on Maggie's shoulder and said to Jane, "I understand Amos."

"Oh?" Jane leaned forward a little as she smiled at Danielle.

Danielle exhaled. "Like Amos, I also left my community. I grew up Mennonite, but I joined the Army anyway, bent on being independent." Her hand slid off Maggie's shoulder. "I hope Amos fared better than *I* did."

"In what way?" Jane asked.

"I couldn't go home." She stood and then looked at me. "I'm sorry. I've said too much."

I wasn't sure what to say, but I met Danielle's gaze as I thought of the photo on her mantel of her dressed as a soldier. If anything, Danielle had said too little.

Thankfully Jane knew what to say. "Danielle, you are always welcome here. And you are welcome to say as much or as little as you want. If you want to say more right now, I want to listen."

Danielle's eyes grew misty. "I will never be able to go back home, but thankfully one person kept loving me—my brother—after everything fell apart."

"When was that?" Jane asked. "When did everything fall apart?"

"After Marc, my husband, died."

I winced. I hadn't expected that.

"My parents had already rejected me when I was eighteen," Danielle said, "but after Marc passed away, I hoped they'd come around. They didn't." Her eyes drifted toward Maggie, who'd slipped away, back toward Miriam and Owen and Ruby. "It's hard being a single mother. Harder than I thought. And it's hard being a widow too. It's not just the loneliness; it's the responsibility. For example, my corn needs to be harvested soon. The man leasing the land just moved. I'm having a hard time finding someone to help."

Jane gave her an empathetic look.

Danielle shook her head a little, causing her blond hair to bounce on her shoulders. "Don't mind me. My mother always said I take up all the space in every room I enter. I hope I haven't done that here."

"Of course you haven't," Jane said.

I agreed with Jane, but I could see what Danielle's mother meant. She had a big personality, especially for having grown up Plain. That, combined with her height and strength and her bright red lipstick, made her larger than life, as Mamm used to say about people—Englischers in particular.

"We've been delighted to have you with us," Jane said. "I hope you'll come back on Thursday."

Danielle glanced at me. "Will you come then?"

"Most likely," I answered. "As long as Mamm feels up to it."

Danielle smiled, just a little. "I would like to come back."

She could, whether Mamm and I did or not.

On the way home, Mamm fell asleep in her chair in the back of the buggy, while Maggie fell asleep on the seat, with her head in her mother's lap.

I thought maybe Danielle would tell me more about her life, but she didn't. She'd gone from talkative to quiet in just a few minutes.

As we neared our farms, Danielle said, "We can walk home from your place."

"But Maggie's asleep."

"She'll wake up. And that way I can help you get your Mamm into the house."

My back hurt from getting Mamm in and out of the buggy and in and out of the house the last three years. "Denki," I said. "I appreciate the help."

When I stopped the buggy by the back-door ramp, Rich came out of the barn. By the time Danielle and I had a groggy Mamm out of the buggy, Rich had reached us.

I introduced Danielle and Maggie to him.

Danielle gushed, "I'm so pleased to meet you."

Rich muttered, "I'll take care of the horse."

As I grabbed the back of Mamm's chair, I said, "I'll have dinner on the table in a half hour."

Maggie asked, "Can I push Regina's chair into the house?"

"You can help," I answered.

"Can you stay for dinner?" Mamm asked.

"Dinner?" Maggie asked. "That's a long time from now."

"Lunch," Danielle responded. "Some people call it dinner."

Maggie pushed harder on the chair. "Can we, Mama?"

Danielle lowered her voice. "Tally, is that all right with you?"

"Of course," I said, although the thought of company made me tired. Taking care of Mamm was a chore in itself, let alone making sure there was enough food for two more and keeping the conversation going and worrying about what topic of conversation Danielle might bring up and how Rich would react.

"We don't have many visitors," Mamm said. "Joanna stopped by yesterday, but before that, I can't think of the last time we had a visitor."

"Jane came by two weeks ago," I said. "With a casserole. Do you remember that?"

"Ach, that's right. Anyway," Mamm said, "Danielle and Maggie, please stay for lunch."

I SUGGESTED Maggie work on the jigsaw puzzle—a map of the world—in the living room with Mamm while Danielle and I worked in the kitchen. Maggie chattered away to Mamm about the room Kenan had made for her under their staircase, while I increased the heat under the stew I'd made before we left for the quilting circle. Next, I dropped biscuit dough onto a cookie sheet while Danielle set the table.

"My parents' kitchen is a lot like yours. Big, with an oak table in the middle. A propane fridge and stove like you have, and the simple cupboards and Formica counters are exactly the same. Even the linoleum. Their house was built about thirty years ago."

I smiled. "That's about when Dat built ours. There was probably a good deal on those particular materials at the time."

Danielle laughed. "Probably."

"Where do your folks live in Ohio?"

"The north central part of the state. My father farms, but there's a family in our district that has a *big* variety store in a remodeled barn that's fairly well known. It's sort of a tourist attraction."

"Oh." We had tourist attractions too. I avoided them at all costs. "Does your family have a car?"

She shook her head. "They use buggies and wagons. They live almost exactly the way you do, except we have a church building for our services instead of meeting in homes."

I shifted the conversation to Maggie. "Do you like homeschooling?"

Danielle grimaced. "Honestly, I'm really bad at it. It's too easy to put it off to the next day and then the next. We'll go home today and do some worksheet pages, but I figure seeing the women quilt and hearing about what life was like during World War I is pretty educational."

I agreed.

"I'm looking at a couple of private schools in town," Danielle said. "I thought homeschooling would be good for us, but now I'm not so sure." She shrugged. "Maggie needs to be around other children, around other people besides me."

By the time the biscuits were done, Rich had come in to wash up. I rolled Mamm into the kitchen, to her place at the foot of the table, and directed Danielle to sit next to Rich, who sat at the head, and Maggie to sit next to Mamm, while I sat on the opposite side of the table.

After Rich led our silent prayer, and as I dished up stew for everyone, he spoke. "Ted"—he glanced at Danielle—"he's our cousin—said the quilting circle is a *feminist* gathering."

Feminist. It wasn't a word I'd heard Rich use before.

Danielle laughed. "I can assure you it is *not*."

"What is it, then?" Rich asked.

I answered, "A quilting circle."

"Ted says Jane tells feminist stories."

I tried not to laugh. Ted was probably teasing Rich, because he knew Joanna was sweet on Rich and she went to the quilting circle.

"Jane does tell stories," Mamm said. "About women from the past."

Rich snorted. "So only women?"

"There's a man, one in particular, in the story she started today," Danielle said. "Plus"—she counted on her fingers—"four more men."

"There are men in all of the stories she tells," I said.

"Her stories are about families," Mamm added.

"I see." Rich put butter on the top of his biscuit. "What else are the stories about?"

"The one today was about an Amish man who joined the Army during World War I," Danielle answered.

Rich shook his head. "That doesn't sound appropriate."

Danielle went on as if she hadn't heard him. "I could relate to the story because I joined the Army when I was eighteen."

Rich's eyebrows shot up. "You were in the Army?"

Danielle answered with a hearty "Yes."

"Are you proud of that?"

"I'm *not* ashamed, but if I had to do it over, I wouldn't have joined," Danielle said. "Although, I met my husband in the Army, so . . ." Her voice trailed off. "My story is different than the man in Jane's story. I wasn't forced to serve, although Amos chose to stop being a conscientious objector and join as a soldier."

"Amos?"

I said, "Amos Berger."

Rich rolled his eyes. "Never heard of him."

Danielle reached over and hit his arm playfully. "No wonder. World War I was a century ago. Were you around then?"

He yawned and then said, with complete seriousness, "Sometimes I feel as if I were."

Danielle shook her head. "You poor old man."

Rich gave her a confused look.

I stifled a laugh at Danielle teasing Rich. He often didn't understand when people were joking. "Berger," I said. "As in Mamm's maiden name. Aenti Frannie and *Onkel* Wayne live on what was the Berger farm, up the road from Jane."

Rich scowled. "We're related to the man in the story?"

"Men," I said. "And most likely, yes." Onkel Wayne had bought the farm years ago. I was certain we descended either from Amos or Ben Berger. I didn't want to ask Mamm and spoil the story though.

Mamm quickly changed the topic—so quickly that I wondered if she was having a hard time recalling the details of her family's history, which had often been the case since her stroke. She said, "Rich, Joanna was at the quilting circle."

At least her short-term memory seemed good.

Rich blushed. "Jah, Ted said she'd been going to the circle. That's probably why he warned me."

I sighed, wondering if Joanna would be able to understand Rich's lack of humor.

Danielle cut Maggie's biscuit in half as she asked Rich, "Is Joanna your sweetheart?"

Rich shook his head just a little as his face grew redder.

"So you want her to *be* your sweetheart."

I sighed again.

Danielle's voice grew softer—and higher. "Does Joanna want to be *your* sweetheart?"

Mamm cleared her throat loudly. "We don't really talk about these things."

"Why not?" Maggie said. "Mama says it's not good to keep secrets."

Danielle reached over and patted Maggie's arms. "There's a difference between keeping secrets and keeping something private. Rich is an adult. He doesn't *need* to tell anyone his personal business. I was teasing him."

Maggie blushed. "Sorry."

"Nothing to be sorry about." Danielle turned toward Rich. "But I'm sorry if my teasing is annoying. I'll stop."

He shook his head but had a befuddled expression on his face. I could tell he was growing frustrated.

On the other hand, Danielle seemed like a different person than she had the day before. Or than she had in the buggy on the way home earlier. Fun. Gregarious. Engaging. She was a puzzle, to be sure.

And so was her brother, Kenan. He'd grown up Old Order Mennonite with Danielle. She'd left to join the Army.

But why had Kenan left?

It wasn't any of my business, and I'd most likely never know. But still, I couldn't help but be curious.

AFTER RICH LED US in a closing prayer, he motioned toward the back door and said, "Tally, I have a question for you."

"I'll be with you in a minute," I said. "After I get Mamm settled in the living room."

"I'll do it." Danielle stood. "Come on, Maggie. Let's go work on the puzzle."

I followed Rich toward the door while Danielle maneuvered Mamm's chair around the table.

I closed the door behind me once on the porch and said, "What is it?"

"Have you made friends with her?"

"With Danielle?"

He nodded.

"She's our neighbor."

"Our Englisch neighbor." Rich crossed his arms. "You don't have to be friendly with her."

"Actually, according to scripture, I do."

Rich frowned. "You don't have to invite her into our home."

"Mamm invited her."

Rich wrinkled his brow. "Oh." He had no problem challenging me on every little thing, but he didn't challenge Mamm. It went against his raising.

"Danielle was teasing you for fun," I said. "Don't take it personally."

He shook his head. "I didn't. I just don't think she's a good influence on you."

I tilted my head. "Why would you say that?"

He frowned. "I guess I'm afraid she might not be a good influence. Nor her brother. What's his name?"

"Kenan," I answered. Rich had a hard time remembering names. And faces. I took a step toward my brother. "I can assure you, put your worries to rest. They're good people. Plus, I don't have the desire nor the time not to follow the rules."

"But you haven't joined the church yet."

I shook my head in disbelief. "When have I had time to join the church?"

He uncrossed his arms and moved backward, toward the steps. "I need to get back to work."

"I need to get back to work too," I said with a little sass in my voice.

What he did was work. What I did was the "dishes" or the "laundry" or "caring for Mamm." My work was never actually referred to as work. It was as if he thought I did all of my chores for fun.

He scowled. I guessed he was confused, once again, as to why I was upset.

I turned and opened the back door, probably closing it behind me a little too loudly.

Danielle came back into the kitchen as I began grabbing plates off the table. "Are you all right?"

I nodded.

"I hope I didn't upset Rich," Danielle said. "I know I can be a little extra."

"No." Was I lying? "He's annoyed with me. As usual."

"He reminds me of my father."

I turned toward her, the stack of plates in my hand. "How so?"

"Super serious. Hard to tease."

That was Rich.

Danielle added, "Rich seems smart and capable though."

I hesitated and then said, "Capable as far as work and making a living. But pretty awkward as far as relationships." My face grew warm. Who was I to talk? "I'm not so good at relationships either."

"Nonsense," Danielle said. "You're wonderful. You've been so hospitable and welcoming to us, in a genuine way."

Her words warmed me. At least I didn't come across the way I felt. Awkward and inadequate.

"At least you understand Rich," Danielle said. "That has to be a big help to him. I was young so I can't be too hard on myself, but I just thought my father was weird. The way he acted—and reacted—didn't help when I decided I wanted to leave. It made everything worse."

I could understand that. It was as if Rich and I spoke different languages most of the time.

Danielle and I continued to clean up while Mamm and Maggie kept working on the puzzle in the living room. Just as we finished, Maggie came into the kitchen, rubbing her eyes and yawning. Mamm followed, struggling to wheel herself across the linoleum.

"We're both tired," Mamm said. "Why don't you help me and then give Danielle and Maggie a ride home?"

"Oh no," Danielle said. "We'll walk."

"I want to go in the buggy again," Maggie pouted.

"Shhh," Danielle said.

"Let Tally give you a ride," Mamm said. "It just started to rain."

"Please, Mama?" Maggie whined, the first time I'd heard her do so.

Danielle shook her head. "Tally has a lot to do without worrying about us too."

"I don't mind," I answered, although it meant I wouldn't be able to walk. Then again, if the rain continued, I wouldn't want to walk anyway. At least not far. "It will just take me a minute to get Mamm settled."

"I can help," Danielle said. "I was a medic in the Army, and I'm a trained medical assistant. I can do patient care."

I glanced at Mamm. It would be nice to have someone else help. Mamm asked, "Do you do transfers?"

"Like a *pro*." Danielle grinned.

Mamm pointed toward the hall. "You can help me to the bathroom. And then into bed."

Danielle placed her hands on the handles of Mamm's wheelchair and began to push her toward the hall.

I pointed toward the living room and asked Maggie, "Do you want to work on the puzzle?"

Maggie shook her head.

"How about if I read you a book?"

She smiled.

I led the way into the living room to the bookcase and pulled *Heidi*, by Johanna Spyri, from the shelf. It was the first book I remembered Mamm reading to me when I was little.

It was also the first time I'd experienced "traveling" through a story. Switzerland didn't seem that far away, nor did the 1800s as I listened to Mamm read the story. I knew my ancestors had come from Switzerland, but I knew nothing about the country. Heidi's story felt both foreign and familiar to me. I loved every word of it and had reread it several times since I was a child.

Maggie scooted close to me as I opened the book and read the first line. "'The little old town of Mayenfeld is charmingly situated.'"

I'd finished page four when Danielle stepped into the room, holding her coat and Maggie's. "Your Mamm is all settled."

"Denki." I closed the book. "I'll go harness the horse."

Danielle held up their coats. "We'll go with you."

"It's pouring," I said.

"We won't melt."

"All right." I stood. "Let's go out the back door."

Once the horse was hitched and we were all settled inside the buggy, I shivered, wet from dashing through the rain. The rain pounded on the roof and bounced off the asphalt ahead of us, making it difficult to hear. But I could make out Maggie saying, "I like you today, Mama."

Danielle pulled Maggie close in a hug. "*I* like me today too."

I kept my eyes on the road, uncomfortable to be witnessing their tender moment.

"Do you think you'll go to Jane's on Thursday?"

It took me a moment to realize Danielle was talking to me. Just as I did, she said, "Tally . . ."

"Sorry. I hope so. If we don't, you should go without us."

"But don't you want to hear more of Jane's story?"

"Of course." I didn't add that the quilting circle was what I looked forward to the most. Which was wrong of me. Church should have been. And then family. But being at Plain Patterns felt like both church and family. Especially when Jane was telling a story. I grimaced. That was probably considered blasphemous. "I'm not sure from day to day how Mamm will be doing."

"What happened to her?" Danielle asked.

"She had a stroke. She did physical therapy and got a little better for a while, but then she plateaued and now she's growing weaker. No one expects that she will ever walk again."

"I'm sorry." Danielle's voice was soft, and her tone was gentle. "What about your Dat? I'm assuming he passed away."

I nodded.

"I know it's hard for you, caring for your Mamm. But I hope she lives for a long time so you have at least one of your parents."

"So do I." It was something that was always on my mind, and more so when I felt overwhelmed with caring for Mamm. At least I had her to care for. When she was gone, all I'd have would be Rich. But it was still a conflict. I couldn't get on with my life until she passed away—and yet when she passed away I'd be without a parent, without a familiar foundation. Of course, if I had a choice, I'd choose for her to live as long as possible, as long as she wasn't in too much pain.

As I turned the horse into their driveway, Maggie asked, "Mama, what are we going to do this afternoon?"

"Take a nap," Danielle said.

"After that?"

"Let's make cookies." Danielle beamed.

Maggie clapped her hands together and then lowered her voice. "Can we make some for Regina and Tally? And Rich?"

"Of course." Danielle patted Maggie's head. "Oh! And we *need* to do school too."

Maggie giggled.

Danielle turned toward me. "Thank you so much for this morning and for lunch. This is the best day we've had in—" She paused.

Maggie chirped, "Forever."

Danielle laughed. "You're nearly right."

After they climbed down from the buggy and reached their front door, I headed home. Even though I was intrigued with Danielle, I was also uneasy. She was needy. Not as needy as Mamm, but definitely needy. Did I have the strength to help her? Even if I had the strength, *could* I help her?

I also had a nagging feeling that Danielle couldn't be completely trusted. Who was the man from the day before? And what was in the pharmacy bag?

God told us to bear one another's burdens, and so fulfill

the law of Christ. Did I—quiet and shy—have it in me to bear Danielle's worldly burdens?

The horse picked up speed as the rain continued to pour down. Could I be Danielle's friend, regardless of our differences? Regardless of Rich's disapproval?

With God's help, I had to try.

CHAPTER 7

It rained for the next twenty-four hours, but by the next afternoon, by the time I helped Mamm into bed for her nap, the sun had come out and had warmed the world some. I grabbed my coat and headed out the door.

As I walked along our cornfield, I thought of Danielle needing to find someone to harvest hers. I needed to speak with Rich. Maybe he and the other Amish men could help. Maybe feeling needed would change his attitude toward Danielle.

I also thought of her saying she feared she wouldn't be able to make her mortgage payments. She didn't seem to have a job. What would she do if she lost her farm? It didn't sound as if she could go home to Ohio.

As I approached Danielle's house, I squinted. There was a vehicle in her driveway. The blue pickup from Monday.

I kept my eyes on the house as I slowed my pace, wondering what I should do. Finally, I crossed the street and headed up the walkway to the house. I'd check to see if Danielle wanted to go to the quilting circle tomorrow. That would be my excuse.

I took a deep breath and forced myself to climb the steps.

I knocked softly at first and then louder, but no one came to the door. I didn't hear any footsteps or voices either. Perhaps they were in the woods again.

I took the trail along the side of the house toward the trees and then stopped at the gate to listen. I didn't hear anyone or anything except for the breeze blowing through the treetops. I wasn't sure how I could explain turning up in the woods, if they were there, to ask if Danielle wanted to go to Plain Patterns in the morning. That seemed, to use Danielle's word, *extra*.

I turned around and headed back to the road. By the time I reached the pavement, I was marching along. I kept going, increasing my speed with each step. Relief washed over me when I reached the far side of my route and I could run. I usually started out slowly, but this time I ran at a sprint for as long as I could and then slowed.

Kenan had given me his phone number. Should I call him? Or would that betray Danielle?

I was a quiet person. I avoided conflict at all costs. I didn't get involved in messy situations between Amish people. Why had I been drawn into drama with an Englisch woman?

I barely knew how to care for Mamm. When to call the doctor. When to push Mamm to do her physical therapy. When to let up. When to encourage her to go to the quilting circle. When to accept she was too tired.

If I didn't know what the right thing to do with my own Mamm was, how would I know what to do with Danielle? Why had I been so sure yesterday that I could be a good friend to her?

But I had told Kenan I'd call him if I saw anything. He specifically asked me to call. And the blue pickup in the driveway certainly made it seem as if there could be a problem.

As I reached the highway again, I slowed back down to a walk. As I neared the farm, I went to the phone shanty instead of the house, pulling the door shut behind me. I dug in my pocket for Kenan's number. For a moment I feared I'd lost it, but then I tried the other pocket and found it in the very tip, worked in as if it were looking for a hole to jump out of.

I leaned against the little counter Dat had put in the shed years ago, picked up the phone, and then dialed the number.

I expected it would go into voicemail, but after five rings, someone said, "Hello?"

"This is Tally," I said. "I'm sorry to call. I'm not sure if I should have or not. . . ."

"What's wrong?"

"I don't know if anything is."

"What is it?"

My anxiety was rising. And it seemed Kenan's was too. "The blue pickup was back at Danielle's when I walked by a while ago. I thought you might—"

"Thank you," he said. "I'm on my way."

The line went dead without him saying good-bye.

A HALF HOUR LATER, after I got Mamm up from her nap, as I put a chicken in to roast, there was a knock on the front door. Leaving Mamm at the kitchen table, I hurried to the door, expecting it to be Kenan.

I was right. He held his baseball cap in one hand, showing his dark hair, which was cut close to his head. "Thank you for calling me."

The afternoon sunshine was gone, and the day had grown cold.

"Come on in." I took a step back into the entryway and Kenan followed me, pulling the door closed behind him.

"I was working close by," he said. "By the time I got there, the pickup was gone, but Danielle and Maggie were both in the study, doing school. They seemed okay."

My face grew warm. "I'm sorry."

"What for?"

"Calling you when nothing was wrong."

"No, I appreciate you calling." He smiled. "I mean, who can really know what the right thing is, right? One counselor I saw thought I was enabling Danielle by being too involved. Another thought I should move in with her so I could keep a closer eye on Maggie."

I didn't know anyone who'd ever been to a counselor before. Some Plain people I knew saw needing counseling as a weakness, but it didn't seem Kenan did.

He shrugged. "But no matter what, I appreciate you calling. I don't know what Dirk is up to. It might be nothing—he might just be trying to help Danielle. But she's been acting strange for the last week or so. I can't tell what's going on."

"What did Danielle say to you?"

Kenan frowned. "That Dirk came to the door, but she didn't let him in."

I tried to keep my face neutral, but I must have failed.

"You're not buying it?"

I shrugged. "It's not my business."

"But I'd appreciate your opinion."

"I didn't see him at the door. He wasn't in his truck." I shrugged again. "Maybe he went for a walk."

"Maybe . . ."

Mamm called out from the kitchen, "Tally, who is it?"

"Kenan," I answered. "Danielle's brother."

"Ask him to come in for a cup of coffee."

I raised my eyebrows, both surprised at Mamm's instructions and sure Kenan wouldn't have time. "How about it?" I asked. "Would you like a cup of coffee? I have a pot on the stove."

"All right." He wore a work shirt and no coat. He looked down at his boots and then up at me. "Should I take these off?"

"No," I answered. "I'll sweep after supper."

I led the way to the kitchen, introduced him to Mamm, and directed him to sit at the table. Then I grabbed three mugs. "Cream?" I asked.

"Black is fine."

I poured the coffees and then put his down in front of him and Mamm's at the end of the table. I pushed her as close as possible and then sat down across from Kenan.

He took a sip. I took a sip too. He took several more, practically draining his cup. Neither of us said anything, and I wondered if perhaps he was as awkward as I was. Mamm slowly sipped her coffee. She smiled at Kenan a few times and then said, "That Maggie is such a well-behaved little girl."

Kenan smiled. "She's wonderful, but she definitely has her moments."

Any child did, but I imagined there were times when Maggie felt pretty insecure. I could tell Kenan did his best to make life safe for her.

Mamm smiled but didn't say anything. It wasn't like her not to be talkative when we had company.

After another awkward silence, I began to say, "Danielle said . . ." just as he said, "Danielle said . . ."

We both laughed.

"You go first," I said.

"She said she enjoyed the quilting circle yesterday and will go with you again tomorrow."

"We enjoyed having her and Maggie go with us." Mamm nodded in agreement, but she seemed extra tired, perhaps because of our excursion the day before. I was unsure if we'd be going in the morning.

"What were you going to say?" Kenan asked.

"Oh, just that I was sorry to hear Danielle say she was having financial problems and wasn't sure if she could keep her farm."

Kenan leaned forward. "Was she serious?"

"I think so," I answered. "She was also concerned about getting her corn harvested."

He lowered his voice. "Her concern about her corn is legitimate, but she shouldn't be having any financial problems. She got a big settlement after Marc died, a death benefit through the union."

Feeling flustered, I said, "I must have misunderstood her." I hoped Danielle hadn't lost her money somehow.

"Who knows." Kenan had a sad expression on his face. "There's a lot she won't talk about with me anymore."

"Did you follow her here?" I asked. "To Indiana?"

Kenan shook his head. "She followed me."

"After her husband died?"

He shook his head again. "I worked with her husband. I got him the job. I was with him when he died."

Before I could get past my shock and figure out what to ask next, Mamm said, "Tally, would you push me back into the bedroom? I want to rest before supper."

I stood and said, "I'll be right back," to Kenan.

"I should get going." He took a final drink of coffee and held up his mug. "Thank you. And like I said, thank you, especially, for calling me."

"You're welcome."

He stood. "I just need to ask one thing, just in case."

"What's that?"

"Do you have any medications in the house?"

"Just my Mamm's blood pressure medication."

"No pain meds? No opioids? Tranquilizers? Or anti-anxiety meds?"

"No. Just baby aspirin and acetaminophen."

"All right. Thank you for answering my question." He tightened his grip on his cap. "I need to get back to work. I'll find my way out."

As I pushed Mamm toward the bathroom, I realized I didn't know what he did. And I still had no idea how Danielle's husband died. But I guessed his questions about whether we had medication in the house had to do with Danielle and the possibility she might be interested in those sorts of medications.

"He seems like a nice young man," Mamm said. "But why did he ask about medications?"

"Maybe just to make sure Maggie is safe here." Now I really was lying.

"Ach," Mamm said. "Do you really think so?"

She saw right through me. I hoped she wouldn't say anything to Rich.

AFTER SUPPER, Mamm said, "I'm going to bed early tonight." For Mamm that meant seven instead of eight.

"Why is that?" I asked.

"I want to be rested for quilting circle tomorrow. Danielle and Maggie are coming with us, right?"

"I believe so."

"That Maggie is really something, isn't she?"

"Jah."

"She reminds me of you when you were a girl."

I tilted my head. "How so?" I was painfully quiet as a child. I still was. Maggie definitely wasn't.

"Smart."

I'd never thought of myself as very smart, and it warmed me a little for Mamm to say she did. Sure, I did well in school—mostly because I loved to read—but I wasn't a quick thinker. I usually thought of the best answer for a discussion long after the lesson was done. Now I thought of what I should have responded to someone a day or a week or a month later. Sometimes even a year later.

Once I had Mamm settled down, I headed for the kitchen just as Rich grabbed his coat.

"Where are you going?" I asked.

"Out." His face remained emotionless.

"Where?"

He shrugged.

I hoped he was going to see Joanna, and I wasn't surprised he wasn't telling me. I sat down on the couch and picked up a dress of Mamm's that needed mending from my work basket. As I patched the tear, the sound of hooves sped by the house. Rich was on his way.

A wave of loneliness swept over me. I put down Mamm's dress and picked up the newspaper we'd continued subscribing to after Dat died, even though I was the only one in the family who now read it.

But I couldn't concentrate on the news and picked up *Heidi* instead. I'd wanted to visit Switzerland since Mamm first read the book to me when I was six. Back then, I didn't realize how far away it was and that the only way to get there was to take a ship or fly.

Some Amish did travel, both by ship and plane. But no one in my family ever had. And I doubted I ever would.

The only way for me to travel was to read.

The next morning, when the sun rose, the weather was cool

but clear. Mamm felt rested when she awoke and was soon ready for the day. I expected Danielle and Maggie to show up any minute by the time I had the horse harnessed, but there was no sight of them.

I pulled the buggy up in front of the back door, set the brake, and then wheeled Mamm down the ramp from the house and up into the back of the buggy.

"Aren't Maggie and Danielle coming?" she asked.

"Maybe not," I answered, mortified that I felt relief. I liked Danielle, but I felt more stressed when she was around. "I'm sorry, I know you were looking forward to them coming with us."

"Go by their house," Mamm commanded. "Perhaps they're just running late."

That seemed intrusive, and I wasn't sure what to do. I'd meddled yesterday for no reason.

I climbed up into the buggy. As we reached the road, the horse veered to the right, and I stopped him. I glanced to the left, toward Danielle's farm.

"Wait!" Danielle was running toward us, carrying Maggie in one arm, who was bouncing up and down and laughing, and a plastic container in the other hand.

I waved and said to Mamm, "Here they come."

Mamm's voice was full of cheer. "*Gut*."

By the time they reached the buggy, Danielle was laughing too. "Sorry we're *late*," she said. "I slept through the alarm. Maggie woke me." It didn't sound good that Maggie had to wake her. How soundly had she been sleeping?

"We were just headed to your house to see if you were coming," Mamm said. "We wouldn't have left without you."

Danielle turned her head. "Aww, that's so sweet of you." They climbed into the buggy.

Maggie waved at Mamm as I snapped the reins and the horse

moved forward, pulling the buggy to the right and onto the road. "We brought you cookies," Maggie said.

Danielle held up the plastic box.

"Denki," Mamm said. "How about if we share them during the quilting circle?"

"Good idea," Maggie said and then pulled a small yo-yo from her pocket.

"Where did you get that?" Danielle asked.

"Dirk gave it to me yesterday," Maggie answered. She turned toward me. "Dirk is our friend."

Danielle didn't say anything.

My face grew warm, so I focused on the road and then said, "Maggie, shall we sing the ABC song?"

Maggie grinned and scooted around on the seat, bumping my thigh with her foot and then belting out, "A, B, C, D . . ." Mamm joined in. I glanced at Danielle. She had her head turned away from me.

When we reached Plain Patterns, Danielle said she'd take care of the horse. "Go on with Regina and Tally," she said to Maggie, handing her the plastic box.

"Climb up on my lap," Mamm said to her. "Tally can push both of us."

Maggie did as Mamm said, with a big grin on her face. Luckily, the chair didn't seem any heavier with Maggie on it. I pushed while Maggie sang the ABC song again.

There was a much smaller group at Plain Patterns than on Tuesday, which was usually the case on Thursdays. Only Miriam was there, with Owen.

After Maggie passed the cookies—oatmeal chocolate chip—to everyone, we gathered around the quilting frame. Maggie didn't join Owen in the play area. Instead, she sat in one of the chairs next to Mamm.

"Jane," Mamm said, "do you have any of those beginner sampler kits? I'd like to buy one for Maggie."

Jane stood. "I do."

"I'll get it," I said.

"They're by the counter," Jane said. "I'll show you."

I took my purse with me, but once I had the kit in my hand and took out my wallet, Jane whispered, "I'll cover it."

I shook my head. "Mamm wants to."

"Well, she doesn't need to know that she didn't." Jane winked.

I appreciated her generosity. Rich was a success at farming, but finances were still tight for us with all of Mamm's medical bills, most of which she didn't know the extent of. The mutual aid fund helped when we needed, but we wanted to pay all we could.

When we reached the back room and quilting circle again, I handed Mamm the kit. She opened the plastic bag and took out the white fabric with a loose weave that was stretched across a small hoop. There was a large plastic needle with a blunt point and a large eye that was threaded with black yarn. Mamm showed Maggie how to practice stitches on the fabric, following the outline of a cat. "You can practice and then when your stitches are small enough, you can quilt with us."

Maggie's eyes grew large. "Thank you."

Jane glanced from Maggie to Danielle and then to me. "I did more research yesterday about World War I and the year after, and about Katie and Ben and Amos in particular. Do you want to hear more of the story?"

"Absolutely," Danielle answered.

I agreed.

"Where was I?" Jane asked, taking her small notebook from her apron pocket.

"Amos had just written another letter to Katie," I said. "He wrote that joining the Army was the biggest mistake of his life."

Danielle nodded. "Yes. That resonated with me."

Jane gave her a sweet smile. "That's right. Amos was in Chickamauga, Georgia, training to go to war."

CHAPTER 8

Katie

As Katie kneaded the dough for bread on the already warm mid-June morning, she thought through the fall and winter months.

She'd followed Mamm's advice and had spent more time with Ben.

The two had gone on long walks in the fall, skated on the Landis pond in January, and taken the Berger sleigh out in February, when the world was blanketed in snow. She enjoyed being active and having someone to share adventures with. Although none of the outings were as fun as the ones she'd had with Amos.

Not once, during any of their outings, did Ben bring up Amos joining the Army. Katie wasn't sure if he didn't know or chose not to speak of it out of embarrassment. She certainly didn't bring it up. In fact, neither of them brought up Amos at all unless it was some memory from the past. When Ben spoke of Amos, it was usually at Amos's expense, to point out one of his foibles. That he was foolish to ride the three-year-old colt that bucked him off. That he hadn't been thinking when he'd tied a rope to the largest willow tree and swung over the creek on it, falling on a rock and breaking his arm. That Amos had deserved to be reprimanded at school when he'd stood up to a teacher who was yelling at one of the Englisch students.

Katie couldn't help but note that she'd admired Amos for all of those things. He'd been helping his father train the colt. Three was plenty old enough to be ridden. They'd all enjoyed swinging on the rope across the creek, including Ben, for many summers, thanks to Amos. Because he fell on the rock, the others knew to avoid it. And he'd done the right thing standing up for the Englisch student when no one else had. The teacher was mean and would have gone after Amos too, if Amos hadn't been bigger than him already. She'd always admired Amos's bravery.

Ben's twisted stories about Amos only drew more attention to how much Katie missed spending time with Amos. But that was the problem. Spending time with Amos could never be the same as it had been before.

When she brought up the subject with Mamm, she encouraged her to give it time. "Ben's a good man," she said. "And he's joined the church. You should too."

"I will." Katie was taking the instruction class and would soon be baptized.

Katie continued to take pies over for Ben and John. More apple pies in the fall and then cream pies through the winter. She also took over a couple of loaves of bread on baking days.

There had been some weeks when she hadn't seen Ben at all, only John. Ben spent more and more time alone in the fields without his father's help. John's arthritis in both his hands and back had grown worse, making it difficult for him to hold and use tools and to lift anything heavy. He'd grown crankier over the last few months, and Katie guessed he was in a lot of pain.

Ben and Seth helped each other when they could, but both farms lacked the farmhands they needed.

Katie missed Amos the most when the *Youngie* from church gathered on Sunday evenings. He'd been the one to start songs for the singings. He'd been the one who pranked the other young men, all in fun. He'd been the one to always help with the setup and the cleanup. Katie always felt in the middle of things when she was with Amos, as if she truly belonged. Now she found herself sitting in the back of the room and hanging around the edges, not interacting with the others. Paulina, in particular, reached out to her, which Katie appreciated. But when she did join in on the conversation, she never felt like herself without Amos nearby.

She was aware of the other couples, of Seth and Paulina in particular. She guessed they would marry soon, most likely in the fall. What if the US hadn't joined the war? What if Amos hadn't joined the Army? She mourned the future she thought she'd have.

Regardless of missing Amos and remembering what she admired about him, Katie had never written him back after his last letter. And he didn't write again. She thought that best. Dat had said she should be a good friend to Amos, but that was when he came home. Not now.

However, she still found herself thinking about him every day. When she pulled her quilts up to her chin at bedtime during the winter, she wondered if he had enough blankets. When she cooked dinner, she wondered if he was getting enough food. And when she checked the mailbox, she hoped to find a letter from him, even though she hadn't responded to his.

Although she did pray for him from time to time, her anger at Amos for giving up his CO status never completely went away. And yet, occasionally in the distant corner of her mind, she wondered if she were in his position, would she have done the same for warmth and enough nourishment?

And now she had something else to think about. There was a bad flu going around that some called the Spanish Flu. Some said it was a fad and would soon be gone, while others believed it could lead to a massive number of deaths. Although she didn't know of anyone who'd gotten it, she'd read about it in Dat's newspapers. Soldiers from France and England had come down with the flu. And now it was in the States too.

If Amos fell ill, would there be someone in Georgia to nurse him?

She put the dough back into the metal bowl, put a towel over it, and placed it next to the stove. After she washed her hands and wiped them on her apron, she decided to walk to the mailbox. Her thoughts of Amos had her longing for a letter again, which made no sense. If she truly wanted a letter, wouldn't she have written him back?

Mamm sat quietly in the living room, staring out the front window. She no longer did much work, not more than a little sewing.

"I'm going to the mailbox," Katie said.

Her mother turned toward her. "All right."

"When I come back, I'll put the bread in to bake. And then start the potatoes." She had leftover chicken from the evening before to serve for dinner.

For years, Mamm oversaw Katie's work, providing instructions and feedback, but it had been weeks now since Mamm had taken any interest in the daily operations of their home.

"Make sure and wear your bonnet," Mamm said. "It's hot."

"I will." Katie hadn't intended to wear her bonnet—it was a quick walk to the mailbox—but she was so relieved to have Mamm tell her what to do that she was eager to please.

She headed to the back porch, grabbed her bonnet and put it on, and then headed down the steps. Seth was dragging the field and Dat was oiling the wheels of the wagon. Neither saw Katie as she walked away from the house.

A flock of swifts flew up above the poplar trees. Katie stopped and tipped her head back, watching as they darted to the right and then to the left and then straight up into the sky. A minute later, they raced to the right and then disappeared from sight.

When she reached the end of the lane, Katie glanced toward the Berger farm. Again her thoughts turned to Amos. If only he'd never left.

She opened the mailbox. It was empty. Not even Dat's newspaper was inside. Sometimes that happened. He'd most likely get two the next day.

Maybe she'd bring Amos up to Ben the next time they went on a walk. Casually. She wouldn't give away that he'd joined the Army, or that she knew he had.

She straightened her back and faced toward town. In the distance, someone walked in the shade on the other side of the road. Unable to move, she stared at the man coming toward her.

As he grew nearer, she saw he wore a khaki uniform and carried a duffel bag. He looked like the pictures of soldiers she'd seen in Dat's newspapers. Handsome young men in pressed uniforms. This man's quick stride exuded confidence, just as the squared shoulders and wide smiles of the soldiers in the photographs did. He wore an Army hat.

She stepped away from the mailbox into the road. "Amos?"

The man stopped and removed his hat, showing his cropped blond hair. His gray eyes were brighter than she'd expected. "Hello, Katie." His voice had become deeper. "How are you?"

"I'm all right, Amos," she answered. "How are you?"

"Just fine." He motioned toward the Berger farm. "I'm headed home."

Her voice caught but she managed to ask, "For good?"

He shook his head. "For a couple of days, if they'll have me. I'm on leave, then I'm headed to New York."

"Oh." Katie folded her arms across her chest. "Did you let your Dat and Ben know you're coming?"

He shook his head. "It will be a surprise. Hopefully a welcome one."

She hoped so too.

"I'd like to see you while I'm here," he said.

She feared seeing him, spending any time with him. Her shaking knees weren't a good sign. She hadn't gotten over Amos Berger. But thinking about him every day when he was a thousand miles away was one thing. Spending time with him would be completely different.

And no matter how she responded to seeing him, shaking knees and all, she was still angry with him.

They stared at each other for a long moment and then he put his hat back on, tipped it, and said, "I'll come by to see you later."

She watched as he continued down the road. He seemed taller and more muscular. He held his head high, and it seemed he carried the duffel bag with no effort.

She walked slowly back to the house, going through the back door. Mamm asked loudly, "Any mail?"

"*Nee*," Katie called back.

Mamm often talked about how they had to go into town to get the mail when she was a little girl, before the rural mail routes were established. Perhaps, now, they would go into town more often if they still had to pick it up.

"Are you all right?"

"Jah." Katie stepped into the front room. "Why do you ask?"

"Your voice sounds shaky." Mamm turned toward her. "And you're pale."

"I'm fine." As she turned to step into the kitchen, Seth came through the back door. "Was that Amos you were talking to?"

Katie froze.

"What did Seth ask?" Mamm called out.

"Nothing." Katie continued into the kitchen.

"It was Amos, wasn't it?" Seth said. "Why is he home?"

"He's on leave." Katie kept her voice low, afraid if Mamm knew she would forbid Katie from leaving the house. "Before he goes to New York."

"Why is he wearing a uniform when he's a conscientious objector?"

She hadn't told Seth that Amos had joined the Army and obviously Mamm and Dat hadn't either.

"You should go ask him," Katie replied.

Seth rubbed the side of his face. "Or you could tell me."

"Katie." Mamm had shuffled into the kitchen and now leaned against the table. "Is Amos home?"

"Jah, he is," Seth said. "I just saw him talking to Katie at the mailbox, and apparently he's joined the Army."

"Well, I knew he'd joined the Army, but what is he doing home? The war isn't over, is it?"

"No, Mamm," Katie said. "The war isn't over."

"He's probably going to the East Coast to ship out to France." Seth crossed his arms. "Too bad he didn't stay a CO. Then he could at least be going as a medic." He shook his head. "Amos Berger is the biggest fool I know."

"Katie," Mamm said, "did you really see Amos out by the mailbox? Did you really talk with him?"

"Jah, Mamm. I did." Katie tried to control her emotions,

but it was useless. Fearing she'd burst into tears, she hurried past Seth and toward the back door.

"Don't go see him!" Mamm yelled.

"I'm not," Katie said. "I just need some fresh air."

She grabbed a basket from the shelf on the back porch and headed to the garden. The strawberries were ripe. Maybe there would be enough to bake a pie or two.

"AFTER MUCH THOUGHT, I think it's the neighborly thing to do to invite John and the boys over for supper this evening," Mamm said while they ate their noon meal.

Earlier she'd forbidden Katie from seeing Amos. Perhaps Mamm thought if he came with his family for supper that would be safer.

Mamm continued, "Considering he won't get much of a homecoming meal from John and Ben."

"What do you think, Katie?" Dat asked.

"I'm going to make strawberry pie. Why don't we invite them for dessert?"

Mamm shook her head. "We need to serve them a meal. I'll help you put something together."

When Katie didn't respond, Dat asked, "Is that all right with you, Katie?"

She nodded but didn't speak as she kept her attention on her food.

Seth piped up, "I'll go over to the Berger place and invite them before I drag the rest of the field."

"Denki, son," Dat said.

Mamm frowned a little. "On second thought, did Amos seem well? He's not bringing that flu home with him, is he?"

Katie lifted her head. "He seemed fine." More than fine. He

may have regretted joining the Army when he wrote his last letter, but over the last eight months something had changed. Today he seemed to be on top of the world.

As Katie cleaned up from dinner, Mamm stayed seated at the table. "I know it's a shock for you to have Amos home. That's why I want them to come to supper. It's best for you to see him with all of us—not alone. By the look on your face, you still have feelings for him. But those will pass in time. It's important that you follow your head in choosing a husband—not your heart."

"Mamm," Katie said. "I have no intentions of choosing a husband anytime soon."

"What about Ben?"

Katie shrugged. Clearly, based on her reaction earlier at the mailbox, her feelings for Ben were nothing like her feelings for Amos.

"I want you to be settled before . . ." Mamm's voice trailed off.

Katie didn't ask her to finish her thought. Mamm wanted her to be married before she died. Katie shuddered.

Mamm quickly changed the topic, instructing Katie to retrieve the last ham from the smokehouse and put it in the oven to bake. After she'd completed that task, Katie mixed up dough for rolls and then the pie crust. Next, she scrubbed the potatoes. She pulled jars of green beans from the pantry, and jars of applesauce too. Mamm, who seemed energized, cleaned the strawberries at the table for the pie.

By five o'clock, Katie had the pies in the cold box with a block of ice to set, and then put the rolls in the oven. By five-thirty, supper was ready.

As she set the table, John Berger and his boys arrived. Amos was wearing Amish attire—a cotton shirt, pants, and work boots. His head wasn't quite as high as it had been on the road, but he smiled when he saw Katie.

She tried to assess if there was conflict between the two brothers. Had Ben just found out that Amos had joined the Army? Ben seemed tense and John seemed more hunched over. Actually, even though his head wasn't held as high, Amos seemed the most relaxed out of the three. He wasn't the broken man Katie had feared he would be.

Mamm directed everyone to sit while Katie placed the food on the table.

John winced as he sat down.

After Dat led everyone in prayer, Mamm thanked Katie for cooking the meal. "I don't know what I would do without my daughter. She keeps this household running."

Katie's face grew even warmer as she passed the rolls to her Dat. Ben sat across the table from her, John sat between his two sons, and Amos sat next to Mamm, at the end of the table.

Mamm addressed Amos. "Tell us how you're doing."

"Just fine," he said. "I can't complain."

"How's Army food?" she asked.

He laughed. "My response to that is, 'I won't complain.'" He glanced at Katie. "I can't tell you how thankful I am for a good homecooked meal."

Katie didn't meet his eyes.

"We have strawberry pie for dessert," Mamm said. "So save room."

"Oh, I will."

"How long are you home for?" Dat asked.

"Only for two days," Amos said. "I'm on my way to Fort Drum in New York."

"And what did you think of Georgia?"

Amos smiled. "It's hot and sticky. Let's just say I'm happy to be leaving Georgia in June and not August."

"What's next?" Seth asked. "After Fort Drum?"

Amos shrugged. "We'll see."

Katie expected Seth to push Amos, to ask him if he was headed to Europe, but he didn't. Instead, her brother passed the green beans to Dat.

The conversation shifted to the weather and how long the hot spell would last.

"Some heat is good, but we'll need more rain soon." John gripped his fork in an awkward manner.

"How were the crops last fall?" Amos asked.

"Just fine." Ben's tone was harsh. "We were shorthanded as far as help, but we all worked hard and managed. Prices were good."

Amos responded, "Because of the war." It wasn't a question—it was a statement. "As much as you'd like to be pacifists and not involved in war, you're still making a profit off of it."

"Son," John said.

Ben smirked.

"Amos is right," Dat said. "It's one of our struggles, isn't it? It's hard to keep from benefiting from what is going on in the world, even though we are to separate ourselves from it."

No one said anything for a long while.

Dat finally spoke again. "I suspect God would want us to use the extra earnings wisely to help those less fortunate."

"I expect so too," John said.

When the men fell silent, Mamm asked Amos how the train ride from Georgia was.

"Just fine," he answered. "I enjoyed seeing the countryside."

Katie imagined he did. Two years ago, she, Amos, Ben, Seth, and Paulina had taken the train to Elkhart for the day. They walked along the St. Joseph River and strolled through some shops downtown. It had been Amos's idea, of course. At the time Ben was interested in Paulina, but soon after that she made her choice of Seth known. Katie wished she'd appreciated that day more instead of taking it for granted, thinking it was only the first of similar days in her future.

After they had their pie, John and his boys went home.

"That seemed strained," Mamm said after they left.

"As expected," Dat said. "But this too shall pass. Someday Amos will come home and need to settle in again. Even if it's awkward, the more we interact with him, the better. It will make it easier for him to return and join the church."

Katie appreciated Dat's wise words, but Amos would never fit in again. She both missed him and resented him.

But she must have missed him more, because once Mamm and Dat went to bed, she headed to the backyard to the oak tree, where she and Amos used to meet.

Seth snuck out of the house without noticing her. Soon, she heard the buggy go by. He was on his way to visit Paulina.

Katie had just about given up on Amos when she heard a stirring in the bushes. When no one appeared, she decided the rustling was an animal.

As she turned toward the house, though, someone called out her name.

CHAPTER 9

Katie?" Ben stepped out of the bushes.

She stifled a groan. Ben was not the Berger brother she wanted to see tonight. She didn't move. Perhaps Dat would come down and tell Ben to go home.

Then again, Mamm would probably stop Dat, wanting Katie and Ben to spend time together.

"I hope I didn't startle you," Ben said as he stepped toward her.

She turned toward him. "You didn't."

His face, visible in the moonlight, was as serious as it had been at dinner. "Can you believe Amos joined the Army?" In the dim light, she wasn't sure if anger flashed in his eyes or not. "What was he thinking?"

Katie shrugged, not wanting to pass judgment on Amos in Ben's presence.

"And the fact he didn't tell anyone. He's such a liar."

"Your father didn't know?" Katie asked.

"Nobody knew."

Katie knew John wouldn't lie to Ben, which meant Ben

hadn't asked him outright and assumed his father didn't know. Just as he was assuming Katie didn't know Amos had joined the Army either. She'd let him continue in those assumptions.

"Amos is weaker than I imagined," Ben said. "I'd guessed his character wasn't the best, but he joined the Army after only a few weeks in Maryland. He barely gave being a CO a chance. He's been training to be a soldier since he was in Maryland—training to be a sniper, of all things."

Katie winced. From what she understood, a sniper preyed on other men. A sniper hunted the enemy.

Ben shook his head. "He's turned his back on God, the church, and his family."

"Are you sure about that?" Katie asked. "Has he said anything about God?"

Ben shook his head. "It's obvious."

"Well, does he plan to go to church tomorrow?"

Ben shrugged.

Katie pressed again. "Are you sure he turned his back on his family?"

"Of course. He joined the Army."

"But he came home to see you."

Ben exhaled loudly. "He only came home to show off. You should have seen him strutting up the lane in his uniform, his head high as if he were something special." He shuddered.

Katie didn't respond. She didn't want to talk about Amos with Ben. She didn't want to hear what Ben thought of his brother.

"You're awfully quiet," Ben said. "You must be as shocked as I am." It seemed he tried to smile, although it looked more like a grimace. "I'm sorry." He sighed. "We all knew you cared for Amos—so did he. You must be hurt."

Katie shrugged.

"But God has not forgotten you. He has other plans. Better plans."

Katie crossed her arms, partly in defense, but partly because of a cool breeze from the woods.

Ben reached out and touched her shoulder.

Katie flinched. This was the most confident Katie had ever seen him.

"My brother is a fool."

Katie stared down at the ground.

"I understand if you don't want to talk. We can discuss this after Amos leaves—again."

Katie didn't respond.

Ben took a step backward. "I hope I haven't upset you. Amos is to blame for all of this. But no doubt, with time, things will work out."

That's certainly what they'd been taught. God's will prevailed in all things. He worked good out of the most difficult circumstances.

"Well, *Guter Nacht*," Ben said.

Katie shivered and turned toward the house. "See you tomorrow."

"See you then." Ben turned and slipped back into the bushes, taking the path back down to the creek and then to the Berger farm, the one that Amos used to walk to see her. The one they all ran along as children.

After Ben left, Katie realized she wasn't ready to go back in the house and settle down for the night, so she walked along the side of the house to the front porch where it was warmer. She would sit on the steps.

As she rounded the corner, a figure stepped out of the shadows. "Have you had a lot of chats with Ben in the last year?"

It was Amos.

She'd thought she wanted to see him, but now she didn't. When had he become ill-mannered? She turned and started to retrace her steps.

"Katie . . ."

The pull of his voice stopped her.

She turned around. "I didn't ask Ben to come here tonight."

Amos grimaced. "Sorry. I didn't have any business bringing Ben up to you. I'm jealous, is all."

She didn't believe him. "Jealous? Why would you be jealous?"

"Because Ben is here while I'm headed to France."

So it was true. He was going overseas.

He gestured toward the lane. "I don't expect you to agree to it, but I have to ask. Will you walk with me?"

Katie's gaze fell behind him, to the darkness of the lane, to the row of poplars on each side. Should she go with Amos? If she didn't, would she ever have a chance to talk with him again?

"All right," she answered. "I just need to go grab a shawl. I'll be right back."

As she started down the stairs with her shawl, she heard steps in her parents' room. Katie froze. The steps stopped and the bed creaked. She waited a long moment and then continued down the steps slowly, one at a time.

When she came out the front door and onto the porch, she saw Amos, out in the open, under the light of the nearly full moon.

She put her finger to her lips and motioned toward the road. Once they reached the lane, she whispered, "One of my parents was awake. I'm not sure which one. But I didn't want our voices to carry to the house."

"I understand."

Before, he would have reached for her hand. Instead, they

walked apart and in silence again until they reached the road. Finally, Katie said, "Tell me about the Army."

"Do you really want me to talk about it?"

Katie nodded.

"I'm getting used to it. I figured out most people are trying to hide what they see as their weaknesses, which makes them act aggressively or defensively. I try to stay humble and honest, without bringing attention to myself."

Katie thought about what Ben said about Amos strutting around in his uniform. She'd seen his confidence, but she didn't believe he was being arrogant. But could he truly stay humble in that environment?

"There are some rough people that I serve with. Men from the streets of New York City. Men who grew up poor in the South and had to scramble to survive. That sort of thing. But I can find something in common with most of the men. Several are Christians. Others like to hunt." He shrugged. "When it comes down to it, they're just men, just like I am."

"What about Georgia?" Katie asked. "How did you like it?"

"It went from hot and sticky to cold and wet, but the countryside is beautiful. Forests. Hills. Rivers. I was able to go hunting several times. The venison was a treat after mostly pork and potatoes." He turned toward her, a faint smile on his face. "Speaking of, I appreciated the meal you fixed for us tonight."

Katie ignored him. "When will you go to France?"

"I'm not sure. I suppose it will take some time at Fort Drum. Much of our time is spent hurrying up and then waiting."

Asking him questions kept Katie focused on the moment—and not her losses. "What do you fear the most?"

He turned his head away from her. "We'll see if I change my mind or not, but right now it's not my own life I'm worried about. It's that I might be required to take the life of someone else."

Katie could see that would weigh on him. "That is troubling."

He blinked. "But I have no one to blame but myself."

Katie wasn't sure what else to say.

After a pause, Amos asked, "How is your Mamm doing?"

"She's been resting more and doing less."

"I'm sorry," he said. "I was grateful for her conversation this evening. She was kind."

"She is kind." Katie wouldn't tell Amos Mamm hoped she'd court—and marry—Ben.

"And your Dat is kind too."

Katie pursed her lips together and then said, "He's concerned about you."

Amos inhaled but didn't respond.

"I'm guessing your Dat is also."

"Jah, although I think he's resigned to my fate."

"What fate is that?"

"Going to France. Having to fight. Being corrupted by the world even more than I've already been."

"Did he say that?"

Amos nodded. "In a letter after I told him I'd joined. He said the ramifications of my decision would play out for the rest of my life."

That was her fear for Amos too.

"He's sorely disappointed in me." Amos stopped and turned toward her. "As I imagine you are too."

It took a moment for her to meet his eyes, but when she did, she saw a glint of emotion.

"Jah, I'm sad." It was true. With Amos beside her, Katie no longer felt any anger. "This isn't what I expected for . . ."

"Us?"

"Jah."

"Nor is it what I expected. I'm sorry."

"It's not your fault the world went to war. . . ."

"It is my fault I joined the Army. I've always been impulsive, as has been pointed out to me over and over."

Ben saw it as a character flaw, but it was one of the things Katie appreciated about Amos. He was willing to take risks. And yet now that very thing she'd admired in him had changed her future forever.

"I've gone too far this time," he said. "I thought joining would mean a year of target practice—not the possibility of ever having to actually shoot someone."

Katie shivered.

They reached the ancient oak tree along the road and stopped, as they used to. Amos leaned against the tree and then Katie did too.

"Tell me about you," Amos said. "What has changed for you?"

Tears stung Katie's eyes. He was what had changed for her. But she answered, "Not much. I'm doing what I've always done. Cooking. Cleaning. Weeding. Washing."

"Courting?"

A lump formed in her throat.

"You should," he said.

She swallowed hard. The sound of hooves coming up the road sent Katie around to the back of the tree. Amos followed her.

On the other side, Katie leaned against the tree again and Amos did the same, but this time his shoulder touched hers. They stood like that as the buggy drove by. Katie watched the lantern on the buggy turn down their lane. Seth had come home early. She might as well stay out longer, until he fell asleep. Otherwise, he'd hear her come in and ask where she'd been.

She leaned her head against Amos's shoulder. She didn't mean to cry, but she couldn't stop the tears. He took her in his arms, pulled her Kapp back, and kissed the top of her head. Then he held her until she finally stopped.

When she did, he said, "I'll walk you home."

Neither spoke until they reached her front porch. Then he whispered, "I don't expect you to wait for me, not at all. In fact, you should court someone else." He put his hands on her shoulders and stared into her eyes. "Even if it's Ben."

She swallowed again.

"But would you write back if I'm able to write to you? A letter from you while I'm over there would mean the world to me, but if your Dat forbids it, I understand."

Katie met Amos's gaze. "He won't."

Amos smiled, just a little. Then he kissed the top of her head again and left without saying good-bye.

THE NEXT MORNING, the Landis family pulled out onto the highway in their buggy just after John Berger and his sons passed by in their wagon.

Katie had cried more when she went to bed and now her eyes felt puffy. Seth gave her a sympathetic look. But she turned her head away from him.

She kept her eyes on the back of Amos's head. Ben sat in the middle of the bench, with John and Amos on each side of him. Again, Amos was dressed in his Amish clothes.

When they reached the Fisher farm, Dat pulled the horse to a stop, and Seth hopped down and helped Mamm from the buggy while Katie climbed down on her own.

The Berger wagon continued on to the barn.

The benches were set up outside of the house, in the shade of a maple tree. Katie sat on the bench beside Mamm, to give her support. Services were hard for Mamm, and she often stayed home. But she'd chosen to come today, perhaps to keep an eye on Katie.

When the single men sat down on a bench on the other side, Mamm whispered, "Did Ben stop by last night?"

Katie nodded.

Mamm smiled and looped her arm through Katie's. "Good. Amos is just a distraction. He'll soon be gone, and life will go back to normal."

Tears stung Katie's eyes, and she blinked quickly.

Mamm didn't notice. "My wish is to see you settled. The sooner, the better."

Katie swallowed hard. "Don't say that."

"Only the Lord knows the numbers of my days."

Paulina Fisher sat down on the bench on the other side of Katie, ending the conversation. Mamm kept her arm looped through Katie's, for extra support. She often did that.

Paulina leaned toward Katie and whispered, "When did Amos come home?"

"Yesterday."

"Is he home to stay?"

Katie shook her head.

"Oh, that's too bad."

Katie didn't respond. Paulina seemed to know how she felt about Amos. Katie turned her attention to the service.

The scripture was Proverbs 3. Katie was familiar with two of the verses and those were the ones she heard. *Trust in the Lord with all thine heart; and lean not unto thine own understanding. In all thy ways acknowledge him, and he shall direct thy paths.*

Could she trust the Lord with Amos? And herself? She feared she'd need to make that decision every day—or become an anxious young woman. Today, she would choose to trust the Lord. But what about tomorrow? And the next day? It was easier to trust when Amos was across the aisle from her.

By the time the service was over, Mamm was exhausted and Dat decided to take her home. He said to Katie, "You can get a ride with the Bergers."

"I'd rather come now, with Mamm."

Seth stayed, most likely so he could spend some time with Paulina, and said he'd get a ride or walk.

When they arrived home, Katie served the cold leftover ham from the night before with rolls and applesauce. Then Mamm went down for a nap and Dat sat in the living room with his opened Bible in his lap but stared out the window.

After an hour of sitting in the front room, lost in her thoughts, Katie said, "I'm going for a walk."

"Where to?" Dat asked.

"Along the creek."

"Don't stay out in the heat too long." He closed his Bible.

"I won't." It was cooler than it had been the day before, but the ride home had been warm. "I won't be long."

The path along the creek started at the old flour mill on the Landis property and veered away from the water and up the bank below the Berger farm. Seth, Ben, Amos, and Katie had worn down the trail from running back and forth between the two farms when they were young. They would play in the abandoned mill, wade and fish in the creek, and swing from the rope hung from the willow tree.

Katie couldn't remember how many times she'd tripped on a root and fallen flat as she ran along the pathway. Mamm's complaints about the dirt on her apron or the tears in her dresses never stopped her. It wasn't until she was eleven, when she bloodied and fattened her lip on a rock when she fell, that she finally slowed down.

The breeze was cool along the creek. A fish jumped. A thrush flew up out of the reeds.

When she was about halfway to the Berger place, a shot rang out. The boys had sometimes target-practiced in the Berger back field years ago. Was Amos using it again? On a Sunday?

She veered up the trail to the field. As she neared the shooting range, someone yelled. She stepped behind a tree.

"Amos!" It was John's voice.

She shifted her body so she could see. On the fence was a line of tin cans. Amos stood with a rifle in his hand.

"Amos!" John shouted again.

"Jah, Dat."

"It's the Sabbath. Why are you shooting?"

Amos's head fell. "Ach. I wasn't thinking."

"Nee, you haven't been thinking at all for the last year."

Tears stung Katie's eyes for Amos.

"I'm sorry, Dat."

"You need to be on your way." John's shoulders were hunched and he leaned forward. "Go ahead and go into town. Get started on your journey to New York."

"You want me to travel on the Sabbath?"

John stepped forward. Ben stood behind their father. John shook his head, as if in disgust. "Why would that matter to you?"

"Fair enough," Amos said. "I'll go change my clothes and be on my way."

If John and Ben had left first, Katie would have revealed herself to Amos. But John walked toward Amos, taking the rifle from his son, and then they walked together toward the house.

Katie stepped out from the tree. Amos raised his hand above his head and waved and then turned and smiled for a quick moment.

Katie considered walking to the road, where she could speak with him before he boarded the train and headed to New York and then on to France. But she talked herself out of it. Perhaps it was the *shohm* she felt for Amos—shame that he'd gone against his father and the church. Against his brother. That he'd gone against her.

Over the next year, she would regret her decision not to meet him on the road that day. At least a thousand times.

CHAPTER 10

Tally

I plunged my needle into a black square and stood to go check on Mamm when Jane stopped telling the story. Mamm's head was tilted to the left a little. She'd given up stitching at the beginning of the story and had simply listened.

Maggie, who had remained by Mamm's side the entire time with her sampler in her hand, asked Jane, "What happened to Amos?"

"You'll have to come back to find out," Jane said.

"When?"

"The next quilting circle is on Tuesday."

"Is that tomorrow?" Maggie asked.

"Hush. Tomorrow is Friday," Danielle said. "Besides, Jane has more important things to do than tell us stories every day."

Jane shook her head. "I believe telling stories is one of the most important things I do, far more important than sales or even quilting."

I agreed with Jane but didn't say so. Just like a good book, her stories were both an escape and a lesson. I needed both in my life.

And from Danielle's interest—and even Maggie's—it seemed they did too.

I knelt down by Mamm. "How are you doing?"

"I'm tired," she said. "Perhaps I overdid it to come today."

"Let's get you home."

Danielle must have overheard me because she said, "Come on, Maggie. Let's go get the horse ready."

"Denki," I said, grateful Danielle could do that for me. It would definitely help get Mamm home sooner.

Jane motioned for Maggie and then opened a cupboard next to the doorway to the front area of the shop. "If you'd like, you may leave your sampler here to work on next time you come to the shop."

Maggie slipped it onto the bottom shelf and ran after her mother.

Mamm and I told Jane good-bye, which took a few minutes, and then I slowly pushed Mamm out the back door and into the sunshine. I squinted against the brightness. I pushed Mamm around the side deck, with the wheels thumping over the slats, to the ramp out front. By the time we reached the buggy, Danielle had it and the horse nearly ready.

As I pushed Mamm up the ramp and into the buggy, my back tightened. I stretched it before I bent over in the buggy to fasten Mamm's chair, but that only made it feel worse. Bending down to secure her chair tweaked it too.

"Where's Maggie?" Mamm asked.

"She's here," I said. "She'll sit up on the seat with us again."

"I was just checking to make sure she was with us." Mamm was definitely tired.

We were all quiet on the way home. When we neared our

farm, Maggie was still awake, and Danielle said, "We can walk home today."

"All right." That way I could get Mamm inside the house sooner. I stopped the buggy by our back door, and Danielle jumped down, followed by Maggie, and opened up the back of the buggy and the ramp. By the time I reached the back, she was pulling Mamm down the ramp, toward the back door.

"I appreciate your help," I said.

"Of course," Danielle said. "Thank you for including us again. I'm really *loving* Jane's story."

I smiled. "So am I."

Maggie waved at Mamm. "Get some rest," the little girl said. "I'll see you soon."

Mamm nodded but didn't speak.

As Danielle and Maggie headed up the lane, I pushed Mamm toward the house. I'd take care of the horse after I got her settled.

Once I had her transferred to the couch with her feet on the footstool, I spread a log cabin quilt Mamm had made the first year of her marriage over the top of her and then hurried and drove the horse and buggy to the barn.

Rich yelled at me from the field. "Is dinner ready yet?"

I shook my head. "Give me a half hour."

He frowned.

I took care of the horse as quickly as I could and then ran back to the house.

I called out, "Mamm!" as I came through the back door and then, "I'm back!" She didn't respond. I hurried into the living room, my coat still on.

Her head was slumped to the side.

"Mamm?" I reached for her face, taking it in my hands. Her eyes were only half open. "Mamm!"

Her eyes rolled back in her head.

My heart raced. I placed my fingers on her neck, searching for her pulse. It was weak.

She opened her eyes and made eye contact. "I'm so sleepy." I could understand her, but the words were slurred together.

I needed help—now.

"I'll be right back." I ran out the front door of the house. Once I reached the lane, I began waving at Rich and yelling. But he was on the tractor and had his back toward me.

I turned toward the phone shanty and began running in that direction.

But as I reached the shanty, a car came around the turn. I squinted. It was Danielle's, the white SUV that was usually parked in her driveway.

I stepped away from the phone shanty and into the road.

The vehicle slowed and then stopped. I ran to the passenger window.

Danielle leaned toward me from the driver's side. "What's wrong?"

"It's Mamm. I think she may be having another stroke. She's in the living room."

"Jump in," Danielle said.

I climbed in, and by the time I closed the door, Danielle had spun the SUV around.

"Whoa, Mama!" Maggie said from the back seat.

"We're going to go help Regina." Danielle gripped the steering wheel. "*Hang on.*"

When we reached the house, Danielle slammed the SUV into Park and jumped down. She was out of the vehicle, calling out, "Come on, Maggie!" as I struggled to open the door.

Maggie sat in one of those booster seats, which she unfastened on her own. She also opened her door as I slammed mine, then pushed her door shut and ran after her mother, who was headed for the front door. They both reached the house before I did.

Danielle flung open the door and yelled, "Regina!"

I followed them into the house.

Mamm was slumped over on the couch now.

Danielle had her fingers on Mamm's wrist. Then she propped Mamm up. "Regina, can you hear me?"

"Jah," Mamm said. "I'm fine." Again, her words were slurred.

"Can you call 9-1-1?" I asked.

"How long will it take for the ambulance to get out here?"

"A while." It had taken a half hour when I called them for Dat and then they'd taken him to the hospital a half hour away.

"The closest hospital is in Bremen. It won't take long for us to get her there," Danielle said. "I have a doctor friend doing an ER shift there right now."

I placed my hand on Mamm's shoulder, but I was thinking of Dat. If only we could have taken him to that hospital. "Can we get her in your SUV?"

"Yes," Danielle answered. "Absolutely."

With Danielle's help, I quickly transferred Mamm into her wheelchair. When I stood up, my lower back caught.

"Are you all right?" Danielle asked.

"I think so." I grabbed the quilt.

Danielle began to push Mamm's chair while Maggie and I trailed behind. I grabbed my purse, which had Mamm's medical information in it, and Mamm's coat and mine as we passed through the back porch. I tucked Mamm's coat around her as we headed down the ramp.

We transferred Mamm into the back seat, I fastened her seat belt, and then I tucked the quilt around her, with her coat on top. I wiggled into my coat as Danielle pushed the wheelchair toward the hatchback.

I followed Maggie around to her door and climbed into the middle of the back seat. Maggie climbed up into her booster seat and buckled herself in. After I fastened my seat belt, I pulled Mamm's head to rest on my shoulder.

Danielle started the engine and pushed something on her cell phone, which was clipped to a holder near the steering wheel. She spoke, saying, "I'm bringing a neighbor to the ER. Probable stroke. See you in a few." I guessed Danielle had left a message for her friend.

Rich started running toward us. I groaned. "Would you tell him what's going on?"

Danielle lowered her window. "We're taking your mom to the hospital."

I leaned forward. "I'll leave a message on the machine as soon as I know what's going on."

Rich frowned. "What are you talking about?"

"Your mom," Danielle said loudly. "She seems to be having another stroke."

Rich started around the car. "I'm coming with you."

I wished he wouldn't, but he climbed into the front seat, taking his straw hat off as he did.

Danielle said, "I know the doctor who's working at the ER today." She stopped at the intersection and waited for a truck to go by. "If it's a stroke, he can give her medicine that might reverse the effects."

"You should call 9-1-1," Rich said.

"We can get her there faster. It could make all the difference to get the medicine as soon as possible."

"Can't the EMTs give her the medicine?"

Danielle shook her head. "Only a doctor can."

"Why not go to the Elkhart or Goshen hospitals? Or Mishawaka? They're all bigger."

"Bremen is closer," Danielle said.

Rich's voice grew louder and more monotone. "Why are you making all of the decisions for our mother?"

I exhaled. Why had Rich come along? "We're going to the hospital in Bremen," I said.

Rich didn't answer me, and Danielle kept driving. We, even Maggie, stayed silent.

Mamm's head remained on my shoulder, and her eyes were closed. I had my hand on her wrist, on her pulse. *God*, I prayed, *please don't take my mother too*. I didn't care if I never did more than take care of Mamm. I didn't want her to die.

I don't know how fast Danielle was driving, but we arrived in Bremen in record time. She finally slowed as we reached the city limits.

When we arrived at the hospital, she pulled up to the emergency entrance. Parked across the lot was the blue pickup. If Rich saw it, he didn't say anything.

"I'll be right back." Danielle jumped out of the car and ran toward a door.

A minute later, she led the way out of the door, pulling a gurney. On the front end, pushing the gurney, was the man who owned the blue pickup.

RICH AND I sat in the waiting room with Maggie while Danielle stayed with Mamm in an exam room.

"Mama used to work here," Maggie said. "Before Daddy died."

"Oh" was all I could manage to say. That explained why Danielle knew exactly what to do. And why she knew the man in the blue pickup, whom Kenan didn't trust but who was now taking care of Mamm.

Finally, I came to my senses enough to say to Maggie, "I'm sorry about your daddy."

Maggie gave me a solemn nod. "I don't always remember him very well, but I look at his picture a lot."

I thought it would be nice if I had a picture of my Dat. Even though I was grown, the image of him was fading for me too. I remembered his blue eyes and bushy brows. And his gray hair and beard. But I couldn't remember his smile anymore, or the sound of his voice.

But I had all of my childhood with him. Maggie hadn't had long at all with her father.

Rich stood and then began pacing, with his hat in his hand. Then he sat back down and said to me, "We shouldn't have come here."

"Dirk and Mama will take care of Regina," Maggie said, sounding much older than she was. "You did the right thing."

I couldn't help but smile, but Rich frowned and shook his head.

Ten minutes later, Danielle stepped into the waiting room. "You and Rich can go in." She seemed shaken. "I'll stay here with Maggie. It's down the hall, the second door on the right."

"How is she?" I asked. Was Danielle alarmed by Mamm's condition?

"As good as can be expected," Danielle answered. "She'll need to be transferred to the Mishawaka hospital for observation and more tests, but she's already been given an IV injection of thrombolytic because of her symptoms and history of ischemic stroke." She turned toward me. "It helped that you brought her medical records."

It meant carrying a big purse, but it was worth it.

"Go on," Danielle said. "She's alert."

Rich led the way, with me following.

When we reached the door to the room, Dirk was coming out and said, "Hello, I'm Dr. Johnson."

"So it was a stroke?" Rich asked.

Dr. Johnson said, "She had all of the classic symptoms and with her history we couldn't take any chances. The anti-clotting medicine will hopefully stop any further clotting and could reverse damage that may have been done."

"Damage?" Rich asked.

Dirk—Dr. Johnson—took a step toward Rich. "Her speech is slurred, and her left hand is stiff. She said it wasn't that way before, which Danielle verified."

Rich frowned again.

"Go on in and see her." Dr. Johnson motioned toward the open door. "I'll be back in a few minutes. An ambulance is on the way to transfer her to Mishawaka."

Mamm was still on the gurney, covered with her log cabin quilt from our house. The faded browns and greens were even dimmer under the bright lights of the exam room.

Rich stepped to one side of her, and I moved to the other. "Mamm," I said. "How are you?"

She grimaced but didn't open her eyes or speak.

"I'm sorry we brought you here," Rich said.

I shot him a concerned look. "Hush."

"Jah, hush," Mamm managed to say. "Danielle did the right thing."

"Don't speak," I said. "Save your strength." I wanted Rich to leave so I could tell Mamm to get better, to not leave me. I'd rather care for her, stuck in our house, for another thirty years than have her die now.

Dr. Johnson stepped back into the exam room. "The ambulance is here." Behind him were two EMTs.

"I'll ride with Mamm," Rich said.

"Sure," Dr. Johnson said. He turned toward me. "It was nice to meet you, Tally."

I didn't think I'd told him my name. Danielle must have.

"Thank you." My voice choked a little. "For taking care of our mother."

Dr. Johnson smiled. "My pleasure. Danielle told me how much you've done for her."

I inhaled deeply, confused and disturbed Danielle had spoken about me to the man Kenan didn't trust.

Dr. Johnson nodded to the paperwork on the counter. "Should I give you your mother's records? Or your brother?"

"Give them to Rich," I said, "since he's going in the ambulance."

"Danielle can take you to Mishawaka," Dr. Johnson said. He handed me the paperwork.

"I'll see you at the hospital," I said to Rich.

He frowned.

I stepped out of the room. When I reached the waiting room, Danielle and Maggie weren't alone. Kenan was sitting with them.

CHAPTER 11

"I'll take Tally." Danielle spoke loudly. "I'm fine."

"You haven't been fine all week."

"You're what makes me not fine," she said. "I really need you to back off. I can't believe you took more time off work. You're going to lose your job."

He shook his head. "My boss is concerned about you too."

"Tell him to save his pity. He's not responsible for me. Neither are you."

They both saw me at the same time.

Kenan stood. "Tally. How is your Mamm?"

"All right, I think," I said. "Rich is going to ride in the ambulance."

Danielle stood and said to me, "And I'm taking you to Mishawaka."

"Then I'm taking Maggie with me," Kenan said.

Danielle pulled her keys from her purse and dangled them for a moment, thinking.

"I want to go with Mama and Tally," Maggie said. "And see Regina."

Danielle's expression grew tense, and she shook her head.

"They won't let you see Regina, baby." She kneeled down by Maggie's chair. "Uncle's right. You need to go with him."

As Danielle stood, Maggie slipped off her chair and then grabbed her mother's leg, sliding down to the floor.

"Maggie, don't do this." Danielle gave Kenan a panicked look.

"I can hire a driver," I said quickly.

Danielle shook her head. "I need to take you. I can talk with the doctors and help you figure out what's going on."

I wanted her to take me, but I didn't want to interfere with Maggie. I wasn't sure what was normal behavior for the little girl—and what was because of her insecurities. I knew what it was like to worry if my mother would take care of me.

Danielle pried Maggie's hands from her leg and lifted her into her arms. "Uncle Kenan will get you some lunch."

Kenan smiled. "And then we'll get ice cream."

Maggie shook her head.

"You'll be helping Regina," Danielle said. "And Tally."

Maggie jutted out her lower lip.

Danielle kissed the top of Maggie's head and said, "I'll be home soon." She slid the girl into Kenan's arms.

Maggie buried her head against Kenan's shoulder and didn't look at her mother again as he carried her out the front door.

"Come on," Danielle said to me. "We need to get you to the hospital so you're there to speak with the doctors. You can't leave this to Rich."

She was right. I couldn't trust Rich to relay to me what the doctors said.

Once we were in her SUV, she said, "Just so you know, Dirk and I are just friends, even though Kenan is sure more is going on. Dirk used to be my boss and he feels bad about what I went through, like he didn't do enough to help me. So that's why *he* puts up with me. I really don't know why Kenan puts up with me though. He's the best brother, better than any sister, but I don't deserve him." She started the engine.

A lump stuck in my throat. I couldn't imagine Rich ever doing for me what Kenan did for Danielle. "Jah," I said. "He seems like a really good guy."

"But he drives me absolutely crazy." She drove around to the front of the ER and turned out of the parking lot. "If Kenan doesn't let up, I'm going to sell the farm and move to South America with Maggie." Then she laughed, which jolted me a little, considering Mamm had just had another stroke and everything felt so serious. But I smiled anyway.

We caught up with the ambulance as it left the outskirts of Bremen and then followed it to the hospital in Mishawaka. They didn't seem to be in a hurry, which Danielle said was a good sign.

When we reached the hospital, she let me off behind the ambulance at the Emergency Department door and then went to park.

The EMT in the cab hopped out and opened up the back of the ambulance. Rich climbed down and then the EMT in the back pushed the gurney out while the other pulled on it.

"How is she?" I asked Rich.

"The same," he answered. "Except she kept asking for you." He frowned, something he'd been doing a lot of in the last hour. A frown was about as much emotion as Rich usually showed.

I stepped aside as the EMTs rolled the gurney toward the door. Mamm reached out for me. "Stay close," she said.

I took her hand. "I will." I walked beside the gurney, holding Mamm's hand on the way in. By the time I'd checked Mamm in, Danielle arrived. A nurse directed the EMTs to push the gurney down the hall.

Rich said, "You should stay out here. It'll be crowded. Danielle can go with me." He seemed to be warming up to her. Perhaps the EMT had told him we'd done the right thing to take Mamm to Bremen.

I shook my head. "I'm going too."

He crossed his arms. "Then I'll stay."

I wasn't going to argue with him. "Come on, Danielle." Last time Mamm was in the hospital, there was so much I didn't understand. I was happy Danielle could explain things to me this time.

We were in the room only a couple of minutes, long enough for the EMTs to transfer Mamm to the hospital bed and leave and for the nurse to take Mamm's vitals, when the doctor came in. He read through Mamm's chart. "There's a note here from a Dr. Johnson."

"Yes," Danielle said. "He administered thrombolytic because of her symptoms and history of ischemic stroke."

I admired Danielle's confidence, and I appreciated her speaking up. I'd forgotten the name of the medication already.

"I see." The doctor read on and then closed the file. "We'll do blood work and a CT scan."

After he left, Danielle said, "I'm going to go get some coffee. Want some?"

I shook my head.

"How about food? A sandwich or something?"

I shook my head again. "Maybe after a while."

She stood and headed to the door.

"Danielle?"

She turned.

"Thank you for your help." I sat down, hoping a change in position would ease the pain in my lower back. It didn't. "I don't know what I would have done without you."

"You would have done fine."

I shook my head. I hadn't done fine the last time.

WHILE DANIELLE WAS GONE, a young woman came in and drew Mamm's blood. And then nothing happened. I kept expecting someone to come get her for the CT scan, but no one showed up. I kept alternating between sitting and standing, but neither made my back feel better.

Finally, Danielle returned. "I saw Rich in the waiting room with Joanna and your cousin Ted. That's his name, right?"

"Jah, that's correct."

"They're going to take Rich home."

"What?"

"Rich said he needed to get back to work, and he asked for you to leave a message about how your Mamm is doing when you know." Danielle shrugged. "Oh, and Joanna said she'd fix Rich supper tonight, so you don't have to."

I rolled my eyes before I realized what I was doing.

"Right?" Danielle said. "As if your main duty is to cook his supper."

I started to laugh. Mamm opened her eyes and smiled.

Danielle snorted out a laugh. "Oh, right. I forgot. That is your main *duty*, at least one of them, as an Amish sister."

For a moment, I envied Danielle's life. She had a brother who catered to her instead of the other way around.

But then I corrected my thinking. God directed my life. I needed to be thankful in all things. Rich worked hard to earn a living for our family. My job was to make sure he was fed and clothed, along with taking care of Mamm.

"Rich also said to tell you that he already let the bishop know your Mamm is in the hospital. He used Ted's phone."

I often wondered if Dat told Rich to be kind to Ted and look out for him. When Dat was still alive, he'd allow Ted to stay with us when he needed to. I knew Rich called Ted sometimes to ask him to stop by the farm for a visit, and sometimes for a ride, but it was the first time I knew of that Rich had called Ted during an emergency.

A young man stepped into the room to take Mamm to her CT scan. "I'll be here when you get back," I said to Mamm.

After she was gone, Danielle asked, "How's your back?"

I rubbed it. "About the same."

"Do you do exercises?"

I shook my head.

"I'll show you a couple of easy ones." She placed her hands against the wall and spread her feet apart. "These are wall push-ups." She leaned in and then pushed herself back out. "Start out with ten at a time and then increase the number." Then she showed me how to do a squat, rotate my torso, and then a back stretch. "See how these work for you. I can show you more if needed."

I thanked her as I practiced the back stretch. When I finished, she said, "You should go get something to eat. It'll be a while before they bring your Mamm back from the CT scan. If not, I'll be here when she gets back."

When I returned to the room after eating a bowl of chicken noodle soup, Mamm wasn't back in the room yet, but Jane Berger was, along with Savannah Mast.

"What are you doing here?" I asked.

"I heard your Mamm was in the hospital," Jane said. "Savannah was at the shop when I got the news, so she brought me here."

Tears, in response to Jane's thoughtfulness, stung my eyes.

"We didn't know Danielle was here with you," Jane said. "I just didn't want you to be alone."

"Denki," I managed to say. "I appreciate you coming."

"Savannah has a doula appointment nearby. She was going to drop me off and come back and get me when she's done. But I can go with her and wait in the car—"

"No," I said. "Please stay. Mamm will be happy to see you."

Savannah smiled. "I'll be back in an hour or so." She turned toward Danielle. "Do you have a phone? Could I text you if I'll be a little later?"

"Of course." Danielle and Savannah swapped numbers.

Savannah was training to be a midwife while working as a doula, as well as looking after her grandmother. She had an energy that I couldn't fathom, but she seemed to thrive on keeping busy.

Right after Savannah left, Mamm returned to the room. She smiled when she saw Jane, who took her hand.

When Jane asked how she was, Mamm whispered, "All right."

"Tired?"

"A little."

I held the cup of water and positioned the straw for her, and Mamm took a long drink.

"Where's Maggie?" Mamm asked Danielle.

"She's with my brother," she replied.

"Too bad." Mamm turned her head toward Jane. "I was hoping you could tell us more of your story, but I don't want Maggie to miss out."

"I can tell Maggie what happens at bedtime," Danielle said quickly.

Jane glanced at me. "Is it all right with you, Tally? I don't want to take away time between you and your mother."

"I think it would be good for all of us," I said.

Danielle pulled one of the chairs along the wall closer to the bed and motioned to Jane to sit.

After she had, Jane said, "This morning feels like a long time ago, so you'll have to remind me where we were in the story."

"Amos was leaving again," I said, "to go to Fort Drum in New York and then ship out to France."

Danielle pulled a tube of lipstick from her purse. "He'd been target-practicing and his father said he was being prideful and needed to leave. Katie was standing behind a tree and saw and heard all of it." She applied the lipstick perfectly, without having to look in the mirror.

"Jah," Jane said. "And Amos waved at Katie and smiled as he left, right?"

I nodded.

"And he'd already asked Katie to write him back if he was able to write her." Jane's eyes had a faraway look in them. "I'm very grateful for those letters. . . ."

CHAPTER 12

Katie

The third week of September, Katie walked to the mailbox in the afternoon as she did every day, hoping that a letter from Amos would finally arrive.

Perhaps his letters had been lost along the way. Maybe a mailbag in France had fallen from a truck and been trampled by a line of marching men. Or perhaps he'd changed his mind about writing to her after all.

Maybe he'd met a girl in New York before he left. Or a girl in France. The ideas in her mind wouldn't stop swirling around and around.

Once again there was no letter from Amos, but there was a newspaper—dated September 19, the day before—for Dat. She pulled it out of the box and read the headline on the front page.

Influenza Reaches Indiana.

Surprised, she kept reading. There were 185 cases of the flu reported in Indianapolis, all among military men. At the mayor's request, school officials were to send home all children exhibiting symptoms and all gathering places were to be fumigated—hotel lobbies, theaters, railway stations, and streetcars. The mayor had also instructed the city police to enforce an anti-spitting ordinance. For the time being, public schools and public places would not be closed, but such action could be taken if later warranted.

She felt for the soldiers, so far from home. Most wouldn't be exposed to the flu if they weren't on Army bases, living so close together. The flu had seemed so far away, as far away as the war. But now it was in Indiana. She doubted it would come to Elkhart County though.

She hoped Amos hadn't been exposed on the ship to France or once he arrived. Perhaps that was why he hadn't written to her.

Katie leafed through the rest of the paper. The only article she could find about the war was that US troops were arriving in France. Underneath that article was a small piece saying one case of influenza had been reported in South Bend. That was forty miles away.

She folded the paper and tucked it under her arm. At least she had one more day this week to hope for a letter. Then it would be Sunday.

But she wasn't sure how long to keep hoping.

She turned back toward the house. The leaves on the trees had begun to turn—bright orange and yellow on the maples, and more muted yellows on the poplars.

The afternoon was bright and warm. Katie picked up her pace. She couldn't let her thoughts wander to Amos, not now.

When she reached the house, Mamm called out to her from the living room. "Katie, would you bring me a glass of water?"

"Just a minute. I need to pump a bucket of fresh water."

She put Dat's newspaper on his desk, went out and pumped the water, and then came back into the house and dipped a glass for Mamm. She still had tomatoes to finish canning and supper to get started. She was feeling overwhelmed with everything she still needed to do. She should have skipped the walk to the mailbox. She could have gone once she'd cleaned the kitchen after supper. Or Dat could have gotten his own newspaper.

No. The reason she walked to the mailbox every day was because if she had a letter from Amos, she didn't want Dat nor Seth to see it.

When Katie returned to the living room, Mamm sat with her head against the back of her chair, her eyes closed.

"Mamm, here's your water."

Mamm didn't answer.

"Mamm?" Katie put her hand on Mamm's shoulder.

"Jah?" Mamm's eyes opened.

Relief flooded through Katie. "I have your water."

"Denki." Mamm reached for the glass, then took a drink. "I must have fallen asleep."

"Do you want to go upstairs and rest?"

Mamm shook her head. "I'm fine."

Katie was sure Mamm wasn't fine. She was dozing off more and more. Climbing the stairs made her winded. And she seldom helped with any of the cleaning or cooking. She rarely even snapped beans or peeled potatoes at the table anymore.

Perhaps it was time for another visit to the doctor.

THE NEXT AFTERNOON on her way to the mailbox, Katie stopped along the field where Dat was repairing a broken fence rail. "Dat," she said. "I need to speak with you. About Mamm."

He stood, stretching his back as he did. "Is she all right?"

"Jah, right now. But have you noticed how she's been dozing off more?"

He shook his head. Of course he wouldn't. He was always out working during the day.

"How about how winded she gets when she climbs the stairs?"

"I have noticed that," he said.

"Do you think an appointment with the doctor would help?"

Dat exhaled, pulled his glove from his right hand, and took his hat off his head. Then he ran his hand through his hair, put his hat back on, and pulled his glove back on his hand. "I'll ask her, but I doubt she'll go."

"Why not?"

"She's convinced there's nothing the doctor can do for her."

"What do you mean?"

"There's no remedy. Her heart valve is most likely damaged. Resting will help her live longer, but it won't save her."

"H-how long does she have?" Katie stammered.

Dat shrugged. "I doubt the doctor knows."

Tears sprang to Katie's eyes.

"It's the Lord's will," Dat said. "Mamm accepts that. We all need to."

Katie couldn't imagine how lonely her life would be without Mamm. Unlike most Amish women, she only had one living sibling. She had cousins who lived in Jackson Township but none nearby.

If Mamm passed away, Katie wouldn't have any woman around to talk with on a regular basis, although perhaps Seth would marry soon and then Paulina would move in with the family. But then Paulina would be in charge of the household—not Katie.

No wonder Mamm was pushing her to marry Ben.

"Katie?" Dat asked. "Are you all right?"

She blinked back her tears as she nodded. "I'm going to go get the mail."

"I'll come in and check on Mamm in a little bit." Dat turned back toward the fence.

As Katie reached the road, a wagon came toward her, from town. She squinted into the afternoon sun. It was either John or Ben. She couldn't tell.

She opened the mailbox. There was one envelope—addressed to her in Amos's handwriting. She quickly slipped it into her pocket as the wagon approached.

It was Ben. He kept his eyes straight ahead and didn't glance her way. At church two weeks ago, he'd said hello to her but only because she was walking with Mamm. Besides that, he hadn't acknowledged her since Amos had been home. She guessed he'd spied on them together that last night.

She watched until the wagon turned down the Bergers' lane. Then she hesitated. If she walked back down the lane and past Dat, he'd ask if there was any mail. She decided to walk up the road and then cut down to the old mill. She'd have some privacy there to read Amos's letter.

Seth drove the team of workhorses, pulling the hay rake over the far field. He didn't seem to notice her. Ben and John would most likely help bale the hay on Monday. Then Dat and Seth would help with the Berger hay in the next few days.

Katie had tried to help with the threshing in late August, but her frequent trips into the house to check on Mamm meant she couldn't contribute much.

It hadn't rained in a few weeks and the dust on the road billowed with each step Katie took. Dust drifted toward her from the horses and the rake. She quickened her step and hurried toward the creek and the mill.

When she reached the trail, she slowed her pace, not wanting to trip on a root. Even though the mill was no longer used,

Dat kept it in good repair, not wanting anyone to venture into it and be met with an accident.

She pushed open the door and in the dim light found her way to the bench by the stone. The creek side of the mill was open, and across the water the trees along the creek swayed in the breeze, the colorful leaves dancing back and forth. Katie took the letter from her pocket and slowly unfolded the paper.

August 15, 1918

Dearest Katie,

I hope this finds you doing well, along with your mother. I pray for her health.

I'll be honest with you. Each day I regret my decision more and more. I shouldn't keep dwelling on this and shouldn't keep repeating myself to you. Forgive me. But I can't help but be honest.

Other soldiers write letters home that are full of cheer because they do not want their loved ones to worry.

I hope to accomplish that feat in my next letter to you.

In the meantime, I'll tell you that my homesickness became nearly unbearable when I left Indiana, but by the time I arrived at Fort Drum, I felt numb.

After finishing our paperwork and the end of our training, we left for New York City, where we boarded the ship. Many of the others suffered from seasickness, but mine wasn't bad as long as I remained on the deck.

We arrived in France three days ago. We are waiting for further orders. The countryside is beautiful, and the people are kind. The weather has been sunny and mostly warm.

I can't complain except for what I fear is ahead of me.

Other soldiers are itching for combat, or so they say, but I dread it. I would appreciate your prayers, if you can find it in your heart to say them.

Sincerely,
Amos

Katie read the letter a second time, her face growing warmer with each word.

The letter brought her no comfort. She knew his request for prayers wasn't for his own safety, but that he wouldn't have to shoot anyone.

She hurried out of the mill and up the bank of the creek. Seth had left the field with the rake and the team of horses, so she crossed it, walking between rows of cut hay instead of taking the road.

Could she trust the Lord? Trust him for Amos's safety? For his future? For her own future? Even though their futures would now never be one?

Katie tried to pray, but no words formed.

Amos had thrown away everything she'd ever dreamed of for the two of them.

And when he'd been home last June, she'd let her guard down.

He'd never return home to stay after this—if he returned at all. He'd be forever changed by the worst the world had to offer. It would consume him, if it hadn't already.

A wave of nausea stopped her. What would it mean if Amos didn't return at all? That he'd been killed?

The letter felt like a hot ember in the pocket of her apron, ready to ignite. Her life would go on much as it always had, but without Amos. His life would be changed forever. Both thoughts brought tears to her eyes.

Before she reached the house, she heard Dat call her name. And then again. "Katie!" There was an alarm in his voice that she hadn't heard before.

She began to run.

When she reached the living room, Dat had Mamm in his arms. "Go tell Seth to get the wagon ready. We need to take Mamm to the doctor."

"No, send Seth to get the doctor," Katie said.

"That will take too long. Go."

Katie ran, yelling her brother's name.

He stepped out of the barn, a harness in his hands. "Dat needs the wagon," Katie panted. "To take Mamm to the doctor."

Together they readied the horses and hitched them to the wagon.

Then Katie ran toward the house while Seth brought the wagon around.

She grabbed quilts from her parents' room and yelled to Dat that the wagon was ready.

Seth went into the house, and Katie hurried outside to make a bed in the wagon for Mamm. It would be a rocky ride for her into town.

Dat and Seth carried Mamm out, making a sling with their hands. Mamm had her eyes open, but her face was ashen, and she could barely hold on to Dat and Seth as they carried her.

"I need you to come with us," Dat said to Katie. "Sit in the back with Mamm."

"Of course." Canning the tomatoes would have to wait.

Katie stroked Mamm's forehead as they bumped along the road.

When they reached town, Mamm said, "Your Dat should have sent for the doctor."

"He wanted to get you care as soon as possible."

"He knows there's not anything that can be done."

"But what if there is?" Katie asked. "Dat must think it's worth trying."

Mamm closed her eyes.

When they reached the doctor's office, a block off Main Street, Dat sent Katie in to see if the doctor was in the office. She waved at Nurse Walden, who sat at the front desk.

"My Mamm needs to see the doctor," Katie called out.

Nurse Walden frowned. "Tell her to come inside."

"I need to know if the doctor can see her," Katie said.

A woman who was heading toward the exit shook her head and rolled her eyes. "These Dutchies. They won't do their part but expect us to jump at their command."

Katie's face grew warm. She'd heard some of the townspeople were resentful of the Amish for not fighting in the war, but she hadn't encountered any comments until now.

Dr. Barker opened the door to the exam room. "Hello, Katie," he said. "Tell your mother to come on in. I can see her now."

CHAPTER 13

On her way back out of the doctor's office to tell Mamm the doctor could see her, a man stepped into the waiting room. He was dressed in a black suit and was blowing his nose into his handkerchief. He didn't appear to be much older than she was.

When Katie came back into the doctor's office with Mamm and Dat, the man was coughing. Nurse Walden stood at the doorway of the exam room. "Come in," she said to Mamm as the man sneezed.

Katie held on to Mamm's arm until Mamm said, "Wait here. I only want your Dat to come back with me."

Reluctantly, Katie sat in a chair across the room from the man. His face was flushed, and his shoulders slumped.

The nurse came back a few minutes later and addressed the man. "It'll be another half hour or so until the doctor can see you."

"I have a sales meeting at Hartman Brothers in fifteen minutes," he said. "I'll come back after that." He blew his nose again, and on the way out of the office, he had another coughing fit.

Katie sat staring at the door to the examination room, willing Mamm and Dat to come out with good news. Perhaps the doctor's first diagnosis had been wrong. Perhaps there was some sort of medication for Mamm. As she prayed silently, her heart softened, and she felt her fear dissipate. Finally, she said a prayer for Amos too. *Bring him home*, she prayed. *Heal him too*.

Soon after, the door opened and Mamm stepped into the waiting room with Nurse Walden at her side.

"Where's Dat?" Katie asked.

"Speaking with Dr. Barker," Mamm said. "Help me out to the wagon."

Katie did as her mother requested, managing to help her up into the bed and back onto the blankets. A few minutes later, Dat came out, carrying a bottle. Hope filled Katie. The doctor *had* given Mamm medicine.

On the way home, Katie sat beside Mamm, who had closed her eyes. Katie wasn't sure she was asleep though. Dat, sitting on the bench, stared straight ahead.

When they reached the house, Dat helped Mamm down and then handed Katie the bottle. "She's to take this tonic twice a day. After breakfast and before bed."

Katie held it carefully, took Mamm's arm, and started toward the house, while Dat drove the wagon to the barn.

"Help me to the sickbed," Mamm said to Katie. "And then bring me a tray for dinner."

The sickbed was in the small room off the kitchen. When Katie and Seth were little, Mamm had them stay in the sickbed when they were ill. That way she could keep an eye on them while she worked in the kitchen.

Katie also guessed the stairs were getting too hard for Mamm.

"What did the doctor say?" Katie asked.

"The same as he said before."

"What about the tonic?"

"He says it might calm my heart."

Katie hoped he was right.

Without much time to prepare supper, she put together a soup from leftover ham and beans. She made biscuits to go with it and opened the last applesauce from last year's apples. She'd be making more applesauce soon.

While Dat and Seth ate at the table, Katie sat with Mamm in the sickroom, coaxing her to eat the soup. It wasn't until it was time to clean up that Katie had a chance to eat. She sat at the table, ate her bowl of soup, and then cleaned the dishes.

She gave Mamm her dose of tonic and tucked her in. Then she returned to canning the tomatoes by the light of the lamp.

"Katie," Mamm said, "you should go to bed."

"I need to finish the tomatoes. The water is almost hot. It won't take long."

The next day, Mamm stayed in the sickroom, and the day after she didn't go to church. Katie stayed home with her.

The next day, Mamm ventured into the front room and also ate her meals at the table, and Katie was hopeful that she was on the mend. But the day after that, she was back in the sickroom with a sore throat and a fever. By evening, she was coughing.

Katie made a bed out of blankets and slept in the kitchen to be close to Mamm. Several times during the night, she rose and mopped Mamm's forehead with a cool cloth. Dat rose long before it was time to do the chores to check on her.

"Maybe you should go get the doctor," Katie said to him.

"It's just a cold," Mamm said. "The doctor can't do anything. I'll keep taking the tonic."

Katie made broths for Mamm, changed her sheets when her

fever broke, and did her best to keep up with the cooking for Dat and Seth and the laundry for all of them. At times, Mamm's lips had a blue tint to them, which worried Katie. It was as if Mamm was freezing—and burning up at the same time.

Thursday, late in the afternoon, Seth cleaned up and went to Paulina's house for supper. Soon after he left, Dr. Barker arrived in his buggy. Surprised, Katie stepped out on the front porch as the doctor tied his horse to the hitching post.

"Dr. Barker," she said. "Did Dat send for you?"

The doctor turned toward her, a confused expression on his face. "Why would he?"

"Mamm's ill. She's been running a fever since Tuesday."

Dr. Barker shook his head. "Where is your Dat?"

"In the barn."

"I'll go speak with him." He tipped his hat to Katie and headed in the opposite direction.

Katie returned to the kitchen and stepped to the sickroom door. Mamm slept fitfully. Sweat beaded on her brow, and she tossed and turned. Katie grabbed the bucket and headed out to the pump for more water, glancing toward the barn as she did. The doctor and Dat stood outside of it, apart, talking.

Once she filled the bucket, she returned to the house. A few minutes later, she heard the buggy leaving.

Several times she went to the back door to look for Dat, but she didn't see him. At the usual time, he came in for supper.

Mamm was still asleep and didn't join them at the table.

After Dat led the two of them in a silent prayer, Katie asked him what the doctor said.

"Jah," Dat said. "I need to talk with you about that."

Before he could say anything more, however, the back door swung open, and Seth rushed into the house. "Is it true what Dr. Barker says? That Mamm has that Spanish flu?"

After supper, Dat tied a white cloth to the front door, as the doctor had instructed him to, as a sign that the family was quarantining. Katie followed him out to the porch.

"We won't tell Mamm what's wrong," Dat said. "If she keeps thinking she has a cold, perhaps she'll do better."

"How can we know for sure she has the flu when the doctor didn't examine her?"

"Because of her symptoms. He doesn't want to expose himself. The man that was in his office last Friday didn't come back to be examined, so Dr. Barker wasn't exposed. The man died at the boardinghouse in town yesterday," Dat said. "Dr. Barker called his place of business in Indianapolis, and they said his wife had died the day before from influenza. It's presumed that's what he had too. The nurse who works for Dr. Barker remembered that you were in the waiting room that afternoon. She thought perhaps you had been exposed and would be ill. That's why Dr. Barker came out to the farm."

Katie did the math in her head. Mamm would have come down with it three days after passing by the man at the doctor's. Now it was three days since Mamm had come down with it. "I'll keep caring for Mamm. You and Seth shouldn't expose yourselves any more than you already have. I'm guessing if I was going to get it, I would have by now."

"The doctor said to leave the doors open when we can, to let fresh air in," Dat said. "And not to let anyone in the house. He said he'd ask the Fishers to let the deacon know."

Seth was listening at the door and said, "Jah, he asked them to spread the word right after he told me to leave at once. Now Paulina won't be wanting to see me anymore."

"Just until this is over," Dat said. "The doctor said we should quarantine for fourteen days. It's just like when you were little and had scarlet fever."

Katie didn't remember that, but she'd been told that Seth and she had scarlet fever at the same time. And then Mamm had come down with it too, which damaged her heart, although Seth and Katie didn't have any lasting effects. She would redouble her prayers for Mamm.

And for Amos too. Not only was he at war, but the influenza was ravaging the troops. He could be fighting two battles at once.

The next morning, when Seth didn't come down for breakfast, Katie told Dat she'd go check on him. She suspected he'd sneaked out late to meet Paulina, even though the doctor clearly told all of them to quarantine. She hoped that was the case, regardless, and that he'd overslept because he was tired. The other option terrified her.

As soon as she opened the door, Katie knew from the stale odor of his room that Seth was ill. He was curled up on his bed with only a sheet covering him, even though the morning was cool. He moaned and turned his head toward her. Sweat glistened on his forehead.

"I'm sick." His lips had the same bluish tint that Mamm's had at times since she'd fallen ill.

"I can see that," Katie answered. "I'll tell Dat and then bring you up some water and fried mush."

Seth didn't respond.

Dat decided that the best thing to do was move Seth's mattress into the front room so Katie wouldn't have to run up and down the stairs, taking care of two patients. Katie helped Seth down the stairs and then Dat brought the mattress down. Katie coaxed water and mush down Seth and then remade the bed. Before she finished, his cough grew so bad that he vomited in the slop jar she'd put beside his mattress.

Seth's fever grew worse during the day, and Katie spent all

of her time going between Mamm and Seth. When Dat came in at noon, he ate cold mush. Katie managed to make chicken soup for supper but no biscuits. She fed Seth while Dat ate at the table and then she fed Mamm. A noise on the porch caught her attention.

She hurried into the front room. Seth stood at the door, wearing only his long underwear. Paulina stood on the porch.

"Go on home," Katie called out. "You can't be here."

"I just wanted to find out how your Mamm is."

"Seth, get back to bed," Katie commanded. She turned toward Paulina. "Go home. Seth is ill. You need to stay away from here."

"Just give me a minute," Paulina said.

Katie shook her head. "Go. Now." She shut the door.

"Katie," Seth whined, "she needs to talk to me."

"It will have to wait. For two weeks." Katie pointed toward the bed. "Settle back down."

ALL KATIE DID was care for Mamm and Seth and try to get some laundry and cooking done. Dat helped when he could, but he had the corn harvest to do completely on his own now. It wasn't safe to hire any hands or ask Ben and John to help. Thankfully, he was still strong and capable.

Most mornings Seth's lips were blue. Katie could see why some called the flu the Purple Death. A few times blood leaked from his nose. Both he and Mamm had horrid coughing fits until their ribs hurt. Seth vomited several more times and had a crippling headache one afternoon. Another time, he said his legs hurt so badly he felt as if someone were torturing him.

Saturday, Paulina came by again, yelling for Katie when she arrived. Katie stepped out the back door and Paulina held up a basket. "I brought you bread, stew, and custard."

Katie wiped away a tear, one of gratitude. "Put it down on the ground. I'll pick it up after you leave."

On Sunday, the last day of September, Dat sat on the porch most of the day and read his Bible. Mamm was better and sat at the kitchen table to eat her soup and bread but then went back to the sickroom.

September gave way to October. The first three days of the month were a blur. By Thursday, Mamm seemed better, but Seth was worse. His fever continued, along with his chills and rounds of sweating. His cough became dry and he hacked continually. His stomach problems worsened too. Katie had to force him to drink water and broth.

Another Sunday passed. Mamm was on the mend, amazingly. Perhaps Dat had been right not to tell her she had the flu.

Finally, Seth seemed to be getting better too. He only had three more days until the two weeks were up. Katie helped him clean up and walk to the table, where he was able to sit for a while. He fed himself a bowl of mush.

Katie sat at the other end of the table and put her head on top of her arms. She awoke to Mamm calling her from the sickroom. She stood, feeling dizzy, and grabbed the chair to steady herself. She wasn't sure if she was getting ill or was just completely exhausted.

The next day was a Saturday, and Paulina came by again with another basket of food.

"Let me sit by her on the porch," Seth said. "I won't get close to her."

"No," Katie said. "Three more days. Not until then."

Katie stepped on the porch. "Denki, Paulina," she said. "Seth is better. If you come back on Wednesday, you can see him."

Paulina pursed her lips together. "Are you sure he's doing better?"

Katie said, "Jah. His fever is gone and he's eating."

"All right. I'll leave the basket and see him on Wednesday."

Katie took it as a good sign when Seth hauled his mattress back up to his room. He came down for a bowl of soup and then went back upstairs. Katie slipped out of the house to go to the mailbox. Most days, since Mamm fell ill, Dat had gotten the mail.

When she reached the mailbox, she leaned against it, exhausted but grateful. Mamm, even with her bad heart, was recovering. So was Seth, even though he'd burned with fever for over a week. And neither she nor Dat had fallen ill, even though they'd both been exposed. She had so much to be grateful for.

She opened the mailbox. There was an envelope—with her name and address, written by Amos. He was still alive, or at least he was when he wrote the letter. She slipped it in the pocket of her apron and started back for the house.

When she reached the kitchen, she sat at the table and read the letter. It was dated September 26, 1918.

Dear Katie,

I can't tell you where we are, but up until today we've only been marching—"sightseeing" is what we call it. Today we saw some action, and it was as bad as I anticipated. Even if my body survives, I'm not sure how my soul possibly will.

It's hard to imagine that I was despondent over not getting enough food to eat or a blanket when I was in Maryland. There is no comparison to what life is like now.

I think about you every day. I pray for you. I pray for your Mamm. I think of our childhood, of running along the creek, back and forth, up and down the path. Of our time in school together, playing baseball and kickball. I would give anything to go back for just one day with you.

Most probably think that I've turned my back on God, but I have to say I've never felt closer to Him. Christ's love and peace is here with me now. I feel both every minute of every day.

Please write when you can. Others in my unit tell me mail is getting through quickly.

Your friend,
Amos

Something had changed in the tone of Amos's letter. He sounded humble. Resigned. Grateful. Obviously no one was writing to him, but he didn't sound as if he was complaining.

Katie slipped the paper back into the envelope and put it in her pocket. This time she would write him back. But as she stood up, another wave of dizziness passed through her.

She'd write to him in the morning. Maybe she wouldn't be as tired then.

That night, when she went up to bed, Seth was coughing. She returned to the kitchen, poured him a glass of water from the pitcher, and took it up to his room. She knocked on his door and heard his moan. She opened the door. He was curled on his bed.

She stepped to his side and felt his forehead. He was burning again. She tried to give him the water to drink, but he refused it.

"Come downstairs to sleep," she said.

He shook his head. "I'll be better after I rest. I'll see you in the morning."

Several times, Katie heard Seth coughing, and it kept her awake. But toward the middle of the night, it stopped. *He's better*, she thought as she finally drifted off to sleep. But when breakfast time came and she went to check on him, she found him ice cold. He'd been dead for hours.

CHAPTER 14

Tally

Mamm closed her eyes and shifted in the hospital bed toward the wall as Jane said, "Well, that's certainly enough for today. I'm sorry to leave the story on such a sad and morbid note though." She patted Mamm's arm. "Regina, don't open your eyes. Just know I'm praying for you. I'll check in with you tomorrow and see what you need."

Mamm nodded.

"Denki," I said to Jane. I was afraid if I said anything more, my voice would crack. I thought of Rich. As much as he annoyed me, I would be lost if he died. Katie was now without a sibling.

Jane gave me a small smile. "In the meantime, leave a message if anything comes up. Or send Danielle to get me."

My eyes brimmed with tears. I knew I could count on Jane.

Savannah arrived, and Jane slipped into her coat. Then they both told Danielle and me good-bye and left.

"What did you think of the story?" Danielle whispered.

I shivered. "I didn't expect Katie's brother to die. Not at

all." I lowered my voice. "I'm worried about her mother." I was worried about mine too.

"Right?" Danielle shook her head. "Life is full of all sorts of twists and turns and tragedies. I guess that's one thing that *never* changes, no matter the year or place."

I agreed. Danielle and I had both experienced that in life. We'd both suffered loss, but I knew losing a husband for her was different than me losing my father. "What about you?" I asked. "What did you think?"

"I'm envious of what Amos wrote to Katie. I wish I would have felt God's peace and love when I was in Iraq. I was so sure God detested me that I couldn't feel anything when I thought of Him." She sighed. "I wonder if Amos was able to keep that way of thinking until the war ended. Until he came home."

I pursed my lips together. "Do we know he came home?"

"I'm assuming he does," Danielle said. "Don't you think he and Katie marry? Jane's last name is Berger."

"Katie might have married Ben."

Danielle wrinkled her nose. "I guess we'll have to see what happens."

"You should get going," I said. "Maggie is probably waiting for you to get home."

"You should come too," Danielle said.

I shook my head. "I'm going to stay here with Mamm."

"No." Mamm's eyes remained closed.

"I'm staying," I said.

"No," Mamm said again. "There's no reason for you to stay. There's nothing you can do. Come back in the morning."

"She's right," Danielle said. "You won't get a good sleep here. They'll eventually move her up to a room. Then they'll come in at least every hour to check on her. Maybe wake her up early for more tests. It's bad enough Regina won't get any sleep, but there's no reason you shouldn't get any too. And you could make your back worse by sleeping in a chair or on the floor."

I grimaced. She was right.

"I'll bring you back first thing in the morning," Danielle said. "Your Mamm will be fine. The nurses and doctors will take good care of her. I'll leave my number in case there's an emergency, so we'll know right away."

"Denki," I said and then reached for Mamm's hand. "Are you sure you don't want me to stay?"

"Go," she whispered.

I squeezed her hand. What if she had another stroke and died during the night? "I think I should stay."

"Go!" Mamm said forcefully. "I want to get some rest."

I took a step backward, a little alarmed by her forcefulness. "All right," I said. "I'll see you tomorrow."

On our way down the hall, Danielle stopped at the nurses' station and asked one of the nurses to add her phone number to Mamm's chart.

Once we were in the car and on the highway headed south toward home, Danielle said, "Speaking of your back . . ." Her words trailed off.

"What about it?" I asked, thinking she had more stretches to show me.

"It got me to thinking. You could use some help with your Mamm, right?"

I shrugged, unsure where she was going with this.

Danielle continued, "What if I became her part-time caregiver? It would give you time with your own pursuits—I mean, if there's something you'd like to do besides care for your Mamm and cook for Rich and clean and do laundry."

I turned my head and glanced out the passenger window.

"I used to want to be a teacher." The sun had just set, and the world was fading away.

Danielle's voice rose. "You could still do that. I can take care of your Mamm during the day."

I smiled at her enthusiasm and turned back toward her. "I'd have to find a teaching job."

"Well." She flashed me a quick grin and then put her eyes back on the road. "Start looking!"

"I wouldn't have any money to pay you until I found a job, until I got paid. And even at that, I won't make enough to pay you what you're worth, what you've been used to."

She brushed the air with her hand. "We can worry about all of that later." She prattled on about what a good teacher she thought I'd be. "You're so good with Maggie. So patient. I've never seen you be unkind to anyone. I wish I'd had a teacher like you when I was in school."

"I would like to teach," I said cautiously. "But I don't know if I'd make a good teacher anymore."

Danielle shot me a puzzled glance. "Why not?"

"I've always been shy and awkward, but it's gotten worse since I've been home caring for Mamm."

"What?"

"It's true," I said. "Maybe the students wouldn't take me seriously."

"Who told you you're shy and awkward?"

I rolled my eyes. "No one had to tell me. I've always known."

"I would *never* think of you as shy and awkward," Danielle said. "Quiet, jah. And often deep in thought. And empathetic. All qualities of a good teacher."

I shook my head.

"I'm going to tell you a secret," Danielle said. "Everyone feels awkward." She grinned. "I've never felt shy, but I've felt awkward my entire life. I believe it's part of the human condition."

I laughed. "I don't believe you."

"Name someone who doesn't feel awkward."

"My cousin Ted."

"Is he a normal person? I mean, I guess I knew some guys in the Army who didn't feel awkward, but they were. They were just too arrogant to realize it."

I laughed again. "Ted isn't arrogant. He's just . . . fun. And sad. It's like he doesn't feel awkward because he doesn't care what anyone thinks."

Danielle smiled. "I think I want to meet this Ted."

"You'd like him," I said.

"Why is he sad?"

"His sister died. When we were young."

"Oh, that is sad."

Danielle slowed as we passed her house. Kenan's truck was in the driveway, and every light in the house seemed to be on. The home seemed so inviting. I could imagine Maggie and Kenan sitting at the table, eating together. Then making cookies. And reading a book. Perhaps she would play under the staircase while he did the dishes or, more likely, Maggie would help him clean the kitchen.

Danielle slowed even more, staring at her house. "I like looking at it as an outsider. Is it a happy house? Do the people who live there have friends? Does the family have purpose?"

"Jah," I answered. "Jah to all three of your questions."

Once we'd passed, she sped up. As we approached my house, she said, "You should try it. Pretend you don't live in your house. What do you see?"

I stared at my house. There was a light in the kitchen window, but that was all. It didn't look very happy. There wasn't anything that made me want to go in—especially knowing Mamm wasn't there. She might not have been a very reliable mother at times, but she was the only mother I had.

"What are you thinking?" Danielle asked.

"That it looks like a nondescript Amish home."

"I think it looks cozy," Danielle said. She stopped the car where I usually parked the buggy. "Here you go."

"Denki," I said. "I really appreciate your help and the ride. I appreciate everything you've done for me. For us."

"You're welcome," she said. "It feels good to be able to help someone else for a change. It's been a while."

I gave her a grateful smile.

"Give me a call in the morning when you're ready to leave," Danielle said. "I'll have to drop you off at the hospital since I'll have Maggie. But I can pick you up in the afternoon. I also can bring your mom home if she gets discharged."

I smiled at the thought of Mamm coming back home so quickly. "See you in the morning."

While the house looked like a typical Amish house from the outside, when I opened the door it didn't sound like one. It did sound like one where the parents were gone and the teenagers were throwing a party. Not that I'd ever been to that sort of thing.

And not that my brother—at twenty-seven—was a teenager. Or would ever throw a party.

Music that I didn't recognize blared, and over it I heard someone yelling, "Supper is ready!"

That voice belonged to my cousin Ted. He must have parked his car by the barn.

I stepped into the kitchen. Ted turned toward me, giving me his impish grin. Without missing a beat, he shouted, "Party's over! Tally's home." Then he grabbed his phone from the counter and turned off the music.

Joanna stepped to the middle of the room and giggled. "Hi, Tally. I'll set the table."

Rich sat at his place, looking awkward. I felt sorry for him. Ted was hard to compete with when it came to having fun, which Rich really didn't know how to have anyway.

"What's for supper?" I asked.

Ted smiled. "Steak. I bought them and cooked them." With his impish grin and wiry frame, he had an elfish look about him. He flipped the spatula, nearly fumbling it, but he caught it at the last moment. He held it up as if in victory.

"And baked potatoes," Joanna said. "I made those."

"We made enough for you," Ted said.

"Denki," I said. "I'll go wash up."

I was fond of Ted, even though he was wild, unpredictable, and irresponsible. We were as different as could be, but he'd always been one of my favorite people. He was two years older than I was and was the class clown when we were in school together. He got his knuckles rapped more times than I could count, but after the teacher turned her back, he'd grin. I would have been mortified, but he didn't seem to mind, and it never stopped him from teasing and acting up.

Any fun I had as a child, I had with Ted. He was always a team captain and chose me first on the playground, even though I was horrible at baseball, kickball, and volleyball. In the last three years, since I'd been trapped at home, Ted had become my window to the outside world.

When I returned from the washroom, the table was set, and Ted had dished up the steaks and potatoes. Rich was pouring a jar of applesauce into a bowl, slopping it over the edge a little, and Joanna was spearing the pickles I'd canned last year from a jar into a bowl.

"How's your Mamm doing?" Ted asked.

"All right," I answered. "I was going to stay at the hospital with her, but she wanted me to come home. I'll go back in the morning."

"I can give you a ride if you need one," Ted offered.

"Don't you work?" I asked.

He shrugged. "I'm between jobs."

That didn't surprise me. "Denki." I grabbed the water pitcher. "But our neighbor Danielle said she could give me a ride."

Rich led all of us in a silent prayer, then Ted said, "Dig in!"

The steak was overdone, and the potatoes were a little hard, but I ate with gratitude. It wasn't very often I ate something I didn't cook.

Instead of commenting on the food, I asked Joanna, "How's your *Gross* Mammi?"

"She'll probably come home tomorrow." She glanced at Rich. "Then I won't be able to get out much."

Rich frowned.

"Well, you'll just have to go see Joanna," I said to him, hoping to prompt him a little.

"Oh," he said.

Joanna smiled.

After supper, she turned to me and said, "We'll clean up."

"Let's play Yahtzee first," Ted suggested.

We used to play that as kids when he visited. I thought it was sweet he wanted to play it now, but not sweet enough that I wanted to join in. I was exhausted. And my back hurt. "Count me out." I yawned. "I'm going to go on up to bed."

Ted laughed. "It's only seven."

"She's probably going to go read," Rich said.

Ted feigned a hurt look. "You'll read but you won't play a game with us?"

"You don't want me to play a game with you. I'd be bad company." I needed some time by myself. I'd been around people most of the day. "Thank you for supper. And for cleaning up."

"Of course," Joanna said. "Enjoy your book."

As I stood, I winced, and my hand went to my lower back.

"Are you all right?" Ted asked.

"I hurt my back." I turned toward Rich. "I'm going to need some help transferring Mamm when she comes home."

He frowned again. "I have a lot of work to get done in the next few weeks."

"I'll help," Ted said.

If I was Englisch, I might have hugged him. But we didn't show affection that way. "That's nice of you."

"You should ask Danielle," Rich said.

I stared at him for a long moment, until he shrugged.

"Have you changed your mind about her?" I asked.

He shrugged again. "She seems to know what she's talking about."

"Jah," I said. "She does." My mind went back to the conversation in the car and a spark of hope ignited. Maybe I could be a teacher after all, with Danielle's help. If I could regain my confidence.

I gave them all a wave and stepped into the front room. I'd finished the last of my library books and hadn't been back for more, so I picked up *Heidi* and headed upstairs with the book.

Reading it would bring back happy memories of Mamm. My relationship with her was complicated, something I could see already in Maggie's relationship with Danielle. But I'd always had Dat around to temper my relationship with Mamm. Maggie didn't have that, although she did have Kenan.

But it was clear Danielle resented Kenan's involvement in

her life. If her husband had lived, perhaps she wouldn't resent his input since Maggie was his daughter. Then again, maybe Danielle would be more stable had her husband lived. Although it seemed her tour in Iraq had been a hard time for her too, along with her husband's death.

I turned on the battery-operated lamp in the bathroom and brushed my teeth, washed my face, brushed my hair, and slipped into my nightgown. Then I padded down the hall to my room and climbed under the quilt that Mamm had made me when I turned eighteen. It was the last quilt she'd made by herself. It was an Amish star pattern made from scraps of dress and apron fabric—shades of blue and green, pink and maroon, lavender and purple, white and black.

I pulled it up to my chin and began to read. Heidi's aunt Dete, after she was offered a job as a maid in the city, took Heidi up to the mountains to her paternal grandfather's place. He lived in seclusion on the *alm*, the high mountain pasture. I could imagine his house, which was made from wood and stone, with small windows to keep the heat inside during the long winter months.

I could imagine all of it. From the very first time I heard the story, I saw an older version of my Dat as Heidi's grandfather, even though Dat wasn't grumpy. The story made me ache for my father, a man who would have made a wonderful grandfather but never had the chance.

I kept reading, trying to transport myself to the Alps of Switzerland, but the noise from below kept landing me back in my bedroom of our own home.

Ted laughed and then yelled, "Yahtzee!"

Joanna screamed, "No!" Then she laughed and yelled, "I hate this game."

I was beginning to also. Nevertheless, my eyes grew heavy.

The next morning, I rose early, thinking of Mamm, anxious to get my chores done and then call the hospital. When I stepped into the kitchen, I gasped. The dishes from the night before were piled in the sink, and empty chip bags were strewn across the counter. The broiler pan Ted had used to cook the steaks was still atop the stove, covered in grease.

I grabbed the empty bags and stuffed them in the garbage. Then I ran the water in the sink over the dirty dishes and got to work. Just as I finished scrubbing the broiler pan, Rich came into the kitchen.

"Any coffee?" he asked.

"Not yet." I knew my voice was tense.

He stood in the middle of the kitchen. "Are you going to make some?"

I began washing the counters without answering.

He filled the coffeepot with water. I doubted he knew where I kept the coffee. Instead of getting it for him, I headed for the back porch and stepped into my rubber boots, grabbed the basket, slipped into my coat, and headed to the chicken coop.

If only I could go for a run. And never stop.

After I tended the chickens and gathered the eggs, I left the basket on the back porch and headed straight for the phone shanty. I doubted Rich could make his own breakfast. He'd have to wait.

There was one message. I hit Play. It was the night shift nurse, saying Mamm had been unsettled during the night. "We'll be doing more blood work this morning," she said. "Call me back if you have any questions."

Feeling anxious, I dialed Danielle's number, wondering if the hospital had called her, but she didn't answer. Perhaps she wasn't awake yet.

I hung up the phone and headed to her house, still wearing my rubber boots. As I neared her house, my heart began to race. Her SUV wasn't parked in the driveway. Where would she be at six-thirty in the morning?

I jogged to her front door, my boots slapping against the cement walkway and then the wooden steps up to her porch. I knocked. And then knocked some more. No one answered.

Finally, I headed back to the phone shanty. I could call a driver, or I could call Ted. His cell number was written on the cover of the notebook next to the phone.

I called Ted. Of course I woke him up.

I explained what I needed.

"Say again," he muttered.

"I need a ride to the hospital. You offered to take me."

"I did?"

"Jah, you did." I paused and then said, "Get here as soon as you can. I'll make you breakfast."

After I hung up, I debated whether or not to call Kenan. I didn't want to. It felt as if I was tattling on Danielle. But then I thought of Maggie. What if she was in danger?

I dialed Kenan's number. After a few rings, it went to his voicemail. I left a brief message. "This is Tally. Danielle was going to give me a ride to the hospital this morning, but her SUV isn't in the driveway, and no one answered the door. I've arranged for another ride, but I thought you might want to know. Good-bye."

When I reached the house, Rich was sitting at the table, drinking coffee. Amazingly, he'd been able to figure it out on his own.

"Ted is going to give me a ride to the hospital. I told him I'd make him breakfast."

Rich's eyes lit up, and he smiled. I couldn't help but smile back.

"Go do your chores," I said. "I'll have breakfast ready by the time you come back."

"Hotcakes?"

"Sure," I said. "And bacon." I'd make scrambled eggs too.

An hour later, Ted and I were on our way to the hospital in his old Nissan with the dented front bumper.

He'd been quiet through breakfast and hadn't eaten much. I figured it was because he'd been up so late the night before, but then he said, "It's been twelve years."

I knew exactly what he was talking about. It was the anniversary of his sister Melinda's death. How could I have forgotten? We'd all been in school together even though we'd been in different districts at the time. Because there were so many children in the two districts, three schools were needed to accommodate all of the scholars. Melinda had been my best friend—my only friend. And she had been Ted's whole world.

"I'm sorry," I said. "I shouldn't have asked you to help me today."

"No." He gave me a quick glance. "I like spending time with you, especially today. You remind me of Melinda, in a good way. And not just that you're the age she would be if . . ." His voice trailed off. "It's not just that. You make me think of happier times. When we were all in school together. When your family would come over for second Christmas. When we used to play Yahtzee together as kids. All of those things."

Too choked up to speak, I nodded. Those had been good times. We all mourned deeply when Melinda died, but I didn't remember Ted's parents or my parents talking with us kids about it.

Melinda had a genetic disease—juvenile Tay-Sachs—that didn't make itself known until she was six. Her cognitive and motor skills deteriorated fairly quickly. She attended school with us until she was eight, about six months after she started needing a wheelchair. It soon became too difficult for her to be in class. She died when she was nine. Ted was eleven when she passed away.

"It should have been me," Ted said quietly.

"What are you talking about?"

"I should have been the one to get sick. To die," he said. "Melinda was the good one. God should have taken me."

"Don't say that."

He shook his head a little. "It's true."

"No," I answered. "It's not true at all." Honestly, I didn't think Melinda should have gotten sick and died, but we were taught to accept God's will. Tears stung my eyes. "Have you felt like this all along?"

He sighed and then said, "Mostly."

"Ted . . ." I wasn't sure what to say. "I'm so sorry."

He stared straight ahead. "I didn't mean to make you feel bad. You have so much on your plate, with Aenti Regina and all."

There was a long moment of silence. I wanted to tell him *not* to feel like God took the wrong person, but I knew me telling him that wouldn't make a difference. "What would make you happy?"

He chuckled. "Is this a setup for you to urge me to join the church? That I'll only find fulfillment when I accept God's will for my life?"

"No. Not at all. I'm just wondering what you need."

He sighed. "I don't know what I need. I'm not happy now. I know I won't be happy if I join the church." He shot me a glance. "I'm stuck."

That sounded miserable—and then I realized I was stuck too. "I kind of understand," I admitted.

"How?"

"Well, I'm not on my Rumschpringe, but I haven't joined the church. I wanted to teach, but instead I'm caring for Mamm, which I'll be doing until she dies. But I don't want her to die, so I can't really teach." I sighed.

"Wow," Ted answered. "I never thought of that. I guess I'm not the only one with problems."

"No," I said. "Your problems are different. You lost Melinda. You were young, and you've carried this guilt—false guilt—all these years." I'd learned about false guilt in a magazine article.

"You've had your Dat die—"

I jumped right in. "It's not the same. Believe me. My Dat was old. He'd lived his life. You lost your sister when she was just a girl."

He rubbed his eye. "I feel bad because I have three other sisters. . . ."

"But they're so much older than you." Ted and Melinda had twin sisters who were twenty years older than Ted, and then another sister, fifteen years older. They were all married. One lived in Ohio and the other two were in Kentucky.

"Jah," he said. "I've felt alone since Melinda died."

"You should stop by more," I said.

He smiled. "You've always been good to me."

"I'm serious," I said. "Mamm loves it when you visit. And I do too." I paused a moment and then said, "I could never take Melinda's place, but I want to be your friend. I really do. Maybe we can figure out how to get unstuck together."

It took a long moment for him to respond, long enough for me to think I'd said the wrong thing. But then he cleared his throat and said, his voice deep and raw, "Denki."

We rode in silence the rest of the way. When we arrived at the hospital, he pulled up to the entrance. "You don't want to come in?" I asked.

He shook his head. "I adore Aenti Regina, but I don't do hospitals."

I understood. Melinda had been in and out of hospitals. Ted had been dragged along more than was probably good for him.

When I reached Mamm's room, she wasn't there, and I had to fight the panic I felt. I talked myself out of my worst fear. If she'd passed away, she would most likely be in the room. But perhaps they'd called right after I left the phone shanty.

As I was arguing with myself, a transportation aide wheeled her back into the room. Relieved, I stepped to her side.

"Where's Danielle?" she asked.

"It worked better for Ted to give me a ride. He said to tell you hello."

Thankfully, she accepted what I said without pressing me. "I'm tired." Her speech seemed fine, but her left hand—which was her dominant hand— was curled a little. Not as much as it had been the day before, but it was definitely affected. "Exhausted, in fact."

"Go ahead and sleep." I'd slipped *Heidi* into my purse before I left the house. I planned to read while Mamm rested. If she slept for long, perhaps I'd take a walk. I wouldn't run, not in public, but a walk would be good.

I'd only read a page when the hospital room phone rang. I answered it, hoping it was Danielle. It wasn't. It was Kenan. "Thank you for calling me," he said. "When I left last night, Danielle seemed fine." He sighed. "Have you heard from her?"

"No," I answered. "I can check on her again when I get back to the house, but I don't know when that will be."

"Thank you," he said. "I appreciate your help. I'm really sorry your mother is in the hospital. And I'm sorry Danielle said she'd give you a ride but didn't follow through. I wish she were more dependable."

"She's been a good friend to me," I said. "I hope she's all right."

"So do I." Kenan said good-bye and then ended the call.

"You should go find Danielle and Maggie," Mamm said. "Call Ted to come get you."

"No," I said. "I need to stay here with you."

Mamm opened her eyes and shook her head. "I can't rest if you're here and we don't know where Danielle and Maggie are. If they're not back at their house, have Ted take you by the Bremen hospital and talk with her doctor friend. Don't stop until you find her."

"And then what do I do?"

"Listen to her. Get her to talk."

"You know I'm bad at that sort of thing."

"Take her to Jane's. Tell Danielle you need to buy some thread. See if Jane will tell the three of you more of the story. That seems to draw Danielle out more than anything."

"Mamm, are you sure? I should be here with you."

"Nee," Mamm said. "Go. I wish I'd had a friend like you. You can help Danielle, I'm sure of it."

I was sure I couldn't, but I could try. There were so many things in life I hadn't tried at all—but I would at least try to be a good friend to Danielle and Maggie. And Kenan too.

Mamm, even though she was ill, had given me hope that I could help. I thought of the verse I'd learned in school that I often recited when I ran. *But they that wait upon the Lord shall renew their strength; they shall mount up with wings as eagles; they shall run and not be weary; they shall walk and not faint.* I wasn't an assertive person, but Mamm was right. I needed to do what I could to help Danielle.

I called Ted. I didn't know if he wasn't far away or if he drove really fast, but twenty minutes later, Ted was out in the parking lot.

I told Mamm good-bye and hurried out of her room.

We drove by Danielle's house first, but her SUV still wasn't there. As we drove through Nappanee, I spotted her SUV parked in front of the café on Main Street. "Pull over," I said to Ted. "Wait here."

When I walked through the door of the café, Maggie jumped up. "Tally!" She had a cinnamon roll and a cup of hot chocolate in front of her.

"Hallo, Maggie," I said.

Danielle's face fell when she saw me. "I was going to give you a ride. . . ." She pursed her red lips. "I'm so sorry. How did you get here?"

I sat down at their table. "My cousin brought me. I've already been to the hospital. Mamm sent me to find you."

Danielle's eyebrows shot up.

I leaned forward. "Kenan's worried about you."

She frowned. "He's always worried."

"You need to text him. He's going to try to leave work if he doesn't hear from you."

"It would serve him right," Danielle muttered.

"Mama . . ." Maggie put a sticky hand on her mother's sweatshirt. "Uncle Kenan loves us."

Danielle turned toward her daughter and sighed. "I know." She took out her phone and keyed in a message. A minute later, her phone rang.

"I'll talk to him," Maggie said.

Danielle shook her head. "You're *sticky*."

Maggie grabbed her napkin and quickly wiped her hands. Then she took the phone. "Hello, Uncle Kenan," she said, turning her face away from her mother. She was silent for a long moment and then said, "Mama couldn't sleep. We got up early and went for a ride. Now we're at the café. I'm eating a cinnamon roll."

Again, Maggie was silent. Then she said, "Okay," and turned toward Danielle. "Uncle Kenan wants to speak with you."

"Tell him to call me in a couple of hours," Danielle said.

Maggie did as her mother asked, told her uncle good-bye, and then handed Danielle the phone again.

"What should we do next?" Maggie asked.

Danielle looked as if she might cry.

"How about if we go see Jane?" I suggested.

Maggie squealed.

"No," Danielle said. "We should get you back to the hospital."

I shook my head. "Mamm's resting. Anyway, I need to get some thread."

"Please, Mama," Maggie said.

"Oh, all right," she said.

"I just need to tell my cousin," I said. "He's out in his car, waiting for me."

Ten minutes later, we were on our way to Plain Patterns. We arrived just after ten. I wondered if Mamm had left a message on Jane's phone—and if Jane had listened to it. Or perhaps it was just Jane's intuition. But as soon as I'd picked out the thread, she said, "I'd love to tell all of you more of the story if you have time to listen."

"I should get Tally back to the hospital," Danielle said.

I shook my head. "Mamm really did want to rest. I'd love to hear more of it."

"Me too," Maggie said.

Jane looked at Danielle. "How about you?"

"As long as *you* have time," she answered.

"I do." Jane lowered her voice and leaned toward Maggie, who was concentrating on her sampler. "This next part might be hard."

"She knows about death. I haven't hidden anything from her," Danielle said.

"I'll go play with the toys if it gets too sad." Maggie continued working on her stitches.

"All right," Jane said. "You let us know." Then she said to Danielle and me, "I might need to wait on a customer now and then, but let's quilt while I tell the story. I was going to try to work on that today anyway. Having you help will make the time go faster."

We all picked up needles, and Danielle said, "Amos had written to Katie again. She'd read the letter right before she found Seth dead."

"Jah," Jane said. "Those were sad times indeed."

CHAPTER 15

Katie

Katie and Dat slowly and carefully carried Seth's body down to the kitchen table, and then Katie began washing him as silent tears streamed down her face. Dat went into the sickroom to break the news to Mamm, who kept asking, "But why did he pass?"

Finally, Dat told her that Seth had the Spanish flu. "You did too," he said. "But you recovered."

After that, Mamm was silent, and then Dat came out of the sickroom and said, "She fell asleep." He stepped to the table and touched Seth's forehead. "I'll go tell the bishop. We won't be able to have a funeral for him, just a graveside service, as soon as possible."

Katie thought about the man in the doctor's office, how he most likely had no idea he had influenza, and how he spread it to Mamm, who spread it to Seth.

If they hadn't taken her to the doctor, this never would have happened. Seth wouldn't be dead. Dat wouldn't be on his own to farm. Paulina wouldn't be without her sweetheart. *Paulina.* Who would tell her Seth had passed?

The tears began again, blurring Katie's vision as she finished washing Seth. Then she dressed him in his only suit. As she worked, she said, "The Lord giveth and the Lord taketh away. Blessed be the name of the Lord." The days of everyone's lives were numbered. She knew that. But she never guessed her strong, healthy brother would die so young.

Dat returned after about an hour. He seemed to want to talk. "Deacon Samuel was in his field, and I had to shout to get his attention," Dat said. "I asked him to come close enough to hear me but not close enough to get infected, in case I'm carrying the disease."

Katie's heart nearly stopped. Dat couldn't get sick. What would they do if he fell ill too?

"Samuel said we'll do the service tomorrow. He'll bring over a coffin this evening." Seth would be buried in the family cemetery on the edge of the property, where their ancestors were buried, going back to when the family first arrived in Elkhart County nearly eighty years ago.

As Katie and Dat spoke, Mamm came out of the sickroom. She was wearing a dress and apron, and her head was covered with a Kapp.

"Mamm," Katie said. "You should be resting."

Mamm shook her head. "I want to be with Seth." She stepped to his side and took his hand.

Dat pulled up a chair and she sat, not letting go of Seth's hand.

After Katie combed Seth's hair and put his hat on his chest, she left her Mamm and Dat at her brother's side and went upstairs to his room. She stripped his bed and then gathered up the bedding and all of his clothes and took them all down to the basement. Then she pulled his mattress from his bed, slid it down the stairs, and dragged it outside.

She looked up at the half-bare maple tree. It seemed to be a sign of her sorrow. She pulled the mattress away from the tree and the dry leaves.

Dat came out with a lit stick from the fire.

Katie wasn't sure if it was necessary or not. No one else would be in the house for weeks, and it was too late to protect Dat and herself. They had definitely been exposed. She hoped since they hadn't come down with it yet that they wouldn't. But she didn't want to take a chance. She could launder everything else.

Dat stayed and watched the fire, while Katie started to boil the water on the stove to wash the bedding and clothes.

As darkness fell, she began hanging Seth's clothing on the far line. When she finished, she moved the basket to the next line and began hanging a sheet. Footsteps caught her attention, and she moved in front of the sheet and squinted into the falling light.

"Is it true?" Paulina stood a few feet away.

"Don't come any closer," Katie said.

"Dat heard Seth passed." Paulina's voice shook. "Is it true?"

"Jah," Katie said. "I'm sorry. He passed during the night."

Paulina fell to her knees and began to cry. "He was going to be a father." She sobbed. "How can he be dead?"

"He was going to be a father." Katie dropped the clothespin in her hand. She longed to kneel beside Paulina and comfort her but not only could she infect Paulina but now her baby too.

"Do your parents know?" Katie asked.

Paulina shook her head.

"Tell them," Katie said. "You need to be cared for. I'll tell my parents too."

Paulina shook her head again. “No, don’t,” she said. “I shouldn’t have told you. I shouldn’t tell anyone.” She scrambled to her feet and ran toward the lane. Katie started after her, yelling for Paulina to stop. But she kept on going, disappearing into the falling darkness.

MAMM WAS BACK in bed when Katie reached the house, but Dat still sat by the table. The lamp was turned down to a soft glow. She stood on the other side of the table, with Seth between them. “Paulina came by,” Katie said. “She was crying.”

“I imagine so,” Dat said.

“She said—” Katie paused. Should she tell Dat? She expected so, out of concern for Paulina.

Dat raised his head. “What is it, Katie?”

She had to tell him. “Paulina said that Seth was going to be a father.”

Dat let out a long sigh. “He brought up marrying her the Sunday before Mamm became ill.”

“She seemed distraught.” Katie closed her eyes, fighting back more tears. “I’m worried about her.”

“Do you think I should go to the Fisher place?” Dat asked.

Dat would have to shout when he arrived, in the dark. Would he frighten the family? Make things worse for Paulina? Katie thought of Ben. She could ask him to go, but then she’d need to tell him why. But perhaps he would deliver a letter for her. Except what if she spread the infection to both Ben and Paulina?

She put her head in her hands. Perhaps she could come up with a message for Ben to relay to Paulina, one that wouldn’t give away the depths of what was going on.

Perhaps there was a scripture that could convey Katie’s message. She thought of the words, *We are troubled on every side, yet not distressed; we are perplexed, but not in despair; Persecuted, but not forsaken; cast down, but not destroyed.* Paulina wasn't persecuted, but she was certainly in despair.

Katie thought harder. The verses were eight and nine from 2 Corinthians 4. In verse six, it started with, *For God, who commanded the light to shine out of darkness, hath shined in our hearts, to give the light of the knowledge of the glory of God in the face of Jesus Christ.*

And the chapter ended with, *While we look not at the things which are seen, but at the things which are not seen: for the things which are seen are temporal; but the things which are not seen are eternal.*

Jah, perhaps that would communicate to Paulina to look to the future as she remembered that God loved her. She needed to look to her future and the future of her and Seth's child, both on earth and in heaven.

"I have an idea," Katie said to Dat. "I'll ask Ben to relay a message to Paulina—Second Corinthians chapter four."

Dat thought a moment and then said, "I think that's a good idea. Go to the Bergers' quickly, before it gets too late."

Katie grabbed a dishtowel to wrap around her mouth and nose, lit the lantern on the back porch, grabbed her shawl, and then hurried out the door. She walked up the road and when she reached the Berger farm, she called out, "Ben! It's me—Katie. I need to talk with you."

John stepped out on the porch, holding a lamp. "Aren't you under quarantine?"

"I am," Katie said. "I'll keep my distance." She held up a towel. "And put this over my face."

"What do you need Ben for?"

"Seth died last night."

John gasped.

"I need Ben to relay a message to Paulina Fisher for us."

John didn't respond for a long moment, but finally he turned toward the door. "Son, come on out. Katie needs to speak with you."

Ben appeared. Katie held her lantern higher. Ben started toward her. When he was about twelve feet away, she held the towel over her mouth and nose and told him to stop.

"I need you to go to Paulina's house for me and give her a message."

"Did I hear you tell Dat that Seth passed away?"

Katie nodded. "That's why I need you to go see Paulina. She knows that Seth passed, but I need you to give her a message."

"I can go in the morning."

Katie shook her head. "I need you to go now."

He crossed his arms. "What do you want me to tell her?"

"I need you to read Second Corinthians chapter four to her."

"That's an odd request," Ben said.

"I know," Katie answered. "But please do it—for Seth, if for no one else. He cared deeply for her."

Ben nodded. "I know he did." He turned toward the house and then back to Katie. "I'll go now."

"Denki." Katie turned and headed home, her feet feeling as heavy as the stone wheels of the flour mill. When she reached the lane, Ben drove by in the Berger wagon. It felt as if it took nearly an eternity for her to reach the house. When she did, she saw Mamm had moved out of the sickroom and gone up to her room. Dat had pulled the tub into the sickroom and had water boiling for Katie.

"I thought you might want a bath," he said.

"Denki."

"Mamm put a towel, a clean nightgown, and your robe out for you."

Tears spilled out of Katie's eyes again. It had been so long since anyone had cared for her. "Denki," Katie said again.

She poured the hot water into the tub and then added cold. She shut the door, peeled off her clothes, and slipped into the water. She held her breath and submerged her face, wishing she could wash away all of her sorrow.

She thought of the words, *For our light affliction, which is but for a moment, worketh for us a far more exceeding and eternal weight of glory. . . .* Seth's death felt like more than a light affliction, but in the vastness of eternity she knew it would be. Still, her heart broke. Seth was dead. But Mamm was alive. Amos was away at war. But as of his last letter, he was alive too.

Was it only yesterday she'd received his letter? It was still in her apron pocket.

After she finished her bath, as she stepped from the water, she felt as if she were leaving her childhood completely behind.

Seth and Amos were gone. Ben was cold toward her. Mamm was dying.

She grabbed the towel. She was no longer a child, but she was uncertain of what kind of woman she would become.

After drying off, she put on her nightclothes. Then she took Amos's letter to Dat's desk and found a piece of paper and a pen.

She began to write, pouring out her soul to him, all of her thoughts and fears, telling him in detail how she felt about everything that had happened in the last year and a half—about him leaving, about when he came home, about how handsome he looked in his uniform, and about how she knew he saw her that day when he was target-practicing because he smiled at her and waved.

That was the last time she saw him. But it wouldn't be the last time ever. He'd be home for good, sometime soon. At least she hoped so. Prayed so.

Then, with her heart heavy, she wrote about Mamm getting the flu, Seth dying, and Paulina being with child.

Her eyes fell to her basket of sewing with the unfinished top of her mosaic quilt. She thought of all her stitches that connected the pieces into blocks. And the stitches to come that would connect the top to the batting and back and then the binding. It was a long, sometimes imperfect, process. She'd had to rip out the stitches of a couple of blocks and start over. She'd likely have to rip out more stitches before she was done. Yet she would continue pulling the thread through the fabric. She was hopeful, even in her grief and exhaustion, that she'd finish the quilt.

It seemed, from the peace Amos had alluded to in his last letter, that the Lord was stitching threads of hope through his story even though he was a soldier.

She whispered a prayer that the Lord would stitch threads of hope through her own story too, whatever it might be.

CHAPTER 16

Tally

The front bell rang, and Jane said, "Excuse me," as she plunged her needle into the fabric.

"That was sad," Maggie said.

"Are you doing okay?" Danielle asked.

"Jah."

Danielle smiled. "Baby, you're talking like a Plain girl."

Maggie giggled, but then her voice grew serious. "I hope Regina doesn't die."

"So do we," Danielle said.

"I think she's going to get better," I said. "She's getting really good care. But someday she'll die, and when she does we'll be sad, but she'll be all right." We didn't assume who would go to heaven—that was up to God. But secretly, I liked to think of Mamm being able to walk again and even run. That was a lovely thought, my mother running. I'd never seen her run in my life.

Maggie raised her head and looked at me. "Are you sure you'll be all right?"

I nodded, swallowing as I did. I didn't speak, sure my voice would give me away and Maggie would realize I was only putting on a brave front, that I didn't feel that way at all. Kids seemed to know when we were trying to trick them.

The door dinged again, and Jane returned. As she sat down and picked up her needle, she said, "Any thoughts as far as the story?"

"I'm wondering which Berger brother was your grandfather," Danielle said. "Ben or Amos."

Jane smiled. "You'll have to stick with the story until the end."

Danielle, with her expression serious, said, "I'm worried about Amos. I keep thinking about what it was like to go to war."

Maggie plunged her big needle into the muslin fabric, stood, and put her sampler on her chair. Then she headed for the toys.

Jane raised her eyebrows at Danielle.

Danielle responded, "She doesn't like it when I talk about Iraq."

"Go ahead," Maggie said. "I'm not listening."

"What happened over there?" Jane whispered.

"Lots. I was a medic, and I was out in the field quite a bit. I met Marc there. He was a linesman—"

"A what?" I asked.

"A linesman. Actually, the Army called them power distribution specialists. He helped install and maintain electrical systems—power lines and that sort of thing—on bases and in theater."

"Oh. And that's what Kenan does here?"

"Yes, for a utility company."

I'd seen men working on the power lines before. It didn't look like a very safe occupation.

"Marc and I met on base in Iraq. We both went off the base

fairly often for our jobs and were counting the days until we went home. There were so many roadside bombings and attacks and IEDs. I was relieved when he flew off in the helicopter on his way to the Baghdad airport to start his journey home. I had one more week and then I'd go to Fort Hood because I was being transferred into another unit. Marc would be waiting for me there.

"Three days before it was my turn to board a helicopter for the first leg of my journey, we got called out into the field. A Humvee had broken down and taken fire. They had two injured soldiers we needed to stabilize and transport. When we arrived, I began running toward them just as the enemy opened fire. I took a bullet in my knee."

I winced.

"I'm pretty sure the sniper aimed at my knee on purpose, from the side. Then again, maybe he was just a bad shot. I was so relieved he hadn't killed me that I kept moving as best I could. The infantry who went with us gave us cover, and we got our wounded back on base. I limped into the hospital, blood dripping into my boot and onto the floor. When they cut my pants open, I nearly fainted from the pain and the mess." Danielle shook her head a little. "I got to head home three days early. But instead of going to Fort Hood, I ended up at Brooke Army Medical Center in San Antonio. I had a couple of surgeries, then PT. Finally, I was sent to Fort Hood, and Marc and I got married there. When I went to my appointment on base, the doctor there said I was on way too many pain meds and cut me off. That was the first time I spiraled out of control."

The front door rang again.

"Oh, I'm so sorry," Jane said. "Excuse me."

Danielle stood. "There I go *again*, saying too much. I'm sorry."

"Don't be," Jane said. "Stay put. I'll be right back."

As Jane walked into the front room, Danielle said, "We should get going. Don't you want to get back to the hospital?"

"I should call Mamm," I said. "And see how she's doing. Hopefully she'll pick up."

Danielle handed me her phone.

Mamm did answer. "Tally, is that you? Can you come get me?"

"You can come home today?"

"Jah," Mamm said. "I can leave this afternoon."

First, Danielle, Maggie, and I went through the Dairy Queen drive-through and got burgers. Then, Danielle gave me a ride back to the hospital. As she drove, she asked, "How's your back doing?"

"It's feeling better today," I answered.

While Danielle waited in the car with Maggie, I went in to collect Mamm. Of course it took longer than I thought it would. The nurse still had to remove the IV and then we had to get Mamm dressed. It took a while to print out the last of the paperwork and give me instructions for her care.

The doctor prescribed a blood thinner, which also meant Mamm would need to have her blood checked regularly. We'd need to hire a driver to take her into the clinic in Nappanee for that, which meant we probably wouldn't be going to the quilting circle as often. But Mamm's health was our priority.

A transportation aide pushed Mamm to the front door of the hospital, while I followed along behind. As soon as we exited, Danielle pulled the SUV around.

Maggie had her window down and waved at Mamm. "Hi, Regina!"

Mamm smiled.

Danielle stopped the SUV, and I opened the passenger door.

Maggie leaned forward in her booster seat and said, "I wish you could sit back here with me, Regina."

"She has more room up here," Danielle said.

Once I had Mamm buckled, I climbed in the back. As Danielle pulled the SUV onto the street, she put her arm out as Mamm swayed a little. The gesture warmed my heart.

When we reached the house, Danielle parked near the back-door ramp and then transferred Mamm into her wheelchair, which was still in the back of Danielle's SUV. Once we were in the house and Mamm was settled in the living room, she turned toward Danielle. "Can you and Maggie stay for supper?"

Danielle shook her head. "Regina, you need to rest."

"I'm going to rest now," Mamm said.

Danielle looked at me. I tried to smile, but I was at a loss as to what to fix for supper for the three of us, let alone company.

"How about if I bring the food?" Danielle said. "Maggie and I'll go fix it and give the two of you some downtime. How about if we plan to eat at six?"

I agreed, overcome with gratitude. Mamm smiled. "Perhaps I'll go take a nap after all."

After Danielle and Maggie left and I'd transferred Mamm into her bed, straining my back just a little again, I scrubbed the kitchen and tidied up the house. Then I made myself a cup of coffee and sat in the living room to rest my back and read a teaching magazine. One of the articles was about learning styles, which I found fascinating. I was definitely a visual learner, but I was pretty sure Rich wasn't. I guessed he was an auditory learner. Ted, on the other hand, was most likely a kinesthetic learner. He'd been bouncing around his entire life.

After an hour, Mamm called out to me. As I stepped into her room, she asked, "Is it six yet? Are they back?"

I shook my head. "It's five," I said. "Let's get you up and ready." I winced a little as I transferred her into her chair.

"Are you all right?" she asked.

"I strained my back is all," I answered.

At six o'clock on the dot, Danielle and Maggie showed up with roasted chicken, mashed potatoes and gravy, roasted vegetables, green salad, homemade rolls, and an apple pie and ice cream.

"Goodness," Mamm said as she watched Danielle unpack everything. "Where did you learn how to cook?"

"I grew up Old Order Mennonite, remember? I was raised to cook like this. I'm a Plain girl at heart." She flashed us a grin. "Just ignore the red lipstick." We all laughed.

I didn't believe there was anything Plain about Danielle, except her cooking—which had a Plain foundation but was also a little fancy. She'd seasoned the chicken with fresh rosemary, thyme, and salt and pepper, which was different than what I used. And the potatoes were mashed with garlic, which I think Mamm wasn't crazy about, but she didn't say anything. Rich did—he actually said the mashed potatoes were delicious and everything else was too. I couldn't remember him ever complimenting me on a meal.

I made decaf coffee to go with the pie and ice cream.

When Rich took the first bite of the apple pie, I suspected that he liked it, based on the expression on his face. But after he swallowed, he said, "This is the best pie I've ever had."

Then he started to blush, which was awfully self-aware—and rare—for him. "No offense, Tally. And Mamm. Your pies are really good too."

I laughed. "I'm not offended. Just grateful to eat all of this delicious food."

When Rich took his last bite of pie, he said seriously, "Maybe you could slip Joanna a few recipes at the quilting circle."

"I'll take copies of your recipes too," I said. Danielle was an excellent cook.

After he finished his coffee, Rich yawned. "I think I'll go to bed early."

I raised my eyebrows, surprised he wasn't going to see Joanna. "Did Beth get out of the hospital today?"

Rich answered, "Jah. Joanna is staying with her, taking care of her now."

"And you're not going over?"

He shook his head. "I'll wait a day."

After Rich led us in a final prayer, Danielle and I cleared the table while Mamm stayed at her place. When we finished, Mamm said, "I think I'd like to go to bed too."

"Before I do the dishes?"

"Jah," Mamm said. "All that good food has made me sleepy."

"I'll help you, Regina," Danielle said.

Again, I felt relief in not having to be one hundred percent responsible for Mamm. Plus, I could save my back for getting Mamm up and dressed in the morning.

"Denki," Mamm said.

"I'll come and tuck you in," I said and then turned to Maggie. "Want to help with the dishes? You can wash."

She grinned.

I washed the glasses and put them in the rack to dry. Then I put the plates in the dishwater and placed a chair for Maggie in front of the sink. As she carefully washed each plate and put them in the rinse water, I dried the glasses and then the plates and put everything in the cupboards. We worked together until all of the dishes were done. Maggie took the job seriously, and as we worked, for the first time I could see why she reminded

Mamm of me when I was little. I took all of my jobs seriously too.

By the time I was Maggie's age, I was doing most of the dishes by myself when Mamm felt "despondent." That was the term she often used. It meant she needed to rest in her room. By the time I was seven, I could cook a meal. By the time I was nine, I could do the laundry.

A few times, Mamm asked me why I never had friends from school come over. All Amish girls worked hard, but I was embarrassed that—at such a young age—I was responsible for most of the housework.

I don't think Dat noticed how much I did. Mamm would cook breakfast, and then I would do the dishes before I left for school, after Dat went outside to start work. I'd fix supper before Dat came in from doing chores. I would get the laundry on the line before I left for school on Monday mornings and then take it down and fold it after school.

There were times when Mamm was better, and we'd work together. There were also times when she mostly stayed in her room for weeks at a time except for coming out for meals. Dat was understanding and kind. Because she only had two children, it wasn't as noticeable as it would have been if she'd had seven or nine or eleven children.

"Tally!"

I turned toward Maggie.

"You weren't listening," she said.

"I'm sorry. What did you say?"

She grinned. "I should spend the night. We should have a slumber party."

I couldn't help but smile at her enthusiasm, but it wasn't a good idea.

"What do you say?" Maggie asked.

"Say to what?" Danielle asked as she came into the room.

"A slumber party," Maggie said. "Just the three of us. It's Friday night, right?" She raised her eyebrows. "We don't have school tomorrow."

Danielle turned toward Maggie. "Did you invite us over? You know that's not polite." She turned toward me. "Although, if we did spend the night, I could help with your Mamm, and that would give you more time to rest your back. What do you think?"

I wasn't sure what to think. What would the bishop think if word got out? Then again, who would say anything? "Is Mamm asleep?" I asked. "I can see what she thinks."

"She's still awake," Danielle said.

I needed to tell her good night anyway. I walked down the hall and slipped through the door to Mamm's bedside.

"Is that you, Tally?"

"Jah." I asked her about Danielle and Maggie spending the night.

"Danielle would be here in the morning, right? To get me up and dressed?"

"Jah," I said again.

"And that will give your back more time to get better."

"Denki." I reached for her hand and squeezed it.

"It's been so long since you've had a friend around."

"Jah. Since Melinda." It had been since Melinda and I were seven, before she ended up in her wheelchair, that I'd had anyone spend the night.

Mamm squeezed my hand back. "It's the anniversary of her death."

I was surprised Mamm remembered.

She asked, "How was Ted today when you saw him?"

"Sad," I answered.

She squeezed my hand again and then closed her eyes.

When I reached the kitchen and told Danielle and Maggie that Mamm had given her permission, Danielle's hand flew to her chest. "We're going to have *so* much fun!"

THERE WAS A MATTRESS that I kept under Mamm's bed that I sometimes slept on that I pulled out into the front room for Danielle and Maggie. Our couch was flat and wide—and was fine to sleep on. Better than sitting on, actually.

Danielle ran to their house to grab pajamas and toothbrushes and changes of clothes for her and Maggie.

While she was gone, I fixed popcorn on the stove while Maggie watched. "We make popcorn in the microwave," she said. "It's easier." She did a little dance in the middle of the kitchen floor. "But I like staying here. It's kind of like camping inside."

That made me smile.

Danielle came back, and we all put on our pajamas and bathrobes and then ate popcorn in the living room.

"Would you read me more of the *Heidi* story?" Maggie yawned. "Before I fall asleep?"

"Of course," I answered.

I picked up the book and began reading. By the time I finished the first chapter—Heidi had just reached her grandfather's home on the mountain and her aunt Dete was leaving—Maggie had fallen asleep.

I closed the book as Danielle asked, "Is *Heidi* one of your favorite books?"

"Jah. Mamm read it to me when I was little."

"What do you like best about it?" Danielle slipped under the covers on the mattress next to Maggie and pulled the covers up to both of their chins.

"Switzerland." I put the book on the table at the end of the couch and then slipped into my bed on the couch. "The mountains. The goats. It's so different than Indiana, and yet it feels familiar at the same time. It's always felt as if I've been there before but in a dream."

Danielle smiled. "I've been to Switzerland." She faced me with her head on her hand.

I felt a flash of jealousy.

"I was stationed in Germany when I was in the Army. I was there for two years and went on trips with friends. France. Italy. Switzerland. I went skiing up in the Alps a few times. The mountains are incredible, especially after growing up in Ohio. The ski villages have these adorable cottages, painted dark brown with green trim, with rocks on the roofs to keep the shingles from blowing off. Of course, in the winter there's so much snow you can't see the roofs. It's enchanting, really. And then in the summer, flower boxes under the windows of the cottages are crammed with red geraniums and blue lobelia. You'd love it."

Danielle had been to Switzerland, not to mention France and Italy. And Iraq. I'd never been farther from home than Elkhart.

"Why did you end up on a farm outside of Nappanee when you've traveled the world?"

"Because Kenan was here. Marc didn't have any family he was close to. Kenan is the only family I have, basically. Kenan had done an apprenticeship out here and then got a job. Marc had the training he needed in the Army to get a job with the same company. So, we came here."

"They both ended up being linesmen, coincidentally?"

"No. I'd told Kenan about what Marc was doing in Iraq. He thought it sounded like an interesting career."

I opened my mouth to ask why Kenan didn't join their church but closed it, fearing it was too nosy.

"This is when you ask me why Kenan didn't join the Mennonite church."

I laughed. "That's exactly what I was wondering."

"Our parents expected him not to have a relationship with me, and he refused to do it."

"Wow."

"Right? I've never had anyone love me as much as Kenan, except Marc. But that was a different kind of love. The thing with Kenan is, I don't actually do anything to make his life better. In fact, I only make it harder—but he keeps loving me anyway." She frowned a little. "What's really sad is that he blames himself for Marc's death, which means he blames himself for my second downward spiral."

Was I supposed to ask how Marc died and why Kenan blamed himself? And what exactly Danielle meant by downward spirals?

She yawned. "All of that's a story—stories—for another day." She smiled, just a little. "Or probably stories I shouldn't tell you at all." A sad expression settled over her face.

Unlike Jane, I had no idea what the right thing to say to her was.

"I imagine you have to get up early," Danielle said. "We should get to sleep."

I wondered what Rich would think in the morning about Danielle and Maggie spending the night. "I'll go check on Mamm," I said.

"Guter Nacht," Danielle said.

"Guter Nacht," I echoed.

Mamm was sleeping soundly, but I stood in the doorway and watched her for quite a while. When I returned, Danielle appeared to be asleep too.

I couldn't imagine anyone more different from me than Danielle. She'd traveled and lived and loved and lost. She wore red lipstick and was loud and brash, at least by my standards. And yet there was something endearing about her, something so human. Something I hadn't seen in anyone in my family and certainly not in myself.

That day I found her in the woods, I never dreamed she could help me. And yet, she had. She *was*. In the future, if she needed help, could I be as generous and gracious to Danielle as she had been to me?

I hoped so, but I wasn't certain. I wasn't sure I had it in me.

CHAPTER 17

During the night, a cry woke me. We had a battery-operated nightlight in the front room for when I needed to check on Mamm in the middle of the night. I turned toward the mattress, guessing the cry came from Maggie, but she was sound asleep.

However, Danielle stared at the ceiling with her eyes wide open and breathed rapidly.

I whispered, "Are you all right?"

She jerked and then turned toward me, her face a blank stare.

"Danielle?"

She blinked. "I'm fine." She turned over, toward Maggie.

When I awoke at five-thirty, Danielle wasn't in bed. Maggie was on top of the covers, on her back, with her arms spread wide, snoring gently. Her dark hair was in a tangle around her face. I rose, pulled the blanket back over her, and then slipped into my robe and followed the scent of coffee brewing into the kitchen. Danielle leaned against the kitchen counter, wearing jeans and a sweatshirt, a wild look in her eyes.

"Are you all right?" I asked, echoing what I'd asked in the middle of the night.

She nodded. "I'm fine. Want some coffee?"

"Jah," I answered. "I'd like some." I hadn't gotten up to the smell of coffee since I was a child. It had been my job to make it since I started drinking it at age twelve. That was the deal Mamm made with me—I could drink it if I made it. I don't think Dat ever had any idea about the deals Mamm made with me.

The other part of the deal was that I had to drink the coffee black. But now that I drank it alone in the morning, I added cream. I got it out of the fridge and added some to two mugs. Then I poured the coffee from the pot on the stove into the mugs and handed one to Danielle.

"Denki," she said. "There's nothing like a hot cup of coffee on a cold morning."

"It is cold, isn't it?"

"It's cold outside but not frosty. I definitely need to get my corn harvested. The drainage in that field isn't good, which makes the corn late to ripen. But I need to get it done before the frost."

That could happen anytime. Rich had harvested our corn two weeks ago.

"What shall I cook for breakfast?" I asked. "What does Maggie like?"

"Oh, the usual. Hotcakes. Bacon. Eggs."

"She's in luck. I can do all three. But first I need to go gather eggs."

"I'll do it," Danielle said.

"You can wear my coat and boots." I pointed to the back porch. "The rooster is always trying to escape. You have to watch him once you let the chickens out into the yard."

She smiled. "Oh, I know how to deal with roosters."

While Danielle was outside, I headed upstairs and got dressed. I didn't want to start the bacon or hotcakes until

Danielle came back in with the eggs, so I went and checked on Maggie again. She was still sound asleep.

When I walked back into the front room after mixing up the hotcake batter and setting the table, Danielle was cuddling with Maggie on the mattress.

"*Guter Mariye*," I said.

She smiled. "That's what Mama says to me every morning."

Danielle laughed. "You know how you said Switzerland felt both familiar and foreign to you at the same time, as if you'd been there before, sometime in a dream?"

I smiled.

"That's how I feel about you." Danielle smiled. "You could be my sister or cousin. From another life. From a dream."

I wasn't sure whether she was serious or not.

"It's a good dream," she said. "A comforting one. Much better than my reality. I never belonged before, but you make me feel as if I belong now." She smiled. "Even though I know I don't."

I wasn't sure what to say and feebly came up with, "You belong here. In our home."

"Denki," Danielle said. "I actually do feel as if I belong here. But will Rich agree when he wakes up, when he finds out we spent the night? And what would your bishop say? Or your Amish neighbors?"

"I'm not sure," I said.

"I can imagine what our bishop would have said." Danielle rolled her eyes. "Sometime I'll have to tell you what all he said to me. I was a wild child from the beginning."

"What about Kenan? Was he a wild child?"

Danielle laughed. "Never. He was definitely the straight man to my comic."

"Comic?"

"Well, I wasn't exactly a comic. More like a trickster."

Maggie scrambled off the mattress, saying, "I heard a car door." She jumped on the couch to look out the window. "Uncle Kenan!" She giggled. "He must be here for breakfast!"

KENAN APPEARED TERRIFIED as he rushed toward the house. Danielle had parked her car over by the barn, and Kenan couldn't see it from the road.

I hurried to the front door and flung it open. "They're here," I yelled to Kenan.

"In your house?"

I nodded and swung the door wide. "Come on in. We're about ready to start breakfast."

He took off his Cincinnati Reds baseball cap, revealing his messy hair. "They came over for breakfast?"

"No, they spent the night."

"What?"

I gestured for him to enter the house. "They're in the front room. Come in."

Once he'd stepped across the threshold, I followed him and shut the door, just as Rich came down the staircase, much later than usual.

"What's happening?" Rich asked.

"Breakfast," I said. "Kenan is going to eat with us." I pointed toward the front room. "And Danielle and Maggie."

Rich followed Kenan into the front room and asked, "Is there coffee?"

"Jah," I answered. "Danielle made it."

"Hi, Rich." Danielle grinned.

Rich ignored her.

She picked up a blanket to fold. "Hi, Kenan."

He shook his head. "You scared me. Why didn't you let me know what your plans were?"

She gave him a sassy grin, flashing her dimples. "Why do you worry so much?"

Forty-five minutes later, Danielle had Mamm up and dressed while Maggie and I dished up platters of hotcakes, bacon, and eggs.

Kenan had gone out with Rich to do the chores. They came in and washed up at the sink on the back porch. Maggie and I put the platters of food on the table as everyone sat down.

Mamm grinned. "It's so nice to have double the amount of people around our table. I always longed for a big family," she said. "This morning, I have five children instead of two."

I wasn't sure how to respond, and I knew Rich didn't know either, but at the same time Danielle and Kenan said, "Thank you for having us." Then they both laughed.

Mamm smiled. "Your mother taught you well."

"Oh, she was a stickler for good manners." Danielle sat next to Mamm and began cutting her hotcakes for her.

Kenan agreed as he started cutting Maggie's.

"So, are there only the two of you?" Rich asked. "Like Tally and me?"

Danielle shook her head and glanced at Kenan.

"There are actually eight of us," Kenan said. "We have six younger siblings."

That shocked me.

"Jah," Danielle said. "There was a lot of pressure on us to set good examples. Kenan did well. . . ."

He shook his head. "No. I left. That was a horrible example." He reached for the syrup and poured a little on Maggie's hotcakes.

"Well, you didn't join the Army or marry an Englischer.

And they still hope you'll come back." Danielle finished cutting Mamm's hotcakes.

Kenan spoke softly as he poured syrup on his own hotcakes. "They hope you'll come back too."

Danielle shook her head a little. "Let's talk about something else."

Kenan cut off a piece of hotcake and ate it. Then he looked at Maggie, his eyes wide. "The hotcakes are delicious. I heard you made these."

She giggled.

I couldn't get past the shock that Danielle and Kenan had younger siblings. It wasn't that I was surprised they had siblings. Most Plain families were large. I didn't know anyone else who had only one sibling, the way Rich and I did.

I'd imagined Danielle and Kenan having married, older siblings who were busy with their own lives. But for Danielle and Kenan to have six younger brothers and sisters meant they'd left so much more than just their parents. Danielle would have helped with those children when they were babies, feeding and diapering them, rocking them to sleep, dressing them, playing with them. I guessed, considering how good he was with Maggie, that Kenan helped too.

Maggie had aunts and uncles. Six more children meant the youngest might be just a few years older than she was.

Rich picked up his coffee mug. "I was thinking about your corn, Danielle. We can harvest it a week from today. Ted will help, and I think I can round up a few other people. We can use my binder." It was quite the speech for Rich.

Kenan said, "I'll help too."

"That's great." Danielle's eyes lit up. "I'll make the food."

"Tally will help with that." Mamm speared a piece of hotcake with her right hand.

"Of course." I was grateful Rich had come up with a plan. Danielle hadn't said anything more about losing her farm, so hopefully that wasn't a possibility.

After breakfast, Kenan said to Rich, "I don't have any plans today. What farm work do you need done?"

"I'm dragging the field with the tractor," he answered.

"Did you know the Amish in Pennsylvania don't use any kind of tractor?" Danielle asked. "Just horses and mules."

"I've heard that," Rich said. "Because if you get comfortable behind the wheel of a tractor, the thinking goes, it's a short hop to sitting behind the wheel of a car."

Danielle and Kenan both laughed.

"Exactly," Kenan said. "So why don't you have a car?"

Rich smiled. "Because I have metal wheels on the tractor. I'm not going to get far on pavement, not enough to make me want to get a car."

"How about during your Rumschpringe? Did you have a car then?"

Rich shook his head. "I've always known I wanted to join the church. I've never been tempted by that." He shrugged. "Besides, our cousin Ted hasn't joined the church. He has a car. I have a ride when I need one." Rich was as talkative as I'd ever seen him. Rich asked Kenan if he was a linesman and then laughed a little. "Did I remember the term right?"

"Jah," Kenan said.

"So, do you know about electrical problems, say in a tractor?"

Kenan picked up his mug. "Like if you need a new fuse?"

Rich shook his head. "I've replaced all of those."

"I can't make any promises, but I'll take a look."

After Rich led us in a closing prayer, he and Kenan headed out to the shed, and Danielle and I cleaned up. Afterward,

Danielle pushed Mamm into the front room, with Maggie following, to work on the puzzle. Mamm wasn't close to finishing it, and I knew she appreciated Maggie's help.

I liked the feeling of having a houseful of people. I couldn't remember a time in my life when I felt as if I belonged as much as I had at breakfast, as much as I did cleaning up the kitchen with Danielle. It felt comforting to belong in real life and not just in a classroom or a book.

AN HOUR LATER, Danielle and I went out to the garden. She did the digging, because of my back, and did the pulling while Maggie and Mamm kept working on the puzzle. We could see them through the window on the side of the house. Every few minutes, Maggie would wave, followed by Mamm.

It seemed Mamm was getting a taste of being a grandmother. Another gift from Danielle.

"Do you often have problems sleeping?" I asked Danielle as we worked.

She stood up straight, the shovel in her hands, and cocked her head. "You're asking me a personal question."

My face grew warm even though it was chilly. "I'm sorry."

Danielle shook her head. "No, it's fine. You just don't do that much." She bent down again and thrust the shovel into the soil. "In fact, I'm touched that you asked." She loosened the soil and then bent down and grabbed a bunch of potatoes. "Yes, I have trouble sleeping. Every single night."

"Does anything help?"

She stood up again. "The thing I hated about the Army the most was the guns." She met my gaze. "Stupid, right? I joined the Army. Of course there would be guns. I had to shoot and qualify it seemed like all the time. In theater, I had to carry a gun even though I never used it. I always wondered if I could have if we came under fire, and when I got shot in the knee, I would have had to if we didn't have combat soldiers nearby."

She tossed the potatoes onto the lawn. "At night I wake up in a panic—not because I think I'm going to get shot, but because I think I'm going to have to shoot someone. Every night, around three-thirty or four, I wake up. That's why I feel as if I understand what Amos was going through."

That made sense.

"Honestly, the pain meds didn't just make my knee feel better. They made my mind feel better too. They kept it from racing and put it to sleep." She shrugged, and her tone turned sad. "I just couldn't figure out how to only take them at night."

I exhaled slowly. I couldn't remember anyone sharing so much of themselves with me. It was a lot like reading.

"What all makes your mind race?" As soon as I asked it, I felt embarrassed. She'd nearly been killed. "I'm sorry," I said. "It's obvious it was being attacked in Iraq."

"No, it's fine," Danielle said. "You're partially right. Part of it is from being shot, but it's more than that. Other things happened in the Army." She hesitated a moment and then asked, "May I ask *you* a personal question?"

What would she want to ask me? "Sure."

"How did you end up with the name Tally?"

I laughed, relieved at how easy the question was. "Rich. He'd heard a little girl in a grocery store called Tally and he liked the name. Mamm thought it was an Englisch name until she checked out a baby name book from the library. It's Hebrew, and it means 'heaven's dew.' Mamm and Dat both liked that, but I have Rich to thank for my name."

"I like it too," she said.

"So do I." And I did. I was such a Plain girl, but at least I had an uncommon name. However, in the last few years, I'd seen the name a few times in the *Budget*, so maybe it was becoming more common.

The sound of horses' hooves turned my attention toward the road as Jane turned into our driveway.

"Look who's here!" Danielle dropped the shovel on the lawn next to the potatoes and waved.

Jane waved back, a big smile on her face. "Hallo!"

Maggie opened the front door and stepped out onto the screened porch.

Jane stopped the buggy by the hitching post, and Danielle ran toward it to tie the reins and help Jane down. "I need to get something from the back," Jane said.

She opened up the rear of the buggy and grabbed a pan. Then she turned toward me and asked, "Tally, can you take a break? I've brought sticky rolls."

I grinned. "Of course."

Once we were all in the house, I made another pot of coffee, and Danielle grabbed a stack of plates and a handful of forks. I pushed Mamm's wheelchair up to the table and then we all sat down.

"Miriam and Owen are watching the shop this morning," Jane said. "I had a couple of errands to run and thought I'd stop by and see how all of you are doing. But it looks as if things are going well."

"We spent the night," Maggie said.

"Here?" Jane asked.

Maggie grinned.

"That sounds like fun." Jane's eyes danced as she connected with Maggie. Jane was one of the people I admired most. In fact, if there was anyone I hoped to emulate in life, besides the Lord, it was Jane.

Maggie asked, "Are you here to tell us more of the story?"

"Do you want me to?"

Maggie grinned again.

Jane glanced around the table. "How about everyone else?"

Mamm nodded.

Danielle said, "Jah. Tally and I were just talking about Amos earlier. I want to know what happened to him."

"All right." Jane took her little notebook from her pocket. "If I remember right, Katie was pouring out her heart to Amos in a letter after Seth died."

CHAPTER 18

Katie

After Katie finished her letter to Amos, all five pages of it, she folded her arms on Dat's desk and put her head down. Too exhausted to cry any more, she fell asleep. Early in the morning, Dat led her up to her room. When she awoke, she could hear rain on the roof and against the window.

She dressed and shuffled down the stairs, still feeling exhausted. Mamm and Dat both sat in the front room. Mamm stared out the window, and Dat sat at his desk, reading his Bible.

Katie cleared her throat, afraid her voice might not work. She croaked, "Hallo."

Mamm turned her face toward Katie, and Dat stood. "Katie." He took a step toward her. "How are you? Are you feeling well?"

"Jah," she answered. "Just tired."

Dat exhaled. "I checked on you a couple of times. You were sleeping soundly."

"Were you afraid I'd fallen ill?"

Dat shrugged.

"I'm fine." Katie's hand flew to her chest. "What day is it? Did I miss the burial?"

Dat shook his head. "It's still Monday, October thirteenth. It's been pouring all day. We're going to do it in an hour. We're hoping the rain will stop or at least slow."

"How are you feeling?" Katie asked Mamm.

"All right." Her gaze drifted toward the kitchen. "It's almost time for my tonic."

When Deacon Samuel came an hour later, it was still raining but not as badly. Mamm had taken her tonic and was back in the sickroom.

"We'll leave her here," Dat said to Katie. He'd already nailed Seth's coffin shut.

The deacon and three other men came into the house, with cloths tied over their faces. Katie grabbed cloths for herself and Dat. If they were contagious, she didn't want to expose the deacon and other men. All of the men wore coats, which dripped from the rain. Even with their wide-brimmed hats, their beards were wet. They carried the coffin out to the wagon, struggling under the weight.

Slowly, the horse pulled the wagon and the men. Dat held an umbrella over Katie and himself and they walked to the corner of the far field, along the road, where the family plot was. Her paternal grandparents were buried there, Steffen and Hanna, along with her paternal great-grandparents, Judah and Emma, whom she'd never met. She barely remembered her grandparents.

Someone, probably the men with Deacon Samuel, had dug the hole. Katie felt gratitude for their care and also for their hard work in the cold rain.

As they reached the cemetery, John and Ben arrived in their wagon. They climbed down from their wagon and stood on the other side of the coffin, their hats pulled down on their heads to block as much of the rain as possible. John nodded at Dat, who nodded back. Ben's eyebrows lifted and then he gave Katie a little wave. It was kind of them to come.

Katie expected Paulina to join them, but no one else arrived.

Deacon Samuel led the group in a prayer and then read from the book of Romans. "'For I am persuaded, that neither death, nor life, nor angels, nor principalities, nor powers, nor things present, nor things to come, nor height, nor depth, nor any other creature, shall be able to separate us from the love of God, which is in Christ Jesus our Lord.'"

The rain dripped off the umbrella and pooled in front of Katie's boots. Samuel kept talking, but Katie no longer listened. Her thoughts kept going to Amos. Where was he? Was he well? Was he in the middle of a battle?

And then she thought of Paulina. Katie wondered what Deacon Samuel would think once he knew Paulina was expecting a child. She would marry another man, who would raise her baby. Perhaps she wouldn't want Katie, Mamm, and Dat to have anything to do with the little one. She felt crushed by the weight. They had lost Seth. Would they lose his baby too?

Finally, Samuel ended the service with a prayer, and Katie bowed her head. At first she couldn't concentrate, but then she prayed for Paulina and the little one she carried. For comfort for Mamm and Dat. For protection for Amos.

And then she prayed for strength for herself. She couldn't be crushed. There was too much for her to do.

As Samuel ended the prayer, someone approached in a buggy. Katie couldn't tell who it was until he climbed down. Phillip Fisher, Paulina's father. He walked quickly toward the group. He called out something, but Katie couldn't make out what it was.

Samuel took a step toward him. He shouted again. "Paulina's ill. So is Barbara and two of the younger children. I need help caring for them. I can't do it on my own."

KATIE HAD BEEN SURE no one else would fall ill. It had been nearly two weeks since Seth had seen Paulina.

Puzzled, she packed a bag and went to the Fisher home to care for the family. When Ben fell ill the next day, Dat brought him to the Fisher home in the wagon, so Katie could care for him too and so that he wouldn't expose John—if he hadn't already.

Once at the Fisher home, Ben confessed to Katie that he'd sat on the porch with Paulina that evening he'd given her the message. Katie felt frustrated. Why hadn't he followed her instructions? And Paulina confessed that she'd snuck over to the Landis home late at night and Seth had come out on the porch to sit with her five days ago.

Katie shook her head in disbelief.

Phillip Fisher and the children who didn't have symptoms tried to stay away from those who were infected, isolating on the first floor while the sick stayed on the second floor, but Katie feared more of them would fall ill. Women in the church dropped off meals for the family so at least Katie didn't have to cook too, but just caring for the ill kept her running all day long and most of the night too, up and down the stairs between the pump, the kitchen, the outhouse, and the bedrooms.

Dr. Barker came and gave Katie instructions. Put fresh linens on the beds as often as possible, and fresh nightclothes on the ill. Wear a covering over your face. Wash your hands. Keep the patients as clean as possible. Encourage the patients to drink fluids and to eat.

He gave her grains of aspirin to reduce fever and grains of opium for sleeplessness, saying, "The more rest the patients can get, the more likely they will be to recover."

Tragically, Paulina's seven-year-old brother passed away the third day. Phillip built a coffin in the barn and then carried it into the house, with a cloth tied to his face, and together he and Katie lifted the little one's washed body inside. Again, Deacon Samuel came, and only a few gathered together to bury the body.

It was obvious to Katie that Paulina, in her nightdress, was with child, and she guessed it was clear to Paulina's mother too, but no one said anything.

Slowly, the others improved, including Ben. By the time all had recovered and the quarantine was over, Katie felt a hundred years old. When it came time for Phillip to drive Katie home, he said to Paulina, "I think it best for you to go with Katie. The Landis family should care for you during this time, lest our little ones start asking questions."

Paulina's face grew red as she turned toward Katie.

"Come with me." Katie couldn't abandon Paulina and her baby. Seth's child.

When they arrived at the house, Mamm gave Katie and Paulina a puzzled look, while Dat simply said, "I'll explain later."

Ben had gone home a couple of days before Katie, and he came over that evening to say hello and thank her for her care. Katie and Paulina were sitting on the porch, both wrapped in quilts against the autumn chill. The doctor said the fresh air would be good for Paulina.

When Ben saw Paulina on the porch, he asked, "Are you staying long?"

"Jah," she answered. "At least for a few months."

Ben's face grew red. Did he know of Paulina's condition? If so, had she told him? Or had he guessed?

Ben stayed until it was time for Katie to start supper. She invited him to join them, but he said, "Nee. I should get home to Dat. He's been unsettled with me being ill." He paused a moment and then said, "And he hasn't had a letter from Amos for a few weeks."

Neither had Katie, but she didn't say anything.

"I'll come back over tomorrow." Ben waved and then headed down the porch steps.

Katie gave Paulina her arm and helped her stand—she was still weak—and they walked in the house together.

Mamm was still spending most of her time in the sickroom, claiming she was too weak to climb the stairs multiple times a day. She called to Katie. "I need to speak with you for a moment."

Once Paulina sat at the kitchen table, Katie stepped to the sickroom door.

Mamm wore a dress and sat up, her back against the headboard. She was covered with a quilt. "I'm nearly out of my tonic."

"Didn't Dat go to the doctor and buy more right after his quarantine ended?"

Mamm frowned. "That was a while ago."

"How much have you been taking?"

"What Dr. Barker prescribed."

Katie hesitated a moment and then said, "I'll go to town tomorrow and speak with him." As she stepped back into the kitchen to stoke the fire, she thought of the opium grains the doctor had given her for the Fisher family and Ben, the ones to help them sleep. The medication worked wonders, and it made her question what was in Mamm's tonic.

That evening, after Katie helped Paulina upstairs to bed, she went back down to stoke the fire in the kitchen stove to help keep Mamm warm through the night. Dat sat in the sickroom with Mamm, speaking softly.

"Katie," Mamm said, "come here."

She stepped to the door and pushed it open a little.

"When is Paulina going home?" Mamm asked.

"I'm not sure," Katie answered. "Phillip doesn't want her at home. He said she was a bad influence on the younger children."

"But why did he send her here?" Mamm asked.

Katie shifted her focus to Dat. "Did you tell her?"

"Not yet."

Mamm turned to him. "What are you keeping from me?"

Dat blushed. For the first time Katie had ever witnessed, her father seemed uncomfortable.

Katie was too, but she could at least speak. "Paulina is carrying Seth's baby."

Mamm sighed.

Dat cleared his throat. "We have an obligation. Seth isn't here to care for her. We must do it."

Tears welled in Mamm's eyes and then started rolling down her face. "I need my tonic, Katie."

Dat left the room while Katie reached for Mamm's bottle. Paulina would be called before the church, once she had her strength back, and then shunned. After she confessed and a period of time had passed, she'd be reinstated. But that didn't mean her parents would welcome her back home. Katie hoped Paulina—and the baby—would stay with the Landis family forever.

But that wouldn't be what was right for Paulina. Or the baby.

Regardless of Mamm's angst, Katie would willingly care for Paulina and the baby as best she could. Just the thought of having a baby—Seth's baby—in the house warmed her like nothing had since before Amos left.

THE NEXT DAY, in the midafternoon, Katie headed into town in the buggy with enough money from the household budget to buy more bottles of the tonic.

When she arrived at the doctor's office, she pulled her cloth over her mouth and face, even though no one else in town wore a covering. There were several people in the doctor's office. One was coughing.

"I just have a quick question for the doctor," Katie told Nurse Walden. "It won't take long."

"Sit down and take your turn," the woman said.

Katie did as she was told, sitting in the chair farthest from the others and keeping her covering over her mouth and nose.

"Are you ill?" the older woman across from her asked.

Katie shook her head.

"I heard the Dutchie around here have the Spanish Flu. Are you sure you're not ill?"

Katie answered, "I'm fine. I just don't want to catch it." She believed she was immune but didn't want to take a chance.

The old woman frowned. "No one in Nappanee has it."

Katie leaned back in her chair. "I'm happy to hear that."

Two patients went in to see the doctor, including the older woman, and then Nurse Walden called Katie's name.

She waited in one of the two rooms for quite a while until the doctor stepped into the room.

"I came to buy more of the tonic for Mamm," Katie said. "But I need to know what's in it."

"Lithium salts and morphine," Dr. Barker said.

"Is morphine like opium? Does it make Mamm sleepy?"

"It relaxes her," Dr. Barker said.

That was good to know, but Katie still had concerns. "She's been taking more since Seth died. She sleeps or stares at the wall most of the time."

"She's grieving."

"Jah, she is. But I'm afraid the tonic is making things worse. She seems numb. Are you sure it's helping her heart?"

"Morphine has been recommended for heart disease." He took a step away from Katie. "I read a journal study about it a few months ago, although there are some who question the findings."

"Could we lessen the amount of morphine in the tonic?"

Dr. Barker hesitated a moment and then said, "Perhaps you could dilute the tonic a little, but you would need to do it gradually. And don't tell her what you're doing. That could make her anxious."

"All right." Katie bought two bottles of tonic from Nurse Walden, who wrapped them in brown paper.

Katie thanked the nurse and then stepped out of the doctor's office and right into a commotion. Church bells were ringing. Someone yelled, "The war is over!"

Someone else shouted, "The ceasefire has been signed!"

"We did it!" another man shouted, one who was just a few feet from Katie. "Our boys made the difference!"

A teenager stood on the corner, waving a newspaper. "Special edition!"

Katie hurried toward him. The top headline on the paper was *Wilson Announces Armistice.* Another headline read *Germany Surrenders.* And a third read *Peace at Last!* Katie bought a copy with the change she had—Dat's copy of the newspaper wouldn't arrive until tomorrow afternoon—and then, with the paper tucked under her arm and the package of tonic in her other hand, she hurried back to the buggy.

The wind turned cold as the horse pulled the buggy down the road. How long would it take for Amos to come home? She imagined it wouldn't be right away. First, they'd have to make their way off the battlefield and then back to a port, where they could board a ship and start the journey home. Perhaps he'd have to return to Fort Drum or to another fort—maybe even back to Georgia—before he could be discharged. Hopefully he would write to her soon and let her know when he would arrive home.

By the time she reached the house, snow had started swirling around the horse. She wrapped the reins around the hitching post and then hurried in the back door of the house. "It's over!" she called out. "Germany surrendered!"

Paulina sat at the kitchen table, peeling potatoes. Dat stepped from the front room into the kitchen, and Mamm followed him.

"We should go tell John and Ben," Katie said. "The buggy is outside." She pulled the newspaper from under her cape and handed it to Dat. "Read it quickly and then we can give it to John."

"May I go?" Paulina asked.

"Jah . . ." Dat took the paper and sat down at the table, spreading it in front of himself.

"I'll stay here." Mamm met Katie's eyes. "Did you forget my tonic?"

Katie shook her head. "I left the package in the buggy. I'll go get it." She stepped back outside into the falling snow.

When Katie returned with the bottles, Dat stood and folded the paper. "I'll wait to read the rest when my paper comes tomorrow."

"Good. The snow is coming down. We should hurry." Katie placed the package on the table.

Paulina finished washing her hands in the basin, then put on her coat and slipped her feet into her boots. A few minutes later, the three of them were on their way.

By the time they reached the Berger place, a layer of snow

coated the ground. Ben started from the barn toward them, and John stepped out onto the porch. "What brings you over?"

Dat held up the newspaper. "Good news! The war is over."

John's usually stoic expression gave way to relief and then sheer pain and then back to relief. Then he said quietly, "I hope my boy will come home." He lifted his gaze to Dat's. "I'm sorry. You'll never be able to hope such a thing again."

Dat climbed the steps and put his hand on John's shoulder. "I want nothing more than for Amos to return. That would make me—all of us—very happy."

Ben reached the porch and said, "Come in. I was just going to make a pot of coffee."

Katie glanced at Dat, who said, "We could take time for one cup. Then we should get back to your Mamm."

Katie agreed. As they started into the house, Paulina fell back. Ben said something to her, although Katie couldn't discern what it was. But Paulina laughed a little, which was the happiest sound Katie had heard in a very long time.

CHAPTER 19

After Mamm had taken a couple of doses of her tonic, Katie started adding water to it. Mamm didn't seem to notice.

One evening, a week after the war ended, as Katie and Paulina cleaned the dishes and Mamm and Dat sat at the table, Mamm said, "You've been a fool, Katie. You've missed your chance with Ben. If Amos comes home at all, he won't stay. He'll move on somewhere else. You'll never marry. You'll never give us a grandchild. This farm will be sold someday, lost to your Dat's family forever."

"Hush," Dat said. "Our family is in God's hands."

Katie's face grew warm, and she resisted looking at Paulina. Why was Mamm talking that way at all, but especially in front of Paulina? She was carrying their grandchild.

That night, as Paulina and Katie crawled into the two beds in the room they now shared, Paulina asked, "Are you interested in Ben?"

"Nee," Katie answered as she blew out the lamp.

"Were you?"

Katie hesitated a moment, staring at the pitch-black ceiling. "Nee."

"It doesn't sound as if you're sure."

"I am. At one time, I believed perhaps I could be interested in him. We went on some walks. I made him some pies. But I wasn't truly interested in Ben—I was angry with Amos."

"But you're not angry with Amos anymore."

Katie sighed. "I'm not."

"And you're not holding on to Ben just in case Amos doesn't come home?"

That was what Mamm had wanted her to do. "Nee," Katie said again. "I'm not holding on to Ben at all."

"Do you *leeva* Amos?"

Did she love Amos? She thought of their trip to Elkhart on the train. Seth and Paulina. Amos and her. Ben, tagging along. None of them had any idea of what was to come.

Did she love Amos? "Jah," Katie answered. "I'll always leeva Amos. I tried to stop, but I couldn't." She'd loved Amos since she was a girl. There was no denying it.

"What if he stays Englisch?" Paulina asked. "Will you leave with him?"

Why was Paulina asking so many questions?

"Katie?"

"No," Katie finally answered. How could she leave her mother and father? She turned toward her friend. "I'm glad you're here. I hope you'll stay."

"I have nowhere else to go," Paulina answered.

"Someday you'll marry. Have more children."

"Don't speak of such things. I have no idea what the future will hold."

"I would prefer you stay here, always, with your baby, but that's selfish of me. I'm praying for a husband for you. In the Lord's time."

"Denki." Paulina began to cry. "It's just . . . it's just . . . all of this. Seth dying. The fact I didn't listen to you and infected my family . . . losing my little brother. Being alone and pregnant." She sobbed. "I don't know what I would do without you, Katie."

"Ach, Paulina," Katie answered. "I don't know what I would do without you either." She was serious. Having Paulina live with them made life bearable after the loss of Seth.

MORE SNOW FELL in between stretches of sunny but cold days. Then the snow melted and rain fell. Dat worked in the fields, doing his best to keep up with all of the tasks. With Paulina in the house to watch Mamm, Katie was free to help Dat. Together, they stacked the haybales. Another day, she helped him repair the fence. Another day, they hauled manure and spread it across the field.

Paulina was shunned and then reinstated in the church a month later. Each day, Katie thought of Amos. Would she know if he were dead? Would she be able to feel it in her heart? She hadn't had a letter from him since the one postmarked the twenty-sixth of September.

At Christmas, the Landis farm had half a foot of snow. John and Ben walked over for a dinner of roasted chicken, mashed potatoes, canned green beans, pickled beets, rolls, and pie made from canned tart cherries. After they finished eating but before Katie served pie, Dat said he needed to go break the ice in the watering trough for the cows.

"I'll do it, Dat," Katie said.

Ben stood. "I'll help you."

Katie felt awkward having Ben go outside with her. Would Mamm get her hopes up again? Would Paulina think Katie had lied to her?

Dat kept a rod by the trough, and Katie, with her gloved hands, grabbed it and dropped it straight down through the ice, which split and broke apart. Then she pulled the broken ice from the trough while Ben watched.

As she placed the rod back against the fence, Ben asked, "How is Paulina doing?"

Katie turned her head and tightened her scarf. "Fine. Don't you think that from observing her?"

It was too cold to tell if his face was red from embarrassment or from the elements.

"Is she feeling all right?"

"Jah," Katie answered. "She hasn't seemed to have any problems, no lasting ones from the influenza."

"That's good," Ben said. "I was worried for her when we all became ill."

Katie turned toward him, meeting his eyes. "How long have you known?"

His face grew even redder. "She told me that night you sent me over with the message."

The night Ben had been infected.

"I felt so bad for her," he said. "She and Seth had planned to marry by the end of November." Ben shook his head as if in deep sorrow. "I hope I can be a good friend to her."

"How good of a friend?" Katie asked.

Ben looked surprised.

"I have no ill intentions," Katie said. "I just wonder what you're getting at. Would you court Paulina?"

Ben's eyes watered, perhaps from the icy wind. He shrugged.

"Well, I can't think of anyone Seth would want to marry Paulina more than you," Katie said. "No one he'd rather be a father to his child than you."

"Do you think so?"

"Jah." Katie placed her fingertips to her cheekbone. "But wait awhile. Give Paulina more time to grieve." Selfishly, she hoped her family would have at least a little time with the baby before Paulina started a new life. She tried to speak, to explain her thoughts, but nothing came out except a sort of gasp.

"It's been a hard year, hasn't it?" Ben whispered.

"Jah." Katie turned toward the house. "The hardest yet."

KATIE CONTINUED WATERING DOWN Mamm's tonic, and in return Mamm turned grouchy and sometimes downright mean. A couple of times, she told Paulina she needed to go home. Katie quickly intervened, chiding Mamm and asking Paulina to pay no attention.

A few times during the night, Katie woke up to Paulina's crying. The last time, Katie asked, "Are you all right?"

"Jah," Paulina said.

"Are you homesick?"

"Jah," Paulina answered. "But not for the home I left. For the home I thought I'd have with Seth."

Katie understood. That was how she felt about Amos.

"You have a place here. Someday, you'll have your own home. You'll have a husband." Katie thought of Ben but didn't mention his name. He was tenderhearted. Perhaps that was what was driving him, which meant he could change his mind. She hadn't wanted Ben to take Paulina away too soon, but on the other hand, she didn't want to get Paulina's hopes up either. Katie stayed silent.

Paulina sobbed.

Katie slipped from her bed and sat next to Paulina and took her friend's hand, holding it until she fell asleep.

The next day, Katie trudged through the snow to the road to

check the mail. She picked up Dat's newspaper. Underneath it was an envelope addressed by Amos.

Tears stung Katie's eyes. She pulled off one glove and slid her finger under the seal. Then she pulled the letter from the envelope. It was dated December 19. He'd made it through the war.

Dear Katie,

As you've heard, the war is over. I am wet and cold and muddy but alive. We have finally made it to a facility with barracks. Many of us are sleeping on the floor, but we are out of the trenches and the rain.

We won't start home until spring.

Thank you for your letter. I've read it over and over and can hear your voice through your words.

I'm sorry the influenza struck your Mamm and took Seth's life. Dat said, in the last letter I had from him, that Ben fell ill too, and you nursed him back to health. Ben is a good man and deserves your care.

Home. I can't imagine it anymore. It seems like a dream.

Your friend,
Amos

Katie slid the letter back into the envelope and replaced her glove. Then she headed back to the house. Amos was alive. He'd survived the war. He hadn't been ill, she assumed.

But his letter was so short, especially considering how long her last letter had been. And the line that Ben was a "good man and deserves your care" stung. Jah, Amos had suggested she court Ben when he was home, but her letter hadn't indicated that she was even considering such a thing.

Amos's letter was a relief but still left her feeling hollow.

When she stepped into the kitchen, Mamm was sitting at the table. "Is it time for my tonic?"

"Jah." They were down to a quarter of the last bottle.

"You need to go to the doctor and buy more."

Katie gave Mamm her medicine.

"It tastes different," Mamm said.

"Probably because it's the end of the bottle." Katie hadn't told Dat nor Paulina what she was doing. And, of course, she hadn't told her mother.

Mamm had been crankier. But she also had been awake more and able to sit up and peel potatoes and help with the sewing, and she'd even helped clean the dishes a few times. She'd been less winded and seemed to have more stamina. It didn't seem as if her heart was any worse.

"How do you feel?" Katie asked. "Better? Worse?"

"Maybe a little better," Mamm said.

At some point, Katie needed to fess up to both Mamm and Dat what she'd done as far as watering down the tonic, but not yet.

Mamm stood. "I'm going to go take a nap."

"All right," Katie said. "We're going to have ham hash for supper." They had leftovers to use up.

"I'll peel the potatoes when I get up." Mamm smiled.

The next day, Katie made it into town to the doctor's office. Again, his office was packed with people, but the worst of the flu was over in other parts of the state, and Nappanee had been spared any more outbreaks, according to the newspaper.

Finally, Nurse Walden called Katie back to one of the rooms.

"I'll get you more of the tonic," Dr. Barker said, stepping toward the cabinet.

"Do you mix the formula yourself?" Katie asked.

"Yes, I do."

"Can you put in less morphine? I've been watering Mamm's down, but she commented on the taste, that it's different."

"How is she doing with the watered-down version?"

"She was cranky for a while, but that's better now. She's sleeping less. Helping more. She's not complaining about chest pain."

He rubbed his chin and then said, "I suppose I could make it with less morphine. Perhaps the lithium salts are helping her spirits. And since the research isn't definite about the effect of morphine on the heart, I'll just put in a little in hopes it will be helpful."

PAULINA DELIVERED a little boy in late February in the sickroom with Mamm's assistance. Katie thought it had been a harrowing birth.

"Nee," Mamm said as she held the little one next to the stove in the kitchen after he was born. "It went quite well. Paulina is a strong woman." Mamm smiled down at the little one, who was sound asleep. "We need to keep them both warm and make sure Paulina gets plenty to eat."

Katie agreed. She would do whatever she could to care for Paulina and the baby, and she was happy that Mamm finally seemed to be leaning that way too.

The next day, Mamm was weary and stayed in bed all day. Katie was sorry helping through the night had exhausted Mamm but was grateful for her expertise during the birth.

As she sat at the table with Katie and Dat, Paulina announced that she'd named her son Seth Landis. "For a first and middle name. I don't know about a last name yet."

"The name pleases me," Dat said, "but it might pain your future husband to have the boy have his father's name."

Paulina responded, "I won't marry anyone it pains."

That evening, Mamm and Dat took turns holding the baby. When Mamm slid the baby into Dat's arms and met his eyes as she did, tears brimmed, but there was also an expression of joy on her face Katie had never seen before.

Katie had her turns with Baby Seth during the middle of the night, changing his diaper and helping Paulina position him for nursing. She felt the same joy she'd seen on Mamm's face.

The year had been miserable with the war and the flu, and then Seth passing. But the baby, no matter, was a blessing. A heritage from the Lord.

Dat must have said something to Ben across the fence when they were checking on the cows about the baby being born because he arrived the next afternoon, carrying a cradle.

Paulina was still in the sickroom, and Mamm said to Ben, "Go say hello. And show her the cradle."

Katie and Mamm sat at the table but could hear Paulina and Ben's soft murmurs.

He said, "I made a cradle for the baby."

"How kind of you," she responded. "I've named him Seth." Katie imagined that Paulina held the little one up for Ben to see.

"Jah, it's good to name him after his father. That way he'll always know."

A minute later, Ben returned to the table. "Denki," he said.

"Come back again soon," Katie told him.

Mamm didn't say anything, but she hadn't been opposed to Ben visiting.

He stopped by at least once a week. He and Paulina would sit in the front room and talk about the weather, about farming, and about the baby.

After one of those visits, Katie overheard Mamm ask Dat, "What does John think about Ben visiting Paulina?"

"He's never talked about it," Dat said. "And I won't ask him. It's between the Youngie."

Paulina's mother came to visit when the baby was two months old. She didn't say much, but she patted Paulina's arm and then held the baby.

When she readied to leave, she turned to Mamm. "Denki."

Mamm nodded.

Having a baby in the house seemed to increase Mamm's stamina. The baby brought comfort to all of them. Katie mourned her brother, but the baby brought her a hope she wouldn't have had otherwise.

Katie continued to write to Amos, even though his last letter had been abrupt and she hadn't heard from him since. She wrote about the baby. That Ben came to visit often. That Mamm was better. That spring was around the corner. That she hoped he'd be on a ship home soon.

The postage seemed an extravagant cost, but Dat didn't complain.

He did, however, mention that food prices were plummeting. "With the war over, we're no longer needed to feed the world," he said. "Hopefully the prices won't go too low."

In mid-June, a letter finally arrived from Amos. It was dated May 23, 1919. She read it while still standing at the mailbox.

Dear Katie,

We are scheduled to leave in a week and will return to Georgia. Hopefully I'll be discharged by the end of July. At this point, unless another opportunity arises, I plan to return to the farm, at least for a short time. Then I'll most likely head west.

I'm not the person I was when you last saw me—you won't want me around for long.

It sounds, from your letters, as if Ben is fond of Paulina. I was selfish not to encourage you to court Ben sooner. He is a good man. Much better than I am. I wish he were courting you, as he was trying to do last time I was home. I'm sorry that changed and if it did because of me.

Don't write back to me. There's not time for the letter to reach me.

I'm afraid you wasted your time writing me all this time, but I treasure your letters nonetheless. I don't know how I would have survived without them.

Amos

He didn't even close the letter with *Your friend*.

Anger welled up in her. But why? It's what she'd expected, that Amos would move on soon, no matter what.

She pulled Dat's newspaper from the mailbox and scanned the front page. A headline near the bottom caught her attention. *Spanish Flu Fells Soldiers Coming Home.* She quickly read the article. Soldiers coming home from Europe were bringing the flu with them. *Americans should be prepared for another outbreak. Soldiers are dying at sea. Others are coming down with the flu once they step on American soil. . . .*

She folded the paper, not wanting to read any more as her anger transformed, once again, into fear.

CHAPTER 20

Tally

When Jane paused, Maggie said, "Don't stop. Please keep telling the story."

Jane smiled. "That's it for now. I need to get back to Plain Patterns so Miriam can get Owen down for his nap."

"Can you stay for a sandwich and bowl of soup?" I asked. "It will only take a minute."

"All right," Jane said. "That will save me fixing my own lunch before I take over the shop." Her eyes twinkled.

Danielle hopped up and began clearing the plates and coffee cups, warming me inside. It was so nice to have someone who wanted to share my work. I pulled out four jars of homemade canned tomato soup from the pantry. After I poured the soup into a stockpot to heat, I pulled the cast-iron griddle from the cabinet. Next, I grabbed two cutting boards.

"Grilled cheese sandwiches and tomato soup." Danielle turned toward Maggie. "Your *favorite*—although Tally is taking it to a new level."

"It's my favorite too." Jane stood. "What can I do to help?"

"You can slice the bread."

After I retrieved everything Jane needed, I sliced the cheese, and then Jane and I both began buttering the bread.

"I'll set the table," Danielle said. "Maggie, *you* can help."

While we worked, Jane said to Danielle, "I've been thinking about your knee and how painful that must have been."

"It was," she said. "But it's not so painful now."

"I know of people who were prescribed painkillers too," Jane said. "I know it can be a bad situation."

"Jah, it definitely can be." Danielle seemed unusually quiet about her ordeal. I guessed she didn't want Kenan to come in and hear her talking about pain meds.

We worked together, and in no time the first batch of sandwiches was done, just as Rich and Kenan came in from the field. After they washed up, Danielle dished up the soup while Jane put a sandwich on each plate and I loaded the next batch on the griddle.

Mamm glowed through lunch. I thought of Katie's mother in the story. She was truly ill—and so was Mamm. But for years Mamm hadn't been physically ill, although I'm sure she'd been mentally ill. On the other hand, the tonic prescribed for Katie's Mamm seemed to make her less mentally healthy.

I couldn't help but wonder what all contributed to Mamm's depression. Did she have anyone she could talk to? Dat was wonderful in many ways, but would he have understood Mamm's pain in not having more children? I guessed he would have most likely suggested she read her Bible and pray. Which was good advice, but Jesus listened and He mourned with those who mourned. Perhaps Mamm had needed more support.

I also couldn't help but think about the tonic Katie's Mamm took. I didn't know a lot about morphine, but considering the opioid problem and the over-prescription of pain meds, that was a connection to the story for Danielle also.

Perhaps she'd talk about it later.

Right after we ate, Jane excused herself to go to Plain Patterns, and Rich and Kenan headed back out to the field.

After Danielle and I cleaned the dishes and kitchen, Danielle helped Mamm get ready for her nap while I read Maggie another chapter. Heidi spent her first day at Grandfather's house, making her bed in the loft, setting the table for supper, and helping Grandfather with the goats.

"Do you have goats?" Maggie asked.

"Nee," I answered. "We have several cows and steers but not goats."

"I wish we had goats."

"Never," Danielle said as she stepped into the living room. "We had them when I was a girl. They're a lot of work and *obnoxious* as all get out."

"I think we should get goats anyway." Maggie stared up at her mother. "Heidi really liked them."

Danielle shook her head and then said, "I'm tempted to get some just to show you how *annoying* they are."

Maggie grinned and then yawned. "I think I need a nap."

"And we need to get out of Tally's hair."

"Nee," I said. "I'm going to start a stew for supper."

"What about your walk?"

I shrugged. "I'll go if I have time."

I covered Maggie with the quilt on the couch and told her to rest.

"I'll help you with the stew," Danielle said.

We sat at the table to peel the carrots and potatoes. "Jane's story just keeps getting better," Danielle said. "I was surprised an Amish woman would take a tonic with morphine in it but then had to laugh at myself. I abused opioids even though I knew better. Desperate people do desperate things—although Katie's Mamm had no idea that the tonic would be addictive."

Although I'd never been that desperate and couldn't imagine what would drive me to that sort of thing, I couldn't say what I might do if I was in enough pain.

"I should talk with Jane more," Danielle said. "I think she understands some of what I went through. When the doctor at Fort Hood cut off my pain meds, essentially cold turkey, I thought I was going to die. I found a contact online but then came the day when he couldn't get meds, or so he said, and he sold me heroin instead. I lived a double life for a few weeks until Marc figured out what was going on."

I didn't know what to say. I'd heard of Youngie in the community trying heroin on their Rumschpringe. Ted had a friend who injured his shoulder and started on pain meds. Later, he used heroin and died of an overdose. Ted was with him. After that, Ted told me that thirty percent of people prescribed pain meds abuse them and one in twenty go on to try heroin. I'd read about opioid addiction in one of the old medical journals I bought at the library sale, about how users often had mood swings and acted in secretive ways.

Ted also told me addiction was a medical problem, but it could quickly become a legal one too. I'm not sure if Ted came up with all that information through his own research or if he talked with someone after his friend died. He also said that the drug companies purposely targeted patients, encouraging doctors to over-prescribe. Honestly, I wouldn't be surprised if Ted had once abused drugs considering everything he knew about the topic, although I doubted he'd ever be direct about that with me.

"I was lucky," Danielle said. "I never lost all my money. Never ended up homeless, like so many vets. Never ended up dead. All thanks to Marc. He saved me."

"You had a part in it too," I said. "You chose to get help."

Her voice thickened. "But only because I had Marc, because I had so much to live for. And because he walked beside me, never shaming me. Always loving me."

I didn't get teary—I didn't do that sort of thing much—but I felt emotional. It must have been wonderful to have that sort of love. What a loss for Danielle.

"You're so innocent," Danielle said to me. "So was I when I joined the Army. I'd never been kissed. Never been drunk. I said the pain meds—in the long run—did more for slowing down my mind than they did for my knee pain, but it was more than that. My second year in the Army, when I was at Fort Bragg, I was attacked by another soldier."

"Oh, Danielle." My breath caught. "That's horrible."

"First, he harassed me, propositioning me and saying lewd things, over and over. I kept a written list with dates, but when I showed it to my sergeant, he said I needed to toughen up, that it wasn't a big deal. A few weeks later, I was walking across the base around nine at night, going back to my barracks, and my abuser attacked me. He tackled me, punched me in the face, groped me, and tried to pull my pants off."

"That's awful."

"I screamed and managed to scramble away from him. As he grabbed at me, a guy stepped out of a barracks and yelled, 'What's going on?' I screamed again and managed to get to my feet and start running while my abuser yelled, 'Nothing. We were just messing around.'"

I shuddered. "Did you get away?"

She nodded. "I was a half block from my barracks. He'd been waiting for me, but I managed to get home before he could run after me again. The guy who stepped out of the barracks didn't go back inside. He waited, and I think it made my attacker pause."

"Wow." I was impressed with Danielle's strength.

"When they say that sexual abuse is about power, I get it. His harassment and then his assault was all about having power over me, both physically and sexually."

"What happened to him when you reported what he'd done?" I asked.

"Nothing—because I didn't report him again." Danielle shrugged. "Look what happened the first time. He gave me a black eye and a bloody lip, but I told everyone I ran into a low-hanging branch. Besides that, there wasn't any other evidence except for some red marks on my arms and legs."

I felt sick at my stomach.

"That attack was worse than being shot in the knee—not that my knee wasn't painful. It was. And I needed the pain meds to get through it. But the assault was what my mind went to when I woke up at night. And during the day when I had a spare moment. So, I was already messed up and then my knee got shot and everything got even worse. The pain meds made me feel kind of normal again." She exhaled and then took a deep breath. "The memories and anxiety would finally calm down. That's what the heroin helped with, especially when my attacker showed up at Fort Hood, while I was still injured. He managed to get transferred there too."

"Oh no," I said. "What ended up happening?"

"He harassed me a few times after he found me on base but stopped after Marc threatened him."

That was sad that it took another man threatening him to make her abuser stop. "How did you stop using?"

"Rehab. I was lucky. Most people never get help. I came to

understand the trauma and that I had PTSD from both the assault and being shot. But because I admitted what was going on as far as my addiction, I was dishonorably discharged."

I wasn't sure what that meant, but it didn't sound good. Especially not for someone who had been sexually harassed and assaulted while in the Army, who served in Iraq, who was shot in the knee while trying to save others, who was prescribed enough pain meds to get addicted—and then was honest about it. It all sounded like a nightmare. A super traumatic one.

"Marc didn't reenlist because of everything I'd gone through, and Kenan got him the job here. We'd both saved some money while in the Army, and we put a payment down on our little farm. I got a job at the Bremen hospital. Then I had Maggie. All the pain seemed behind me. But then after Marc died, I fell apart again. I started writing myself prescriptions for painkillers. It was a couple of months until I got busted. By then I was addicted again, and Kenan hauled me back to rehab. This time in Elkhart."

It was my turn to pause and then ask, "Do you mind my questions?"

"No," Danielle answered. "Ask whatever you want."

"What about now?" I ventured. "Are you using again?"

"Not opioids. But Dirk has gotten me some sleeping aids." Danielle cut a potato into chunks and plopped them into the bowl. "I take them sometimes because if I go without sleeping for very long, I get an intense urge to use opioids again. Kenan doesn't think it's safe for me to take the sleep aids because of Maggie. And he's right. If the house burned down or she was injured, what good would I be to her?"

"Was that what was in the pharmacy bag the day I found you in the woods?"

"Yes," she said. "I hadn't slept for three nights. Dirk was

going to have a picnic with us but was called back to work." She began peeling another potato. "I decided to take one pill, thinking it would just calm me down—not put me to sleep. But it did. Kenan was right. I put Maggie in an unsafe predicament. I'll never do that again."

"What are you going to do?"

She shrugged. "I've been taking a half pill at night. That usually helps me sleep until four or so, which is enough. I'm not sure I could drive after taking that, but I could wake up and get Maggie out of the house if there was a fire or call Kenan or 9-1-1 in case of an emergency."

"So, are you dating Dirk?"

"No," Danielle said. "He's been a good friend to me is all. Kenan doesn't like him, but he's fine."

I'd finished peeling the carrots, cutting them into chunks, and then tossed them into the bowl. Then I stood to braise the stew meat.

"You should go for your walk," Danielle said. "It's good for your back. I can keep an ear out for your Mamm until you get back, while I finish the stew."

"Would you?" I asked.

"*Go.*" She smiled. "It means a lot for me to be here. It's a comfortable feeling that I don't experience much anymore."

CHAPTER 21

As I walked, I thought of the doctors who over-prescribed the pain medication. Did anything happen to them? Or the drug companies that encouraged doctors to prescribe the medication? Were the patients who became addicted the only ones to pay?

I reached the far side of the loop and started running, slowly at first, hoping it wouldn't make my injury worse. It didn't. If anything, it helped relax me more and loosened my back. After about five minutes, someone called my name. I squinted toward the field where Kenan and Rich were working. Kenan jogged toward the fence, waving.

I immediately slowed to a walk. "What are you doing over here?"

He held up a post-hole digger. "I told Rich I'd work on the fence line. He's coming on the tractor with the posts." He'd reached the fence and leaned the digger against a fence pole that was already set. "Mind if I walk with you? Or jog, if you prefer."

"We can walk." I'd never jogged with anyone before.

For a moment, neither of us said anything. I liked that about Kenan. He seemed awkward like I was. He appeared to be at a loss for words quite often too. Finally, Kenan said, "Thank you for being such a good friend to Danielle. She seems better today."

"I enjoy spending time with her," I said. "And with Maggie too."

"So do I," Kenan said. "I just feel as if I'm enabling Danielle a lot of the time. It leaves me with a bad feeling."

He'd mentioned that before. "What do you mean exactly?"

"I feel as if I rescue her when I shouldn't. As if I'm trying to control her all the time instead of letting her fail."

"She told me you got her back in rehab after her husband died."

He nodded.

"Was that enabling her?"

"No." He sighed. "That was the right thing to do. She's just hard to figure out sometimes."

I stretched my stride to match his. "But letting her fail might mean Maggie could get hurt."

"That's what keeps me over-involved."

"Have you thought about moving in with them?"

He literally shuddered. "I don't think that would be a good idea."

"Why not?"

"I'm too suspicious. And most of the time I'm wrong. I was convinced she and Dirk were in a relationship, but they're not. I made a fool out of myself over that one."

"Would it have been bad if they were?"

Kenan shrugged. "I'm not sure. At the time, I was convinced it would have been. Probably because I thought it was too soon after Marc died." He shook his head. "See? I'm controlling and over-involved."

It sounded like a true dilemma.

"Remember when you told me that Danielle was worried about losing her farm?" Kenan asked. "That alarmed me because she got a large sum from Marc's life insurance policy. I was afraid maybe she'd spent it. No, not afraid. Sure. I was certain she'd blown all the money, but I had no idea on what. When I asked her about it, she said she *feels* as if she might lose the farm. There's no evidence she would. She still has the majority of her money invested or in savings. She only draws out so much for monthly expenses. But she *felt* as if she were going to lose the farm, and I jumped to conclusions. She can be so doom and gloom."

I felt horrible, as I was the one responsible for that episode. "Does she feel that way because of what she's gone through?"

"Definitely," he said. "She wasn't that way when we were kids."

I thought of all the times Mamm hadn't been logical when she was distraught. "I think sometimes people believe what they fear."

"That could be," he said. "But it's hard for me to understand."

"I think it's hard for a lot of people to understand." I thought of Danielle's red lipstick. Did she wear it to remind herself not to be all doom and gloom? "But on the other hand," I said, "Danielle can be a lot of fun too."

"Definitely," Kenan said again. "She made my childhood one long parade, as you can imagine. She had a wild imagination and always came up with games and these whole entire settings from books she'd read for us to interact in—after chores were all done, of course. We played *Little House on the Prairie* for years. She was so bent on having fun that she'd help the rest of us complete our work in record time so we could play with her."

"What was she like when you were teenagers?"

"*Druvvel.*"

I laughed at the Pennsylvania Dutch word for trouble. I thought of Danielle saying she'd never been drunk before she was eighteen. But she didn't say she didn't drink before then.

"She was definitely a wild child," he said. "She found a group of friends who were a mix of Mennonite and Englisch Youngie. They went hiking together, played volleyball, and went on camping trips. They partied some, but looking back, it seems fairly innocent. Still, our parents were horrified. She was their firstborn. They expected her to be obedient. If Danielle had been a younger child, I don't think it would have been so bad. But they expected her to set a good example. They didn't know what to do with a strong-willed child, especially a daughter. It was as if the more disappointed they became in her, the more reason she gave them to be disappointed."

He smiled a little. "But she was a hard worker around our farm all through her teenage years," he said, "and she helped Mamm with the cooking and cleaning and caring for the younger children."

I thought about how helpful Danielle was around our house.

We came to the end of the field, and I stopped, not wanting to take him too far from his work. "Do you like it here in Indiana?" I asked. "Do you plan to stay?"

"I'll stay as long as Danielle and Maggie do."

"If they leave, will you go back home?"

"Probably not. I miss my siblings, but I don't have a life there anymore."

The rumble of the tractor's metal wheels stole our attention. Rich stared but didn't smile.

"I better go," Kenan said. "I'm enjoying working with Rich. I've missed working on a farm." He took a step backward and then said, "It's cool that you run."

My face grew warm. "I don't, really."

He shook his head. "No. You really were. I do road races sometimes. You should do one."

I laughed, glancing down at my apron. "Dressed like this?"

"Jah, why not?" he said. "You have good form, and you were moving pretty fast. You'd do great."

I shook my head and waved. "Have fun working on the fence."

He smiled, turned, and then began jogging back toward the tractor.

I wondered if he had a girlfriend in Nappanee, if he hoped to marry, and if he wanted a family. He'd make a good husband and father. He was so good with Maggie, and he was devoted to Danielle, even though he was frustrated with her and worried about her.

Once I rounded the corner, where Rich couldn't see me, I began to run again.

AFTER I RETURNED, I told Danielle she and Maggie should go home. "My back feels better," I said. "I can transfer Mamm."

Danielle yawned. "Call if you need anything."

Rich, Mamm, and I had a quiet supper. I put Mamm to bed early and then read more. Sunday morning, an off week for church, Rich left to spend time with Joanna. At least that's where I assumed he went. He didn't say a word.

Late in the morning, Kenan showed up with a basket of fruit and a tray of muffins. He took me by surprise, but I did my best not to show it. Had he come to see me? I nearly laughed at myself. He was super nice, but I doubted he'd come to see Mamm. But I couldn't figure out why he would come see me.

I made another pot of coffee, and I moved Mamm out onto the porch. There was a bit of chill in the air, but the day was bright. I tucked the log cabin quilt under Mamm's legs and pulled it up to her chin.

"I didn't make the muffins," Kenan said. "I bought them."

"Really?" I teased.

He grinned. "You could tell, right?"

"I did wonder if you made the fruit."

He laughed.

I took an orange from the basket and peeled it, splitting it between the three of us.

Even though she had a cup of coffee, Mamm started to doze.

Kenan spoke softly. "I hope I didn't say too much yesterday."

Ach, that explained why he'd come. He needed to explain himself, something I could relate to. He hadn't come to see me after all. "I really love Danielle," he said. "It's been hard for me to know how much to help her, but I've never regretted helping her. Nor will I ever stop."

I admired that about him, and I felt some of that care toward me too, which I hadn't experienced much in life, honestly. Not that people didn't care about me. They did. Dat had. Mamm did. Rich did in his own way. But it was something I knew. Not something I felt. Kenan was different.

I smiled. "I've never known a brother as devoted as you are."

He shrugged. "I don't know about that. But Danielle's always been really good to me too. I never would have left home if she hadn't talked me through it."

"And you don't regret it?"

He lowered his voice even more. "No. Our parents' intentions were good, but they were so strict that it came off as uncaring, sometimes as neglectful. Punitive. I didn't realize it then, but looking back it's pretty clear. I always knew Danielle loved me, but I wasn't sure about my parents."

"Ouch," I said.

"I helped our next younger brother leave too. He's in Colorado now. All three of us who left are doing better than the ones who stayed. Although, from what I've heard, our parents aren't as hard on the younger ones as they were on us. You can't imagine how angry they were when Danielle joined the Army."

"Why did she choose the Army?"

Kenan answered, "She didn't feel as if she had any other options."

I winced.

"When I left, she sent me money so I could move here and start the apprenticeship."

"Why did you decide to be a linesman?"

He smiled. "Well, when you grow up without any electricity, it's pretty fascinating. I always wondered how those lines sent electricity to everyone's houses except for ours." He laughed. "When Danielle explained to me what Marc did, I wanted to do the same." He smiled again.

I smiled back at him.

His face grew serious. "Sadly, my work is what led to Marc's death."

I'd been curious but now I dreaded knowing. Still, I asked, "What happened?"

"Marc was up on a pole, and I was below him. He was stringing a line and made contact with a live wire and fell backward, toward me. He was buckled, so he didn't fall off the pole. There's a famous photo of one linesman giving another mouth-to-mouth and saving the man. I remembered that photo, and I did my best. But he was already dead."

I gasped. "How horrible."

Kenan exhaled slowly. "We just passed the anniversary a few weeks ago, which is always hard. Especially for Danielle."

"Of course it would be. The job sounds dangerous."

"It is," Kenan said. "It's the tenth most dangerous job in the US."

"What's more dangerous?"

"Loggers. Roofers. Farmers. That sort of thing."

"Farmers?" I'd never thought about Rich's work as being dangerous. "What about police officers?"

"They're lower on the list," Kenan said. "I think firefighters are higher than police—even higher than linesmen."

"Interesting."

"I'm not sure where soldiers fall on the list. For Danielle, and I think many others, the dangers were far greater than combat. I know the rate of addiction is about the same as in the general population, even though the military tests regularly for drugs. The suicide rates for both soldiers and veterans are also high."

He paused and I waited, wondering if he would say more. Finally, in a low voice, he said, "I'm afraid she's using again."

It seemed he'd been afraid of that all week. "Do you have new evidence?"

He shook his head. "It's the way she was acting earlier this week. Secretive and tense. It's the way she acted after Marc died, when she started using."

I paused for a long moment, again unsure of what to say. Finally, I settled on, "How horrible for all of you to have Marc die, and in such a tragic way."

"It was. The hardest thing I've ever done was tell Danielle. Marc was tough on the outside. You could tell he grew up in a rough neighborhood and had been in the Army. But he was a big teddy bear. He would do anything for the people he loved. I know Maggie doesn't remember him enough to realize what she's missing, but she'll have a different life without him than she would have had with him."

I knew how different my life was after losing my Dat, and I'd been grown when he'd passed.

Kenan finished his coffee and then said, "Well, thank you for listening. I appreciate it."

"You're welcome," I responded. "Thank you for the muffins and fruit."

He stood and turned toward Mamm. "Please tell Regina good-bye for me when she wakes up."

"I will." I stood and watched him walk down the steps and toward his pickup. He turned and waved. I smiled and waved back.

As I was ready to wake Mamm and roll her back into the house, a buggy turned into our driveway. It wasn't Rich and it wasn't Jane.

I squinted. It was Bishop David and his wife, Catherine. I shook Mamm's shoulder. "We have company."

She stirred. "Danielle and Maggie?"

"No. David and Catherine." It wasn't often that they visited.

Mamm raised her head. "Oh." The last time the bishop had stopped by was just after we'd been added to his district.

David parked the buggy and helped Catherine, who held a paper bag in her hands, down.

"Hallo," David called out as he waved.

I waved back. "*Willkomm.*"

"Guter Mariye. I wanted to check to see how you're doing, Regina," David said.

Catherine held up the bag. "And I brought doughnuts."

I imagined her making a big batch Saturday and then delivering them as she and David visited people in our district on the off Sundays.

As they came up onto the porch, I said, "I'll make a pot of coffee."

"Oh, don't do that on our behalf." Catherine laughed and then lowered her voice. "Neither one of us needs any more liquid."

I smiled and took the doughnuts from her and put them out with the muffins. "Help yourselves."

Catherine took a chocolate muffin and David took a poppy-seed one. Mamm and I each selected a doughnut.

"How are you doing?" David asked Mamm.

"Good," she said. "No different, really." She smiled. "Considering I had another stroke, I'm fortunate to be feeling the same as I did last week."

David smiled.

"Our neighbor Danielle got me to the hospital in Bremen," Mamm said, "where Dr. Johnson gave me medicine that stopped the damage and reversed some. Then the ambulance took me on to Mishawaka for further testing."

"That's what Rich told me," David said.

"I only had to spend one night there," Mamm explained. "I'm glad to be home. Danielle and her daughter have visited. Jane visited. Danielle's brother Kenan visited. All of that has helped."

Catherine cocked her head. Was she wondering about Kenan?

"Is Rich around?" David asked.

Mamm shook her head. "He's visiting Joanna Yoder."

David smiled, just a little. "That's nice to hear." He rubbed his hands together. "What do you need? Is there anything we can do?"

Mamm glanced at me. I smiled and then said, "I can't think of anything. Danielle brought us a meal on Friday night and then fixed stew for us last night."

"She sounds like a good neighbor," Catherine said.

"She is," Mamm answered. "And her daughter Maggie is a treasure."

"Who are they?" David asked.

"Englischers, although Danielle grew up Mennonite in Ohio," Mamm explained. "They live down the road, the next place on the right."

"I see," David said. "I'm glad they've been able to help."

"So am I." Mamm smiled.

I was too, but I wasn't going to say it out loud. I didn't want David to become concerned.

I asked Catherine about her grandchildren, including the twins who were toddlers and kept all of them entertained.

After a few minutes, I said, "I should take Mamm inside. Would you like to join us?"

"Oh, we can't stay." Catherine stood. "We have a few more stops to make."

David stood too. "Tell Rich to leave me a message if there's anything you need. If not, we'll see you next Sunday."

"You will indeed," Mamm said.

After they left, I wheeled her back into the kitchen while I put away the doughnuts and leftover muffins.

Out of the blue, Mamm said, "I wonder what *you* need."

"What do you mean?"

"In this life. Part of me hoped you'd be married by now, although if that happened it would be harder for you to care for me too."

"I don't want to be married," I said. "I haven't courted anyone. How could I be married?"

The light in the kitchen shifted as a cloud passed over the sun. "But what will happen to you when I'm gone?"

"Don't talk that way," I said.

As I readied Mamm for her nap, she said, "I heard you reading Maggie the *Heidi* book. Do you remember when I read it to you?"

"Of course," I said. "That's why I appreciate it so much. It's still one of my favorite stories."

"I'm sorry," Mamm said.

"Sorry for what?"

"That I wasn't a better mother to you."

"You were fine," I said. "Just fine."

"You're being kind. I was depressed, although I don't think I realized it at the time. I relied on you to do too much of the work." As I transferred her into bed, Mamm said, "I thought of myself first in so many ways. Before I was married, I didn't enjoy my life because all I wanted was a husband. Then when I had a husband, I didn't enjoy my life because I wanted children. Then when I finally had two children, I wanted more. I wasted so much of my life on what I didn't have."

"Mamm . . ." That was so sad I wasn't sure what to say.

"You're not like me. If you never marry, you'll be fine. But I see you with Maggie, and I know you would be a good mother. A much better mother than I was."

"Don't say that, Mamm."

"It's true." She was in her bed now, her head on her pillow. "I also know you would make a good teacher. It doesn't matter that you're quiet. You're good with children. You're good at both learning and teaching. I've heard you with Maggie in the kitchen, explaining things to her. Asking her about what she likes, what she wants. Giving her tasks to do but explaining each step. You might think that comes naturally to others because it comes naturally to you, but it doesn't." Mamm met my eyes. "You have a gift."

It was the nicest thing my Mamm had ever said to me. I blinked away tears. "Denki. That means a lot."

"I hope you'll marry. Or teach school. I think either would provide a good life for you."

I knew Mamm always wanted me to marry. What Amish mother didn't want that for her daughter? That was what we were raised for. But the fact she considered teaching a viable future for me was a surprise. I was beginning to believe, once again, that teaching would be the most fulfilling option for me. But that would mean Mamm would die, and I didn't want that. Unless Danielle *could* care for Mamm, meaning I *could* teach.

A coldness swept through me. But if Kenan was right and Danielle was using again, then I couldn't trust her with Mamm. As much as I adored Danielle, I couldn't take a chance with her caring for Mamm. Not now.

"Did I ever tell you I wanted to be a teacher?" Mamm asked.

"No. I would remember if you had."

"I did, right up until the time I was offered a position." Her eyes met mine. "I turned it down."

"Why did you do that?"

Tears welled in Mamm's eyes. "I was twenty and afraid. Afraid I would be a bad teacher."

I couldn't imagine Mamm as a teacher, but I didn't know what she was like when she was my age.

"That's what I admire about you," Mamm said. "You're never afraid to take a risk. You'll make a wonderful teacher—and you won't be afraid."

"Oh, but I am afraid," I said. "Terrified."

"But you took the job. You were going to teach."

I didn't respond.

"Tally?"

"Jah," I answered. "I took the job. But now, I feel less confident about teaching."

Mamm frowned.

I wasn't sure why we were still talking about this. "But I've been thinking more about it lately." I smiled. "I'll figure it out."

Mamm smiled back at me, and she seemed to be satisfied with my answer. "That's my girl." Then she yawned and said, "Would you read me a chapter from *Heidi*? Don't start at the beginning. Start wherever you left off with Maggie."

I headed to the front room, grabbed the book, and returned to Mamm's room. In chapter three, Heidi went with Peter up on the mountain with the goats. An eagle screeched over them, Heidi gave her bread and cheese to Peter, and she saved a goat from going over the rocks.

Halfway through the chapter, Mamm started snoring. I kept reading anyway until the end of the chapter, wishing I'd been reading books to Mamm all along at naptime. It was good for both of us.

CHAPTER 22

The next day, I read Mamm chapter four. Grandfather bundled Heidi on a sled and took her down to Peter's hut to visit his grandmother. The visits became frequent, and Grandfather fixed the broken shutter and other things on the hut while Heidi visited with Peter's grandmother.

Heidi brought out the best in people.

Maggie did that too. And so did Danielle.

It was Monday afternoon. I hadn't seen the two since Saturday. Two days. The longest I'd gone without seeing them since we became friends. Why did it seem like so much longer?

I was like the grandmother in *Heidi*. Transformed by a neighbor and always wondering when she would visit again. Why was Danielle staying away? Was she avoiding us on purpose?

I decided to stop by and say hello while I was on my walk. First, I put the book on Mamm's nightstand and then kissed her on the forehead, something I never did. I remembered, vaguely, that she used to kiss me that way sometimes. I stared at her for a long moment. At the wrinkles around her eyes and mouth. At the blue veins in her eyelids. At her clenched fist.

Then I turned away and headed to the back porch to put on my running shoes. Rich was working on the tractor when

I walked by. He didn't see me. As I neared Danielle's house, I noted her SUV in the driveway and smoke coming from the chimney. All looked normal, but when I knocked on the door, no one answered. Perhaps Maggie was napping. Perhaps they both were.

Dejected, I headed back to the other side of the highway, thinking about Danielle and feeling mortified that I'd been so bold in asking her such personal questions about her addiction.

Tomorrow was Tuesday. Hopefully she'd want to go to Plain Patterns to hear more—perhaps the rest—of Katie's story. However, I couldn't imagine that Mamm would feel up to going. I hoped Danielle and Maggie would go on their own. Then they could tell me the story.

On the straight stretch on the back side of my route, I started to run, picking up speed with each step. I felt as if I was nearly flying. I'd never run so fast. The freedom and power I longed for flooded through me. I thought of Kenan's mention of the road races he ran. *Could* I do something like that someday?

I kept running, reciting out loud the verse from Isaiah that I'd memorized in school. "'. . . they that wait upon the Lord shall renew their strength; they shall mount up with wings as eagles; they shall run and not be weary; and they shall walk, and not faint.'" I thought of the eagle in *Heidi*. Of its strength. Of its screeching. The wings of an eagle were powerful.

I didn't slow until I reached the phone shanty, and then I maintained a quick walk.

After I reached the house, I slipped out of my running shoes and then seared a roast for dinner. I put it in the oven and then peeled carrots and potatoes, which made me think of Danielle and her help on Saturday. I listened for Mamm's call as I worked.

Once I'd finished with the vegetables, I put them in the Dutch oven with the roast. Then I went to check on Mamm. She was still and didn't even stir as I approached her bed. She appeared peaceful. I stepped closer.

Something was wrong. I watched her chest, waiting for the rise and fall, the rise and fall. It didn't come.

"Mamm." I touched her forehead with my fingers, on the same spot where I'd kissed her earlier. Her skin was cold. "Mamm!" I grabbed her wrist and felt for a pulse. I couldn't find one.

I sat on the edge of the bed for a long while, staring at her, and then lowered my head into my shaking hands. I had been weary of caring for her, but I hadn't wanted her to die. I couldn't stop shaking.

I went to find Rich in the field. Walking did me good because by the time I reached him, I'd gained control of my body. Slowly, I said, "Mamm has passed away."

He turned toward me with a blank stare on his face. Finally, he asked, "Are you sure?"

I nodded.

He turned and marched toward the house. I followed, moving as if through a thick fog. It seemed as if I couldn't see more than an inch in front of my face.

By the time I reached the house, Rich was coming out. "I'm going to go get Danielle. She'll know what to do."

"We need to call the undertaker," I said. "The same one who took care of Dat."

"All right," Rich said. "We can do that after I get Danielle. Go sit with Mamm until I get back."

Still surprised at Rich's turnaround when it came to Danielle, I knew I'd feel better too if she were with us. She always knew what to do.

I did as Rich directed, but this time I climbed up on the other side of the bed and sat beside Mamm, my head against the headboard. I didn't touch her. She was gone, but it was comforting to be close to her. I mourned for Mamm, for all she never had. How I wished she could have found joy in what God had given her, in the good husband and the two children. But then I whispered a prayer of gratitude. She had her weaknesses, jah, but she kept trying. Kept moving forward. I regretted that she hadn't shared more of her sorrows and grief with me.

I thought of Katie's story and her prayer that the Lord would stitch threads of hope through her own story even after she'd lost so much. Right now, in my own story, those threads of hope seemed pretty frayed. Life felt like a tattered old quilt that needed to be repaired. But I wasn't sure with what.

I took comfort in knowing Katie had survived trying times. Surely I could too.

I don't know how much time passed before Danielle came through the bedroom door, followed by Rich. "I'm *so* sorry, Tally." Danielle stepped to the side of the bed and touched Mamm's arm. "Tell me about when you found her."

"When I got back from my walk, I put a roast in the oven and then came to check on her," I explained. "She was cold and had no pulse."

"She looks so peaceful."

I agreed. "What do you think happened?"

Danielle shook her head. "There's no way for me to know."

"I'm wondering if she had another stroke."

Danielle's eyes filled with tears. "That's a possibility."

I asked, "Where's Maggie?"

"Kenan came and got her." Danielle motioned for Rich to step closer. "You should say your good-byes to your mother, either out loud or silently. Whichever feels most comfortable."

I felt I'd already said mine, but I agreed. This time I put my hand on her arm, which was covered by the quilt.

Rich stepped to the bed and put his hand on her other arm. Neither of us spoke.

After a while, Danielle said to Rich, "You should call the undertaker when you're ready."

He lifted his head and met my gaze. "Who else should I call?"

"The bishop," I answered. "And would you leave a message for Jane too? Her number is on the front of the notebook in the shanty. And call Joanna. See if someone else can sit with Beth so she can sit with you."

He nodded.

"Oh, and call Ted too. He can tell Aenti Frannie. And maybe he can run errands for us tomorrow too."

The undertaker soon arrived and took Mamm to the funeral home to be embalmed, and then David arrived. Danielle had cleaned up the peelings in the sink and made a pot of coffee, and we all sat at the table. David said the visitation would be Wednesday evening and the service and burial would be on Thursday. He finished his coffee and then stood. "Catherine and I'll both be here on Wednesday, and Jonah will come over tomorrow." Jonah was the deacon and would see what Rich and I needed. We would have help with cleaning, chores, and preparation of the food. That was what the Amish did.

"We have supper for tonight," I said. "There's no need for anyone to bring anything." I wasn't ready to interact with others yet. "If we have help tomorrow, that's soon enough."

"All right," David said. "I'll make the calls."

After he left, Rich went out to do the chores, and Danielle asked, "How are you feeling?"

I sighed. "Kind of numb."

"That's normal," she said.

I hadn't felt this way when Dat died, probably because I needed to be alert for Mamm.

Danielle reached across the table and took my hand. "You are not alone."

A knock on the front door startled me.

"I'll get it," Danielle said.

I wasn't ready to interact with anyone and considered going into Mamm's room and closing the door. But then I heard Jane say, "How is she?"

Tears welled in my eyes. I did want to see Jane.

Another voice—Kenan's—asked Danielle, "Do you want us to stay? Or go to your house?"

"Can we stay?" Maggie asked.

"No," Danielle said. "You should—"

I was on my feet. "Wait." I hurried into the front room. Jane, Kenan, and Maggie all stood just inside the door, facing Danielle. "Please stay." I wasn't ready to be alone. "I made a roast. There's plenty for everyone."

"Are you sure?" Kenan asked.

"Jah, I am."

Kenan's eyes gazed down at me. "I'm so sorry, Tally."

"Denki," I managed to say.

"We're all here for you. We want to help."

A lump formed in my throat, so I nodded instead of speaking. I believed Kenan.

Maggie took my hand. "I'm sorry about Regina too."

I returned Maggie's squeeze and then motioned toward the kitchen with my free hand, leading the way.

"Is Rich doing chores?" Kenan asked. At my nod, he said, "I'll go help him." He slipped ahead of us and out the back door. As we sat around the table, I stared at Mamm's place and thought of the joy Maggie had brought to her. Of how happy she'd been at the table just two days before when Jane told us more of the story over sticky buns.

"I thought more people would be here," Jane said.

"I asked the bishop to tell people to wait until tomorrow morning," I said. "I didn't feel up to a crowd."

"Jah," Jane said. "Being inundated with help can be both a blessing and a bane."

"I'm grateful you came," I said.

Jane smiled and took a covered bowl from her bag. "I brought you a broccoli salad that I'd made this morning for my supper."

"Do you need anything else?" Danielle asked.

"I was going to make biscuits," I said.

"I'll do that." Danielle stood.

"Denki." Having Danielle as a friend was like having a sister, albeit an older sister who was a little wild but super capable and not afraid to take charge.

"Jane," Maggie said, "would you tell us more of the story?"

"Not now," Jane said. "We're here to sit with Tally, to ease her grief."

"Actually," I said, "I think that would be a good way for the four of us to be together. And I believe Mamm would want you to tell it." I just wished she could have heard the rest before she died, but it didn't matter now—certainly not to her.

"As long as you're sure," Jane said.

I nodded.

"Where were we?"

"Katie had finally received a letter from Amos that he would soon leave Europe," Danielle said. "And then, in that day's newspaper, there was an article about the flu spreading through the troops returning home."

"That's right," Jane said. "Katie was afraid he'd survived the war only to become ill—or worse, to die—on the ship bringing him home."

CHAPTER 23

Katie

In June of 1919, President Wilson signed the Treaty of Versailles after arriving in France the previous December. It was reported that he came down with a common cold in early April, which delayed the process.

Dat read the article out loud to Mamm, Paulina, and Katie and then held up the front page, showing a photograph of President Woodrow Wilson and British Prime Minister David Lloyd George during the Paris Peace Conference. President Wilson wore a black top hat.

"His face looks gaunt," Dat said. "My guess is he had the flu, not a cold."

"Why wouldn't it be reported as such?" Mamm asked.

"He wouldn't want other world leaders to know," Dat said. "It would make him appear weak. But he must have been dreadfully ill for the negotiations to stop between April and June. Members of Congress are saying he didn't negotiate the issues they wanted and believe he was too ill to do so." Dat flipped the newspaper to the next page. "Not once has Wilson given a statement about the pandemic or spoken in public about it, let alone about his own health."

Mamm clucked her tongue. "Even though thousands of people have died?"

"Jah," Dat said. "I suppose he also thinks addressing the issue would make him and the government seem weak for not stopping it, so it's better to just ignore it. It's too bad he can't just speak the truth."

Katie agreed. The flu had taken Seth, a healthy young man, from them. It felt personal. It *was* personal. Others, even though they survived, had been dreadfully ill. The disease, which according to the newspaper was spreading across the country again, was nothing to ignore.

Mamm took over the task of sharing baked goods with Ben and John, taking over loaves of bread, sticky buns, and pies. Dat took her over in the buggy because she couldn't walk that far. Paulina asked to go with her once, but Mamm said she thought that was too forward.

Baby Seth was strong and healthy. He smiled and laughed and began turning over, thrusting himself around on the floor. Both Mamm and Dat enjoyed holding him. So did Katie. The baby had brought hope to a household that would have otherwise been filled with grief.

Ben stopped coming around to see Paulina by the middle of July. At first Katie figured he was busy with farming. But it was soon obvious it was intentional. Several times Paulina cried herself to sleep. She mentioned a few times that she wondered if she should ask her parents if she could move back home. Katie was sure it was because of Ben. In the middle of August,

Katie marched over to confront him one afternoon when she was supposed to be checking the mail.

He was in the tack room connected to the barn, repairing a harness. "Ben Berger," she said, "I didn't suspect this of you."

"Suspect what?"

"That you would lead Paulina on and then ignore her."

His face grew red, and he lowered his head. "I've been busy."

"She's confused. And hurt. You implied you were interested in her."

He looked up from the harness. "Did you tell Paulina that?"

"Of course not." Katie shook her head. "Did you not mean what you indicated before?"

"I thought I did."

"Are you afraid about what others might think?"

He shook his head. "I don't listen to gossip. And I don't talk with anyone except Dat." He sighed. "But yes, I am worried about what others might think."

Katie crossed her arms.

"I'm not like you," Ben said. "Or Amos."

"What do you mean?"

"Daring."

"I'm not daring," Katie said.

"You are. You risked your life to take care of others who were ill."

"I did what I needed to."

"You've stuck by Amos even when he's been a fool." Ben shook his head. "I have a question for you."

"What is it?"

"Are you still waiting for Amos to come home?"

Katie wasn't sure what to say. Jah, she was anticipating Amos coming home but not with any sort of expectation.

"If he was coming home, he'd be here by now," Ben said.

"I'm guessing he headed west. You're wasting your time waiting for him."

Katie didn't respond.

Ben kept talking. "So you can quiz me about my feelings for Paulina, but I don't have a right to speak the truth about Amos?"

"No, you don't. Paulina is sleeping in my room, crying because of the way you've treated her, while you have no idea what the truth about Amos is." Katie spun around and left the tack room. She hoped Ben hadn't shifted his affection toward her again. It made no sense that he'd seemed so fond of Paulina—even building the cradle for Seth—and now completely ignored her.

What had happened to change his mind, besides Amos not coming home?

Even though Amos had told her not to, she'd kept writing to him. As long as he was still in the Army, the letters would be forwarded to him. If he'd been discharged, she hoped the letters would be returned to her. Then she'd know he wasn't coming home.

She also hoped, since John hadn't heard otherwise, that Amos was still alive. But she had no idea how long it took for the Army to make those sorts of notifications.

Two weeks later, Dat cleared his throat after he ended the prayer at the beginning of supper and said, "Amos is back."

Katie kept her eyes on her plate, but her heart raced.

"He arrived home last night."

"Oh." Mamm took a biscuit from the basket. "I thought he'd probably headed west by now. That's what Ben thought too."

Katie dropped her fork. As it clattered to the floor, Mamm

shook her head. Katie quickly picked it up. Had Mamm been talking to Ben about Amos when she delivered the bread?

Amos had written to Katie that he might *head west* in his last letter. Had he written that to John too?

"Is Amos doing all right?" Paulina asked.

Dat paused. "I think so. John didn't give me many details."

After she cleaned up after supper, Katie left Mamm holding Baby Seth at the table and Paulina heating water on the stove for the little one's bath and headed upstairs.

Katie opened the bottom drawer of her bureau and took out the letters from Amos. She knew she'd left the packet tightly tied, but the string was loose now. She untied the string and opened the top envelope, the last letter from Amos. She always placed the letters back in the envelope the way Amos did—with the trifold showing. But now it was in backward.

KATIE WENT ABOUT HER CHORES, feeling unsettled, for the next three days. A couple of times, Mamm suggested she take a peach pie over for Ben.

"Why for Ben, Mamm?" Katie finally asked. "Why not for Amos?"

"Well, for all three of the Berger men," Mamm said.

Katie shook her head. "Paulina should make a pie for Ben."

"Nee," Mamm said. "Ben isn't interested in her." Mamm hesitated a moment and then said, "He's interested in you, Katie. He always has been."

"What have you done?"

"What do you mean?"

"Did you talk with Ben? Did you tell him Amos planned to go west?"

Mamm's face reddened.

"Why would you do that? Ben cared about Paulina," Katie said. "She would have had a good husband. Baby Seth—your grandson—would have had a good father."

Mamm crossed her arms. "I want you to be taken care of before—" She stopped.

Tears stung Katie's eyes. "Before?"

"I die."

"Is your death imminent?"

"I don't know the day or hour, none of us do. But I won't live to be old. I won't live to see you have a family if you don't start soon."

"Mamm . . ." Katie pursed her lips together. "That's no reason for you to try to manipulate Ben, and me, at Paulina's expense. You need to trust God."

"God gave you a mother for a reason," Mamm said. "It's my job to help you choose a husband."

"Nee, it's not. You've raised me. You've done your job. If you believe I'm behaving foolishly, tell me. But please stop manipulating people."

Mamm wrinkled her nose.

"In my bottom drawer are letters from Amos, ones that I carefully tied. He wrote about heading west, something you mentioned and said Ben had too. Did you read the letter and then tell Ben what Amos wrote?"

Mamm's eyes welled with tears. "I want you to have a husband, a home, a family. That's all."

"I already have a home and a family."

"Ach, but perhaps not for long," Mamm said.

"I'll trust God with that."

More tears flooded Mamm's eyes. "I was trying to help you."

"Well, you've only made things worse." Katie rubbed the side of her face. "I'm fond of Ben. He's a good man. But I don't want to marry him. I'll never want to marry him. I'd rather never marry." Katie started for the back door. "I'm going for a walk."

"Wear your bonnet," Mamm said. "The sun—"

Katie was already out the door, without her bonnet. She debated whether she should march over to the Bergers' place and confront Amos for not coming to see her yet but decided against it—for now.

Instead, she headed for the creek.

She ducked into the mill and sat on the cool stone. The rushing of the creek calmed her racing mind some. She took several deep breaths and then said a prayer. *Lord, help me to trust you. Help me to forgive Mamm. She means well, I know.*

If Mamm had still been taking the high dose of tonic that she had been previously, she most likely wouldn't have had the energy or motivation to snoop through Katie's drawers. But Katie still hadn't told her she'd watered down her tonic and then gotten Dr. Barker to change the formula. She should have. She'd been deceitful with Mamm, just as Mamm had been deceitful with her.

She wasn't sure what to do. *In all thy ways acknowledge him, and he shall direct thy paths.*

Lord, she prayed, *direct my path as clearly as Seth, Ben, Amos, and I wore the path along the creek*. She unclasped her hands and spread them wide.

She wanted to see Amos again, to make sure he was all right. And then she'd leave him alone.

Katie stood and left the mill, heading along the creek, taking the long way back to the house.

As she came around the bend in the creek, she saw someone standing at the edge of the water, staring up into the sky. Katie shaded her eyes. An eagle soared overhead and then drifted away, disappearing in the top of a tree.

Her eyes fell to the figure by the creek. The man turned toward her. At first, she thought he was old. His frame was thin, and he appeared frail. He turned away from her and started walking west.

Although his shoulders slumped, she recognized his walk.

"Amos!"

He kept going.

"Stop!"

He didn't.

Defeat swept through her, but it was quickly chased away by anger—her prayer quickly forgotten. She hurried after him, just as she had when they were children, picking up speed until she was running. He picked up his pace, not looking back once. She gained on him and just as she could almost reach out and grab him, she tripped on a root and went sprawling onto the path, her arms flying forward.

As she lifted her head, Amos turned. He paused a moment but then hurried back to her.

She met his eyes. They were sunken in, and his cheekbones were much more prominent than she remembered. "Why didn't you stop?"

He extended his hand toward her. "Are you hurt?"

She ignored him. She rolled to her side and then to a sitting position, her back toward him. She was covered with dust. She brushed her hands together.

He stepped around her until he was in front of her and offered his hand again.

This time she took it. From his pull to lift her to her feet, she could tell he was weak.

"What happened to you?" she asked as she brushed off her apron.

His face reddened.

"Are you ill?"

"I was," he answered. "I came down with the flu on the way home. Half the soldiers on the ship did."

Katie winced. "I read about that happening. I was worried about you."

"I know," he said. "I received your letters. I spent some time in the infirmary at Camp Meade and your letters caught up with me."

"Why did you make me run after you?"

He turned toward the creek. "I'm not going to stay home long."

"Let me guess—you'll be heading west soon."

He turned back toward her. "That's what you want, right?" His eyes flashed. "That's what you told Ben."

"I didn't tell Ben anything."

"How would he know if you didn't tell him? You're the only one I wrote that to."

"I didn't say anything to Ben. But my Mamm might have."

"You told your Mamm?"

She shook her head. "She read the letter. It was in my bottom drawer."

"You saved my letter?"

"Letters. I saved all of your letters."

"Oh."

"Why are you going to leave?"

He shrugged.

"Amos . . ."

His eyes grew watery, and then he pointed up the trail. "I should get back home."

Katie exhaled. Seeing him hadn't helped at all. She stepped aside and let him pass by, and then watched as he walked slowly, shuffling along. Her anger dissipated. Something had happened to Amos. He wasn't the man he had been just over a year ago. Not at all. Just like he'd said in his last letter.

She felt ill. In her heart, she knew he wouldn't be leaving anytime soon. He needed to recover first.

She thought of when John, Ben, and Amos had come for supper the last time Amos was home as she walked back to the house. There would be none of that this time. Everything had changed.

When she reached the house, Mamm was napping in the sickroom, Paulina was upstairs with the baby, and Dat was working in the barn. She sat down at Dat's desk. He had a stack of newspapers on top again. She knew he'd saved them for a reason.

There were ten or more. *World War Ends With Treaty of Versailles* from June 28 was the first one. She worked backward. The next was a paper from June 1 with the main headline *Einstein's Theory of General Relativity Tested.*

Next was from March 5. The main headline was *Communist International Founded*. Katie skimmed the article. The group resolved to "struggle by all available means, including armed force, for the overthrow of the international bourgeoisie . . ." That sounded like something Dat would be interested in following, but it was far away—in Russia.

The next paper was from February 8, and the main headline was about a general strike in Seattle, Washington, involving 65,000 workers. That number of laborers was hard to imagine. The next paper was from December 5, and the headline was *Wilson Leaves for Paris*.

The next-to-last newspaper, dated December 1, was folded to an inside story. The headline was *Meuse-Argonne Offensive Largest in US Military History*. She skimmed the article and then read it again. The battle began September 26, stretched along the entire Western Front, and didn't end until the Armistice on November 11, for a total of forty-seven days. It involved 1.2 million soldiers and resulted in 350,000 casualties, including 26,277 American lives lost and 28,000 German lives. The losses were worse because of the inexperience of the troops and because the Spanish flu spread through the trenches.

Something niggled at Katie's mind. Amos's next-to-last letter was dated September 26. Had he survived forty-seven days of battle? Were some of those Americans who died his friends? Was he responsible for some of those German deaths? She shivered. If any of that was true, then he went through that and then fell ill on the ship coming home—ill enough to end up in the infirmary.

Katie looked back at the article. One of the units mentioned in the article was the 52nd Infantry, the Ready Rifles. Dat had underlined the words. Was that Amos's unit?

The last newspaper was the one from November 11, the day the war ended.

Katie opened the side drawer of the desk, wondering if there were more newspapers or clippings. If so, they weren't in the side drawer. She opened the top drawer. There were several small newspaper clippings. She pulled them out. Each one was about the 6th Division, the 52nd Infantry, or the Ready Rifles. The articles dated back to early the previous summer. Dat *had* been tracking Amos.

Katie put the clippings in the drawer and sat for a moment, pondering what Amos had gone through. But what could she know for sure? She had no idea what he'd experienced except for the report of the number of deaths and injuries. But it had to have been horrid, whatever the details were.

She stood, filled a glass with water from the pitcher, and then headed out to the barn to speak with Dat.

He sat on a bale of hay, scratching the ears of a gray kitten.

As Katie approached, the kitten scampered away. She extended the glass to him. "I thought you might be thirsty."

"Denki." He took the glass and drained it in one long drink.

"I need to tell you something," Katie said.

"Oh?" He looked up at her and then patted the bale of hay. "Sit."

Katie did, and then said, "I watered down Mamm's tonic. Then I spoke with Dr. Barker and asked him to take most of the morphine out of the formula but leave the lithium salts."

Dat rubbed the back of his neck. "Morphine was in the tonic?"

"Jah," Katie said. "I started watering the tonic down in January and then by March it was the new formula and there was no longer much morphine in it. The doctor said morphine might be good for the heart, but he can't be certain. But the morphine made her drowsy and out of sorts. I deceived Mamm though. I never told her what I was doing."

"That's why she's been doing better?"

"Maybe."

"She's been irritable at times but not sleeping as much. And more of a help, jah?"

"Jah," Katie said.

"I need to think for a moment," Dat said. After a long pause, he said, "I will take responsibility for this. Do not tell your Mamm. I think it's best she doesn't know. You saw a problem and addressed it. Perhaps the lithium salts are mostly helping her."

"It seems so," Katie said.

"Let's leave it at that. Anything else?"

"Jah," Katie answered. "I went through your top desk drawer and saw the clippings about Amos's infantry division."

"You shouldn't go through my desk."

"I know." Katie hesitated a moment and then said, "I also went through your newspapers, the ones you've saved. I found the article about the battle, the one that lasted forty-seven days—"

"The Meuse-Argonne Offensive."

"Jah," Katie said. "It sounded horrible. I can't imagine what Amos went through."

Dat's voice was barely a whisper. "Nor can I."

"I saw him down at the creek just now." Katie blinked, doing her best not to cry. "He's frail and broken."

Dat turned toward Katie, his eyes full of concern. "I imagine he is."

"He says he does want to go out West," Katie said, "but he seems too weak. I doubt he'll even be able to help much on the farm."

"Give him some time," Dat said.

"I don't know if there is any time."

"You can't rush these things." Dat wiggled his fingers and the kitten darted back to his side. As Dat petted her, he said to Katie, "There's a thing called shell shock that some soldiers go through, believed to be caused by the relentless bombardments during the war. I read about it soon after the war began—an article in the newspaper quoted a medical journal. The symptoms include ringing ears, amnesia, headaches, dizziness, tremors, and a sensitivity to noise. Some call it mental shock."

"You think that's what Amos has?"

"Jah, from what John said, I do. And Amos is still recovering from the flu too."

"You told me to be a friend to him when he came home, but I don't know if that's possible. Not if he doesn't want me as a friend."

"Don't give up on him," Dat said. "Take a pie over. Write him a note. Do what you would have done before. But don't push him. Don't question him or corner him for any answers. He needs time to heal."

Before Amos had been carefree. And optimistic. They both had been. And when she'd worried about Mamm's health, he'd always treated her kindly, with understanding. Could she do the same for him?

Dat stood. "Katie?"

"I'll try," she said.

"That's all you can do."

CHAPTER 24

When Jane stopped the story, none of us urged her to keep telling it. I felt drained and wasn't sure I wanted to know how the story ended for Amos. Did he live long enough to go out West? War and the flu had taken a heavy toll on him. His was a sad story, for sure.

Danielle appeared as if she might cry. Amos's shell shock was a lot like her PTSD. Perhaps his story was resonating with her in a negative way.

Maggie stood and walked into the living room. I followed a few feet behind her. She stopped at the puzzle of the world and picked up a piece. Guessing she needed to be alone, I returned to the kitchen.

Danielle and I set the table, and then I pulled the pot roast from the oven. Just before it was time to eat, Joanna and Ted arrived. That made eight people for supper. I added two more place settings. Soon Maggie wandered back from the living room, and Kenan and Rich came into the kitchen.

Joanna stepped to Rich's side. She didn't touch him or really even say anything, but she leaned toward him and their arms touched. Rich's face relaxed. She tilted her head and whispered something, although I couldn't tell what it was.

Ted rubbed his eyes and said, "I'm sorry to hear about Aenti Regina."

"Denki," I said.

He didn't say anything more.

The mood was somber. Jane said what a privilege it was to be present. "Regina would have enjoyed this meal with all of you."

"Jah," I said. "She especially enjoyed the interactions around the table these last few days. She always longed for a houseful of Youngie, and she had that recently, more than ever before. It made her happy."

After supper, Kenan took Jane home. Then Joanna said she needed to get back to her *Gross* Mammi, but she'd return by the next evening. Ted rose to take her. Rich walked them outside with the lantern and then went back to work in the barn.

As Danielle and Maggie helped me clean up, Maggie said, "I'm going to start school."

"You are?" I glanced at Danielle.

She wrinkled her nose. "There's an opening at a private school in town. It's kind of an alternative school where the curriculum is tailored to what the students need, and the staff is pretty easygoing. She'll start next week."

I'd heard about that school and at one time had thought about applying for a job there. "How nice," I said to Maggie.

She shook her head and then in a serious voice said, "I don't want to go." She looked at Danielle.

"They said I can stay with you the first day, remember? And the next if you need me to. Until you've adjusted."

Maggie began to cry. Between sobs, she spit out, "Why did Regina have to die?" After another sob and a raggedy breath, Maggie gasped, "Why did Daddy have to die?"

Danielle sat down on a chair and pulled Maggie onto her lap. I sat down beside them. Once Maggie calmed down, she climbed off Danielle's lap and onto mine. My arms felt full, wrapped around the little girl.

I thought about asking Danielle if she and Maggie wanted to spend the night again but feared it was all too much for Maggie. Her grief was deep, and I didn't want to bring up more bad memories for her by having her in our house without Mamm.

"You two should go home," I said.

"We'll come back in the morning." Danielle stood. "We'll bring breakfast."

"Only if Maggie is doing all right," I said. "I don't want this to be too hard for her."

After they left, I finished cleaning the kitchen, put my nightgown on, and then climbed into Mamm's bed to read. After a while, I heard Rich come in from the barn and then go upstairs. I could hear the water running for his nightly shower. Then all was quiet.

Too quiet.

The next morning, Danielle and Maggie arrived at six-thirty with bacon, scrambled eggs, and French toast, all packed in an insulated bag and still hot. Maggie climbed up onto the couch and pulled Mamm's log cabin quilt over her head.

"Someone's grumpy." Danielle poured herself a cup of coffee.

I felt out of sorts too.

"How are you doing?" Danielle took a sip.

"All right," I answered. "Sad about losing Mamm . . ."

"What else?" Danielle asked.

"Oh, it doesn't matter now. I mean, I'm trying not to think past today, and then tomorrow, and then the service on Thursday."

Danielle gave me a little smile. "You're trying not to think about your future, right?"

"I'm at a loss as to what to do."

"You mean you don't want to stay here and cook for Rich?"

I smiled.

"You don't have to decide now." Danielle patted my shoulder with her free hand. "When do you plan to join the church?"

"I think I'll wait a year or so. Maybe I'll have a Rumschpringe after all."

"Really?"

"Not to run wild." I smiled. "That's not me. But to have a chance to do what I want to do."

"Like teach?"

I shrugged. "This sounds silly," I said, "but Kenan said there are road races. I'd like to train for one and run in it."

"Well, that is *running*. . . ." Danielle laughed.

I joined her. But then I said, "I can assure you I won't be running wild."

Rich came in from the barn, and we ate, although Maggie didn't join us. After Rich went back outside, Maggie shuffled to the table and ate while I started cleaning up.

A knock fell on the front door.

"I'll go get it," Maggie said.

"It's a crew to help us clean," I said to Danielle.

"I expected that. We'll get going."

"Will you come back later?"

She nodded. "We need to go into town to run some errands and do some shopping. We'll be back later this afternoon."

"Denki," I said.

The five women who Maggie led into the kitchen helped me clean the house from top to bottom. They stripped Mamm's bed, washed the linens, and aired the quilt. They swept and mopped and dusted and polished. They cleaned the refrigerator and stove and sink and counters. They cleaned out the woodstove and laid a fire. Then they worked outside, tidying up the garden and the flower beds, sweeping the walkways, porches, and ramp.

A handful of men helped Rich clean out the shop. The church wagon would arrive the next day to set up for Thursday. The community would bring food for a meal after the service, so we wouldn't have to worry about that either.

Maggie and Danielle returned an hour after everyone left and had supper with us—bean soup and biscuits that one of the women made. Before they left, Danielle asked Rich to help her rearrange the furniture in the front room to make room for Mamm's casket, saying I needed to rest my back.

The next day, in the midafternoon, the undertaker arrived with Mamm's body secure in the plain casket and put it on a stand that he provided in the front room, next to the puzzle of the world that Mamm didn't have a chance to finish. Perhaps Maggie would.

The next few hours were a blur as people came for the viewing. Ted came with his parents, Aenti Frannie and Onkel Wayne. Our aunt stayed near Rich and me, greeting people we didn't know. Some were distant cousins of Mamm's and friends from her childhood. I was surprised by the number of people. Of course David and Catherine came and the other ladies from Plain Patterns, including Savannah, along with her boyfriend, Tommy.

Danielle came without Maggie—Kenan had come by to watch her—at eight o'clock. She didn't wear her usual red lipstick and wore a modest skirt and blouse. She was subdued, and her face was pale. She stepped close to the casket and stared at Mamm for a long while. Danielle had been a big help with Mamm—but I think Mamm had helped Danielle too.

Before Danielle left, she whispered, "I'll be back in the morning. What time will the service start?"

"Eight-thirty."

Danielle smiled, just a little. "I'd forgotten how early Plain people start their life events. Weddings start at the same time, right?"

"Jah, but our eight-thirty is like everyone else's ten-thirty or eleven."

"That's true," Danielle said. "Besides, it's character building to get up early and be functional. I've got the getting-up-early part down—it's being functional that's hard for me."

I wasn't sure what to say. Was she feeling worse? Was it because of Mamm's death?

"See you in the morning." Danielle slipped out the front door.

The next morning, the women in our district took care of the food, and the men set up the benches in the shed and did the chores. As people arrived for the service, some of the younger men took care of the buggies and horses.

When Aenti Frannie and Onkel Wayne arrived, they appeared as stoic as ever, but Ted's eyes were rimmed with red, and he kept his head down.

Joanna arrived, followed by Danielle, Maggie, and Kenan. I was surprised Kenan took a day off work. He made his way to the men's side and disappeared from view. Jane walked by, along with Miriam. I guessed Derek, who Miriam would marry in a month, had Owen with him. Savannah and her grandmother, Dorothy, followed Jane and Miriam.

I could see the corner of the casket from where I sat. I had no idea what the preacher spoke about. He read several scriptures, but I couldn't seem to follow his words.

Finally, after the service was over, the pallbearers carried the casket out to a wagon, and then Rich and I climbed in a buggy and followed it to the cemetery, a mile away. Others followed behind us.

I choked back tears as the casket was lowered into the ground. Joanna stood next to Rich. For a moment, I felt painfully alone, but then Ted stepped to my side. He knew the pain of losing someone he loved.

Ted stayed next to me until the burial was over. "Denki," I said. "Are you coming back to the house?"

He pulled his hand down over his face. "Of course."

By the time we arrived, the benches had been turned into tables in the house, and the meal of casseroles, salads, and ham-and-cheese sandwiches on rolls was ready to serve. I didn't remember eating, but I must have. I wanted to sit with Danielle, Maggie, and Jane, but instead I thanked people for coming and said I appreciated their presence. It was all true—but I was overwhelmed.

Danielle stayed with me, along with Jane and Miriam and the other women, when it was all over. Maggie sat on her mother's lap, leaning against her chest. Danielle had her hands wrapped around her daughter. "I've forgotten how important it is to have a community at a time like this," Danielle said.

"Who helped you when Marc passed away?" I asked.

"Kenan." Danielle stared past me. "We had a small graveside service."

Jane waited a long moment and then said to Danielle, "Why don't you bring Tally by the shop in the morning for the rest of the story? That might be a needed escape."

Danielle focused on me. "What do you think?"

"I'd like that. It'll give me something to look forward to."

Maggie looked up at Danielle. "I'd like that too."

Soon after, Maggie started whining and asked if they could

go home. "In a little bit," Danielle said, a hint of annoyance in her voice.

"No, now." Maggie crossed her arms.

"You should go," I whispered to Danielle. "It's been a long day." Mamm's death and the service seemed to be wearing on both of them.

"All right." Danielle sighed. "I'll see you tomorrow."

The women in our district finished cleaning up the kitchen and storing the extra food in the refrigerator, and Rich told the men in the district they could go on home. "Kenan will help me with the chores," he said.

Joanna stayed in the house with me. As we sat at the kitchen table, drinking the last cups of coffee, she chattered away about her *Gross* Mammi. "She seems to be doing fine," Joanna said. "A neighbor is staying with her while I'm here. Rich is going to give me a ride home after he does the chores." She smiled. "He said he'd have supper with me."

I smiled back. That was fine with me.

Joanna gave me a furtive look.

"What is it?" I asked.

"Can I ask you a couple of questions?"

I tensed. The last thing I wanted to do was speak for my brother. "Have you asked Rich your questions?"

"I've tried."

When I didn't respond, she said, "It's just that he doesn't talk much. And when I talk, I'm not always sure if he's listening, although then he'll say something—just a few words—to let me know that he was."

"Jah," I said. "Rich has never been very expressive."

Joanna stayed surprisingly quiet. Finally, she said, "He seems kind. He is to me at least. Mammi Beth says that's what's most important. She said I'll have other women to talk with, but if he's not kind, he won't make a good husband."

"Jah, he's kind," I said. "Kind to people and animals both. Sometimes, because he's not aware of other people's emotions, it might seem he's not kind. But it's never intentional. Try talking with him about how you feel and see what his reaction is. See if he can learn to acknowledge your feelings when you tell him, even if he can't discern them."

"Denki." Joanna drank the last of her coffee and then said, "That's good advice."

A half hour later, Rich and Kenan pulled up to the house in the buggy. I went out with Joanna so I could tell Kenan thank you. Joanna jumped up in the buggy, and Rich called out, "Don't stay up for me."

I smiled. "I won't."

Kenan turned toward his truck.

"Thank you for all of your help," I said. "Would you like a cup of coffee before you leave? You could drink it on the porch. It's already made."

"If that's all right."

I nodded. We'd be on the porch. But it was still a bold move on my part.

"Sure," he said.

"Wait here," I instructed.

"I will," he answered. "After I get my coat out of my truck."

I placed cheese and crackers on a plate, along with a few snickerdoodle cookies that were left over from the meal, and then poured a cup of coffee for Kenan and grabbed my cup that was still half full.

After I placed everything on a tray, I put on my coat and carried it out to the porch. Kenan sat at the table, looking at his phone. He stood quickly, slipped the phone in his pocket, and held the door for me, all in one swift movement.

I put the tray on the table, and we both sat down.

"Danielle seemed quiet today," I said. "So did Maggie. I'm afraid the service brought up sad memories for them."

"I'll check on them on my way home." Kenan took a sip of coffee and then said, "I've been thinking about Marc a lot today too. After we pulled him down from the pole and the paramedics pronounced him dead, which we already knew, I drove to Danielle's house. She worked three days a week back then and was home with Maggie the day it happened. Danielle howled for hours after I told her. I finally called Dirk, and he came out and gave her something to calm her down, which was a mistake. Neither of us knew her history then."

I tilted my head.

"Jah," Kenan said. "She'd gone through rehab and everything before they moved here but didn't tell me. Dirk was her supervisor in a medical environment, and she failed to include the information on her application too."

"Oh."

"Anyway, I called my parents that night and begged them to come out. I told them Danielle needed them. That I needed them. That their granddaughter needed them. But they wouldn't. I haven't spoken to them since."

"I'm sorry."

"It's been really hard. I think Danielle saw your Mamm as a mother figure, and as a grandmother figure for Maggie."

"That's definitely how Mamm saw herself. Both Danielle and Maggie brought her a lot of joy."

Kenan picked up a cracker and held it between his fingers. "Isn't that the way life is? Something starts to look good and then—bam—everything changes again. The only thing permanent is change."

I probably hadn't experienced that as much as he had, even though now both my parents had passed away. I still lived in the community I was born into.

"I'm going to reach out to a Mennonite pastor here. Not Old Order but maybe my parents would listen to him," Kenan said. "I've heard he specializes in fostering reconciliation in families."

"Do you think your parents would be interested?"

Kenan shrugged. "I'm not sure. I'm going to meet with the pastor and see if I can get Danielle to go with me. If our parents don't want to reconcile, then I'll let it go and not bring it up again."

"I'm sorry," I said again. "Do you still suspect Danielle is using again, like you mentioned the other day?"

He grimaced. "I shouldn't have said anything."

I pressed him. "Do you?"

He shrugged. "Hopefully I was just being paranoid." He met my eyes and said, "I'm sorry. We buried your Mamm today, and I've been going on and on about my own family's problems. That's rude of me."

"No," I said. "It's fine. I want to know as much as you want to tell me. I care about Danielle and Maggie." I cared about Kenan too, but I wasn't going to say it out loud.

"Thank you," he said. "As much as Danielle frustrates me and as much as she's struggled with addiction, she's the most kindhearted person I know."

I tilted my head again. "You know what? She's one of the kindest people I know too." Jane was the other. "I've never had a friend like Danielle."

The conversation turned to farming. "I've enjoyed helping Rich," Kenan said. "I hadn't realized how much I like farm work. It was stressful with my father as a kid, but it's different with Rich. He makes it all about working with living things and shaping them into food."

"Are you considering a career change?" I teased.

He chuckled. "I don't think so." Then he grew serious. "How about you? What are your plans now?"

I stared off toward the road. "I'm not sure."

"Danielle said you would like to teach."

I turned my head toward the barn. "I don't know that I'm ready."

"What's holding you back?"

"Lack of experience." My eyes met Kenan's.

"How can you get experience without becoming a teacher?"

I smiled. "I worked as an aide when I was seventeen. And I've read a lot about teaching. But I've lost a lot of confidence in the last few years. I'm not sure I have what it takes."

"What do you mean you're not sure you have what it takes?"

"I'm quiet."

"I hadn't noticed."

I smiled.

"I had teachers who were gregarious and teachers who were quiet," Kenan said. "I don't think that really had any bearing on whether they were good teachers or not."

I shrugged, and we both grew quiet.

"Well," Kenan said finally, "you need time to mourn your Mamm. Don't feel as if you need to make any decisions now."

"I'd need to join the church before I taught, anyway. I haven't even taken the class yet."

"Really?" His eyebrows shot up. "I just assumed you'd joined the church."

I shook my head.

"Interesting." His dark eyes met mine and held my gaze.

I leaned back in my chair. When he didn't say anything, I asked, "What is it?"

"Oh." He smiled a little. "Sorry, was I being intense?"

Maybe not intense—but whatever it was, I liked it. It was if he was looking into my soul.

"I think I was being intense. Danielle says it's freaky when I do that." He smiled again. "I was just thinking . . ."

I held my breath, waiting.

He continued, "I was thinking that there's always hope. Too often we expect the worse or fear things won't work out. But they always do. God never stops working."

Tears stung my eyes. I hoped he was right.

He finished his coffee and then said, "I better go check on Danielle and Maggie." He held the door for me so I could carry the tray into the house, and then, through the screen, told me good-bye.

I sliced up an apple and ate it alongside the rest of the crackers and cheese for my supper. Then I put on my nightclothes and climbed into Mamm's bed again and read the rest of *Heidi*. Nature was important in the story—the mountain air, the hiking, sledding, and tending the goats—but the relationships were truly restorative. Heidi changed Grandfather, Peter, his grandmother, and Clara—pretty much everyone she came in contact with. Danielle was that way too, and yet she had her own challenges and struggles and sorrows.

I must have fallen asleep before Rich returned home. I slept heavily, so much so that when I awoke in the morning, I forgot for a minute where I was. But then I remembered. And I remembered that Mamm was gone.

Danielle was late picking me up to head to Plain Patterns, and I began to fear the worst. Had she had a hard time sleeping?

Did she take too many pills? Had she started taking something else?

I could see why Kenan was in over his head trying to help Danielle. It could make a person start feeling a little crazy.

I walked to the road, glancing toward Danielle's place and toward town. I could see her SUV coming down the road. What had she been doing?

I stepped to the side as she pulled into the driveway. As I opened the passenger door, she asked, "Ready?"

"Jah." I climbed in and then looked into the back seat at Maggie. "Hallo," I said. "How are you?"

She gave me a thumbs-up, but she didn't look very enthusiastic. "We had to go to the store." She yawned. "Mama woke me early."

Danielle looked into the rearview mirror. "Take a little nap on the way to Jane's."

Maggie yawned again but didn't close her eyes.

Danielle seemed to be acting normally. She was alert. Her driving was fine. She looked in the rearview mirror more than necessary, but perhaps she was only being cautious.

By the time we reached Plain Patterns, Maggie had fallen asleep. Danielle unbuckled her and carried her in, while I followed around the side of the shop to the back, up the ramp that I knew Jane's brother had built just for Mamm. We entered through the back door. Jane sat at her desk with her reading glasses on, pecking away on an old-fashioned typewriter.

"Hallo." She turned toward us as she kept typing. "I'm just finishing up my column for the hundred-year anniversary of the 1918 Armistice." She hit a few more keys and then stopped. "That's all for now." She stood. "Aww, Maggie's asleep." Jane's blue eyes twinkled. "She's such a sweet thing."

Danielle smiled. "She is."

Jane pointed toward the little kitchen counter. "I made an apple crisp for us. I'll dish up."

Danielle sat down with her coat on and Maggie still in her arms. I took my coat off and picked up a needle, ready to quilt.

"Tally," Jane said, "you just enjoy your crisp and the story. Quilt if you'd prefer, but don't feel as if you need to."

I put the needle back into the fabric and went to help Jane serve the crisp. As I walked back to the frame, I noticed her *Gross* Mammi Katie's quilt on the other frame. Jane had put a new binding around it. "You're making good progress," I said.

"Slowly but surely," Jane said.

I stepped closer to it. "Just think. These squares were made from Katie and her Mamm's scraps, from dresses they wore and shirts her Dat and Seth wore too."

"I think about that every day," Jane said.

The squares of fabric were fragile on their own. One would think material that was a hundred years old would have frayed long ago. But here, all sewn together, the fabric lasted decades longer than the original garments ever would have. There was strength in the pattern they'd become.

I put Danielle's crisp on the seat beside her, on her right side so she could eat it while she held Maggie.

"I remember where I left off on Monday." Jane pulled her notebook from her pocket. "Amos had come home, still weak from having the flu and shaken from the war."

"That's right," I said. "Amos was shell shocked."

Danielle pulled Maggie closer. "Today he'd be diagnosed with PTSD."

"Jah," Jane said. "During and after World War Two, it was called combat stress reaction."

"And during Vietnam I don't think they called it anything at all," Danielle said wryly. "I think they just blamed the soldiers."

"I remember those days," Jane said. "I've heard there was a lot of self-medicating going on by the US soldiers who served in Vietnam. A lot of drug use, proportionate to their level of despair."

"I've heard that too," Danielle said.

"Anyway . . ." Jane took a bite of the crisp, chewed it, and swallowed. "Those were difficult times after the first World War and at the end of the flu pandemic for Katie as she worried about those she loved. As far as Amos, she tried to take her Dat's advice not to question him or corner him. She could only hope, in time, that he would heal."

CHAPTER 25

Katie

The early September day was warm and sticky with no hint of fall in the air as Katie walked to the mailbox, even though her days of hoping for a letter from Amos were long over. It seemed so odd that when he'd been halfway across the world, she'd felt closer to him than now, when he lived next door. Life hadn't turned out at all as she would have thought a couple of years ago. Jah, Mamm was sickly, but the rest of life had seemed predictable. Even when Amos left as a CO, she'd figured he'd soon be home and then life would resume its natural course.

But everything had changed. And she didn't feel as if she'd done a very good job of adapting. In fact, a restlessness she'd never felt before stalked her.

After she pulled Dat's newspaper from the day before—September 4th—out of the box, she read it, as was her habit now. The main headline was *President Wilson Makes Indianapolis Stop on Train Tour*. The president was on a monthlong tour of the United States, from Washington, DC, to San Diego,

California. He'd stopped in Indianapolis the day before, at the Indiana State Fair on Big Thursday. His blue train car was called *Mayflower*, and he was promoting the League of Nations, hoping for a peaceful future for the world.

President Wilson certainly got around. He'd spent six months of the year so far in Europe, and now he was traveling to the far corners of the United States.

She skimmed the rest of the front page. Farm prices had fallen even more, and a farmer in Jackson Township had lost his farm to the bank. How horrible.

She raised her head. Someone was whistling.

Amos was walking up the road. His gait was slow, but he held his head higher than the last time she'd seen him.

"Hallo, Katie." He took off his Englisch hat and wiped sweat from his brow. His blond hair had grown out.

"Hallo." She squinted up at him. "Have you come from town?"

He nodded. "I took the train to Indianapolis yesterday morning. I had some business with the Army about my discharge."

She held up the newspaper. "Did you see the president?"

"I did, at the Coliseum last night. He believes if we don't work with European nations to create the League of Nations, there will be another war within a generation."

Katie exhaled. That was hard to imagine. Hadn't the Great War been the war to end all wars? Wasn't that what had been promised? "Do you blame the president?"

"For?"

Katie felt her face grow even warmer, and she guessed it was growing red.

His voice had an edge to it. "For what I went through?"

She nodded.

"No, I only blame myself. President Wilson had a hard decision to make. If we hadn't fought, the war would most likely still be going on. More would have died. I've heard, as it was, forty million died from injuries and disease."

Katie couldn't imagine that number of people.

"I don't envy the decisions a leader has to make," Amos said. "If only the whole world was nonresistant . . . but the truth is, I grew up with the teaching and still didn't embrace it. I can't expect others to live by it." He smiled a little. "Even though we'd all be better off."

Katie agreed. She was encouraged he was talking to her. Hoping he'd continue, she asked, "How was it to travel again?"

"Better than I thought it would be," he said. "I'm slow but am able to walk a distance now. It gives me hope I can travel much farther next time." He tipped his hat and then said, "I'd better get on home."

Tears stung her eyes as he walked away. He'd gone south to Indianapolis—and he'd come back. Next time, he would go west. And then he'd be gone for good.

She felt as if she'd been kicked in the stomach. Maybe things would be better after Amos left. Maybe both of them could get on with their lives, although she had no idea how hers would change. There wasn't anyone she wanted to court. She'd spend her days caring for Mamm, and then for Dat, when he was old. Eventually, she'd need to hire someone to run the farm. She would need to somehow knot the unraveling threads of her life.

Instead of going to the house, she went to the shed, where Dat was working on the thresher. "President Wilson was in Indianapolis yesterday evening."

"I heard he was going to be."

"Amos went."

"Really?"

"Jah. He just passed by, coming from town. He took the train back this morning."

"Is he feeling better?"

"He said he's getting his strength back." She handed Dat the newspaper. "You talked about him being shell shocked. What caused it?"

"The machine guns, grenades, artillery, poisonous gas, warplanes, zeppelins, tanks. Bombs dropping from the sky. The constant bombardment, along with the fear of being hit. Most likely for Amos, and most other soldiers too, he also feared killing others."

Katie said, "It's hard to imagine forty-seven straight days of fighting."

"Jah, God didn't create man to live that way. Living in trenches filled with mud and water and worse. Fighting, both at a distance and hand to hand. Nee. He created us to love our neighbors—not kill them." Dat held the newspaper against his chest. "Of those who survived, many have missing limbs. Others have lungs ruined by the gas. Others have lost their minds. Many would say Amos was fortunate, but the war took a toll on him too. However, we know God's love is a healing balm. Jesus *is* the great physician of the mind, the spirit, and the body."

Katie remembered Dat's words as she walked to the house. She'd been taught her entire life that Jesus was the great physician. But whom He chose to heal—and whom He chose not to—was a great mystery to her. Mamm had survived the flu. Seth had not. Mamm would most likely die soon of her bad heart.

Would the Lord heal Amos of his wounded heart?

TOWARD THE END OF SEPTEMBER, President Wilson's train tour abruptly ended after he fell ill in Colorado, and he and his entourage returned to Washington, DC. There were rumors that he'd had a stroke, but nothing was confirmed. Dat speculated that the flu had left him in poor health and more susceptible to further illness.

October arrived. The days grew cooler, the leaves fell, and Paulina started talking about going to Ohio to stay with a childless, elderly aunt and uncle. "I feel as if I'm languishing," she told Katie one morning as she walked out to the chicken coop, the baby on her hip. "I think it would be easier for all of you if I figure out something else."

"Nee," Katie said. "We all want you here."

"I know your Mamm and Dat like having Baby Seth here, but I don't want to be a bother."

"You're not," Katie said. "Please don't think about leaving. Your home is here."

Paulina's eyes filled with tears. "I need a husband, and I may never find one here."

Katie opened the gate. "Give it time. The Lord has a plan for you." If only Mamm hadn't meddled by talking to Ben, he and Paulina might have been married by now. She grew clammy, remembering she had meddled too. On Christmas Day she'd asked Ben to wait to court Paulina because she, selfishly, wanted time with the baby before Paulina left their home. What if Katie hadn't meddled either? She'd been as bad as Mamm.

Feeling convicted, Katie explained her part in it and apologized to Paulina. "I wanted Ben to court you. I just didn't want him to take you away too soon."

Paulina stayed quiet for a long moment and then said, "I forgive you." Then she sighed and said, "I doubt it's the Lord's will that I marry Ben."

Katie wished with all of her heart it was. What would be better than to have Paulina and Baby Seth so close? Paulina was a sister to her. Baby Seth was her joy. The thought of them going to Ohio made her feel ill.

In mid-October, Katie went into town and bought two more bottles of the lithium salts for Mamm from Dr. Barker. This time he didn't add any morphine. Then she went to Hartman Brothers to buy sugar and the backing for her quilt. She chose a solid blue that matched the calico border. She'd been working on the same quilt for over two years, and she hoped to finish it soon.

As she walked back out to the buggy, she saw Ben dart around the corner. She called out his name and then hurried after him. He stepped into an alley.

"Ben Berger!"

When he didn't appear, she followed him into the alley. He stood a few feet in front of her.

She marched up to him. "Stop avoiding me."

His hat was pulled down low on his forehead. He exhaled slowly.

"How are you doing?" she asked.

"Fine."

"How's your Dat?"

"Fine. I told him he needs to look harder for a wife since neither I nor Amos have any hopes of finding one."

Katie ignored him. "How is Amos?"

He rolled his eyes. "Not so fine."

"What do you mean?"

"He yells during the night. Kicks the wall. It's as if he's possessed."

"Or having nightmares."

"You've probably noticed he hasn't gone to church once since he's been home."

Katie had but she wasn't going to admit it to Ben. "I've

noticed you at church, but you've been aloof and avoiding me and everyone else."

He shrugged. "The sooner he leaves, the better."

"You can't mean that."

"I absolutely mean it. And I tell him that every day."

"Ben, what's happened to you?"

"Amos never should have come home. He especially never should have written to you."

"What do you know about that?"

"I found some letters you sent him."

Katie's face grew warm.

"How many letters did you send?"

She shrugged. "A few."

"I found twenty-three."

That was more than she would have guessed.

"And to think at one time I thought you were interested in me."

Katie raised her head and met Ben's gaze. She could hardly understand her feelings toward Amos, let alone explain them to Ben. But that wasn't his business anyway. "My Mamm never should have interfered as far as Paulina. And I shouldn't have asked you last Christmas to wait to court—"

"Stop." Ben exhaled again. "I won't talk about this."

Katie wanted to grab his shoulders and shake him, but instead she walked away without saying good-bye. She'd lost her entire childhood—all of her friends. Seth was dead. Ben was angry with her. Amos would soon leave. So would Paulina. Mamm would die. She'd never felt so alone in her entire life.

The next day, as Katie walked to the mailbox in the drizzling rain, she caught sight of a second person in the field with Dat. *Seth*. No, of course it wasn't. She stepped to the fence and lowered the hood of her cape. Why was Amos helping Dat plow the field when the Bergers had so much work of their own?

She squinted. Amos looked as if he'd gained some weight from the last time she she'd seen him, and he appeared stronger. He was handling the horses while Dat picked up stones.

Katie kept walking. Now she dreaded what she might find at the mailbox—like a letter from Paulina's aunt and uncle, asking her to come. There was a newspaper for Dat, but that was all.

That evening, after she'd cleaned the kitchen and sat down to finish stitching the border on her quilt, she asked Dat, "Why was Amos helping you today?"

"I hired him," Dat said. "He wants to make some extra money, and I can't keep up with everything on my own."

"Why does he want extra money?"

"It seems there are some debts as far as the farm that he wants to pay off. He's worried about the falling crop prices, what that could mean for next year."

"Oh." Katie guessed he was saving money to move out West too.

A WEEK LATER, Mamm had gone to bed early and Paulina was putting the baby to bed as Katie knotted the last stitch after securing the calico border to the quilt. It was time to get ready to do the actual quilting. She laid the blue backing on the front-room floor and then layered the batting—made from carded wool—on top of it. Next, she placed the quilt top on both. As she pinned the three layers together, she heard a knock at the back door. Dat was at the kitchen table, reading the paper, so she didn't rise to answer it. Most likely it was a deacon on church business.

Dat said, "Gut'n Owed."

A deep voice asked, "Vyt, do you have a minute?"

Katie froze. It was Amos.

"Jah," Dat said. "Sit down at the table with me. How about a piece of peach pie?"

Katie had made the pie that afternoon, using peaches she'd canned in August.

"Denki," Amos said.

"I think there's some coffee left too," Dat said. "It might be a little strong."

"I prefer it strong," Amos said.

They were quiet for a moment. Katie wasn't sure what to do as she listened to the clatter of dishes. If she stayed, she'd be eavesdropping. If she went upstairs, she'd be interfering with the baby's bedtime routine.

She could go ahead and start basting the layers of the quilt, but she was afraid Dat and Amos would hear her moving around and think she was eavesdropping, which she would be. She stayed put.

More dishes clanked and then chairs moved. Finally, it seemed they sat down.

"I need your advice. . . . Or maybe I just need to talk with someone."

"Either way," Dat responded, "I'm listening."

Amos's voice was low. "I can't decide if I should join the church. . . ."

Katie sat up straight.

His voice rose in volume a little. "Or leave altogether."

Her shoulders slumped.

"I feel like a broken wagon. Or more like the broken wheel, split down the middle and impossible to repair, on the broken wagon. I'm not as strong as I was, but I'm definitely doing better than when I first arrived. Most of the fall work is done.

I paid off the debts for the seed with the money I'd saved from the Army and the money I earned as a hired hand, so the farm is in good shape now."

It sounded as if he'd been working for more farmers than just Dat.

"I'm not sure Ben can keep up with the farm work, but I'm hoping if I leave, he'll get more help from the community. I don't feel as if anyone wants to come around the farm with me staying at the house."

That made Katie sad.

"Nor do I feel as if anyone wants me to stay."

Dat spoke. "We want you to stay."

"Who do you mean, exactly, when you say 'we'?" Amos asked.

Dat cleared his throat. "I should speak for myself. I want you to stay."

Tears stung Katie's eyes. Did she want Amos to stay? She'd thought it would be easier for both of them if he left, but what was easier for her shouldn't matter. She knew God's plan for Amos wasn't based on what was easiest for her. That wasn't the way God worked.

"Katie!" Paulina yelled from the stairs. "Could you help me for a minute?"

Katie hurried to the stairs, stepping as lightly as she could. Once she was halfway up the stairs, she called out, "Jah. On my way." Katie hoped it would sound to Dat and Amos as if she were upstairs and not listening to their conversation.

The words *broken wheel* jarred in her head as Katie hurried down the hall to help Paulina. Poor Amos.

Over the next two weeks, Katie worked on her quilt, which was now stretched over the frame in the front room, pushing her needle through the three layers over and over, whenever she had a spare minute. Paulina and Mamm helped when they could, with Baby Seth crawling under the frame.

Now, instead of hoping for a letter from Amos, she looked for Amos on the way to the mailbox—both in the fields and on the road, mulling over and over if she should talk with him. She played over possible scenarios in her mind.

What if she told him she was finally ready to talk about *us*? Even though she was two years too late? She'd been so sure he would be too changed by being a soldier for them to ever marry, even if he joined the church. Had she thought he'd be damaged goods? Now that she saw him wounded but working to get stronger, she felt differently. But could she tell him that?

Would he care if she did?

A few times, she saw him in the distance on the Berger property but not in Dat's fields and never on the road. One time, when she reached the mailbox, she turned toward the Berger farm and started walking. But she only made it halfway before she changed her mind. If Amos was with Ben or John, what would she say?

Several times, she walked along the creek, hoping Amos would be down there alone. But he never was.

On the second Tuesday of November, the first anniversary of the Armistice, Katie walked to the mailbox in the afternoon. The day was overcast and cool, but it wasn't raining. When she reached the road, she glanced toward town. A buggy she didn't recognize was headed that way. Just ahead of it was Amos, with a pack on his back.

Her heart raced. He was leaving without saying good-bye.

As she debated what to do—yell? run after him?—Amos turned and waved at whoever was in the buggy. It stopped when it reached him, and he climbed in.

The sound of a wagon coming from the direction of the

Bergers' place caught Katie's attention. Ben waved and then yelled, "Have you seen Amos?"

Katie pointed toward town. When Ben reached her, she said, "He just climbed into a buggy."

"He's leaving," Ben said. "I saw a note in his room that he didn't intend for us to find until later."

"Did you tell your Dat?"

Ben shook his head. "As much as I don't want to, I'm going to go get Amos and force him to come back. We need his help."

"But you wanted him to leave." Katie's voice shook. "You told him that every day."

"Well, jah, I thought I wanted him to leave. But I didn't think he would actually do it." Ben pursed his lips and snapped the reins. He took off without saying good-bye.

Katie didn't waste a minute watching the wagon roll down the road. She grabbed Dat's newspaper out of the mailbox and began running toward the barn. When she reached it, Dat looked up from his workbench, alarmed. "Is your mother all right?"

She caught her breath. "Jah."

"The baby and Paulina?"

She nodded. "I need the buggy to go into town." She started toward the tack room. "Why didn't you tell Amos to stay that night he came to talk with you?"

"Because he has to make that decision."

"Well, he did. He's leaving. He's headed to town right now."

"Katie . . ."

She grabbed the harness. "I need to go tell him good-bye, that's all." She was willing to trust the Lord with Amos—but she wasn't willing to let him go without telling him farewell. No matter his future and her future, Amos meant too much to her for that to happen.

"Of course you do," Dat said. "I'll help you harness the horse."

The ride into town seemed to take forever. She pushed the horse as fast as she could but didn't catch up with Ben or the buggy. Both had too much of a head start. She feared her effort was in vain.

When she reached the train station, she spotted Ben in his wagon, ready to leave. She yelled for him to wait and pulled up behind him. After setting the brake, she jumped down.

"You're too late," he said. "Amos won't listen to me. He's stubborn as ever."

Katie spun around. She needed to see him. She needed to tell him how she felt about him. That she loved him. She started for the station as a whistle blew. A plume of smoke rose, and the engine began to roll. Katie hurried to the end of the station. The train clacked on by.

She was too late.

She turned back toward Ben.

Still in the wagon, he lowered his head as she marched toward him.

"Did you listen to him?" Katie's voice was loud, louder than it should have been. "Did you ask what he went through over there?"

"He brought this on himself."

Katie winced. She hadn't done anything more than Ben had. She hadn't sought Amos out. She didn't make him feel like he belonged. Dat had told her to be a good friend to Amos, but she hadn't been. Instead, she'd been angry with him because of her own pain. How could she have been such a fool?

"He was obligated to help us after what he did." Ben placed his palms on his thighs. "He ruined everything. You obviously still care about him, regardless of what he's done."

"Of course I care about him," she said. "I always have. He may not care for me but—" Her voice broke. "But I didn't show him that I cared. I'm so sorry I didn't."

"Did you hope to leave with him?" Ben asked.

"He never asked me to," Katie answered. If he had? The way she felt now, she would have gone with him. Her heart sank. Except she wouldn't have. She needed to care for Mamm.

She reached up and touched Ben's hand. "I'm sorry. This has been hard on you too. It's been hard on all of us."

"You're right. And I've been a fool too. A self-righteous one. To both Amos and Paulina."

Katie drew her hand back. "It's not too late, as far as Paulina."

Ben exhaled slowly and then looked beyond Katie. She turned. Amos stood behind her. He hadn't been on the departing train.

Another train whistle blew, and Amos disappeared into the station.

"Amos!" she called out. "At least let me say good-bye!" She ran after him into the lobby of the station, scrambling around a couple with three children, and then out to the platform. Without turning back toward her, Amos bounded up the steps of the train, boarding the passenger car. The whistle blew again.

She watched him take his seat through the window. He buried his head in his hands. The train whistle blew again.

Amos was leaving.

She turned back toward the station and stumbled through the lobby, gasping for air. When she reached the street, Ben's wagon was gone.

Lord, she prayed, *give me strength*. Life hadn't turned out the way she'd hoped, but she couldn't give in to despair. When she reached her buggy, she leaned against it, inhaling deeply.

"Katie!"

She turned.

Amos ran toward her.

Katie stood straight and stepped toward him. When he reached her, she said the line she'd rehearsed, whispering, "I'm ready to talk about us."

Amos took both her hands in his. "I've been waiting years to hear you say that, Katie Landis."

He helped her onto the seat of the buggy and then climbed up beside her. She snapped the reins as he said, "Let's go home."

CHAPTER 26

Tally

I relished the end of the story as Maggie, who had woken up once Jane had started, jumped off her chair and said rather loudly, "So they did get married?"

Jane slipped her notebook into her pocket. "Jah, they did." She patted the chair beside her. "Come sit by me."

Maggie hurried to her side, and Jane put her arm around the girl, speaking directly to her. "Amos joined the church the following spring and then they married the next autumn. Amos moved into the Landis home. Katie's love, along with the help of John and Vyt and eventually Ben and Paulina and others in their congregation, brought healing. Serving others, especially Katie and their children, further strengthened Amos. He helped both his Dat and Vyt farm, so he and Ben essentially kept both farms going, guiding them through the farm depression of the 1920s."

"I know about the Great Depression in the 1930s," Danielle said. "But what happened to farms in the 1920s?"

Jane answered, "From 1919 to 1920, corn tumbled from one

dollar and thirty cents per bushel to forty-seven cents, causing huge losses for farmers. Also, the Amish, with their horses and wagons, were competing with Englisch farmers' tractors and threshing machines for the first time."

I asked the obvious. "But both the Landis and Berger farms survived?"

"Jah," Jane said. "Lots of farmers throughout the entire country lost their farms during the 1920s—the Great Depression started early for them—but not the Landis and Berger families. By the time the early 1930s began, both farms were stable, although times were definitely hard until World War II started, causing a need for an increase in farm production again."

I jumped to my next question. "Were Ben and Paulina my great-great-grandparents?"

"Jah," Jane said. "Their grandson was Frank Berger, your grandfather."

"Who sold the farm to Onkel Wayne, long before I was born?"

"Jah, Frank sold the farm to Wayne," Jane said. "Then it became the Glick Farm."

"Glick," Danielle repeated. "Is that Ted's last name?"

I nodded.

"Will he inherit it?"

"I have no idea." I glanced at Jane.

"Ted may still join the church. Time will tell."

I couldn't imagine it, but I guessed Jane had seen crazier things in her lifetime. If not, I guessed one of his older sisters and her husband would end up with the farm.

"How much longer did the flu pandemic last?" Danielle asked.

"Until the spring of 1920. The troops coming home from

Europe brought a second wave with them, causing more death and heartache. The symptoms and effects were horrid, along with the mortality rate."

"What about President Wilson? Did he recover from his stroke?" I'd read a lot of presidential biographies but not one about him yet. I'd have to see if there was one at the library.

"No," Jane said. "He didn't recover. He did have a stroke and was bedridden and incapacitated for the rest of his presidency. His wife, Edith, acted as Wilson's proxy for the duration of his presidency, which was over in a year."

Jane went on to say that it was believed, according to his doctor, that President Wilson did become infected with influenza in April 1919 in France and it weakened him so much that he was unable to negotiate all that he wanted as far as the Treaty of Versailles.

"Some believe he suffered neurological damage from the flu," Jane said, "and that most likely contributed to his later stroke. Ironically," she added, "as Vyt pointed out, the president didn't mention the flu pandemic in public during his entire presidency. Either way, his failure to talk about the horror of the pandemic or mourn with those who mourned seemed to be politically motivated."

"How many people in the US died from the flu?" Danielle asked.

Jane took out her notebook. "I have the stats in here somewhere," she said as she flipped through the pages. "Here it is. From 1918 to 1920, over 675,000 people died in the United States and fifty million worldwide. One-third of the world population became infected with it. The US military lost more troops to disease—63,000 soldiers—than to combat, which killed 53,000 soldiers." Jane closed the notebook. "Katie had always been gifted with caring for others, from the time she was a girl bandaging Amos's wounds to caring for her mother to nursing those ill with the flu. She continued, throughout her life, to care for her family and neighbors when they fell ill."

I appreciated that about Katie. She knew she was good at nursing others and she did it. She was also good at loving Amos, and once she figured things out, she went after him without knowing how he'd respond. She took a chance.

Was I good at teaching? Was I willing to pursue it with passion?

Jane closed her notebook and then addressed Maggie again. "Would you like to see Katie's house and the old mill?"

"Jah," Maggie said.

Jane glanced at Danielle. "Would that be all right?"

"I'd like that."

"Do you feel up to it, Tally?" Jane asked me.

"Jah," I answered. "I do." The story had taken my mind off Mamm. More time with Jane, Danielle, and Maggie probably would too.

JANE LED THE WAY OUT the back doorway of the quilt shop and along the side deck to the back and along the garden that still needed to be put to bed. Then she led the way down to the creek, toward the old mill. "We won't go inside," she said. "Andy—my brother—does his best to keep it safe, but I'm not sure if he has any repair projects going on or not."

The mill was two stories high and painted white.

"It's a grist mill," Jane said. "My great-great-great grandfather, Judah Landis, built it before the Civil War. Judah dammed the creek and dug raceways to move the water to the mill and then back away from it. It hasn't been in use in over a century. Andy has talked about tearing it down but hasn't been able to bring himself to do it."

Jane led the way down a narrow path to the mill, where we peered through an opening in the side. "There are two quartz stones that used to crush the wheat. Andy did remove the wheel that was on the creek side years ago because it was rotting. There were locks that directed the water over the wheel."

I found it all fascinating, partly because I didn't realize how close the two farms were when I was growing up. We were never allowed to play by the creek when we were little, and by the time we were old enough to, Melinda was ill and I stayed up at the house with her.

Danielle yawned, likely not because she was bored but because she didn't sleep well. Jane stepped back up to the main path and pointed east. "There's a trail that goes up to the house in about a hundred yards."

"Is this the trail Katie and Amos ran along when they were children?" Maggie asked.

Jane nodded. "And Seth and Ben too." When they reached the trail, Jane directed Maggie to lead the way as she said, "The house is where Katie lived with her Mamm, Dat, and Seth. Katie and Amos had nine children, including my father, Andrew. My brother was named after him. I grew up in the house until Andy built the *Dawdi Haus* where I live. It's where I first opened Plain Patterns. Then Andy built the current quilt shop for me a few years ago."

"You've had Plain Patterns for a while," I said.

"Nearly ten years."

"Any plans to retire?"

She chuckled. "Funny you should ask. Maybe not retire, but maybe change things up a little. I've felt a little restless."

I knew that feeling.

"I'd like to travel," she said. "Do more research. But I'm not sure yet." She smiled at me. "Which means I need to wait on the Lord and see how He leads."

It felt as if Jane's words weren't just for her but for me too.

Soon we reached a lawn with pavers partially sunk into the ground. Maggie leaped from paver to paver, and the three of us followed. Ahead was a large two-story white house. Along the back was a screened porch. "Go to the back door," Jane called to Maggie.

Maggie stopped on the steps of the porch, waiting until we caught up. Then Jane opened the back door and stepped inside. "Andy? Rhonda?"

"Hallo, Jane!" a man's voice called out.

"I have friends with me." Jane motioned for us to follow her. "I wanted to show them the house."

As we stepped through the screened porch, which had a sofa and a few rocking chairs, and into the kitchen, a man with a long gray beard and a balding head met us. "Willkomm," he said.

Jane spoke to us, saying, "This is my brother Andy. Andy, you know Tally."

"Jah." He gave me a sympathetic look. "I'm sorry about your Mamm."

"Denki," I responded.

Jane gave me a caring smile and then said, "And this is Danielle and her daughter, Maggie."

"Pleased to meet you," Andy said.

"Likewise," Danielle answered as she nudged Maggie.

Maggie spoke quietly. "Pleased to meet you too."

"Do you mind if I show them around?" Jane asked.

"Go ahead. I'm the only one here. I'll stay out of your way."

I glanced around the kitchen. Obviously, with its maple cabinets and stone countertops, it was nothing like it would have been in 1917, but the wood floors were most likely the same, and the oak kitchen table looked to be at least a hundred years old. I could imagine Amos sitting at the table, speaking with Vyt, while Katie eavesdropped from the front room.

I pointed to the far side of the kitchen. "Is that the sickroom?"

"Jah," Jane said. "But it's used as a pantry now." She turned and we followed her through the kitchen and into the front room. It was larger than I had imagined, with bookcases on either side of the fireplace at the end of the room and a large window that overlooked the porch. I glanced through it, imagining Katie and Amos slipping away in the dark toward the road. Then I thought of Katie's quilt spread out on the floor as she pinned the layers together before quilting it. I shivered.

Jane pointed toward the other end of the room. "Let's go upstairs," Jane said. The staircase was open and made of oak.

Maggie led the way again, up to the landing, where she stopped. Jane pointed to the first door. "This was *Gross* Dawdi Vyt's room when I was little." She opened the door. Inside was an old bed with a red-and-white bear's paw quilt with a black border spread over the top.

"Who made the quilt?" I asked.

"Mammi Katie," Jane answered. "For *Gross* Dawdi Vyt's eightieth birthday, which means the quilt was made in 1945 and is . . ." She raised her eyebrows. "Over seventy years old."

"It's beautiful."

Jane stepped to the bed and placed her hand on the quilt. "Mammi Katie did good work."

We went on down the hallway to the next room. "This was Katie's room as a child." It had two single beds with simple patchwork quilts. "Paulina stayed in here with her. As I researched her story, there were things I remembered that Mammi Katie had told me years ago, such as that a friend of hers lived with the family for a while before they both married. I didn't realize until now that her friend was my great-aunt Paulina."

"Do you remember Paulina and Ben?" I asked.

"Jah." Jane led the way back into the hall. "I remember both of them well. Once Paulina and Ben married, she and Baby Seth moved into the Berger home, and she took care of John as he aged. Paulina and Ben had five more children, including your great-grandfather, Tally. They were always close with Mammi Katie and Dawdi Amos. Katie and Paulina remained as close as sisters."

"So, tell me how you and Joanna are related?" Danielle asked.

"Joanna and I aren't really related. Beth is Joanna's step-grandmother and my first cousin. Beth's mother, Martha, was my aunt, Katie and Amos's oldest daughter, which is why she inherited the quilt, most likely. And then it was passed down to Beth, who is insisting that I keep it now."

It warmed my heart that Jane would own the quilt her Mammi Katie had made.

When we reached the first floor again, Jane stepped back onto the porch and told Andy good-bye and then she led us out the front door.

"I'm looking forward to tomorrow," Jane said to Danielle.

"What's tomorrow?"

"Harvesting the corn. Derek will help the men, and Miriam and I will both bring food."

"Oh yeah." Danielle smiled. "Thank you. I'm looking forward to it too."

As we headed back to Plain Patterns, Danielle fell quiet again. Maggie had been unusually quiet too.

"Are you two all right?" I asked.

Maggie yawned. "I'm not tired."

I laughed and then said, "Danielle?"

She kept walking.

"Danielle?"

She stopped. "What?"

"Are you all right?"

She nodded. "I'm fine."

I wasn't so sure.

CHAPTER 27

On the way home, Danielle seemed distracted. She passed a tandem bike with an older Amish couple on it, and then came up on a semi too fast. I gasped and managed to say, "Truck!"

She slammed on the brakes. "Sorry."

I glanced in the back seat to see if Maggie was doing okay. Her eyes were droopy, and she didn't seem to register what had happened. When I glanced back again, she was asleep.

"What did you think of the rest of Jane's story?" I asked.

Danielle shrugged.

I didn't say any more.

She turned toward town instead of toward home. "Where are we going?" I asked.

"I need to pick up something."

"Danielle," I said, "what's going on?"

"Nothing," she said. "I need to stop by a friend's place. And then I'll get you home." Her usually expressive tone was flat.

The closer we came to town, the more suspicious I became. Is this what Kenan had meant when he said he noticed changes in Danielle when she started using? Or was I being overly suspicious too?

When we arrived in town, she turned off Main Street and then after a few blocks pulled into the driveway of a two-story house.

"I'll be right back." Danielle put the SUV in Park, grabbed her purse, jumped down, and strode up to the house.

A middle-aged woman came to the door, and Danielle stepped inside. Maggie slept soundly. Not sure what I was looking for, I opened the glove box. There was a vehicle manual, a vinyl folder, and a pen.

With frequent glances to the porch in front of me, I opened the console between the seats. There was a bottle of Tylenol and a hairbrush. I didn't open the bottle. I didn't know enough to tell if what was inside was Tylenol or something else.

I opened the bottom part of the console. There was an empty prescription bottle without a label on the front.

The door of the house closed, and Danielle started down the steps. I closed the console.

Danielle didn't have anything in her hand, but she could have easily put something in her purse. Her step seemed a little lighter. She climbed in the SUV and said, "Ready?"

I nodded.

She didn't say anything more, but as we neared my house, I said, "I'd like to go home with you and Maggie."

"What?"

"I want to go to your house."

"Why?"

"Because I'm concerned."

Danielle paused and then asked, "About?"

"About you. And Maggie."

She kept driving, staring straight ahead. "Why are you concerned?"

"I'm not sure," I said. "I just know I need to go home with you."

"I told you I wasn't getting anything from Dirk."

"I believe you," I said. "But you could be getting something else—like from the woman at the house you just stopped at. I need to make sure you and Maggie are safe."

She didn't respond, but she did drive past our farm without stopping.

When we reached Danielle's house, I unhooked Maggie, who was still asleep, from her booster seat and then carried her into the house after Danielle unlocked the door. "You can put her down in her room." Danielle closed the door. "She'll probably wake up soon, but maybe not."

After I came back into the living room, I offered to make lunch.

"How long are you going to stay?" Danielle asked.

"As long as I'm needed."

"We got home safely," she said. "You're not needed."

"Did you take something?" I asked.

"Just one." She paused. "Okay, two. I took two."

"Two what?"

"Pain pills."

"And then you drove."

"I'm fine," she said. "Besides, what should I have done? Asked you to drive?"

I ignored her, heading toward the kitchen as I asked, "How about a sandwich?" When she didn't answer, I kept going and opened the fridge, pulling out sliced turkey, a block of cheese, and a head of lettuce. A loaf of bread was on the counter.

I made two sandwiches, placed them on plates, and carried them out to the table. Danielle was on the couch, curled up.

She said, "That story of Jane's was really hard to take today."

I thought it had been uplifting but didn't say so. "In what way?" I asked.

"Amos. The way he talked about being broken—like a broken wheel. I totally get that. Every day, I feel as if another piece of me breaks. But then Amos was all right. It was as if all of a sudden, things were perfect."

"Jane didn't say things were perfect. She said the healing was gradual for Amos and that he and Katie gained strength by helping others."

"Well, that's more than I'll ever have. Maybe if Marc hadn't died . . ."

I didn't respond. I took an afghan from the back of the rocking chair and put it over the top of her, tucking it in around her neck, the way I had for Mamm. She met my eyes but didn't smile.

I sat down beside her. "What do you need?"

She exhaled and then muttered, "To confess."

I waited for her to speak again.

"I've been lying to everyone," Danielle said. "I did stop using, I promise. Dirk brought me sleeping aids, that was all. But for the last few days, I've been getting pills from that house in town." She leaned against the back of the couch. "I haven't been taking a lot, just a couple in the afternoon when Maggie's resting or playing. That's all. It just takes the edge off. Helps me get through the rest of the day."

"Did you take any when you were at my house, after Mamm passed?"

"No."

I turned toward her, tucking my foot underneath me. "What made the difference?"

"Being around other people. My mind doesn't go crazy."

"What does your mind do if you don't take them?"

"What I already told you."

I leaned toward her. "What made you start taking them again?"

"Grief." Tears filled her eyes.

I reached out and touched Danielle's arm. "Tell me more."

"It was a dream come true to befriend you and your Mamm. To go to Plain Patterns with you. I felt a sense of belonging. Of community. This sounds so selfish. . . ."

"No, it doesn't. Go on."

"You lost your mother. I only lost someone I'd just met. I feel ridiculous." She wiped a tear away. "But it was after she died that I searched for the pills. The feeling of belonging when we stayed with you had been so strong—and then to have your Mamm die like that did me in." She brushed away a tear. "And here I am, a hot mess again."

"You lost more than someone you just met," I said. "You'd already lost your family. Then your sense of safety while you were in the Army. And then your husband. You've had loss after loss. It's no wonder my Mamm's death affected you the way it did."

Danielle put her head in her hands. "It wasn't just the grief of your Mamm. I just lied again." She let out a raggedy breath. "I've been using the last few weeks, not just since your Mamm passed. Dirk did bring me the sleeping aids, but that's not what put me to sleep. It was the combination of the two."

I steadied myself, trying not to react. She'd lied. I felt betrayed. But now she was telling the truth . . . at least I hoped she was. I managed to say, "You need support."

"I was hoping you and your Mamm and Plain Patterns would be the support I needed."

I shook my head. "I can be your friend. So can Jane. But we're not qualified to help you." I squeezed her arm. "I read about a counseling service in Goshen that's organized to help Plain people."

Danielle groaned and pulled away from me. "I've tried therapy a few times. And I'm not Plain anymore."

"Still, a therapist there might help you figure out things other therapists couldn't. They would understand your family dynamics better."

Danielle shook her head. "You sound like Kenan. Stop worrying. I'll be fine." She pulled away from me, yawned, and closed her eyes. Clearly our conversation was over.

I returned to the kitchen and called Kenan's number on the landline, leaving him a voicemail. "I'm at Danielle's. We need you to stop by as soon as possible."

Then I stepped to the dining room window. I needed to let Rich know where I was at some point, but I didn't want to leave Danielle and Maggie alone. I sat down at the table and started eating my sandwich.

"Tally?" Maggie stood bleary-eyed in the middle of the living room. She turned and pointed toward Danielle. "Is Mama sick again?"

"She's sleeping," I answered.

Maggie began to cry and headed for her room under the staircase. I followed her, but she pulled the door closed behind her.

I kneeled. "Maggie?"

"Go away," she said.

"Come get me if you need me." I retreated back to the table, not sure what else to do.

Danielle stirred and lifted her head. She muttered, "Is Maggie okay?"

I shook my head. "She's crying."

"Because of me?"

"Jah."

Danielle leaned her head against the back of the couch. "Will you help me?"

"Jah, I'll help any way I can." I thought of Kenan's frustration in helping Danielle. I had no reason to think that my helping her would be any easier, but maybe the two of us together could do more than he could alone.

Maggie began to cry loudly.

Danielle moaned.

I returned to the door to the little room. "Maggie," I said, "come out now if you'd like. Or you can wait until Uncle Kenan comes. He should be here soon to help us sort everything out."

"Why is Kenan coming?" Danielle asked.

I ignored her, sitting down beside the little door, my back to the wall.

Maggie stayed silent.

We stayed like that for a half hour until Kenan opened the door and called out, "Where is everyone?"

"Uncle!" Maggie tumbled out of the staircase room and hurried past me.

Danielle scowled and then grabbed a pillow off the couch and buried her face in it.

Maggie bounded toward Kenan and into his arms. When he stepped into the living room, he asked, "What's going on?" over Maggie's head.

"We need to talk." I nodded toward Danielle. "The three of us."

Kenan lowered Maggie to the floor and then said, "Do you want to go play in your room under the staircase?"

She shook her head. "I just came out of there."

"Would you make me a sandwich?" he asked. "I'm going to talk with your mama and Tally for a little while."

Maggie didn't seem happy to be sent to the kitchen, but then she said, "I'll make one for me too. I've been practicing."

Kenan gave her a fist bump.

I sat next to Danielle, and Kenan pulled the rocking chair closer to the couch. "What's going on?" he asked again.

Danielle glanced at me and then back at Kenan. "I've been using some, just to take the edge off. I'll quit now—I promise."

He leaned forward in his chair. "I suspected you were. The rehab in Elkhart has added an outpatient clinic. We should give them a call right now."

"I really don't think I need rehab," she said. "Tally knows. You know. I'll quit. And Tally mentioned a counseling center in Goshen. I can do that."

"Danielle," I said, "I think counseling would be good, but it's not set up for addiction recovery. You'd need to do both."

Kenan jumped in. "You're doing this for Maggie, remember? You promised if you used again—even a single pill—you would go back."

Tears flooded Danielle's eyes. "Who will take care of Maggie?" she asked. "While I'm gone during the day? I don't have daycare like I did before."

"I'll take care of her," I blurted out. "I told you I would help, remember? Just a while ago."

Danielle swiped at her tears. "That's too much to ask of you."

"You're not asking," I said. "I'm offering."

Danielle didn't respond for a long moment but finally said, "If you're sure."

"Absolutely," I answered. "And she'll be going to school soon too."

"Let's call right now," Kenan said. "And see when you can start. And then we'll look into the counseling center."

Danielle shook her head. "Let me think a minute."

Instead of responding, Kenan stepped to the window. I registered the sound of tires on the gravel of Danielle's driveway. Kenan looked worried. "It's a sheriff's car."

"Oh no," Danielle said.

"What do they want?" I asked. But I knew. Someone had most likely been watching the house in town.

Kenan said, "I'll go talk to him."

As Kenan closed the front door behind him, Maggie came out from the kitchen, carrying two sandwiches on big dinner plates, holding them as even as she could. But one of them tipped and the sandwich began to slide.

"Watch it!" Danielle yelled, which scared Maggie. She yanked the plate, causing the sandwich to fall onto the floor.

"Maggie!" Danielle yelled again. "What are you doing?"

Maggie jerked her head up, and the other sandwich fell off the other plate.

"Let me help." I hurried to her side and scooped up both of the sandwiches. Then I looked her in the eye and said, "Let's go in the kitchen and sort this out. Maybe all we need is new slices of bread."

Maggie's lower lip jutted out.

"It's all right," I said. "Accidents happen."

As I helped Maggie in the kitchen, the front door opened and closed and Kenan said, "Danielle, this is Officer Pitt. This is my sister Danielle Roman."

"Ma'am," the officer said.

I couldn't hear Danielle's response, but I could hear the officer say, "You were seen buying illegal opioids this morning, which is a serious charge."

There was a pause, and then Kenan asked, "Where's Tally?"

"In the kitchen with Maggie," Danielle answered.

The officer must have stepped closer to Danielle and lowered his voice because I couldn't hear any more of what was said.

I threw away the slices of bread that landed on the floor, and Maggie started spreading mustard on the fresh slices. Kenan stepped into the kitchen and said, "Tally, the officer has some questions for you. I'll stay in here with Maggie."

I washed my hands, which were shaking a little. After wiping them on a dish towel, I went into the living room and sat next to Danielle. The officer, who was still standing, introduced himself and then said, "Were you with Mrs. Roman today?"

"Jah," I answered.

"We had a report today of a white SUV outside a residence where the occupant was selling opioids. Did you visit a house on Maple Street at approximately 11:45 this morning with Mrs. Roman?"

"She stayed in the car," Danielle said quickly.

"Is that correct?" the officer asked.

"Jah," I answered.

"Kenan!" Danielle shouted. "Would you come here?"

"What about Maggie?"

"She needs to hear what I'm going to say too."

I'd read enough mysteries to ask, "Do you need a lawyer?"

She exhaled sharply. "I have one. But I don't want to call him, not yet. Right now, I just need Kenan."

He came into the room and said, "Tally is absolutely not involved in any of this."

"She stayed in the car," Danielle said. "She had no idea what I was doing."

After a few more questions, Kenan pulled out his phone and showed that he'd called the rehab center while in the kitchen. "Danielle has an appointment for Monday morning. The receptionist said she thought there would be an opening within the week."

"That's good to know." The officer jotted something down in a small notebook and then said, "The lead detective is willing to give you immunity if you agree to testify against the woman selling the opioids."

Danielle grimaced.

"But even if you agree to testify and are granted immunity, we'll still need to notify the Department of Child Services," Officer Pitt added.

My heart sank at the seriousness of the charge, but it made sense. Danielle had purchased illegal drugs and used them while Maggie was in her care.

Danielle clutched her stomach. Her frantic gaze landed on Kenan. "I've really messed up, haven't I?"

"We'll get through this." He glanced at Maggie, who frowned and headed back to the kitchen.

"Of course I'll testify against the woman." Danielle leaned forward and spoke quietly. "I'll do whatever I need to."

Kenan cleared his throat. "Danielle has been through rehab before. She got addicted to opioids after being badly injured in Iraq. Then her husband was killed a few years ago."

"The anniversary of Marc's death was three weeks ago. I took it hard," Danielle added. She explained about not being able to sleep and then Mamm having a stroke. She paused a moment and then said, "And then Tally's mother just passed away. I took that hard too."

"I see." Officer Pitt jotted a few more things down in his notebook and then asked, "Are you taking any other illegal substances? Or any other medications that haven't been prescribed?"

She shook her head. "I had some sleeping aids, but I took all of them."

"Who prescribed them?"

"Dr. Johnson. He works at Bremen Hospital."

After writing in the notebook again, Officer Pitt slipped it into his pocket. "I'll be in touch. The detective on the case will be too. And expect a call from DCS. Continue pursuing rehab, but be prepared for court-ordered therapy too."

Danielle stood and extended her hand. "Thank you."

Officer Pitt shook her hand and said, "I agree with your brother. I believe you'll get through this."

After the officer left, Maggie came back into the room and crawled into Danielle's lap.

Kenan looked over at me. "I have the rest of the day off. I'll stay here with Danielle and Maggie and spend the night."

Danielle didn't protest.

"I'll go ahead and go home, then," I said.

Kenan said, "I'll walk you out."

I turned toward Danielle. "The guys can do the harvest tomorrow without the rest of us coming. You don't have to host us."

She shook her head. "I want to. Let's stick with our plan. I don't think anything will happen by then."

"I'll be over by eight." I took my coat down from the peg by the door. "I'll bring rolls and leftovers from yesterday."

"Thank you," Danielle said.

Maggie, who'd been so quiet, smiled. "That will be fun."

I smiled, said good-bye, and then headed out the door, with Kenan following. He walked down the steps with me. Then he asked, "I'm so sorry you've been pulled into all of this."

"I'm fine," I answered. "I'll see you tomorrow."

Kenan met my gaze and held it as intensely as he had on the porch. I met his gaze and held it until I felt as if I might cry. Then I quickly turned away and started to walk home. Instead of turning to the left, though, I turned right and started running, not waiting for the backstretch. It all felt like too much. Mamm dying. Danielle using again. I ran hard and fast. I cried for Mamm. And for Danielle. I cried for myself and the uncertainty ahead of me. Then I ran faster, and as I ran, I felt stronger.

I'd done the right thing today, even though it was hard.

Being Danielle's friend wasn't always easy, but it was making me a better person. In some odd way, I felt as if I was finding myself, my voice, my own story.

When I reached home, as I headed toward the ramp, Rich came out the back door. "Where have you been?"

"Over at Danielle's. Then I went for a—" I hesitated. "A run."

He shook his head a little.

I asked, "Will it still work to harvest Danielle's corn tomorrow?"

"Jah." He scratched the back of his neck. "Ted is going to help. And David."

"Jane said Derek will too. And Jane and Miriam will bring food." I met my brother's eyes. "Denki. I really appreciate your help."

Rich shrugged and continued on toward the barn.

I spent Friday evening making dinner rolls for the next day. We had an abundance of cold cuts I planned to take for sandwiches, and three salads that needed to be eaten.

Again, at bedtime, I climbed into Mamm's bed. Before I fell asleep, I read the rest of *Heidi*. Of course it had a happy ending—Clara and Heidi were to be lifelong friends. Clara's father had promised to care for Heidi once Grandfather couldn't. Heidi had greatly enhanced Clara's life, and Clara and her family had improved Heidi's life too. More importantly, genuine relationships had grown and flourished.

I hoped the same would be true for Danielle and me.

Danielle had helped me find myself, much as Heidi helped Clara find her strength. But I knew I'd helped Danielle too. That was the way God worked. He brought us together, no matter how broken, for a reason.

CHAPTER 28

The next morning, I was up at my usual time—long before dawn. I quickly did my chores, scrambled eggs, served breakfast, cleaned up, and then packed up the buggy, including our two folding tables and eight folding chairs. Rich already had the workhorses hitched to the binder, and he started over ahead of me.

When I arrived, Jane and Miriam were unpacking their buggy while Derek held Owen. A few minutes later, Ted's car pulled in, and Joanna climbed out of the passenger seat, laughing. Then Ted climbed out. He was laughing too.

I glanced toward the binder. Kenan had the gate to the field open, and Rich was driving the horses through. He hadn't seen Ted and Joanna sharing an amusing moment. I cautioned myself not to read anything into it—and I realized then how much I hoped Joanna and Rich's relationship worked out.

Danielle, who had her red lipstick back on, stepped out on the porch, followed by Maggie. Owen started wiggling, and once Derek put him down, the little boy ran to Maggie. Savannah and her boyfriend, Tommy, arrived next. As Tommy headed to the field, Savannah headed to the house, carrying a pan of sticky rolls. A diamond on her finger sparkled.

"What is that?" Danielle squealed.

"What?" Savannah teased.

Danielle laughed. "That *ring* on your finger."

Savannah held up her left hand as she held the pan with her right. "Exactly what it looks like." She beamed. I'd always really liked Savannah, which made me all the happier for her. Tommy grew up Amish, and Savannah stayed with her grandmother during the summers while she was growing up. Now they both attended a Mennonite church—not Old Order like the one Danielle and Kenan grew up in, but a more progressive church. They were making their life together work. I also liked that they'd taken so long before deciding to marry. They'd been friends and then dated for quite a while. By now, they knew each other well.

Bishop David showed up next, after I'd completely unloaded my buggy. He waved and headed toward where the other buggies were parked.

Once I was in the house, I could see Danielle had dark circles under her eyes. When we were in the kitchen alone, I asked how she was doing. "Tired," she answered. "Mortified."

"Please don't be mortified."

"You shouldn't have to know about all of my—" She stopped as Joanna came into the kitchen.

"What can I do?" she asked.

"You can set up the tables and chairs out in the yard," I said. "I'll get a pot of coffee started to go with the snack."

Once Joanna left, I said, "Danielle, I'm your friend. I need you to accept what I can do for you, just as I accepted all you did for Mamm and have done for me—and will continue to do. Jesus called us to serve one another."

"He did." Then she reached over and touched my arm. "Denki." She lowered her voice and said, "A lady from the Department of Child Services called last night. She wants to schedule a home visit next week to see what Maggie's current living situation is. Kenan has offered to move in with us while I'm in rehab, and I mentioned to her that you are my neighbor and have agreed to help watch Maggie too. Will you come over for the home visit?"

"Of course," I said.

Danielle's shoulders relaxed. "Denki. The lady sounded encouraging once I explained I have an appointment for rehab. She said Child Services will work to keep Maggie with me as long as she is safe and I am getting the help I need, which I'm certain will include weekly drug tests."

I exhaled in relief. "That all sounds hopeful." I agreed with Kenan and Officer Pitt. I believed Danielle would successfully navigate her current situation too.

The rest of the day went like any other Amish workday, except that we had more Englischers among us than usual. By noon, the men only had a couple more hours of work. They took time off to wash up and then sit down to eat. We had soup, sandwiches, and salads, along with peach pies that Jane had made for dessert. Danielle spoke at the end of lunch, thanking everyone for their help. "I just wish Regina was here with us," she said.

I gave her a grateful smile.

Later, as we cleaned up the kitchen, Savannah told Danielle about the church she attended. "I'd love to have you visit with us sometime," Savannah said.

"I'll think about it," Danielle answered.

Once we finished, Maggie and Owen played on the lawn while Savannah and Miriam sat on the steps and chatted. Jane and Danielle sat on the porch with me.

Danielle said, "It was hard for me to hear the rest of Katie and Amos's story, but I need to thank you. It helped me through a rough day yesterday." She went on to tell Jane a little of what happened. "I'll start rehab again, hopefully by next week."

Jane reached over and patted her hand. "You're doing the right thing."

"I know," Danielle said. "With Kenan and Tally's help, plus motivation from Maggie. I'd *never* make it on my own."

"None of us would," Jane said.

"Sadly, I know I've already scarred Maggie."

Jane gave Danielle a tender look. "Every family has patterns," Jane said, "that are passed through generations. Amos's shell shock affected his children. Of course your PTSD and addiction has affected Maggie. No one gets through life without some kind of trauma. But you're doing your best to make a healthy life for her. Trust the Lord for healing, for you and for Maggie. But don't expect perfection out of yourself. That's not a possibility for any of us."

"Denki." Then Danielle said, "Tally has the name of a counseling center in Goshen. I think getting therapy for me, along with family therapy with Maggie, from someone who understands my Plain background might help."

"Good idea," Jane said.

I wished Mamm and I had that sort of resource when I was young. Perhaps that would have helped her come out of her dark places.

The gathering wound down gradually. Tommy and Savannah left first to go check on her grandmother.

Next, David left. Then Jane, Miriam, and Derek, leaving Danielle, Maggie, and me on the porch. Joanna was at the fence, watching Kenan, Rich, and Ted finish the work.

A blue pickup turned into the driveway.

Maggie, who was playing with her yo-yo on the lawn, turned toward Danielle. "What's Dirk doing here?"

"I don't know." Danielle stood.

He climbed out of his pickup. "Hi, Mags."

She waved and kept playing.

He started toward the porch. When he saw me, he said, "Tally, I was sorry to hear about your mother."

"Thank you," I answered.

Danielle took a step toward him. "What's up?"

He motioned toward his pickup. "Could I speak with you for a moment, in private?"

"Do you mind speaking in front of Tally? And Maggie?" Danielle glanced back toward me. "I don't want it to seem as if I'm keeping any secrets."

"Sure." He shoved his hands in the pockets of his jacket. "I had a visit from an Officer Pitt this morning. He had a few questions about the sleeping aids I prescribed."

"I should have texted you—"

"No. It's fine. But I have a confession to make. The pills I brought you weren't prescription pills."

"What?"

"It was a supplement. I was trying to see if something homeopathic might help. I didn't know you were using at the time or what reaction the combination of the two might cause."

"Isn't that illegal?" Danielle asked. "To give me something other than what you indicated you would?"

He raised his eyebrows. "I told you I would bring you something to help you sleep. I never said what it was."

Danielle shook her head.

"I'm sorry," he said. "I should have been honest with you. I showed the officer the bottle of supplements and explained to him that there wasn't an actual script written. He seemed to believe me."

"So, he won't report you to the medical board?"

"There's nothing to report." He sighed. "Anyway, I'm sorry. I promise I will be transparent with you if you ask for my help again."

Danielle crossed her arms. "Whatever you gave me did help."

"The supplement might have helped—or maybe it had a psychological effect." He took a bottle from his pocket. "Either way, here's more of the supplements in the original bottle. It's an herb. Totally natural. But check with your primary doctor if you decide to continue taking it."

Danielle took the bottle. "Thank you."

"See you around." Dirk patted Maggie on the head as he walked by, and she glanced up at him with a grin.

I was relieved Dirk hadn't brought Danielle sleeping pills when he knew she'd had an addiction problem, and I couldn't help but think of how Katie weaned her Mamm off the large dose of morphine from the doctor. Sometimes people needed *less* help, as both Katie and Dirk had done, not more.

"Danielle!" Kenan was jogging toward us. "What did Dirk want?"

"Nothing. He wanted to explain something to me," she said. "I'll tell you later."

As Rich drove the binder through the gate Kenan had opened, Joanna walked with Ted toward his car. I feared she'd leave with him. But she didn't. First of all, because he didn't leave. After tossing his sweatshirt in his car, he walked toward the porch. And second of all, because Joanna walked toward Rich. She climbed up on the binder beside him. With a rare grin, Rich called out to me, "See you at the house."

I invited Danielle, Maggie, Kenan, and Ted over for supper. "We have lots of leftovers," I said. "Turkey and ham and mashed potatoes."

"Sounds great," Kenan said. "Do we have time for a walk first?" He grinned. "I know of a loop."

I smiled.

"What do you think, Danielle?" Kenan asked.

"Sure," she said. "A walk sounds like a good idea." She turned to Ted. "Want to come with us?"

He gave her his impish grin. "I told Rich I'd help him with the chores, but he probably won't mind if I take my time."

By the time we were on the back side of the loop, Maggie had grown tired. Ted hoisted her onto his back and then began to run. The rest of us began to run with him, with Kenan staying at my side.

I wasn't sure exactly what I wanted, but I was going to figure it out. Starting with my Rumschpringe. No, I wasn't going to run wild. But I was going to start seriously running.

But for now, I'd concentrate on helping Danielle with Maggie, getting them both through the time of rehab ahead of them as a family. After that, I'd see what God had for me.

I thought of Jane's words along the banks of the creek, that she needed to wait on the Lord and see how He would lead her. I thought of Katie too. Life hadn't turned out the way she'd expected it to, but it had turned out beautifully just the same.

Like Jane—and Katie—I felt restless. But I was also confident that God would provide.

ON MONDAY MORNING, Danielle, Maggie, and I went to Maggie's new school. After Danielle completed the paperwork, she explained to the head teacher that she had a medical appointment she needed to go to. "Can Tally stay with Maggie for the day?"

"That's fine." The woman was middle-aged and seemed kind. She turned her attention to Maggie. "We're so glad you're here. I'll walk with you and Tally to your class."

I was sold on the school right away. In some ways, it was similar to an Amish school with its mixed-age groups in the classrooms and hands-on work. Maggie's class had five-, six-, and seven-year-olds, a dedicated teacher, and jobs for the students to do, such as wiping down the tables before and after lunch and cleaning up after themselves.

But in other ways it was very different. Before lunch, the children played a math game using marbles. After lunch, while the teacher read to them, they all knitted, even the boys. Maggie didn't know how, but I was able to quietly teach her while the teacher read *Pippi Longstocking*, another book I loved as a child—and still did.

At the end of the day, Maggie's teacher mentioned the head teacher was looking to hire a part-time aide to float among the classrooms. "Do you know of anyone who would be interested?"

"Actually," I answered, "I do."

EPILOGUE

Jane

October 18, 2019

Nearly a year later, just after three on a Friday afternoon, Jane put out a platter of chocolate chip cookies on a table in the middle of the quilting circle. For now, she'd put away the frame.

Miriam called out from the front room of Plain Patterns. "Savannah just turned into the parking lot. She has Dorothy and Wanda with her. And here comes Catherine. Joanna is riding with her."

There was a long pause and then Miriam added, "My Mamm is here, with Ruby."

Jane headed toward the front room. Miriam still stood at the window, Owen on her hip. "What about Tally?" Jane asked.

Miriam pointed. "There's Danielle's SUV. I'm guessing Tally is with her."

"Maggie?" Owen asked.

Miriam gave him a squeeze. "She's here too."

That was everyone Jane expected.

Owen wiggled down from Miriam's arms and yelled, "Maggie's here!"

"Use your inside voice," Miriam chided.

A few minutes later, the three children, with Maggie in charge, played in the corner while the women gathered around the table.

Savannah now had a wedding ring on her finger. She and Tommy had married a month ago, in an outdoor ceremony on her grandmother's farm.

Catherine spoke first. "I have good news."

Savannah's eyes lit up. "Oh?"

"Sophie is expecting a baby. She's past the first trimester. She told me to ask all of you to pray."

Jane's hand flew to her chest.

"Of course we'll pray" Tally said.

"Absolutely," Savannah added.

Sophie and her sweetheart, Jasper, had married six months earlier. Sophie had lupus and Jane knew she wondered if she'd be able to have children at all. Catherine wouldn't usually mention a pregnancy this early, even though it was past the first trimester. Jane guessed Catherine was more worried about Sophie and the little one than she let on.

"How many grandchildren will this be for you?" Tally asked Catherine.

"Nineteen." Catherine beamed. "I have a special calendar just to keep track of the birthdays." Most Amish grandmothers had some sort of system. Some had nearly a hundred grandchildren and great-grandchildren. Some had great-great-grandchildren.

"How was the marathon?" Savannah asked Tally.

She smiled. "Did you notice I'm limping?"

Savannah shook her head.

Tally grinned. "I finished it in just under four hours."

"Wow!" Savannah's eyebrows shot up. "That's great! How about Kenan? How did he do?"

"Worse than he should have," Tally answered. "He stayed with me the whole time." She leaned back against her chair.. "And we waded in Lake Michigan after the race, even though it was chilly by the time I finished."

"What did you wear?" Joanna asked.

Tally glanced down at her cape dress and apron. "Not this."

They all laughed.

"I wore running pants with a long lightweight jacket," Tally said. "I didn't look quite like the other women in the race, but I didn't exactly stand out either."

"Where else, besides Chicago, do you plan to travel?" Jane asked.

Tally smiled. "The Grand Canyon is definitely still on my list. Maybe next spring." She glanced at Danielle. "Right?"

Danielle nodded.

Joanna sighed. "That sounds like so much fun." Running a household had been a struggle for her the last few months.

"How's the cooking coming along?" Miriam asked Joanna.

"Well, I haven't poisoned Rich yet, so that's good."

They all laughed.

Rich and Joanna had married last May. Jane glanced toward Tally, wondering whether she would join the church or not. The young woman was hard to figure out sometimes. Jah, she was quiet, but there seemed to be a lot going on in her head—and in her life.

Tally worked part-time at Maggie's school and had been living in her own apartment in town for the last six months. Jane knew she spent quite a bit of time with Kenan, who seemed to be a worthy young man. She didn't know if they were serious or not, or even actually dating or courting or whatever they would call it. What she did know was that Tally had come into her own over the last year. She was a confident young woman now.

Danielle had also grown. She testified against the woman selling opioids in town, which broke up that operation. And she finished her addiction treatment last April, fulfilled the requirements of Child Services around the same time, and then started her individual therapy and family counseling with Maggie in Goshen. She also started a program in Elkhart to become a phlebotomist. Kenan had lived with Danielle and Maggie for the last year, but Jane had heard he planned to move out.

After a pause, Danielle said, "I have a job interview on Monday for a position at the Red Cross." Danielle smiled. "It will be part-time, so I can drop Maggie off at school and pick her up, just like I've been doing."

"Wunderbar," Jane said.

"And of course, Tally is still at the school. That's what made this all work for Maggie." Danielle leaned her head toward Tally, who sat on the other side of her. "I don't know what I would have done this last year without you—without all of you."

Jane smiled. "That's a perfect transition into what I have planned for today. I have a quilt for you, Danielle." She stood and walked to the cabinet next to the doorway and pulled out the mosaic quilt that Katie Landis Berger had made. "I finally finished repairing this a few months ago, but for the last year I knew this quilt was meant for you."

Jane stepped toward Danielle, through the circle, and placed the quilt on her lap.

Danielle shook her head. "I can't take it. It's a family heirloom."

Jane simply smiled and said, "Our family has a plethora of heirlooms. I want you to have it."

Danielle wiped a tear away, and Jane thought of the young woman being estranged from her own family. She had Kenan—but she also had Tally, Savannah, Miriam, and the others. Kenan had worked with a Mennonite pastor in the area to attempt to reconcile with their mother and father. Danielle had said they made enough progress to be able to speak with one another, and she was hopeful, in time, that perhaps their relationships would heal.

Maggie joined the circle and stepped to her mother's side, running her hand over the quilt.

Jane said, "Amos Berger experienced war and trauma and estrangement, just as you have. He found healing through Katie's love. You've found healing through love too—the love of your husband, the love of your brother, the love of your friends. This quilt is a symbol of that love, of that comfort."

"Thank you," Danielle sputtered. "I'll treasure this forever." She looked from Jane to Tally. "But I think you should give this to Tally."

"No," Tally said. "It's perfect for you."

"Jah." Jane stepped out of the circle again. "Besides, I have another quilt for Tally." She returned to the cupboard and took the sunshine-and-shadows quilt they'd all worked on a year ago from the bottom shelf. She turned toward Tally and placed the quilt in her arms. "This is the last quilt your mother worked on. Her hopes for you are stitched through it along with all of ours, no matter where you land."

Danielle put her arm around Tally and Maggie patted Tally's arm, but in true Tally fashion, she didn't cry. She did say, graciously, "Denki. This is the most thoughtful gift I've ever received."

Then she cleared her throat and said, "Joanna and Danielle already know this, but I do know where I'm going to land."

Jane's voice gave away her surprise. "You do?"

"I've been hired full time at Maggie's school. I'll continue to live in town." She placed her hands as if they were on an invisible steering wheel. "Kenan taught me how to drive, and I hope to get my license soon and then buy a car."

Maggie grasped the end of her braid. "We're all going to the Mennonite church now. Even Mama." Her mouth turned down into a pout. "I wanted all of us to join the Amish, like Rich and Joanna, but Mama said no. And Tally and Kenan don't want to either."

Jane threw her hands up in the air. "I guess you do know what your plans are." She heard Ted had been going to the Mennonite church where Savannah and Tommy attended as well.

Tally smiled at Maggie and then said in a respectful tone, "You can visit Rich and Joanna and help with their chores and whatnot whenever you want."

Maggie nodded. Then she beamed and swung her head up and down, her long single braid bobbing on her back as she said, "I'm going to join the Amish when I grow up."

"Jah." Danielle laughed. "I won't be surprised if you do."

"Danielle," Jane said, "no matter what, both you and Maggie are part of our community. All of you"—she glanced at Tally—"are part of us and will remain so."

"Denki," Tally and Danielle said in unison.

Jane had planned an announcement of her own, but as she opened her mouth, she hesitated. Miriam caught her eye and smiled. Jane cleared her throat, feeling nervous about what she had to say as all of the women in the room turned their attention back to her.

Life was one change after another. Nothing ever stayed the same, at least not for long.

"Jane," Danielle said, "do you have something more to say?"

Jane nodded. "I have an announcement to make too. I hope to do some traveling and more writing in the near future. Miriam will be in charge of the shop and the quilting circle while I'm gone." Jane focused on Tally. "Don't answer me now, but I was wondering if you would be interested in taking over my column."

"Oh, I don't need to think about it," Tally said. "I'd love to. At least during the school year and next summer. But I might need the summer after that off." Her eyes sparkled.

Jane tilted her head, wondering if that meant Tally and Kenan planned to marry in two years.

"Where do you plan to travel?" Tally quickly asked.

Jane couldn't help but smile. "Switzerland, next summer. Lord willing."

"I'll definitely be available then, if you want a traveling partner."

"Absolutely." Jane had broached the subject with Tally before, but things had been up in the air for her at the time. "I'm so glad you'll be able to join me."

Tally grinned. "Just think of the stories we'll have to tell."

"Exactly." A deep joy filled Jane as she looked around the room, from one woman to the next. She beamed. "And I'll look forward to hearing the next chapters of all of your stories too, once we return home."

Acknowledgments

When I came up with the idea for the historical story in *Threads of Hope*, it was 2018, nearly two years before COVD-19 changed our world. When it came time to write the story, I was isolating at home and living through the worst pandemic in the last one hundred years—while writing about the 1918–19 pandemic.

Researching and writing about the hard things our ancestors survived always encourages me, but writing about a past pandemic while living through one absolutely fascinated me. Never before, when I've written historical fiction, have the stakes in current life been as high (or nearly) as in the story I'm writing. I was reminded, over and over, how precious life is.

Although I don't recall specific stories from my grandparents about the 1918–19 pandemic, nor about World War I, I held all four of them in my thoughts while I wrote the story. Three of them were vibrant young adults during that period, hardworking and determined. The fourth was still a child, on her way to living a full, rewarding life. All created lives, homes, and families that continue to impact me today. Most importantly, they loved the Lord and lived out their faith in quiet but lasting ways.

Perhaps I also thought of my grandparents as I wrote because

I became a grandmother for the first time during the pandemic (Welcome, Harlow!). The stakes are higher now—as is my gratitude to the Lord and therefore my joy.

Some of the books that helped me in my research for this story are *Pandemic 1918: The Story of the Deadliest Influenza in History* by Catharine Arnold; the Smithsonian's *World War I: The Definitive Visual History* by R. G. Grant; *WWI: Tales from the Trenches* by Daniel Wrinn; *They Called It Nappanee: 1874–1974*; and *Echoes of the Past: Experiences of the Plain People* compiled by Freeman L. Yoder and Lizzie Yoder.

As with all of my novels about the Amish, I am indebted to my good friend Marietta Couch for being a sounding board for my ideas, for sharing her expertise, and for reading my manuscripts. As always, any mistakes are mine and mine alone.

As with every book I've ever written, I'm grateful to my husband, Peter, for his support, which includes his military and medical knowledge and his overall optimism and upbeat attitude. When I'm on deadline, his steadiness sees me through.

I'm also thankful for the encouragement of my agent, Natasha Kern; the expertise of my editor, Jennifer Veilleux; the amazing work of the entire team at Bethany House Publishers; and last but not least, my readers. Thank you!

Leslie Gould is the #1 bestselling and award-winning author of many novels, including the NEIGHBORS OF LANCASTER COUNTY series and the SISTERS OF LANCASTER COUNTY series. She holds an MFA in creative writing and enjoys research trips, church history, and hiking, especially in the beautiful state of Oregon where she lives. She and her husband, Peter, have four adult children and one grandbaby.

Sign Up for Leslie's Newsletter

Keep up to date with Leslie's news, book releases, and events by signing up for her email list at lesliegould.com.

More from Leslie Gould

Dumped by her fiancé a week before the wedding, Savannah Mast flees California for her Amish grandmother's farm, where she becomes unexpectedly entangled in the search for a missing Amish girl. When she discovers her childhood friend, Tommy Miller, is implicated as a suspect, she must do all she can to find the Amish girl and clear his name.

Piecing It All Together • Plain Patterns #1

You May Also Like . . .

Few are pleased Sophie Deiner has returned to her Amish community, but a sudden illness leaves her no choice. She befriends a group of migrant workers but is appalled by their living conditions. She soon finds her advocacy for change opposed by her ex, the farm foreman, and that her efforts only make things worse. Has she chosen a fight she can't win?

A Patchwork Past by Leslie Gould
Plain Patterns #2
lesliegould.com

In this captivating dual-time series, three young Amish women find inspiration and encouragement for their uncertain futures in the stories of their brave ancestors who lived during the Revolutionary War, the Civil War, and World War II.

The Sisters of Lancaster County: *A Plain Leaving, A Simple Singing, A Faithful Gathering* by Leslie Gould
lesliegould.com

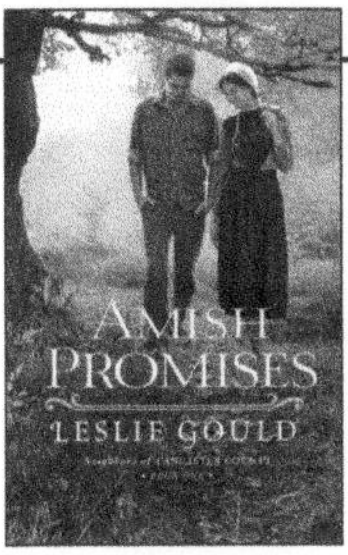

When a military family and an Amish family become neighbors, their lives are soon linked in unexpected ways—through conflict, then friendship, and finally, love.

The Neighbors of Lancaster County: *Amish Promises, Amish Sweethearts, Amish Weddings* by Leslie Gould
lesliegould.com

More from Baker Publishing Group

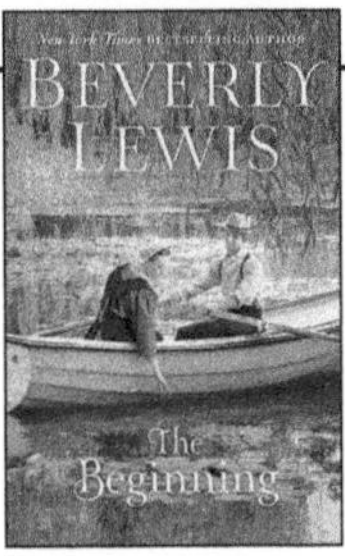

Susie Mast's Old Order life has been shaped more by tragedy than by her own choices. But when she decides to stop waiting on her childhood friend and accept another young man's invitation, she soon realizes her mistake. Will family secrets and missed opportunities dim Susie's hopes for the future? Or is what seems like the end only the beginning?

The Beginning by Beverly Lewis
beverlylewis.com

Eager to begin a new chapter as a Lancaster County tour guide, Anna searches for the answers of her grandmother's past and an old stone wall—both a mystery due to the elderly woman's Alzheimer's. And when Anna grows close with a Mennonite man and an Amish widower, she's faced with a difficult choice. Will she find love and the truth, or only heartbreak?

The Stone Wall by Beverly Lewis
beverlylewis.com

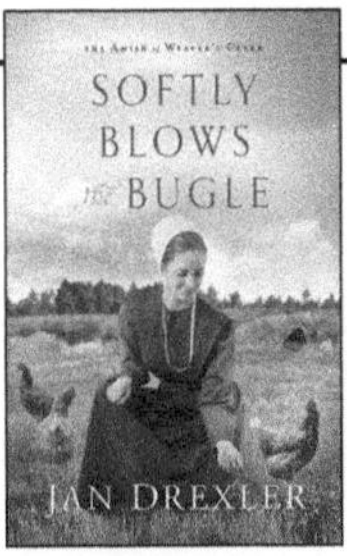

After a disastrous marriage, Elizabeth Kaufman is determined to never be at the mercy of any man again. When Aaron Zook returns from the battlefield, he never imagined the Amish way of life his grandfather had rejected would be so enticing—and a certain widow he can't stop thinking of. Will he be able to convince her to risk giving her heart away once more?

Softly Blows the Bugle by Jan Drexler
The Amish of Weaver's Creek #3 • jandrexler.com

BETHANYHOUSE